DARK ROVER'S GIFT

THE CHILDREN OF THE GODS

I. T. LUCAS

Published by Evening Star Press, LLC.

EveningStarPress.com

ISBN: 978-1-962067-76-8

FENELLA

Fenella stretched an arm across the empty space beside her, and the lazy smile she'd woken up with wilted into a frown.

Din's absence felt surprisingly wrong.

Exhausted after her shift, she'd opted to return to Shira's place alone and just collapse into bed after a quick shower, but now she regretted that decision. She missed having Din's arm draped across her waist, his breath warm against her neck, and hearing the soft murmurs he made while dreaming.

A week ago, she would have scoffed at anyone even suggesting that she could get used to a male's presence in her life so quickly.

Somehow, Din had gotten under her skin, and it hadn't been just because of his impromptu declaration of love on the way home last night. It was about him rolling up his sleeves and helping clean up after closing so she could finish things earlier, it was the stroll down

When a text notification from Din caught her eye, she rushed to open the messaging application.

Good morning, my love. Call me when you wake up? I'll come to pick you up for the party.

My love.

The endearment still tasted new. It wasn't the same as, 'how are you, love?' Or 'what can I get you, love?' *My love* sounded different, and it sent a surge of warmth through her, followed immediately by a flutter of fear.

Fenella pushed herself upright, her sore muscles protesting, but not as badly as she'd expected them to. Immortality had many perks, chief among them being rapid recovery. Once she had a cup or two of coffee in her, she would be as good as new.

Padding barefoot into the kitchen, she expected to find Shira there, or at least a half-full coffee carafe and the lingering scents of breakfast, but the kitchen was empty and smelled faintly of cleaning solution.

A twinge of concern flickered through her.

"Shira?" Fenella called out as she walked toward her roommate's door.

Finding it closed, she knocked gently, then with more force when no answer came. "Shira? Are you in there?"

Given how well the houses in the village were soundproofed, Shira might not have heard her. Fenella hesitated only for a split second before pushing the door slightly open.

The bedroom was empty, the bed neatly made as if it hadn't been slept in.

A spike of anxiety followed.

Yesterday, Shira had promised to come to the bar provided that nothing materialized from the hookup she'd been planning, but since she hadn't shown up, perhaps she'd decided to spend the night with the guy.

It shouldn't be a cause for worry.

After all, she was an immortal, stronger and faster than any human female and many human males and possessing the ability to thrall. She was in no danger from some human dude, even if he was up to no good.

But what if he'd slipped her a roofie?

Were immortals immune to those?

Thankfully, it had never happened to Fenella, but that was because she was always super careful with her drinks. She never let them out of her sight and held on to them until she was done drinking.

Returning to her bedroom, she retrieved her phone and dialed her roommate's number.

After several rings, the call went to voicemail.

"Hey, it's me," Fenella said after the beep. "Just checking to see if you're okay since you didn't come home last night. Call me when you get this."

She terminated the call and tried to tamp down her worry.

Shira is fine, and I'm overreacting.

After a moment's hesitation, Fenella called Din.

"Good morning, love," he answered almost imme-

Fenella was just finishing her updo when the doorbell rang, and she opened it to find Din balancing a cardboard tray containing two large coffee cups and a paper bag that emitted the heavenly scent of fresh pastries.

"Caffeine delivery," he announced with a bright smile that had his left cheek dimple.

Fenella relieved him of the tray. "You're officially my favorite person."

"I aim to please." He leaned to plant a soft kiss on her cheek. "You look lovely."

"Thank you." She cast him a smile. "You look good yourself, Professor."

"Oh, this old thing?" He waved a hand over his outfit of black jeans and a gray button-down shirt, then followed her inside and closed the door behind him.

Fenella laughed. "That sounds like something Max would have said."

When Din didn't laugh back, she realized her mistake. "Didn't mean to imply that it was a lame joke."

He took a seat at the counter. "So, where is Shira off to this morning?"

Talk about a change of subject.

Fenella set the coffee on the counter. "I don't think she came home last night. Yesterday, she said something about a possible hookup after work, so I assume that she spent the night with the guy. I'm trying not to worry."

diately, sounding amused. "Or should I say good afternoon?"

"Good morning to you, too," Fenella said. "What's the point of working late if you can't sleep in?"

"Fair point. How are you feeling?"

"I missed you this morning. Any chance you want to come over and have breakfast with me? Shira's not home, and I don't want to eat alone."

She rolled her eyes at the words that had just left her mouth. Since when did she have a problem with doing anything without company?

"I'll be there in twenty minutes with coffee and pastries."

"You're my hero." She made a loud kissing sound. "See you soon."

Twenty minutes was just enough time to figure out what to wear for an outdoor party and get herself dolled up.

Would a pair of leggings and a button-down blouse work?

Or should she put on a dress?

She still had the one she'd borrowed from Jasmine, although given that Jasmine didn't want the dress back, it wasn't really borrowed. Fenella had worn it to meet Din at the café when he'd first arrived at the village, but she still didn't have the right shoes to wear with it other than the flip-flops Jasmine had given her.

Oh well, Din had seemed impressed then, so it couldn't be too bad. Besides, it wasn't as if she had a lot of options.

The lie came easily. He hadn't thought about Fenella's missing roommate since they'd gotten out of the house.

"Maybe she's already here." Holding on to his arm, Fenella rose on her tiptoes and scanned the growing crowd.

Din followed her example, his gaze sweeping across the gathering, looking for Shira's distinctive red curls. The crowd had grown considerably in just the last few minutes, with perhaps a hundred immortals now mingling on the green. Then he saw it—a flash of fiery red among the sea of more subdued hair colors.

"There she is." He pointed toward the far side of the lawn, where Shira stood talking with a dark-haired man Din didn't recognize. "Near that big tree over there."

As Fenella followed his gaze, relief washed over her face. "Thank God. I was starting to worry." She tugged at his arm. "Come on, let's say hello and give her grief about not letting me know where she was."

As they approached, Din studied the man with Shira. He was tall and lean, dressed in dark jeans and a button-down shirt similar to Din's own outfit. There was nothing remarkable about him other than the intensity with which he listened to whatever Shira was saying.

"Shira!" Fenella called when they were a few yards away.

Her roommate turned, her face lighting up. "Hi!" She waved them over.

15

Fenella gave her new friend a quick once-over as they approached. "I tried calling you this morning. I was worried when I saw that you weren't home. I left you a voicemail message."

Shira at least had the grace to look sheepish. "I'm sorry. My phone died, and I didn't have my charger with me." She turned to the man beside her. "This is Ruvon. Ruvon, these are my friends, Fenella and Din."

"I know," Ruvon said, his voice soft and his handshake firmer than Din had expected from his slight build.

Something about him seemed vaguely familiar, though Din couldn't place where he might have seen him before.

"Ruvon works for Kalugal. He handles his security systems," Shira said.

Ah. That explained it. Din wasn't well acquainted with Kalugal's men.

"I heard that you started working at the Hobbit Bar," Ruvon said to Fenella.

"I did," she confirmed. "Last night was my first."

Ruvon smiled for the first time since the conversation had started. "Your psychic readings were the talk of the village this morning. Perhaps I'll stop by tonight to get one. Should I bring a specific object or would anything do?"

"Bring your wallet." She winked. "I bet it hides many interesting stories."

the row of displayed artifacts in the pavilion and the fascinating stories he'd told her, and it was a hundred and one little things she couldn't think of right now that had felt so right when they'd happened.

I'm in love with you, Fenella.

The words reverberated in her head, exhilarating, terrifying. She wanted to be loved, but at the same time, she didn't want to be tied down by the bonds it implied.

It wasn't that she was afraid of commitment or that she wanted the freedom to pursue other men. It was much more fundamental than that.

She was scared of losing Din.

It wasn't about him walking away and leaving her or anything else as mundane as that. She might have harbored those kinds of fears when she was young and naive and hadn't witnessed the random cruelty of the world. Now she was afraid of losing him permanently to an act of terror or even a fatal accident, and that wasn't theoretical given the landing gear malfunction during his flight from Edinburgh to New York.

A miracle had saved him and the other passengers. According to the news commentator, water landings rarely ended well.

With a sigh, Fenella reached for her phone on the nightstand, squinting at the screen. Noon already?

The birthday celebration for Kian and his daughter was starting in two hours, which didn't leave much time to prepare.

"She'll probably return in time for the party," Din said. "She wouldn't want to miss that."

"I'll keep a lookout for her." Fenella pulled the cups out of the cardboard tray and handed one to Din. "What do we do if she doesn't show up?"

He frowned. "I don't know what the procedure here is, but the Guardians probably have a protocol they follow when a village resident goes missing. We can just tell Max and let him handle the rest." He removed the pastries from the bag—chocolate croissants by the look and smell of them.

Fenella snatched one out of his hand and took a bite. It was warm, and the chocolate melted on her tongue. "This is heavenly."

The intensity with which he looked at her mouth and the glow in his eyes made her breath hitch.

She licked her lips. "Hungry?"

"Very."

"Eggs?" she teased.

Din leaned closer to her, their lips almost touching. "No, not for eggs."

"Toast?" she breathed.

"I love you," he said, his chocolate-scented breath fanning over her face.

If she let him kiss her now, they would never get to the party or they would get there after everyone else had left. Normally, Fenella wouldn't have minded, but it was the boss's birthday, and she would have to be an idiot to do anything to antagonize her very generous host.

She placed a finger over his lips. "I'm not saying those three words back to you. Not yet. But I'm willing to say that I'm glad you're here."

Din kissed her fingertips before moving her hand away. "That's more than enough for me. For now."

The guy was just too good to be true.

Oh, to hell with it.

She closed the distance between them, pressing her lips to his. The kiss was gentle at first, a sweet hello, a reconnection, but it quickly deepened into something more urgent. Din's hands came to rest at her waist, pulling her closer to him.

When they finally separated, they were both breathless.

"So, what would you like for breakfast?" she said, trying to sound casual. "I offered eggs and toast, and you said no to both."

Din laughed, the sound sending a pleasant shiver down her spine. "Let's stick to the pastries. There will be enough food at the party."

"I have to admit that I prefer this delicious croissant to anything else. It is worth waking up for." Fenella licked a smudge of chocolate from her thumb.

After a moment, she checked her phone to see if Shira had returned her message, but there were no new notifications on the screen.

"Maybe I should call the library?" She wiped her hands on a napkin. "Is it open on Saturday?"

She didn't know which library Shira worked in, and in a city the size of Los Angeles, there were probably hundreds of them. Ingrid should know, though. The woman knew everything about everyone.

"I'm sure it's open," Din said. "But I doubt anyone would know where Shira is. Unless the hookup was someone she works with?"

Fenella shrugged. "She didn't say who it was. I think she would have mentioned it if he were a coworker."

2

DIN

The summer sun warmed Din's face as he and Fenella walked toward the village green, but even more warming was the knowledge that she'd missed him this morning.

Getting such an admission from a woman who was so fiercely protective of her independence was invaluable, but he tried not to strut like a peacock and to keep his jubilant mood at bay. If he made too much of it, Fenella might never admit such things to him again.

When they reached the village square, Din was stunned by the transformation that had been accomplished overnight for Kian and Allegra's joint birthday celebration. What was usually an open expanse of grass was now a festival of color. Streamers in pastel shades crisscrossed overhead, tied to temporary poles that had been erected around the perimeter. Beneath this canopy, white-linen-covered tables dotted the area, each centerpiece featuring paper flowers with doll fairies suspended by wire between them.

A raised platform stood at the far end of the green, no doubt where the Clan Mother would give her speech and Kian would make an appearance with his daughter.

"Wow," Fenella breathed. "I can't believe how quickly this was done. Yesterday, it was just a lawn with neatly trimmed grass." She waved a hand at the buffet that lined one side of the area. "Who cooked all that?"

"I guess the Odus." Din pointed with his chin at the three butlers standing behind the tables with aprons tied around their suits. "Ogidu, Okidu, and Onidu, I think. I have a hard time telling them apart. You know they are a kind of cyborg, right?"

She nodded. "They are not identical, but they still look like triplets to me."

"Ogidu is Annani's butler, Okidu is Kian's, and Onidu is Amanda's, and it looks like they have combined their efforts to prepare this party."

"That's incredible." Fenella stared at the three figures. "I wonder what it would feel like to have one of those. It's like having the artificial intelligence chatbot installed in an actual body." She looked up at him with a smile. "Soon, there will be one in every household, but I don't think they will look quite as human as these."

"Which one would you prefer?" he asked. "The human-looking type or one that is obviously a robot?"

She pursed her lips. "I'm not sure. I need to think about it."

He chuckled. "What is there to think about?"

She gave him a look that seemed to question his intelligence. "A human-looking robot could be fun because I could treat it as a friend and have talks with it. On the other hand, it's much easier to tell a robot to clean the toilet and then power down for the night, because I want my peace and quiet. I don't need to think about hurting its feelings or anything like that."

"There's something to that," Din acknowledged. "The Clan Mother and her children have always treated the Odus as if they were part of the family, so now that they are gaining sentience, there is less concern about them turning out evil."

Her eyes widened. "Are you serious? These cyborgs are sentient, and there is a chance that they could turn against the clan?"

"I don't think that even partial sentience can override their base programming to not harm Annani and her family, but I'm not an expert on those things." He craned his neck to scan the crowd for William and Kaia, who were the experts, but it seemed like they hadn't arrived yet. "It's an excellent question, though, and we can ask William when he gets here."

Fenella's attention was already on something else. "Oh my God, look at that cake!" She tugged him toward the center of the buffet.

The enormous cake dominated the table—a masterpiece of confectionery architecture. Six tiers high, each layer was frosted in gradients of pastel colors that flowed seamlessly from one to the next. Delicate sugar flowers cascaded down one side, and crowning the top was a porcelain doll that resembled a beautiful baby girl dressed in layers of tulle.

"It's gorgeous," Fenella said. "Do you think Allegra will be wearing a dress like that? I can't wait to see her."

Din shrugged. "Maybe."

He was more interested in who had baked the cake. If it were Gerard, they were in for a treat. Otherwise, it would probably be meh.

Fenella's gaze lingered for a moment longer on the cake and then moved to scan the gathering crowd. Looking down at her outfit and the flip-flops on her dainty feet, she grimaced. "I feel underdressed for the occasion. The dress is nice, but these flip flops are too casual."

"You look beautiful, and flip-flops are perfect for an outdoor party on the grass. The females in heels will be sinking into the lawn all afternoon."

He loved the sundress she was wearing and how it hugged her curves in all the right places. Her dark hair was swept up in an elegant knot, showcasing her graceful neck, and he had a hard time refraining from trailing kisses all over it.

"I guess," Fenella said without conviction.

"If you want, I could take you shopping in Los Angeles."

Her eyes brightened. "That would be lovely, but I

need to get paid first." She gave a rueful laugh. "I just realized I didn't even ask Atzil how much he's paying me. I was so excited to have the job that it completely slipped my mind."

"You just wanted to have a purpose, not a paycheck."

She laughed. "Unlike you, Professor, I need to earn my keep. But I almost forgot about the tips. Atzil let me keep everything from the tip jar, which was pretty generous. That alone should cover at least two decent pairs of shoes."

Din's heart squeezed at her excitement over the modest sum. He wanted to shower her with everything she needed—clothes, shoes, jewelry, anything that would bring her joy. But he knew better than to offer. Fenella valued her self-sufficiency above almost everything else.

It was something he admired about her but also found frustrating.

Would that change when they moved in together? *If* they moved in together?

Or perhaps only an official marriage ceremony would soften her stance on accepting his support. Some women cared about such things. But he was getting ahead of himself. Fenella had already made it clear that she wasn't ready for declarations of love, let alone discussions of marriage.

"What's wrong?" Fenella nudged him with her elbow. "You've got that brooding professor look."

Din forced a smile. "I'm just worried about Shira."

The lie came easily. He hadn't thought about Fenella's missing roommate since they'd gotten out of the house.

"Maybe she's already here." Holding on to his arm, Fenella rose on her tiptoes and scanned the growing crowd.

Din followed her example, his gaze sweeping across the gathering, looking for Shira's distinctive red curls. The crowd had grown considerably in just the last few minutes, with perhaps a hundred immortals now mingling on the green. Then he saw it—a flash of fiery red among the sea of more subdued hair colors.

"There she is." He pointed toward the far side of the lawn, where Shira stood talking with a dark-haired man Din didn't recognize. "Near that big tree over there."

As Fenella followed his gaze, relief washed over her face. "Thank God. I was starting to worry." She tugged at his arm. "Come on, let's say hello and give her grief about not letting me know where she was."

As they approached, Din studied the man with Shira. He was tall and lean, dressed in dark jeans and a button-down shirt similar to Din's own outfit. There was nothing remarkable about him other than the intensity with which he listened to whatever Shira was saying.

"Shira!" Fenella called when they were a few yards away.

Her roommate turned, her face lighting up. "Hi!" She waved them over.

Fenella gave her new friend a quick once-over as they approached. "I tried calling you this morning. I was worried when I saw that you weren't home. I left you a voicemail message."

Shira at least had the grace to look sheepish. "I'm sorry. My phone died, and I didn't have my charger with me." She turned to the man beside her. "This is Ruvon. Ruvon, these are my friends, Fenella and Din."

"I know," Ruvon said, his voice soft and his hand-shake firmer than Din had expected from his slight build.

Something about him seemed vaguely familiar, though Din couldn't place where he might have seen him before.

"Ruvon works for Kalugal. He handles his security systems," Shira said.

Ah. That explained it. Din wasn't well acquainted with Kalugal's men.

"I heard that you started working at the Hobbit Bar," Ruvon said to Fenella.

"I did," she confirmed. "Last night was my first."

Ruvon smiled for the first time since the conversation had started. "Your psychic readings were the talk of the village this morning. Perhaps I'll stop by tonight to get one. Should I bring a specific object or would anything do?"

"Bring your wallet." She winked. "I bet it hides many interesting stories."

3

FENELLA

Ruvon actually blushed, which made him look more like the shy boy next door than a scary ex-Doomer.

Also, he obviously wasn't Shira's hookup from last night. Or was he?

Shira hadn't explicitly said that she was meeting a human.

"Shira, can I borrow you for a moment?" Fenella touched her roommate's elbow.

Shira looked a little uncomfortable. "Of course!"

"I'll get us something to drink," Din offered.

Fenella gave him a grateful smile. "Thank you. That would be lovely."

"I'll see you all around," Ruvon said before following Din to the buffet tables.

Fenella waited until she was alone with Shira. "I was worried about you. You should have called me or texted me about spending the night with the guy."

A flash of irritation crossed Shira's eyes. "I don't recall you asking for my permission when you spent nights with Din."

The retort caught Fenella off guard. "That's different."

"Is it?" Shira crossed her arms. "How?"

"Din is in the village," Fenella countered, keeping her voice low. "Your library and your mysterious hookup are outside of it in the human world, and no one is safe out there, not even an immortal like you."

Shira's expression softened. "I forgot what you've been through. It should have occurred to me that you would panic. I'll text you next time, I promise."

Fenella's first instinct was to deny Shira's implication that she'd panicked because she was vulnerable, but what was the point when she was right?

"I'm sorry for overreacting, but I called you and you didn't answer. I also left you a voicemail. Wouldn't you have worried if you were in my shoes?"

Shira had already explained about her phone dying on her, but it was no doubt charged by now, and she'd had ample opportunity to call Fenella to let her know that she was alive.

A hint of embarrassment colored Shira's cheeks. "I saw that you'd called but didn't check the message. I was in a rush to get ready for the party, and I figured I'd see you here anyway."

"Makes sense." Fenella let out a breath. "So, how was the hookup? Worth all this brouhaha?"

Shira snorted. "Not really. He was underwhelming,

to be honest, and normally, I wouldn't have spent the night, but I fell asleep."

"Humans can't keep up," Din's voice came from behind Fenella. He handed her a champagne glass, a smirk playing at the corners of his mouth. "It's not their fault that they don't have our stamina."

Shira raised an eyebrow. "Stamina is not everything. I've tried a couple of Kalugal's men before. They had the stamina, but they lacked skills."

Fenella nearly choked on her champagne. Was Ruvon a former lover? Or perhaps he was Shira's next conquest?

Din opened his mouth, no doubt ready with a witty comeback, but then a sudden hush fell over the crowd, and Fenella turned to see what had caused it.

The Clan Mother had appeared on the podium, though Fenella couldn't recall seeing her walk through the crowd to get there. One moment the stage had been empty, and the next, Annani stood at its center, resplendent in a flowing silk gown.

"How did she do that?" Fenella whispered to Din.

"Do what?"

"Get there without anyone noticing?"

Din shrugged, looking as puzzled as she felt. He lifted his finger to his lips, indicating she should stop talking.

Fenella wondered if there was some sort of secret passage beneath the village green, but it seemed absurd to have an elaborate tunnel system just so the

Clan Mother could make dramatic entrances at parties.

More likely, the goddess employed some mind trick to divert everyone's attention from her as she approached, making herself visible only when she wished to be seen.

Either way, it was impressive.

"My beloved children," Annani's melodious voice carried across the green without the help of amplification. "We gather today to celebrate a most joyous occasion—the two thousand and first birthday of my son Kian, and the first birthday of my granddaughter, Allegra. The actual birthday date passed a while ago, and we are celebrating a little late because emergencies kept popping up, forcing us to postpone the party. Thankfully, today we are all here, the sky is clear, and we are finally ready to celebrate."

The crowd broke into cheers and applause, their faces upturned to the goddess with fond, happy expressions. They truly loved her, and Fenella understood the sentiment. The Clan Mother was warm and friendly, and once Fenella had gotten used to the glow, the unearthly beauty, and the power emanating from the tiny female, she'd become comfortable in her presence.

"Two thousand and one years ago, I was blessed with the birth of a strong, beautiful boy," the goddess said. "When I held him for the first time, I felt a love so encompassing, so overwhelming, that I knew I would move mountains, part seas, and challenge the heavens themselves to keep him safe. After the birth of my first daughter, I thought that I could never feel a love so strong again, but a mother's heart has no limits. I love all of my children with the same intensity."

Fenella's gaze drifted to Kian, who stood at the edge of the stage with Allegra in his arms. The clan's leader appeared almost embarrassed by his mother's effusive praise, though there was no doubting the affection between them.

"That same love now extends to my precious granddaughter." Annani's voice softened as she looked at Allegra. "And to each of you. Love is what drives all that we do. It binds us and guides us, and it is the force that sustains us. Without love, there is nothing."

Fenella stifled the urge to roll her eyes. Love might play a part, but she doubted it was the only motivation for the goddess's actions. From what she'd learned since arriving at the village, Annani had been manipulating global politics for thousands of years, playing a chess game against the forces of darkness represented by the Brotherhood.

Still, she couldn't deny the emotion in the goddess's voice when she spoke of her family. That, at least, was sincere.

The goddess continued, "As we celebrate these two milestones today, I ask you all to reflect on what truly matters in this existence. Not power, not wealth, not even the gift of life itself—but the connections we forge with one another, the love we give and receive."

Her luminous gaze swept across the crowd, and for

an unsettling moment, Fenella felt as if those ancient eyes paused on her briefly. A shiver ran down her spine.

"Even I, who have lived for thousands of years, continue to learn this lesson," the goddess said. "Joy can be fleeting and pain can feel overwhelming, but every ending brings with it a new beginning, every loss an opportunity for growth."

Fenella felt a tightness in her chest at these words. They struck too close to her own experiences—the constant reinvention of herself, the severing of connections for safety's sake, the walls she'd built to survive.

"Look around you." The Clan Mother spread her arms wide. "See the family we have built together, the haven we have created. This is what we fight to protect. Together we stand against the darkness."

As the word 'darkness' triggered images of a dingy cell and a monster who called himself a doctor, the festive village green receded, and the goddess's voice faded.

Then Din's arm slipped around her waist, anchoring her to the present. "You okay?" he whispered.

Fenella nodded, grateful for his steadying presence.

"—into this new year with hope and purpose," Annani was concluding her speech. "May Allegra grow strong and wise, surrounded by love. May Kian continue to lead with compassion and vision. And may all of you, my cherished family, find the peace and happiness you deserve."

A thunderous round of applause broke out as the Clan Mother raised her hands in blessing over the crowd. Fenella clapped along, her mind still churning with conflicting emotions.

Part of her wanted to believe in Annani's vision of family and security, and to accept that after decades of running, she could finally stop, could belong somewhere. But another part, the survivor who'd learned to trust nothing and no one, remained wary of pretty words and shining promises.

"Let us honor Kian and Allegra." The goddess gestured to the side of the platform, where Kian stood with Allegra in his arms.

The little girl was dressed in a fluffy confection that mirrored the doll atop the cake, her blond curls adorned with a tiny tiara. She stared wide-eyed at the crowd, her small arm wrapped around her daddy's neck.

"She's adorable," Fenella whispered.

"She is," Din agreed.

As the applause died down, Kian stepped forward with Allegra, who seemed upset, and murmured something to his mother, who nodded with a smile and waved her hand. Music began to play from hidden speakers, and as the goddess announced that it was time to feast, the crowd's attention shifted to the buffet tables where the Odus were beginning to serve food.

"Hungry?" Din asked.

Fenella nodded. "I could eat."

As they joined the line forming at the buffet, Fenella scanned the crowd, spotting Kyra and Max near the cake. Jasmine and Ell-rom were swaying to the music, two tall and striking figures who stood out even among this extraordinarily good-looking crowd.

Din followed her gaze. "Your new cousin seems happy."

"She does." Fenella watched Jasmine laugh at something Ell-rom whispered in her ear. "I still can't wrap my head around being related to her. What are the odds?"

As they inched forward in the buffet line, Fenella's mind returned to the Clan Mother's speech. For all her skepticism about Annani's political machinations, she couldn't deny there had been wisdom in those words about love and connection. She'd spent so long avoiding attachments, convinced they would only lead to pain when she inevitably had to flee.

Yet here she was, surrounded by people who cared about her—Din, Kyra, Jasmine, even Shira in her own way. People who accepted her, broken pieces and all.

What would it be like to stop running? To let herself belong?

"Your mind seems to be a million miles away," Din said as they reached the front of the line and began filling their plates.

"I was thinking about the Clan Mother's speech."

Fenella selected a stuffed mushroom. "All that talk about love and family being her driving force."

"You don't believe her?"

Fenella shrugged. "I believe she loves her family. However, she has been manipulating global affairs for thousands of years. You can't tell me that's all motivated by maternal instinct."

"What do you think drives her then?" Din added a slice of beef to his plate.

"Power, maybe? The desire to shape the world according to her vision?" Fenella selected a few more appetizers. "Not that I'm criticizing. From what I've gathered, she stands against the Brotherhood, which puts her firmly on the side of good in my book."

As they moved to the end of the buffet table, their plates laden with an assortment of delicacies, Fenella spotted two vacant seats.

"Shall we?"

When they settled at the table, Fenella cast another glance at the podium, now empty. The Clan Mother had vanished as mysteriously as she'd appeared, leaving Kian and Syssi to circulate among the guests with Allegra.

"I still want to know how she does that disappearing act," she muttered.

Din chuckled. "Some mysteries are better left unsolved. The Clan Mother loves to maintain an air of enigma around herself. She has quite the penchant for drama."

"She does?" Fenella speared a piece of glazed

salmon with her fork. "The Clan Mother doesn't need any tricks to make herself seem more. She's the most powerful being on Earth." She took a bite and chewed for a moment, still thinking about the appearing and disappearing acts. "I hate unsolved mysteries."

"Is that a warning?" Din asked.

"More like a disclaimer." Fenella grinned. "Just so you know what you're getting into with me."

"I think I have a pretty good idea." His expression turned serious. "And I love every little bit of you."

The warmth in his voice made her heart clench. She might not be ready to say the words he wanted to hear yet, but in moments like this, she was tempted.

4

DIN

Instead of answering in kind, Fenella smiled and then dug into her plate with renewed gusto. Din knew that he had hit a nerve. She was still skittish, still reluctant to acknowledge her feelings for him; nevertheless, having her back in his life felt right.

It wasn't the passionate infatuation of fifty years ago, but something deeper, more substantial. He loved her—her strength, her humor, her resilience, the way she was slowly opening herself to possibilities after a lifetime of caution.

He wanted to be part of her future, to build something lasting with her. He wanted to wake every morning to her tangled hair and sleepy smiles.

But she wasn't ready for any of that.

"Oh, look." She waved at someone behind Din. "Kyra's entire gang is here. I should say hello." She rose to her feet. "Do you want to come?"

He glanced at their half-eaten meals. "I'll stay to

guard the plates. Otherwise, the Odus will collect them, and all this great food will go to waste."

She nodded. "I'll be right back."

When she walked away, Okidu—at least Din thought it was him—stopped by their table with a tray of champagne flutes.

Din selected two, nodding his thanks, and put one next to Fenella's plate.

"Quite the turnout," a familiar voice said from behind him.

He turned to find Max standing there, looking as cocky as ever.

"Indeed. The entire village seems to be here."

"No one in their right mind would miss Kian's birthday." Max grinned. "And doubly so when the Clan Mother was expected to deliver a speech. Everyone loves her speeches." His gaze shifted to where Fenella stood with Kyra and her sisters. "How are things progressing with our flame-haired barmaid?"

"Fenella is not a redhead," Din corrected automatically.

"Figure of speech," Max waved a hand. "She's certainly fiery enough to qualify, regardless of her actual hair color." He leaned closer. "Seriously, though. Everything okay?"

"Perfect." Din smiled. "It's not easy, but if I wanted easy, I wouldn't be in love with Fenella."

Max lifted an eyebrow. "So, the love word has been unleashed?"

Din laughed. "You couldn't have phrased it more

accurately if you tried. Fenella reacted to it as if I had shot her, but she's getting used to the idea."

"Give her time," Max said, clapping him on the shoulder. "She's always been skittish, and then trauma left scars that need healing." His gaze drifted to where Kyra stood chatting with Fenella and her sisters. "It needs to at least scab over."

Din nodded. "I'm here for her."

Max studied him for a moment. "Have you given more thought to your academic commitments?"

"I'll finish the term remotely. After that, I'll request a sabbatical." Din took a sip of champagne. "Or I'll resign if necessary. The university is the least of my concerns."

"Got your priorities straight." Max took a champagne flute off a passing tray carried by one of the Odus. "Just don't let Fenella know that you are making her a priority. Make it about yourself needing a change of pace or something of that nature. Being made the center of someone else's life will make her hackles rise."

Max was right, but Din didn't feel comfortable about masking his intentions. Then again, all was fair in love and war. If he wanted to win Fenella over, he needed to wage war with her insecurities and her reluctance to acknowledge her feelings and stay put in one place long enough to sprout roots.

"I'll take your advice under consideration," he said noncommittally.

Max raised his flute. "To second chances."

"And to not wasting them," Din added, returning the toast.

As they drank, Din's gaze once again sought Fenella across the lawn. She had extricated herself from Kyra and her gaggle of relatives and was now making her way toward him.

She moved with natural sensuality, her hips swaying and her sundress fluttering around her knees. Her face was relaxed, happy, and her lips were curved in a small smile that seemed reserved just for him.

She was beautiful, but it was her inner spirit, her resilience and fierceness that shone through.

"Here comes trouble," Max murmured with amusement, excusing himself with a salute and a grin.

"Did I scare him away?" Fenella asked as she sat back in her chair and lifted her fork.

"I doubt it. He just wanted to get back to Kyra."

Fenella looked up and smiled. "Right as always, Professor. Max is stealing her from her sisters and taking her to dance."

Din frowned. "Is there dancing?"

"Yeah." She waved with her fork. "Look over there."

He turned to look in the direction she'd indicated and saw that several couples were already dancing on a wooden platform. "Do you want to join?"

"Sure. As soon as I'm done eating." She put another piece of salmon into her mouth.

"Fenella! Din!" Syssi approached them with Allegra sitting on her hip, tiny fingers playing with her mother's dangling earrings. "Are you enjoying the party?"

"Very much so," Fenella said, her smile warm as she reached for Allegra's hand. "Happy birthday, little princess."

"Thank you," Allegra said with surprising confidence for someone who was supposed to be just one year old. "My cake is pretty."

Fenella's eyes widened. "Yes. It is. Especially the beautiful doll on top."

Allegra frowned. "Mine."

"Of course." Fenella sounded like she was stifling laughter.

Syssi sighed. "That decoration was why my little hellion didn't thank the guests for coming like we'd rehearsed. She wanted that doll before anyone could take it, and she refused to speak."

"Can't blame her." Din winked at the child. "The doll is very pretty."

"Don't encourage her." Syssi adjusted Allegra on her hip, turning toward Fenella. "I hear you've become quite the sensation at the Hobbit."

Fenella laughed. "Word travels fast."

"In a village this size? At the speed of light," Syssi said. "Everyone's talking about your psychic readings."

"It's just a bit of fun," Fenella said with a dismissive wave. "I have a knack for making up stories about people."

"Perhaps you're picking up more than you realize," Syssi suggested.

Before Fenella could respond, Bridget walked up to Syssi. "Sorry to interrupt, but Kian's looking for you."

"Thank you for telling me." Syssi turned back to them. "It was a pleasure chatting with you. Please, enjoy the party, and don't leave without saying goodbye."

As Syssi and Bridget walked away, Din noticed Fenella staring after them with an odd expression.

"Something's wrong?" he asked.

"No, nothing." She took a sip of champagne. "I just had a passing thought about how different my life is now compared to only a few weeks ago. I went from prisoner to bartender with paranormal abilities and newfound relatives." A rueful smile curved her lips. "And I've acquired a devastatingly handsome Scottish professor who tells me he loves me."

Din's heart skipped at her words. "I hope you count me among the good things in your life."

Her eyes met his, vulnerability and determination warring in their depths. "Of course it's good. For now."

His heart sank.

She leaned over and pressed a soft kiss to his lips. It was just a brief contact, appropriate for their public setting, but the meaning behind it lifted his heart from where it had dropped to a moment ago.

It had turned the meaning of *for now* into a promise instead of a threat.

5

KIAN

Kian spotted Syssi making her way through the crowd with Allegra perched on her hip. His daughter's sparkly tiara had slipped to one side, and her chubby fingers were tangled in Syssi's necklace, but she looked utterly delighted with the attention she was receiving from everyone who stopped to coo at her.

His heart swelled at the sight of them.

In his two thousand years of existence, nothing had prepared him for the fierce, all-consuming love he felt for his daughter and her mother. Before Syssi had entered his life, he'd dedicated himself to the clan, but now these two precious ladies were his entire world, and the clan's business took a back seat, at least as far as his heart was concerned. It still took too much of his time and left too little for what really mattered.

"There they are," he murmured to Amanda, who stood beside him on the platform. "Perhaps this time,

Allegra is ready to say a few words to her guests and wow them with her advanced vocabulary."

Amanda snorted. "The prodigy miracle child."

"That's right." He wasn't embarrassed in the least for thinking that the sun came out in the morning to shine on Allegra's golden curls and the moon came up at night just to sing her a lullaby.

"She certainly has your stubbornness," Amanda said. "It's right there in the set of her jaw."

"Can't deny that." He sighed. "As Syssi likes to say, it's the flip side of the same coin. You can't have determination and assertiveness without stubbornness, right? If she were sweet and mellow, she wouldn't have what it takes to be a leader."

Amanda nodded. "I agree a hundred percent, especially since the same can be said about me."

"Daddy!" Allegra cried when she spotted him, reaching out with grabby hands, nearly strangling Syssi with the necklace still clutched in her fist.

"Careful, sweetheart," Syssi untangled their daughter's fingers from the jewelry. "You're going to break Mommy's necklace."

"Come to Daddy, sweetheart." Kian lifted Allegra from Syssi's arms, planting a kiss on her rosy cheek. "Are you ready now for your big speech, Princess?"

Allegra nodded solemnly. "I say thank you."

"That's right," Kian confirmed, catching Syssi's eye with a smile. They'd practiced the simple words with Allegra for days, though whether she'd stick to the script was anyone's guess.

Allegra bobbed her head again, but there was a gleam in her eye that made Kian suspect she had ideas of her own.

She was supposed to have said the line after his mother's speech, but she'd refused because she'd wanted to get the doll first. It had taken Syssi some time to explain that no one was going to take the doll because if anyone but her did that, Uncle Gerard would be angry, and everyone was scared of Uncle Gerard.

It hadn't been a lie either and, evidently, even Allegra knew the power of Chef Gerard.

"I want to talk there," Allegra pointed to the microphone on the platform.

"Come on, then," Kian said. "Let's give the people what they want."

Together, the three of them climbed the steps to the platform. The crowd's attention immediately shifted toward them, and a hush fell over the lawn.

"Hello, everyone," Kian said into the microphone. "Thank you for joining us on this special day. Allegra has something she'd like to say."

He held the microphone up to his daughter's mouth, but suddenly confronted with the reality of addressing the crowd, Allegra ducked her head shyly against his neck.

"It's okay, sweetheart," Kian murmured. "Remember what we practiced?"

Allegra peeked out at the assembled guests, her blue eyes wide. Then, as if making a decision, she reached for the microphone with determined hands.

Kian surrendered it, keeping a firm grip on both his daughter and the mic to prevent any disasters.

Allegra took a deep breath, then proclaimed in a clear, high voice, "Thank you for coming to my birthday. Eat the cake, but don't touch the doll. She's mine."

As the crowd erupted in laughter and applause, Kian looked at Syssi, who was covering her mouth to stifle her own giggles.

He took the microphone back, bouncing a now-beaming Allegra on his hip. "Well, you heard the birthday girl. The cake is for eating, but the doll is spoken for."

More laughter rippled through the crowd. Kian scanned the faces below, feeling a surge of gratitude for this community they had all built. Two thousand and one years of existence, and these were the moments that made it all worthwhile.

"Before we cut the cake," he continued, "I want to extend my heartfelt thanks to Amanda for organizing this wonderful celebration. As always, her ingenuity and creativity have made this day perfect."

Amanda waved from her spot near the buffet, her arm linked with Dalhu's.

"And special thanks to Gerard for the incredible cake that has everyone talking," Kian added. "It's not only beautiful but, I'm assured, delicious as well."

Gerard, standing beside the dessert table, gave a not-so-modest bow.

"And now," Kian announced, "I'd like to invite Jasmine to come up and lead us in singing 'Happy Birthday.'"

As Jasmine ascended the steps, Ell-rom watched her from below, his eyes full of pride.

"Thank you, Kian," Jasmine said, taking the microphone. She turned to face the crowd. "Everyone ready? One, two, three..."

As everyone broke into song, their voices rising in harmony, Allegra's face lit up with delight. Syssi leaned against his side, her hand resting on their daughter's back, and for a moment, the world narrowed to just the three of them amidst the music.

When the song ended, they moved to the cake table where Gerard stood ready with a knife. He handed it to Kian with a flourish.

"The honor is yours, Regent," Gerard said with a wink at Allegra.

Kian positioned the knife at the base of the towering creation, then paused. "Do you want to help?" he asked his daughter.

She nodded with a solemn expression and put her little hand over his.

"Ready?" he asked. "Push down."

Together, they cut into the bottom tier of the cake, eliciting more applause.

"And now." Kian lifted Allegra higher. "The moment our princess has been waiting for."

He allowed her to reach up and remove the doll that crowned the cake. She clutched it to her chest with a triumphant grin, as if she'd just claimed a hard-won prize, ignoring the frosting that she was smearing over her party dress.

"Mine," she declared again, just in case anyone had missed her earlier announcement.

"Yes, yours," Syssi agreed, smoothing her daughter's curls. "But what do we say when we receive a gift?"

Allegra looked down at the doll, then back up at her mother. "Thank you," she said dutifully, though Kian wasn't sure if she was thanking Gerard for the cake or the universe at large for the doll.

As the Odus took over and began slicing and distributing cake, Kian spotted Kalugal and Jacki standing at the other side of the buffet table with little Darius in his father's arms.

"Look who's here," he said, pointing in their direction. "Your cousin Darius is back from Egypt. Do you want to say hello?"

"Darius," Allegra repeated, then looked at her doll and shook her head.

"He's not going to take your doll away, sweetie."

She shook her head again.

"I'll take her," Syssi said. "Say hello for both of us."

She took their daughter, who was now having an intense one-sided whispered conversation with the doll.

Kian kissed Syssi's cheek, then Allegra's, and then made his way toward Kalugal, Jacki, and their son.

"Happy birthday, cousin." Kalugal pulled Kian into a brief embrace.

"Thank you for cutting your trip short to be here," Kian said, offering his hand to Jacki. "I know how much you've been looking forward to exploring Egypt."

Jacki smiled. "It was time to come home. Egypt is fascinating, but it's very stressful there these days."

"How so?" Kian asked.

The political situation in Egypt had been tense for years, but he hadn't heard of any specific threats to tourists lately.

"It's just the general vibe. We needed a cadre of bodyguards with us at all times. It became rather oppressive after a while."

"The Brotherhood's influence has grown there," Kalugal added in a lower voice. "I had to keep a low profile and use my Professor Gunter disguise."

"It was still an incredible trip," Jacki said. "Despite the security concerns, it felt like a treasure hunt. The digs were fruitful, and the markets were a treasure trove! I found several pieces that set my intuition humming."

Jacki's psychometric abilities made her uniquely suited for archaeological work. Her ability to touch an object and glean its history was very useful, but it also potentially exposed her to things she would rather not see, so she was discriminating about the objects she allowed herself to touch.

"We brought some interesting finds back with us," Kalugal said. "I can't wait to show them to the family."

Kian's curiosity was piqued. "What kind of finds?"

A mysterious smile played across Kalugal's lips. "I'd rather keep it as a surprise for later. I don't want to compete with your birthday celebration."

Kian raised an eyebrow but didn't press the matter. Kalugal enjoyed drama almost as much as Annani, and Kian had no problem letting his cousin have his moment.

"As you wish," Kian said. "By the way, have you met our guest Din yet? He's an archaeology professor at the University of Edinburgh. I thought you two might have a lot to chat about."

"I haven't had the pleasure of meeting the professor yet."

"Let me introduce you," Kian offered. "He's mentioned something about some artifacts from predynastic Egypt, but I might be mistaken."

"Predynastic?" Kalugal's interest was immediately captured. "That's an era that's always fascinated me. The transition period was when early Egyptian culture was still forming its identity. This is when the gods' influence was most prominent."

Kian scanned the crowd, finally spotting Din and Fenella sitting at a table near the dance floor.

"There they are," Kian said, pointing them out. "Let's walk over and I'll make the introductions."

6

DIN

D in held on to Fenella's hand as they both watched couples twirling on the dance floor.

His mind kept circling back to the two small words that carried so much uncertainty.

"For now."

"You are brooding again," Fenella said. "You've got that professor face—all furrowed brow and distant eyes."

"Sorry." He shifted to face her. "Do you want to dance?"

"Sure." She started to rise when Kian walked over to their table with Kalugal and his wife and son.

Din had seen Kalugal and Jacki during their visit to Scotland when they'd stayed at the castle, again when he'd visited the village for special occasions, and once again during the wedding cruise, but they'd never been formally introduced.

He still found it difficult to wrap his head around Kalugal being Navuh's son—the offspring of the Brotherhood's founder and leader, the big bad wolf himself, and at the same time being Annani's nephew and Kian's cousin. It had been bizarre, to say the least, to find out that Navuh was mated to Annani's sister Areana, and that she had given him two sons.

All the other sons Navuh claimed as his own were not related to him by blood.

Kalugal and Lokan were part of the clan now, but Lokan was still straddling the fence, pretending to work for his father while feeding the clan information about the Brotherhood.

"Din, Fenella," Kian greeted them as he reached their table. "I'd like you to meet Kalugal and Jacki and their son, Darius."

Din rose to his feet, Fenella following suit.

"Kalugal, this is Professor Din MacDougal," Kian said. "He is visiting us from Scotland. And this is Fenella, a new member of our community with a long history connecting her to the clan."

Kalugal extended a hand to Fenella first. "Enchanted. I've heard about your performance at the Hobbit Bar. I can't wait to see you in action."

"I'm there tonight." She shook his hand. "Bring an object for me to read and I promise to embarrass you in front of everyone."

Kalugal laughed. "Perhaps I shouldn't come then."

Jacki smiled as she took Fenella's hand. "We'll come

together, and you can embarrass me if Kalugal refuses to play along."

"I'll play." Kalugal turned to Din. "Professor, it's a pleasure to meet a fellow archaeologist, although I have to admit that my academic title is fake. I'm self-taught."

Din accepted the handshake. "Your collection of artifacts is quite impressive."

Kalugal looked delighted at the praise. "What portion of it have you seen?"

"Only the pieces displayed in the pavilion," Din said. "But they're extraordinary. The predynastic figurines, in particular, are fascinating."

"Predynastic Egypt is one of Kalugal's particular interests." Jacki took the squirming baby from her husband's arms. "Kian mentioned you specialize in that era?"

"Among others," Din said. "Naturally, my particular interest is evidence of advanced civilizations predating our conventional historical timeline, but those are hard to come by."

"Evidence of gods." Kalugal's lips curled in a knowing smirk. "That's why I entered the field as well." He chuckled. "In academic circles, admission of such interest would be career suicide. But here, there is no need for scholarly euphemisms."

"We've just returned from Egypt," Jacki said. "The political situation is tense, and it's not safe, but it was still worth it. We managed to acquire several remarkable artifacts."

"Which brings me to why I wanted to meet you," Kalugal added. "We're hosting a brunch tomorrow at our home to show the family what we've brought back, and since you're an archaeologist, I'd like to invite you and Fenella to join us."

Din blinked in surprise. A family gathering at Kalugal's home was not how he imagined spending his Sunday morning, and he was sure he would be acutely uncomfortable with the clan's royalty present.

When he glanced at Fenella, she looked equally taken aback.

"That's very kind, but I wouldn't want to intrude on a family event."

Kalugal waved a dismissive hand. "Nonsense. Your expertise would be valuable. Besides, Fenella is family now, isn't she? She's part of the in-laws, so to speak, and you are her companion."

It took Din a moment to process what Kalugal had meant by his comment. Fenella was loosely related to Jasmine, who was mated to Ell-rom, Annani's half-brother, but the connection was so distant that it was nearly irrelevant.

"We'd be honored," Fenella said before Din could formulate a response. "What time should we arrive?"

"Eleven," Kalugal said. "You can find the location on the village map."

"Are you certain we wouldn't be intruding?" Din tried again.

"Family is a fluid concept." Kalugal clapped him on his back. "Blood relations matter less than the bonds we choose to form. I'm inviting you because I believe your insights will be valuable and because of Fenella's newly discovered talent."

Din swallowed. There was something in Kalugal's tone that brooked no argument, and he wondered whether the guy was using compulsion on him.

He wouldn't do that in front of Kian, would he?

"What sort of artifacts did you find?" Din asked, changing tack.

Jacki's eyes lit up. "That's the surprise."

Kalugal turned to Fenella. "Your psychometric ability might become useful as well."

She glanced at Jacki. "That's your talent also, I've heard."

"Yes," Jacki confirmed. "Mine is unpredictable, though. Sometimes I touch an object and see the past, and sometimes I see the future. Most often, though, I get nothing."

Fenella's eyes widened. "It's the same for me, but I thought it was because I'm new to this. Kyra and Jasmine seem to amplify my ability, though. I don't think I can sense anything without them."

Kalugal regarded Fenella with curiosity in his smiling eyes. "Then I sure need to invite Kyra as well. She is with Max, correct?"

"Yes," Kian said. "Max is now in charge of the dungeon, so his security clearance has been bumped up. But Din and Fenella are civilians."

Kalugal didn't seem perturbed by what Kian was implying. "Don't worry about confidentiality, cousin. I can ensure that whatever needs to remain a secret stays a secret."

Obviously, the guy could compel anyone, including immortals, to keep a secret.

The exchange made Din even more curious about the artifact Kalugal was going to reveal.

"Tomorrow at eleven," Kalugal said before departing with his family and Kian.

"Well, that was interesting." Fenella watched them walk away. "It seems that I've been upgraded from Jasmine's distant relation to someone worthy of brunch invitations to the inner circle."

"It would seem so." Din rubbed his jaw. "I'm sorry if I seemed reluctant. I just wasn't expecting to be invited to a family gathering."

"It's a bit intimidating, I have to admit."

He nodded. "Kalugal is an interesting guy. Do you know that he's a three-quarter god?"

She frowned. "What do you mean?"

"His mother is a full-blooded goddess, Annani's half-sister, and his father is a half-god, half-human. That makes Kalugal and his brother Lokan three-quarter gods, which is more than Kian and his sisters, who are only half-god, half-human."

Fenella shook her head. "Does it matter? Does it change the clan hierarchy?"

"Not really. I just find it hard to believe. We didn't know all that before Kalugal and Lokan joined the clan. We also didn't know that Navuh's other sons are not really his. He just claims all the boys born to his immortal concubines, but he is entirely devoted to Areana, proof that even monsters can have a redeeming quality."

Fenella tilted her head. "How many sons does he claim to have?"

"I don't know." Din chuckled. "Many, I guess. Their portraits are hanging in a room in the office building. Dalhu, Amanda's husband, sketched them for the clan. He is also a former Doomer, but he is not part of Kalugal's men. He found his way to the clan in a different way."

"I bet there is a fascinating story there." She shook her head. "I'm constantly learning new things about this immortal community, but every time I think I get the gist of it, I discover new fantastic stories. Is there a book somewhere that documents everything in a systematic manner?"

"Unfortunately, there isn't." He wrapped his arm around her waist. "We believe that oral transmission of history is the best way to preserve it."

She frowned. "You can't be serious."

"I wish I wasn't. I have no idea why no one's undertaken the task of documenting our history." He sighed. "It's a complex world we inhabit. Gods and immortals, ancient grudges and new alliances. Sometimes I wonder if humans have any idea how much of their history has been manipulated by forces they don't understand, and it is still being manipulated to this day."

"Does it bother you?" Fenella asked. "Knowing the

truth when the rest of your colleagues at the university are fumbling in the dark?"

Din considered the question. "It used to. I'd sit in academic conferences listening to theories that completely missed the mark, wanting to stand up and tell them the truth. But no one would believe me even if I did. Humans prefer to cling to dogmas and stories that fit the narrative of their beliefs. Truth matters very little to them."

"Very philosophical, Professor," Fenella said. "I imagine it makes writing peer-reviewed papers challenging. 'Ancient Aliens' isn't exactly a respected theory in archaeology."

Din was surprised that she was familiar with the show. "You have no idea. I've had to become an expert in implication and suggestion, presenting evidence in ways that hint at the truth without explicitly stating it."

"Well, tomorrow you can speak freely," Fenella said. "No need to couch your theories in academic jargon when you're among fellow believers."

"True," Din agreed. "Though I'm still trying to wrap my head around Kalugal's invitation. I understand why you were included—your connection to Jasmine, plus your psychometric abilities, makes you a valuable guest. But why does he need me there? I'm sure he doesn't expect me to know more about archaeology than he does."

Fenella's eyes sparkled with mischief. "Maybe he's just curious about the guy who obsessed about a bartender for fifty years until he got to be her boyfriend."

"Boyfriend?" Din raised an eyebrow. "Is that what I am?"

"Well, you're certainly not just a friend," Fenella said. "And 'lover' seems a bit old-fashioned, don't you think?"

"I prefer 'devoted admirer,'" Din suggested. "Or perhaps an enamored suitor." He caught her hand, bringing it to his lips.

Fenella's laughter faded, replaced by a curious intensity. "You're serious, aren't you? About us, I mean."

"I told you I love you. I don't say those words lightly. In fact, other than my mother, you are the only woman I've ever said that to."

A complex mix of emotions crossed Fenella's face —hope, fear, longing, uncertainty. "It's all happening so fast, Din," she said quietly. "You need to give me more time."

"We have plenty of it," he assured her. "Take as long as you need."

7

FENELLA

Fenella stared up at Kalugal's house, her expectations shattered. The structure was modest, almost humble by village standards, with a red door that provided the only splash of color against the neutral exterior and was the sole indicator that what lay on the other side was not as humble as the exterior suggested.

She recognized the door from a luxury homes magazine she'd browsed through at the clinic. It was an Italian designer piece that cost a fortune.

"That's an interesting front door," Din muttered. "It looks heavy."

"That's because it is. This whole thing swings on a pivot."

He looked at her with a frown. "How do you know that?"

"I've seen it in a magazine. The price quoted was twenty-five thousand dollars."

His eyes widened. "Just for the door?"

She nodded. "Just for the door before installation."

Shaking his head, Din rang the doorbell, and moments later, the door swung open just as Fenella had explained, pivoting to reveal Kalugal himself, dressed casually in a dark blue short-sleeved shirt and jeans that fit him so well Fenella was sure they had been custom-ordered.

"Welcome to my home." He stepped aside to let them enter. "I do appreciate punctuality, and it seems like you are the only ones who actually showed up on time."

"Are we the first to arrive?" Fenella asked.

"Indeed." Kalugal closed the door behind them by giving it a slight push. It locked with a pneumatic hiss. "Which is fortunate since I can give you a tour while we wait for the others."

The entry foyer was tastefully decorated but unremarkable other than the departure from the Mediterranean style Fenella had grown accustomed to throughout the village. Here, the slant was a little more contemporary.

"This way." He beckoned them forward. "We can use the lift or the stairs. Which do you prefer?"

"The stairs," Fenella said.

"Okay then." He led them toward a pair of glass doors that seemed to be leading into a sitting room.

When he opened them, though, they revealed a wide staircase that descended into a vast open living area bathed in natural light from above. The ceiling—

or rather, what should have been the ceiling—was a series of geometric skylights that allowed sunlight to spill into the space below. The room stretched far beyond what the footprint of the aboveground structure could possibly contain.

"It's built underground," she breathed.

"Most of it." Kalugal's lips curved with satisfaction at her stunned reaction. "Come, I'll show you the rest."

They followed him down the stairs into the main living area, an expansive space with multiple seating arrangements, a state-of-the-art entertainment system, and floor-to-ceiling bookshelves along one wall. The furnishings were luxurious without being showy—comfortable leather sofas, plush area rugs, and occasional tables that looked handcrafted even though they were all in contemporary style.

"This is incredible," Din said. "How much square footage are we talking about?"

"Just under twelve thousand," Kalugal replied.

Fenella's jaw dropped. "Twelve thousand? Where is it all hiding?"

Kalugal waved his hand. "Mostly underground. No structure in the village can be more than one story aboveground, and footprints are restricted to maintain the village's low profile from aerial observation. But I employed a creative solution around the restrictions."

He led them through an archway into a formal dining room, large enough to seat twenty people comfortably, explaining that it could accommodate double that by extending the table.

They continued to a large gym that rivaled the one in the clan's underground complex, and a library. Several corridors led to what Fenella assumed were bedrooms.

"I would show you the kitchen, but Atzil hates anyone intruding on his domain when he's cooking, so you'll have to wait for after brunch, and maybe he'll show you around since you two are working together."

Last night, Atzil had muttered something about having to wake up early and prepare brunch, but he hadn't seemed upset about having to work on the weekend. On the contrary, he'd been excited about hosting the Clan Mother and the rest of the family.

"The skylights are essential," Kalugal continued his tour. "Without natural light, living underground would be depressing. But they're designed to be completely concealed when needed." He tapped a control panel on the wall, and a section of one of the skylights darkened, a seamless panel sliding into place above it. "At night, the underground part of the house disappears from aerial view, and in case of a breach, I can seal it off completely, turning it into a bunker."

"Brilliant," Din said.

"Thank you." Kalugal tapped the panel again, and the skylight reopened, flooding the room with light once more. "In my opinion, that's a much smarter approach to security than Kian's. My cousin focuses on maintaining the village's aesthetic uniformity, with everyone living in similar-sized homes, which is a noble idea in theory, but impractical in reality. As leaders of our communities, Kian and I need larger spaces for entertaining guests, and we also have larger households, or at least I do."

As he led them back to the dining room, Fenella swept her gaze over the artwork hanging on the walls and the statues perched on pedestals.

Compared to all this splendor, the Clan Mother's home looked provincial.

How rich was Kalugal?

Was he richer than Kian?

It appeared there was a competition going on between the cousins, but it seemed like the kind that was inevitable between two alphas and not anything worrisome or malicious. It was good-natured.

"Hello." Jacki entered the room. "I see that Kalugal gave you the tour already."

Her blond hair was pulled back in a simple pony-tail, and her outfit of white wide-legged pants and a pink silk blouse was casual and elegant.

Kalugal wrapped an arm around her waist. "I didn't show them the kitchen. Do you want to risk it?"

She assumed a horrified expression. "And risk my life? No, thank you. No one goes into that kitchen until Atzil is done."

Fenella laughed. "You make him sound like a tyrant. He's such a nice guy. The best boss I ever had."

Jacki rolled her eyes. "Atzil suffers from a split personality. I don't recommend you get acquainted with the one that's in control while he's in the kitchen.

Can I offer you anything to drink? Coffee, tea, mimosas?"

"Coffee would be wonderful," Fenella said. "But if the kitchen is off limits…"

"We have a coffee station." Jacki leaned closer to Fenella. "Kalugal had to make ours fancier than Syssi's."

"I heard that," Kalugal said. "I just wanted us to enjoy great coffee."

Rolling her eyes, Jacki threaded her arm through Fenella's and led her to the living room to show her the sprawling bar, which could easily rival the Hobbit's and included a commercial La Marzocco espresso machine, which the Hobbit didn't have.

"That's bigger than the one they have in the village café," Din commented.

The grin on Kalugal's face was so big it was almost comical. "Of course it is."

"Should we wait for the others?" Fenella asked as Jacki started making cappuccinos for the four of them.

"They can join us when they get here." Kalugal looked at his watch, which seemed like a luxury item and probably cost as much as a car. "I think I made a mistake and told everyone to get here at eleven-thirty instead of eleven."

"You did," Jacki said.

"Oh." He cast them a sheepish smile. "My apologies for the mistake. I hope you don't mind."

Fenella had a feeling that he had done that on purpose, although she couldn't understand why he needed to use subterfuge. He could have just told them that he was inviting them earlier so they would have time to chat.

"No, of course not," Din said. "We can talk about your digs until they get here."

Fenella didn't mind general talk about archeology, but if they started throwing academic terms around that she wasn't familiar with, she would get bored pretty quickly.

"Are you also an archaeologist?" she asked Jacki as they sat with their coffees on the comfortable sectional.

"I'm not. My interest is mostly by association." She smiled at her husband. "I've always wanted to go see a dig, but Kalugal didn't want to take me to Egypt while Darius was still little. We finally went after you were rescued, but we cut our trip short to return for the birthday celebration and for other reasons." She cast Kalugal a quick glance. "We might go back after Kalugal takes care of some urgent business matters."

"What's your background, then?" Fenella asked before taking a sip from the heavenly-smelling cappuccino.

Jacki put her cup down. "My background has little to do with what I'm doing these days, which is managing our charitable organization." She smiled. "Lately, I've been busy restructuring our charity to maximize government funding streams."

Fenella raised an eyebrow. "That sounds complicated."

"It is," Jacki said. "But fascinating once you understand the system. Our foundation, which primarily focuses on rehabilitation services for trafficking survivors, was funded primarily by the clan and Kalugal's contributions. The funds collected through charity galas and the like were not substantial. Now we get millions in government grants and subsidies."

"I had no idea the government provided that much support," Fenella said.

"Most people don't." Jacki's eyes lit up. "There are dozens of federal and state programs with overlapping mandates, each with its own funding streams. The trick is knowing how to position your services to qualify for multiple sources without violating any regulations."

"It sounds like a system that could be easily abused," Fenella said.

"Oh, it absolutely is," Jacki agreed. "The amount of fraud is staggering. Organizations claiming to provide services they never deliver, inflating client numbers, misappropriating funds for administrative 'overhead' that somehow includes the CEO's vacation home, mega-yacht, private jet, and so on. But in our case, one hundred percent of the money goes directly to benefit survivors. I don't even take a salary."

"Did you study nonprofit management?" Fenella asked.

Jacki laughed, the sound both rueful and proud. "I didn't attend university at all. I grew up in the foster care system, bouncing between homes until I aged out at eighteen. Street smarts were my education." She took a sip of her coffee. "Ella—Julian's wife—is the one with the formal education in nonprofit administration. She handles the paperwork and compliance. But all the monetary shenanigans?" She tapped her temple. "Those were my ideas."

Kalugal's arm slid around his wife's shoulders, his expression adoring. "Jacki's the real genius in the family."

"Stop it," Jacki protested. "I'm like a bulldog with a bone when I'm on a mission, but I don't come close to your intellect." She turned to Fenella. "Kalugal speaks seventeen languages fluently and can calculate orbital mechanics in his head."

Fenella chuckled. "I don't even know what that means."

Should she feel inadequate?

Well, of course. Compared to these two geniuses, she was an average nobody.

Her greatest accomplishment was mixing killer drinks.

"I can show you some of the artifacts while we wait for the others." Kalugal rose to his feet once they were done with their coffees. "I keep most of my finds in the vaults, but I have a few things on display around the house."

As they followed their hosts, Din leaned close to Fenella's ear. "Those two have a mutual admiration club," he whispered, his breath warm against her skin.

Fenella stifled a laugh and leaned to whisper back,

"It's kind of adorable." She paused, then added with a mischievous smile. "I think you're a genius, too. No one can grill a perfect steak like you do."

Din's eyes widened in mock surprise before they both dissolved into quiet laughter, drawing curious glances from their hosts.

Once they surveyed the few pieces scattered along the hallways, they returned to the dining room.

"Who else is coming?" Fenella helped herself to a glass of cucumber water from a carafe on the sideboard.

"The Clan Mother, of course," Jacki said. "Kian and Syssi, Amanda and Dalhu, Alena and Orion, Max and Kyra, Jasmine and Ell-rom, Morelle and Brandon. I hope they bring the kids."

Fenella smiled. "Yeah, me too. I would love to get to know Allegra. She seems like a character."

"She definitely is." Jacki poured herself a glass. "Darius adores her."

"Where is he?" Fenella asked.

"With Shamash. He'll bring him later." She leaned against the sideboard. "Shamash used to be Kalugal's butler of sorts, more like a personal assistant, but he turned out to be so good with Darius that he's our nanny now."

Fenella couldn't imagine a former Doomer as a babysitter, but if Jacki was comfortable leaving her baby boy with the guy, he had to be a good person.

8

ANNANI

Annani stood by the window of her village home, her hand on the glass that was warmed by the sunlight filtering through the leaves of a maple tree. She smoothed her other hand over the side of her dark purple gown, chosen specifically because it minimized the appearance of stains.

Spending time with her newest batch of grandchildren was a delight, but their little fingers were not always clean, and she did not want to worry about her clothing. Later, her faithful Odus would do their best to wash the stains out, but if they failed, it would not be a big loss. She was not attached to any garment, and the seamstress she employed to make her gowns would love to create new ones for her.

At the humming sound of an electric cart approaching, a smile bloomed on her face, and a few moments later, the golf cart she had been expecting stopped in front of her house. Kian got out, leaving Syssi and Allegra in the vehicle as he strode to her front door.

Her son rarely did anything at a leisurely pace, always moving with purpose and determination. She wished he could slow down and just savor life like she was doing, and maybe one day he would, when Allegra was all grown up and ready to take over for her daddy.

When the doorbell rang, Annani put her sunglasses on and walked over to greet her son.

"Mother." He bowed nearly in half to kiss her cheek. "Your chariot awaits."

Annani laughed. "I still remember those, and this lovely golf cart is much more comfortable to sit in, but not as impressive to look at."

Smiling, he offered her his arm. "We can make it a project and build a golf cart that looks like a chariot. I'm sure the kids would love it."

"Indeed." She leaned on him not because she needed to, but because it felt nice. "Any idea what Kalugal's surprise might be?"

"I suspect it's an artifact of some significance. What else could he have brought over from a dig in Egypt?"

As they reached the golf cart, Allegra's face lit up, her small arms reaching out to Annani. "Nana!"

"Hello, my little princess." Annani bent to receive the enthusiastic hug from her granddaughter. "And how are you this beautiful morning?"

"Look!" Allegra held up the porcelain figurine from her birthday cake, its delicate features gleaming in the sunlight. "She's so pretty."

"She is indeed." Annani examined the doll with appropriate solemnity. "But you must be very careful with her. Porcelain breaks easily if dropped."

Nodding with a serious expression on her sweet face, Allegra clutched the doll closer to her chest.

Kian offered his hand to help Annani settle into the back seat beside Allegra's car seat, and once everyone was situated, he set off along the winding paths of the village.

"Sparkles, see?" Allegra pointed to the doll's elaborate costume. "Also on shoes. And her hair is like mine." She patted her own blonde curls for emphasis.

"Does she have a name yet?" Annani asked.

Allegra frowned, thinking for a long moment before lifting the doll in front of Annani's face. "She is Princess Sparkle."

"Princess Sparkle is perfect," Annani declared, earning a beaming smile from her granddaughter.

As the cart wound through the village, Annani's thoughts turned to Kalugal's invitation and the hint of a special revelation.

"I keep trying to guess what Kalugal found in Egypt." Syssi echoed Annani's thoughts. "He mentioned artifacts, but that was it. The guy sure likes to build up suspense."

"The most memorable artifact in Kalugal's possession, as far as I am concerned, is that small figurine of

Wonder—or Gulan as she was once called." Annani paused, memories of her childhood friend contrasting with the woman she had become as Wonder. "When Jacki held it, she saw visions of what happened to the caravan Gulan was traveling with when the earthquake struck."

"I remember," Kian said. "Jacki reacted strongly to it, and Kalugal was worried."

Annani adjusted the folds of her gown. "The strange thing is that Wonder herself never held the figurine, and whoever carved it could not possibly have known about the earthquake or who Wonder was at the time. The only plausible explanation is that it was a figurine of someone who merely resembled Wonder. But then it does not make sense that it held echoes of what happened to her."

"Maybe the carver had a vision of her," Syssi suggested. "Perhaps he or she had seen Wonder tumbling into the chasm while trying to save people, and that person imparted the vision on the figurine."

"That is actually the explanation that makes the most sense," Annani agreed. "Some humans possess second sight."

Like the old woman who had told her that she would find Khiann again. At the time, Annani had neither believed nor disbelieved the prophecy entirely. It had given her a glimmer of hope, and now, five thousand years later, it had grown into more than a glimmer.

Why had it taken her so long to detangle what had actually happened?

No body had ever been found, so the only evidence had been the oral testimony given by Mortdh's warriors. Their minds could have been manipulated by her father to implicate Mortdh and get rid of a powerful enemy. It did not mean that her father had engineered Khiann's death or even had anything to do with it. It only meant that he had capitalized on an opportunity.

Ahn might have even suspected that Khiann had fallen victim to the earthquake and was buried somewhere in the desert, but had waited until after the trial to tell her. He had no way of knowing that neither he nor the other gods would survive long enough to search for Khiann.

But that did not make much sense either.

If Ahn's plan had materialized and Mortdh had been entombed for the crime of murdering Khiann, once Khiann had been dug out of the desert and resurrected, the gods would have demanded that Mortdh be resurrected as well. The punishment for attempted murder of a god was not the same as the punishment for actually killing another god.

"Mommy, Nana, look!" Allegra's voice cut through Annani's jumbled thoughts. She pointed excitedly at a butterfly dancing on the warm currents of air beside their slow-moving cart. "Butterfly is pretty!"

"Yes, sweetheart, it's beautiful." Syssi leaned to kiss the top of her daughter's head.

"I think it has something to do with our search for Khiann." Kian's words sent a jolt of hope through Annani's chest. "Kalugal wouldn't have cut his trip short just to attend our birthday celebration, and he wouldn't have specifically requested that Fenella join us along with Din."

"Ah, yes. Our archaeologist guest." Annani kept her voice steady despite the turmoil of emotions rioting inside of her. "I am pleased to see how well he and Fenella have reconnected. As always, watching the Fates' matchmaking is fascinating. They make the most unlikely pairing, and yet they are perfect."

"Maybe they work so well because they are not perfect," Syssi said. "Those two were separated for fifty years, but I suppose that they had some growing up to do before they were ready to commit to each other."

"Time means little when souls recognize each other," Annani said softly. Her thoughts drifted again to Khiann and her infatuation with him that had blossomed into love. "True connections transcend the constraints of time and circumstance."

Kian slowed the cart as they passed the bridge leading to Kalugal's section, and as he stopped in front of the small house with a distinctive red door, Annani observed it with interest.

The door was new, another small act of rebellion on Kalugal's part, his refusal to conform to the village's Mediterranean vibe.

"We've arrived," Kian announced.

"Let me out!" Allegra demanded, already struggling against the straps of her car seat.

"Patience, munchkin." Syssi unhooked the safety belts, lifting her daughter out of the seat. "Remember what we talked about? Inside voices and gentle hands."

Allegra nodded solemnly, though Annani caught the mischievous gleam in her eye that suggested these rules might be forgotten once she was reunited with her little playmates.

She was a bossy little girl, a natural leader, and the other children had accepted her authority without a fight.

Anticipating the lovely time she was going to spend with her grandchildren, Annani experienced an expectant joy. Still, beneath it all, there was the persistent melancholy that she had learned to hide so well that even she sometimes forgot it was there. It was the longing for the one who should have been by her side through all these millennia, raising their children and grandchildren together and watching their clan grow.

But the Fates had had different plans, and her children had been fathered by humans who had embodied some of Khiann's qualities but never all of them.

There was no one like Khiann, her one and only love, and hopefully, they would one day be reunited.

Kian rang the doorbell, and moments later, the door swung open to reveal Kalugal.

"Clan Mother," he greeted her with a respectful bow. "Kian, Syssi, and the little princess. Welcome to my home."

Annani had told Kalugal a thousand times to call her by her name, but he refused, either calling her Clan Mother or Aunt Annani when Darius was present.

"Uncle Kal!" Allegra wriggled in her mother's arms. "Look. Princess Sparkle. She wants to meet Darius!"

Kalugal's expression warmed as he bent to the child's level. "What a splendid idea. Darius is playing with Evie, so you can show them your doll at the same time."

Allegra nodded eagerly.

As Syssi followed Kalugal inside with Allegra, Kian offered his arm once more to Annani. "Shall we, Mother?"

They stepped into the house, following the sounds of conversation and children's laughter down into Kalugal's impressive underground domain. The main living area was already filled with family members.

Annani's gaze drifted to the children. Allegra was showing her doll to Darius, and Evie was watching with interest, patiently waiting her turn to be introduced to Princess Sparkle.

A pang of sadness touched Annani's heart again as she watched Kalugal's beautiful little boy. Areana would miss her grandchild growing up because she was a willing prisoner of her mate, restricted to the lavish harem that Navuh had put her in. Annani's and Areana's own sons had offered to free her, but Areana had refused.

For better or worse, Navuh was her truelove mate,

and she would never leave him, not even to see her grandchild grow.

Darius's first words, his first steps, the gradual unfolding of personality and talent—they could never be reclaimed once passed. These precious moments would be lost forever to her.

9

KALUGAL

Kalugal savored the gentle hum of conversation flowing around his dining table, the satisfaction of a successful gathering curiously comforting.

His family and guests were enjoying Atzil's culinary masterpiece of a brunch while stealing curious glances his way.

He'd kept them waiting deliberately.

The art of suspense was something his cousin didn't understand and therefore had never mastered. Kian was always so direct, so focused on efficiency, and there was merit in that, but it also sucked all the fun out of life, and when one lived for as long as they did, having fun was vital.

There was value to the anticipation, the curiosity, the guessing, all heightening the eventual revelation.

"More mimosas?" Kalugal offered, gesturing to the crystal pitcher.

"Please." Fenella held out her glass.

She seemed particularly impatient, even more so than the rest of the family, who were more familiar with his antics, her eyes darting between him and the door to his study where he'd stored the artifact.

Din tried to maintain his scholarly composure, but Kalugal caught the professor's fingers tapping rhythmically against the tablecloth.

Atzil emerged from the kitchen with another platter of delicacies and placed a tray of miniature quiches on the table.

"Atzil, you have outdone yourself," Annani said, her luminous skin casting a subtle glow even in the well-lit dining room. "The spiced lamb was exquisite."

Atzil's face brightened at the goddess's praise. "Thank you, Clan Mother. Would you care for more of the poached eggs with smoked salmon? You seemed to enjoy them."

"Perhaps later," Annani said. "I am saving room for whatever delights you have planned for dessert."

Atzil bowed his head and retreated to his kitchen, but not before Kalugal noticed the smile tugging at the corners of his mouth.

From down the corridor, childish laughter echoed, punctuated by Shamash's deeper voice.

"Sounds like Shamash keeps the children entertained," Jacki said. "I was worried that he couldn't handle the whole gang, but he seems to be doing just fine."

Kalugal nodded. "He's a natural, and he has endless

patience, which was needed during Darius's colic phase. The guy just enjoys taking care of children."

"Perhaps he needs to find a mate," Orion suggested, his arm draped casually around Alena's shoulders. "Start a family of his own."

Kalugal sighed. "I hope he finds someone, but regrettably, my men and the clan ladies do not seem to be meant for one another. Even Atzil and Ingrid are not regarding their union as fated, which is sad. They are both still hoping to someday find their one and only."

There was a long moment of silence as they all contemplated the disappointing reality. There had been so much hope when Kalugal and his men had first joined the clan, but the Fates seemed to have other plans for members of their integrated community.

"Speaking of Shamash," Jacki turned toward the corridor as the man himself appeared, Darius balanced on his hip. "Is everything all right?"

Shamash nodded. "The children wanted to show their creations to everyone, and by children, I mean their ringleader." He tilted his head in Allegra's direction.

Clutching the porcelain doll in one hand and a colorful drawing in the other, Allegra ran up to Annani. "Nana. I drew Princess Sparkle for you."

The drawing was just a scribble, but Annani made all the appropriate noises, praising her granddaughter's artistic acumen.

Darius squirmed in Shamash's arms, pointing at Kalugal. "Papa!" He held up a piece of paper with something that looked like a triangle scribbled on it.

"Is this a pyramid?" Kalugal stood, walking over to take his son from Shamash. "Let's see this masterpiece."

"Pimid," Darius said.

"Very impressive," Kalugal declared after examining the vaguely triangular scribble. "Perhaps you'll be an architect like your namesake."

When Darius regarded him with a pair of dark eyes that seemed to understand more than they should at his age, Kalugal hugged his son to his chest and kissed the top of his head. "Do you want to stay here with Mommy and Daddy or do you want to go back with Shamash to play?"

As an answer, Darius twisted in his arms and reached for Shamash.

"I guess it's back to playing." Kalugal handed the boy to his assistant.

Allegra seemed to agree with Darius and followed Shamash out of the dining room.

Kalugal waited until they were gone before turning to his guests. "I believe I've kept you all in suspense long enough."

"I'd say," Kian grumbled.

Fenella and Din exchanged a glance, while Kyra leaned forward, her hand automatically rising to the pendant at her throat.

"Jacki and I discovered quite a remarkable item

during our time in Egypt," Kalugal continued. "An item I believe may be of particular interest to you, Clan Mother."

Annani's luminous gaze fixed on him, a flicker of something crossing her features. Was it hope he detected there for a brief moment?

"If you'll excuse me," Kalugal said, "I'll get the artifact."

In his study, he walked over to the safe, which was concealed behind a panel in the bookshelf. The combination was unnecessary—the lock responded to his DNA—but he maintained the pretense of entering a code for any watching eyes. The panel slid aside, revealing a velvet-lined interior where the cloth-wrapped figurine waited.

He lifted it carefully, the weight solid and familiar in his hand. He and Jacki had found it in the marketplace and would have missed it if not for the red-painted long hair of the exquisite figurine catching Jacki's eye. How it had gotten there, who had created it, and why it bore such a striking resemblance to his aunt remained unanswered questions, but he knew Annani would appreciate the unique gift.

Returning to the dining room, Kalugal was gratified to see that conversation remained suspended, all eyes turning to the bundle in his hands.

"Clan Mother." He walked to where Annani sat at the head of the table. "I present to you this gift, though it is rightfully yours in ways I cannot explain. Not yet, anyway."

He placed the cloth-wrapped object in front of her and then stepped back.

Annani's fingers were steady as she unwrapped the protective cloth, layer by layer, and as the final fold fell away, a collective gasp rippled around the table.

The figurine was small, no larger than her palm, but it was exquisitely detailed. Carved from some pale stone that gleamed with an inner light reminiscent of Annani's own skin, it depicted a woman with cascading red hair that flowed nearly to her knees. The face was upturned as if basking in sunlight, a gesture so familiar that several of those present glanced between the statue and Annani herself in astonishment.

"It's you," Kian breathed. "Down to the smallest detail."

Annani remained silent, her fingers tracing the contours of the miniature figure with wonder.

"How is this possible?" Amanda leaned forward, her eyes blazing with curiosity. "Did you have it dated? Is it a find from the era of the gods?"

He shook his head. "It's not nearly as ancient. Perhaps a couple of centuries old, if that. We found it among many others in an open market. We would have missed it if not for the hair. It caught Jacki's attention."

"I have never visited Egypt," Annani said. "But even if the carver met me in another country, my skin would not have been glowing. I only let my glow come out when it is safe among my people."

"Perhaps it is a copy of an older artifact," Din suggested. "The carver might have found a figurine that survived from the gods' era and copied the design."

"That's what we thought," Jacki said. "I read the figurine psychometrically, but I saw very little. A few snippets from the carver's life—an artisan who worked primarily with wood but occasionally chose to work in stone for special commissions or for his own enjoyment. One of the snippets I got was him working while looking at another figurine, but the impressions were too faint and fractured for me to follow."

Morelle leaned forward. "The original figurine would be the key, wouldn't it?"

"My thoughts exactly," Kalugal nodded. "That's why I want to suggest an experiment." His gaze fell over Fenella, Kyra, and Jasmine. "Three women bound by blood, each with unique talents that amplify when combined, might crack this mystery."

Fenella got his meaning right away. "You want us to try reading it together."

He nodded. "The carver was exposed to the original, even held it in his hand. He might have imparted what he'd absorbed from the original figurine into his creation, and with your combined power, you might be able to access it."

"It's worth trying," Kyra said, her hand closing around her pendant. "Although what would that achieve?"

Kalugal smiled. "Finding out the identity of the

original carver would be a good start. Perhaps it's the same person who carved Wonder's figurine. That person knew her fate, so perhaps he also knew Khiann's."

Annani's eyes lifted from the little statue, hope and caution warring in her expression. "What makes you think that this is connected to Khiann?"

"It's just a hunch," Kalugal answered honestly. "But consider the precision of the likeness, the care with which it was crafted. Someone went to extraordinary lengths to create this representation of you, Clan Mother, and the Fates made sure that Jacki and I found it. It does not seem like a coincidence."

A heavy silence fell over the room as the implications settled over them.

"We will give it a try," Jasmine said, looking at Fenella and Kyra.

Fenella nodded, but Kalugal noted the wariness in her posture. She didn't look confident in her ability.

"When do you want to do this?" she asked.

"No time like the present," Kalugal said, casting a glance at Annani. "It's up to you, Clan Mother. Are you ready to do this now?"

Annani cradled the figurine, her expression softening as she gazed at the miniature version of herself. "My heart cannot bear further delay, not when hope stands before me."

She held out the figurine, offering it to Jasmine, who sat closest to her. "If you are willing, I would be grateful for the tiniest morsel of information the three of you can glean."

Jasmine extended her hand. "Of course."

"Perhaps we should move to the living room," Kalugal suggested. "Where there is more comfortable seating, and you three can arrange yourselves however works best for you."

As the group rose from the table, Kalugal caught Jacki's eye across the room. She offered him a small smile of encouragement. They had been right to gift the figurine to the Clan Mother and involve Fenella, Kyra, and Jasmine. Whether it would lead anywhere remained to be seen, but even the smallest chance was worth pursuing.

Kalugal followed the others into the living room, waiting for everyone to find a spot to sit before claiming one for himself. Fenella, Kyra, and Jasmine sat on one of the larger sofas, and the others arranged themselves in a loose semicircle, with Annani taking the armchair directly across from the three women.

"How do we do this?" Fenella asked.

"We should all be touching," Jasmine said. "Like we did before."

Fenella nodded. "Let's do this."

As Jasmine unwrapped the figurine and placed it on the coffee table, Kalugal felt the air in the room grow heavy with anticipation.

The moment had arrived, and he had a feeling it would be even more monumental than any of them had expected.

FENELLA

Fenella settled deeper into the plush sofa, acutely aware of the weight of expectation from every corner of Kalugal's living room. The figurine sat on the coffee table before them, its pale stone surface catching the light from the skylights above, the glow mimicking the goddess's but not quite.

Such a small thing to carry such enormous hope.

The last time she'd attempted psychometry with Kyra and Jasmine bolstering her ability, the visions had hit her like a freight train. She wasn't eager for a repeat performance, especially not with an audience of immortal royalty watching her every move.

"We should sit closer together and hold hands," Jasmine suggested, scooting towards Kyra. "We need physical contact with each other."

Fenella moved in from the other side as Kyra's hand rose to touch her amber pendant. "This is like a supernatural séance," Fenella muttered, then caught Din's encouraging look from where he was sitting in one of Kalugal's fancy chairs that didn't look comfortable.

All these modern pieces were mainly designed to look good. Function was a secondary consideration.

Jasmine chuckled. "I wouldn't call it a séance. We're not trying to contact spirits. It's just reading the echoes left behind in the stone."

"Right. Echoes." Fenella wiped her palms on her pants, annoyed at herself for being nervous. She'd faced down drunken patrons, survived decades on the run, endured unspeakable abuse, and here she was, intimidated by what secrets a tiny statue might hold. "Let's get on with it then."

Jasmine carefully lifted the figurine and handed it to Fenella, who cradled it in her left hand while extending her right toward Kyra. "Ready when you are."

Kyra took her offered hand, and Fenella noted how steady and warm Kyra's hand was compared to her own slightly clammy palm.

With Fenella in the center and Kyra and Jasmine flanking her, the three of them focused inwards and... nothing happened.

"Should we close our eyes?" Kyra asked.

"It might help with focus," Jasmine agreed.

Fenella nodded, though the idea of blocking off sensory input while surrounded by people made her even more nervous than she already was. It went against the survival instinct she'd honed over fifty years of running.

She had to remind herself that she was among friends and had nothing to fear. Din was there, her newly discovered cousins were beside her, and the Clan Mother herself sat across from them, radiating the kind of power that no enemy would be stupid enough to underestimate.

There was no safer place on the face of the Earth for her. She could do this.

"Alright." Fenella forced her eyes shut. "Here goes nothing."

At first, there was only darkness behind her eyelids, the sound of her own breathing, and the small sounds everyone around her was making—the soft rustle of fabric as someone shifted position, and the faint whir of air conditioning.

Still, nothing was coming through.

The figurine might as well have been mass-produced in China for all the psychic impression it was giving off.

"I'm not getting anything," she started to say when Jasmine's hand tightened around hers.

"Give it a moment," Jasmine murmured. "Some-times it takes time to—"

The vision slammed into Fenella with the force of a battering ram. One moment she was sitting on a comfortable sofa in Kalugal's underground mansion, and the next she was somewhere else entirely, seeing through eyes that weren't her own.

A workshop. Small, cramped, with stone dust dancing in shafts of sunlight streaming through a single window. The air tasted dry and gritty, carrying the sharp tang of worked stone and the underlying sweetness of wood shavings. Through the borrowed eyes, Fenella saw hands—not her own, but weathered and strong, marked with the countless small scars that came from years of working with tools on wood and stone.

The carver.

She was experiencing his memories, seeing through his eyes as he worked.

The figurine took shape slowly under his patient hands, each stroke of the chisel deliberate and careful. This wasn't his usual medium—Fenella could feel his slight uncertainty with the stone, the way he had to adjust his technique from the wood he typically worked with. But there was something driving him, a compulsion that went beyond a simple task of producing something pretty that people would pay to own.

His thoughts came to her not in words she could understand—the language was unfamiliar to her—but in impressions and emotions that transcended linguistic barriers.

Devotion.

That was what she felt strongest. This man was devoted to his task because he felt inspired and moved.

The scene shifted, jumping forward in time like a

fast-forwarded movie. Now the figurine was nearly complete, needing only the finer details. The carver set down his tools and reached for something on a high shelf—another figurine wrapped in soft cloth.

When he carefully unwrapped it, Fenella's breath caught in her throat—or would have, if she'd been in control of the body she was experiencing this through.

This was the master figurine he was copying, and it was exquisite. Where the copy was merely beautiful, this was transcendent. The stone seemed to glow with an inner light that had nothing to do with the shafts of sunshine filtering through the workshop window. Every line, every curve spoke of an artist who had captured more than just the likeness of Annani but also some of her essence.

The carver handled it with the reverence one might show a holy relic. His thoughts were a jumble of awe and longing, though for what, Fenella couldn't quite grasp. He studied the original carefully, comparing it to his own work, and she felt his frustration at his inability to capture that ineffable quality that made the original so extraordinary.

But he was close.

The workshop door opened, and a woman entered —his wife, Fenella understood through the warm rush of affection that colored the carver's thoughts. She said something in that unknown language, her tone gently chiding. The carver responded with words Fenella couldn't understand but a tone she recognized—the universal sound of a husband promising he'd be done soon, just a few more minutes.

The woman approached, bringing with her the scent of baked goods. She looked at both figurines, the original and the copy, and even through the carver's eyes, Fenella could see her expression soften with wonder. She reached out as if to touch the original, then pulled her hand back, clearly thinking better of it.

More words were exchanged, and then the woman left, but not before pressing a kiss to the carver's weathered cheek.

Alone again, he returned his attention to the figurines, the original and the copy he was making.

Putting the copy on his worktable, he lifted the original, turning it over in his hands to examine it from every angle, and as he did, the bottom came into view. There, carved into the base in tiny, precise characters, was an inscription.

The script was unfamiliar—not quite pictographic but not alphabetic either. The symbols seemed to flow into each other, creating a pattern that was both artistic and functional. Fenella forced herself to focus, to memorize every line, every curve, every minute detail of the inscription.

The carver ran his thumb over it, and through his touch, Fenella felt something. A resonance, as if the carved symbols themselves held their own memories. The carver must have felt it too because his hands trembled slightly before he carefully set the figurine down.

The vision jumped forward again. Now the workshop was busier, with children helping to clean and wrap various carved items, preparing them for sale. The copy of Annani's figurine sat on a special shelf, complete and painted in bright colors, and in his hand was another copy he was working on. The carver would look at it sometimes with an expression of mingled pride and dissatisfaction. He'd come close to capturing the original's beauty, but he still wasn't happy with the result.

Days blended into one another in that strange, compressed way of memory. Fenella saw glimpses of the carver's life and the steady rhythm of his work. Always, the original figurine remained wrapped and hidden, brought out only when he needed to reference it for some detail or simply to marvel at its perfection, and the first copy he'd made sat on the worktable, serving as the model for many more just like it.

None achieved the perfection of the original, though, which frustrated the carver to no end.

She wanted to tell him that perfectionism was a horrible trait that led to nothing but misery, but the connection between them flowed in just one direction. Besides, the man was long gone, probably spending many years trying to reach the perfection of the original and never quite making it.

On occasion, he would take out the original just to look at it, to run his fingers over that inscription at the base, and each time he did, Fenella paid attention, committing the image of those symbols into her memory.

The workshop was filled with other pieces—wooden carvings mostly that weren't as intricate, practical items and decorative ones alike. The carver's wife and children would take them to sell at the market, returning with coins and supplies.

It was a decent life, filled with the small joys of family, but always, the carver's thoughts would return to the original figurine and the mystery it represented. Who had carved it?

How had he captured such ethereal beauty in stone?

The vision began to fade, the workshop growing dimmer, the sensory details becoming less distinct. Fenella tried to hold on, to glean just a bit more information, but it was like trying to grasp smoke.

Then she was back in her own body, sitting on Kalugal's sofa with her eyes closed and her hand clasped around the figurine. The transition was jarring—from the dry heat of the workshop to the climate-controlled comfort of the underground mansion, from the scent of stone dust to the lingering aroma of Atzil's cooking.

Fenella opened her eyes, blinking against the sudden brightness. Her head spun slightly, and she felt a little disoriented. This time, however, she felt energized instead of drained.

"Oh, wow. This was incredible," she said. "I was actually there, with all of the sensory input. I felt the heat, I smelled the wood and the stone and even the carver's own sweat."

"Gross," Jasmine murmured. "I could have done without that input."

"You felt it too?" Fenella asked.

Jasmine nodded, and so did Kyra.

"Did you see the inscription?" she asked, looking between Kyra and Jasmine. "The carving on the bottom of the original figurine?"

Jasmine nodded, her eyes bright with excitement. "I did. I need a piece of paper to write it down before the image fades."

"You didn't understand it either?" Kyra asked.

Jasmine shook her head. "No, I hoped you did."

"It wasn't Arabic or Farsi." She grimaced. "The vision was blurry for me, and I didn't get the same sensory input as the two of you. I think I was seeing it through Fenella's eyes rather than experiencing it directly."

"We need to write it down," Fenella turned to look at Kalugal. "Or rather, draw what we saw before we forget the details."

Kalugal rose to his feet. "I'll be back in a moment."

He returned promptly with several sheets of paper and pencils. "Here," he distributed them among the three of them.

Fenella grabbed a pencil, her hand moving almost of its own accord as she tried to recreate the symbols. It was harder than she'd expected. The inscription had been small, precisely carved, and she'd been seeing it through someone else's eyes. But she did her best, drawing each symbol as accurately as her memory allowed.

Beside her, Jasmine and Kyra did the same, and while they worked on the inscription, everyone else watched them with bated breath. The room was silent except for the scratch of three pencils on paper and the barely audible breathing of their audience.

"That's the best I can do." Fenella stood up and walked over to Kalugal. "I hope you can decipher the language."

When he frowned, her heart sank.

Kyra and Jasmine handed him their creations next, and as he laid them out side by side on the coffee table, Fenella could see that they'd all captured the same basic symbols, though with slight variations in detail and proportions.

Kalugal studied the drawings intently. "I think this is written in the old language," he said finally.

Gathering up the papers, he walked over to where the Clan Mother sat. "You are more fluent in the old script than I am. Perhaps you can read what it says?"

Annani accepted the papers, and the silence in the room was absolute as everyone waited for her to speak.

11

ANNANI

Annani took the papers from Kalugal with surprisingly steady hands, perhaps because she did not expect any profound revelations from the inscription, but Kalugal was right about the text being written in the old language, and she got excited.

She had not seen it written in so very long that deciphering the script was an effort. Like a schoolgirl, she had to focus on each symbol and sound it out in her mind.

The problem was that the symbols were imperfectly rendered—understandable given that Fenella, Kyra, and Jasmine had been drawing what they had seen rather than writing it—but the underlying structure was there, waiting to be deciphered.

Her fingertips traced over the penciled lines as she began the slow work of translation. The first symbol was clear enough, though Jasmine's version showed it slightly more angular than it should have been. The second required more thought. Was that curve meant to connect to the line below it, or was it separate? She compared the three drawings, looking for consensus among the variations.

"What does it say?" Kian's voice broke through her concentration, tinged with an impatience she recognized all too well.

"Patience, my son," she murmured, not lifting her eyes from the papers. "The old language is not like modern tongues. Each symbol carries layers of meaning, and the way they combine can change the entire message. I must concentrate."

She sensed rather than saw Kian's frustrated shift, but he held his tongue. The rest of the room remained silent, the weight of their collective anticipation disturbing her focus.

The third symbol crystallized in her mind, and with it, the beginning of understanding. Her breath caught as the meaning began to unfold before her. Could it truly be...?

"Mother?" Amanda sounded concerned. "Are you alright?"

Annani did not answer immediately, too focused on confirming what she thought she was deciphering. The fourth symbol, the fifth—yes, yes, it was becoming clearer. Her heart began to race with excitement.

The final symbols fell into place like tumblers in a lock, and the complete message revealed itself to her.

For a moment, she could only stare at the papers, scarcely able to believe what she was seeing.

"Blessed be the memory of the most radiant princess who was taken from us too soon," she read aloud.

There was a collective intake of breath from her audience, but Annani was not finished. Below the inscription, there was a name that made her vision blur with sudden tears.

"Esag, son of Agnon."

The papers trembled in her hands as the full implications crashed over her. Esag was alive. Khiann's best friend still lived.

"Who is Esag?" Ell-rom's question came from her left.

Annani set the papers on the side table beside her chair, needing a moment to compose herself. When she looked up, she found every eye in the room fixed upon her.

"Esag was Khiann's squire," she said, her voice steady, but emotion colored her words. "But he was much more than that. He was Khiann's dearest friend, despite the difference in their stations. They were as close as brothers."

She paused, gathering the threads of memory that stretched back over five thousand years. "Esag was also the great love of my dear friend Gulan's life—or Wonder as you know her now."

"Isn't she happily married to that tall Guardian?" Kyra asked.

"Yes, she is, but as a young girl, she was desperately in love with Esag, who was also a redhead." Annani laughed. "My dear friend seems to have a thing for red hair." She patted her own long locks. "Back then, though, she was very different from the confident female you all know as Wonder. She was shy and reserved, embarrassed about her height and her tremendous strength. Never mind that those were the exact qualities my parents had chosen her for. They wanted my companion to be an added layer of security." Annani smiled. "What they did not know was that I pulled poor Gulan, who was a very careful and reserved girl, into taking part in every conceivable mischief I could think of. But back to Esag. Once I started seeing Khiann, Gulan was seeing much more of Esag, and she would blush whenever he spoke to her. It was quite endearing."

"Did he return her feelings?" Jasmine asked.

Annani's smile faded. "Esag liked Gulan, and he enjoyed her company, but he was engaged to be married to another—a match arranged by his family when he was barely more than a boy."

She could still picture Gulan's face whenever someone mentioned Esag's intended bride, the way she would wince and try to force a smile.

"Gulan convinced herself that Esag did not love his fiancée," Annani continued. "Which was true enough—he found Ashegan vapid and vain. But not loving his intended did not mean that he was willing to give up all the status and wealth that the match secured for him and his family. He had his younger sisters to think of, and the matches they could secure if he was mated to the well-connected Ashegan."

"So, what happened?" Fenella asked.

"Gulan held on to the hope that Esag would break the engagement. She waited, certain that eventually he would realize they were meant to be together and end things with Ashegan. But then she learned that Esag had set a date for his wedding with his intended, and her heart broke. It could not have happened at a worse time, either, right before my wedding to Khiann." Annani's voice caught at speaking her beloved's name.

She could still remember the despair in Gulan's eyes, but back then, Annani had been too preoccupied with her upcoming nuptials and the happiness bubbling inside of her to pay closer attention to Gulan and realize that her friend was falling apart.

"Gulan was devastated," Annani said. "She managed to maintain her composure through the celebration, but after helping me prepare for my wedding night, she escaped, but she left me a note, explaining why she had to run."

The memory of the tear-stricken note Gulan had left behind was still vivid in Annani's mind.

"What did the note say?" Morelle asked.

"She said that the pain of losing Esag, or rather the dream of him, was too much for her to bear. If she stayed, she would have to watch him join with another, and Gulan knew that she would not survive that. She asked me to forgive her for not saying goodbye in person. She knew I would have tried to stop her." Annani looked at Kian. "I am so glad that she ran, though. She would not be here today if she had stayed behind."

He nodded. "Absolutely."

Annani took a long steadying breath. "When Khiann learned that Gulan had fled, he was furious at Esag for leading her on, and he worried for her safety traveling alone. So, he did what seemed sensible at the time."

"He sent Esag after her," Kalugal said, understanding dawning in his voice.

"Yes. Esag and two other immortals. I think their names were Roven and Davuh, but I might be wrong. It has been a day or two since." She chuckled. "Khiann reasoned that Esag would have the best chance of convincing Gulan to return."

"They never made it back," Brandon stated rather than asked.

"No. They had been gone for many weeks, but they never found her, and then the world ended." Annani's voice went flat, emotionless—the only way she could speak of that time without her voice breaking. "In an instant, everyone I had ever known or loved was gone. Everyone except those who, by chance or the Fates' design, were far enough away to escape the poisonous wind that followed the bombing."

A heavy silence fell over the room as the weight of that loss settled over them anew. Even those who had heard the story before seemed affected by hearing it again.

"I always hoped," Annani continued after a moment, "that Esag and his companions had traveled far enough to escape the destruction. That perhaps they had found Gulan and the three of them had survived together somewhere. But after we found Gulan, or rather she found us, I knew that they had never reached her, and I had no way of knowing if they made it out alive. Until now."

She gestured to the figurine that sat on the coffee table, where Fenella had placed it after their viewing.

"Somehow, Esag survived," she said, wonder coloring her voice. "And he carved my likeness in memory of me, believing me dead along with all the others."

"Wonder will be overjoyed to hear this," Alena said. "Even if she no longer carries a torch for him, knowing he lived—"

"Yes," Annani agreed. "She mourned him along with all the others we lost. To know that her first love survived will bring her great comfort."

"Wait," Kalugal said suddenly, his eyes sharpening with realization. "If Esag carved your figurine, then he must have been the one who carved Wonder's figurine as well."

Annani felt her breath catch as the implications hit her. "Of course. Of course! It makes perfect sense."

"But there's still something that doesn't add up," Kalugal continued, his brow furrowed in thought.

"When Jacki touched Wonder's figurine, she saw visions of the earthquake, of Wonder falling into the chasm. How could Esag have known about that? He was nowhere near when it happened."

"Did you ever check for an inscription on Wonder's figurine?" Annani asked.

Kalugal nodded. "Of course I did. It was one of the first things I looked for. But there was just one symbol, which indicated the price. I still don't understand how he could have imparted onto the figurine knowledge he couldn't possess."

"Maybe he did," Annani murmured.

"What do you mean?" Jasmine asked.

Annani leaned back in the armchair and steepled her fingers. "When I knew Esag, he was a young immortal with no particular paranormal talents beyond the standard abilities of our kind. But that was over five thousand years ago. It is entirely possible that he has developed additional abilities in the millennia since. He might have seen what happened to Gulan in a vision."

"Wouldn't he have looked for her?" Fenella asked. "If he knew that she survived and he had feelings for her, he should have looked."

Annani shook her head. "The desert is vast. Where would he have even started?"

"Right." Fenella sank back into the couch. "It's the same problem we have with finding Khiann. We don't know where to start, and we are no closer to answers after solving the mystery of the figurine than we were before."

Annani felt a pang of not-quite disappointment, but something close to it. Learning that Esag lived was a joy in itself, but Fenella was right. It did not bring them any closer to finding the answer to the question that burned brightest in her heart.

"Actually," Kalugal said slowly, "I wouldn't discount this discovery just yet." He shifted his gaze to Annani. "We need to find Esag by following the trail of figurines. If he has developed visionary abilities and saw what happened to Wonder, then perhaps he also saw what happened to Khiann, and more importantly, Esag was familiar with the caravan routes. He might have recognized some landmark that can bring us to at least the general area of where Khiann is buried."

Hope bloomed in Annani's chest. "The Fates are constantly delivering more clues that lead us to Khiann. We need to follow them."

"I agree." Kalugal's eyes gleamed with the thrill of the hunt. "The figurines are our breadcrumbs to finding Esag. That Egyptian artisan had an original to copy from. Where did he get it? Who sold it to him or commissioned the copy?"

"The trail is very old," Max said. "But I trust the Fates to show us the way."

"Where do we start?" Syssi asked. "Egypt is a large country, and figurines are sold everywhere. Only now, most of them are made in China."

Jacki chuckled. "That's why an original like this one

stood out." She waved her hand at the figurine. "There won't be many of those around, and we can hire locals to scout for them. Once more are found, we can focus the search there."

"We'll need to be subtle," Brandon cautioned. "The political situation in Egypt is volatile, and the Brotherhood's influence there grows stronger by the day. We can't afford to attract the wrong kind of attention to our efforts."

"Don't worry about it," Kalugal said. "I have the perfect cover for searching for artifacts. Professor Gunter is well known in archeological circles." He cast a glance at Din. "What do you think? Would you like to sink your teeth into this project?"

"I would love to." Din glanced at Annani. "Finding Khiann is more important than the Holy Grail, even if I can't boast about it to any of my colleagues."

"Jacki and I can return to Egypt and help with the search as well," Kalugal said. "I have plenty of local contacts that I can deploy." Kalugal's gaze swept over Fenella, Kyra, and Jasmine. "Perhaps our three talented ladies would consider joining the expedition? If we find Esag, or even just more of his work, the immediate availability of their combined abilities could prove invaluable."

Fenella looked uncomfortable at the suggestion. "I've just started a job at the Hobbit Bar. I don't want to lose it."

Annani had a feeling that it was more about leaving the safety of the village than the new job.

"I am sure Atzil will hold the position open for you," she said. "And you will not be traveling alone. You will be well protected at all times."

Kyra reached for Fenella's hand, but her eyes were on Annani. "I'm not keen on leaving my sisters alone in the village while I go exploring in Egypt, but this is important to the Clan Mother, and we owe you more than I can put into words. You are the only reason we have a civilization at all. Without you, we would all still be living in the Dark Ages." She shivered. "Women would have been treated everywhere as they are treated in Afghanistan. As less than human, caged and abused."

Fenella's back straightened. "Fifty years ago, I would have dismissed what you've just said as a crazy conspiracy theory, but I know better now." She turned to Annani, her eyes shining with unshed tears. "I know now that we owe it all to you, and I also know that we need to unite behind you and help you hold back the tsunami of hate."

Annani swallowed. "Thank you, child. I appreciate your confidence in me, and I hope that I will live up to your expectations, but some tidal waves might be too powerful even for me. Good does not always triumph over evil."

"Evil will not win on my watch," Fenella said with so much conviction that Annani was tempted to believe her. "Maybe finding your Khiann will be just the thing we need to reverse the trend."

It was a beautiful sentiment, but Khiann was only her salvation, not the entire world's.

He had not been a particularly powerful god, and since he had spent the last five thousand years in stasis, he had not grown in power during that time. If Annani were incredibly lucky, he would be found exactly the same as when he had been lost.

Kian looked at her with understanding in his eyes. "Let's find him first and then fight to save the world."

She nodded. "My heart tells me that we must not delay. If Esag is out there, and if he has knowledge of what became of Khiann..." She couldn't finish the sentence, couldn't voice the hope that threatened to overwhelm her.

"There is no reason to delay," Kian promised. "We just need a few days to organize things."

"I have a few business meetings I can't postpone," Kalugal said, "But in the meantime, I'll have my people begin searching for genuine artifacts. We might be able to narrow down our search area before we even leave."

Annani looked around the room at these people— her family by blood and by choice—and felt a swell of emotion that threatened to spill over as tears. For five thousand years, she had believed Khiann was lost to her forever. Now, for the first time, she had more than just vague hope. She had a trail to follow, breadcrumbs left by an old friend who had mourned his people in the only way he knew how.

"Thank you," she said. "Whatever comes of this search, know that your efforts are greatly appreciated."

12

KIAN

The return of the children brightened Annani's mood, Allegra immediately making a beeline for her grandmother with Princess Sparkle clutched in her hand. Darius giggled happily when Jacki scooped him up into her arms and kissed both of his cheeks.

Evie toddled up to Amanda with her arms outstretched.

"Well, hello, sweetheart." Annani gathered Allegra into her lap. "How was your playtime with Shamash?"

Allegra cast the guy a haughty look that Kian didn't know how to decipher and then launched into an animated tale about Princess Sparkle's adventures in the playroom, largely incomprehensible due to her excitement.

"It is time for whiskey and cigars," Kalugal announced. "My smoking lounge is finally completed, and I have some excellent Cuban cigars." He rose from his seat.

The guy had a smoking lounge?

Kian had to admit that the idea held appeal, and he was curious to see his cousin's latest extravagance. Besides, he was more than ready for some relaxing time with a good whiskey and a genuine Cohiba.

"You didn't tell me that you were building a smoking lounge." Kian followed Kalugal up.

"It was a spur-of-the-moment stroke of brilliance, realizing that my library could serve a dual purpose. Is there anything better than relaxing with a book, a cigar, and a shot of whiskey?"

"You won't hear any arguments from me. I agree that it's a brilliant idea, especially since it means that you will be stocking your own cigars from now on and not be mooching off me."

Kalugal laughed. "It occurred to me that I owed you quite a number of cigars, and that perhaps you would visit me more often now that I have this beautiful space dedicated to the things you love."

Kian put a hand over his heart. "I'm touched. You built it all for me?"

"Of course." Kalugal clapped him on the back. "My men enjoy unwinding there as well, and it means they don't hog the living room, so Jacki is happy." He turned to the rest of his guests. "Who else is joining us?"

"Count me in," Max said immediately.

When Brandon, Din, Orion, Dalhu, and Ell-rom

rose to their feet, Kalugal lifted a brow. "It's not a gentlemen-only invitation. Any of you ladies care to join?"

"Phew, gross." Amanda waved a dismissive hand. "I hate the smell. Enjoy your cigars, boys."

"I'd love to try," Morelle said, "but perhaps another time. I think I'll stay here with Annani and the little ones."

She must have noticed that beneath Annani's brave façade, her sister was struggling with the emotional impact of learning about Esag.

"Another time, then," Kalugal agreed easily. "Gentlemen, follow me."

As he herded them through yet another corridor in the labyrinth that was his home, the temperature dropped slightly, but since everything was climate-controlled, Kian had a feeling that it was done deliberately to create the right ambiance.

Everything about Kalugal's domain spoke of careful planning and attention to detail.

When they reached the smoking lounge, it was exactly what Kian had expected from his cousin—impressive to the point of being ostentatious. The centerpiece was a massive skylight that Kalugal demonstrated could open completely, ensuring proper ventilation. The furnishings were leather and dark wood, arranged in several conversation groupings that encouraged intimacy while maintaining sight lines to the whole room. A fully stocked bar dominated one wall, with the crystal decanters catching the light from carefully positioned fixtures. The other walls were lined with bookcases, stocked with leather-bound editions of whatever was available in that format. In fact, Kian suspected that the books had been purchased for their decorative value and not their contents, even though Kalugal was a well-read guy. Perhaps there were hidden bookcases behind the ones that were just for display.

"This is very nice," Kian said. "I like it when you go all out."

"You mean to say it's excessive?" Kalugal suggested with a self-deprecating laugh. "Perhaps it is, but then you know my motto. If you have the money, why not?"

Kian couldn't even argue that the money could have been better spent on more deserving projects because Kalugal and Jacki were donating enough of their time and wealth to the rehabilitation of trafficking victims, and Jacki had proven to be a genius at getting the government to fund a large share of the operation. He didn't like that a hefty portion had to circle back to fund the politicians' campaigns and award contracts to their family members, but that was how the cookie crumbled, and as much as he would have liked to, he couldn't right every wrong.

"It's exquisite," Brandon said, running an appreciative hand over the back of a leather chair that probably cost more than most people's cars.

"Thank you." Kalugal moved to the bar, pulling out glasses with his usual flair. "Whiskey preferences, gentlemen? I have quite a selection."

As they stated their preferences—ranging from Orion's request for "whatever's best" to Ell-rom's uncertain "whatever you recommend"—Kian studied the space more carefully. Every detail had been considered, from the ventilation system that would prevent smoke from lingering to the placement of tables at the perfect height for resting a glass while seated.

His cousin had created a sanctuary where people could let down their guard, where difficult conversations could happen over shared indulgences, and where loyalty was built one interaction at a time.

Perhaps the next council meeting should be held in this lounge...

Oh, so that was Kalugal's plan. Clever bastard. He knew exactly which bait Kian would take.

"The humidor is through here," Kalugal said, leading them to a temperature-controlled closet that would have made any cigar aficionado weep with envy. "Please, select whatever appeals to you."

Kian chose a robusto that smelled of earth and promise, while the others made their selections with varying degrees of expertise. Din, surprisingly, showed considerable knowledge, helping Ell-rom navigate the options with patient explanations about wrapper types and flavor profiles.

Soon, they were seated on the comfortable chairs, the ritual of cutting and lighting their cigars providing a familiar rhythm. The first draws filled the air with aromatic smoke that the ventilation system whisked away just slowly enough to let them appreciate the scent.

"Now this," Max said, leaning back with a contented sigh, "is civilized."

"My thoughts exactly," Kalugal agreed, savoring his own cigar with obvious pleasure. "I invite my men to join me here after a long day in the office. They seem to appreciate both the gesture and the quality of the spirits."

Kian took a sip of the whiskey Kalugal had poured him—something Scottish, old, and expensive—and felt some of the day's tension begin to ease.

Leaning back in the comfortable armchair, he took another sip from the superb whiskey before turning to his cousin. "You mentioned noticing an increased presence of Doomers in Egypt. Max reports the same from Iran."

"What did you find?" Kalugal asked Max.

"They're embedded deeper than we feared, and there are a lot of them. They are not just engaged in influence operations like they used to be in the past, but actual integration with the Revolutionary Guard. They had intel on our movements that suggests either exceptional intelligence gathering or inside information."

"Or both," Kian said.

Kalugal's expression darkened. "That mirrors what I observed in Egypt. The Brotherhood's presence there isn't just growing—it's metastasizing. They're not content with influence anymore. They're building actual power structures, bases of operation. I wouldn't be surprised if they are planning to take over when the time is right."

"Sleeper cells?" Dalhu asked.

"Nothing sleepy about them," Kalugal said. "There are so many of them in Cairo that I suspect they are getting ready to take control of key institutions. The religious establishment, the military, and naturally, the intelligence services. They're playing a long game, and you are falling behind, cousin."

The words hung heavy in the smoke-tinged air. Kian took another draw from his cigar, using the moment to organize his thoughts. The situation was worsening by the day, approaching the irreversible, and he was low on options.

"You are not telling me anything I don't already know." He finished the whiskey in his glass and put it on the side table next to his armchair. "Your father outsmarted me, and I find myself playing catch-up. I need to come up with a more aggressive approach. I've been thinking about forming a specialized task force of gifted females who could exert influence on key figures in the government. I hate using Navuh's tactics, but what choice do I have? By taking the higher moral ground, I might be dooming the whole of humanity to slavery under the Brotherhood's banner." He closed his eyes briefly. "Everything my mother has worked for, all the rights she restored for women, it will all crumble."

Kalugal sighed dramatically. "As I've said many

times before, cousin, humans are too dumb to appreciate what they have and too easily manipulated. They fall for the same play time and again, believing the blatant lies, the propaganda, while the elites are robbing them blind and sending them into the meat grinder."

"You're not helping," Kian grumbled. "I need solutions, not commiseration."

Kalugal puffed on his cigar. "Your idea of a female spy force is not particularly original, but that only means that I think it might work. Beautiful, immortal women who can thrall are a formidable asset. They could counteract the Brotherhood's manipulations. The problem is how many would be willing to do that? Furthermore, the females you have in mind are mostly mated to Guardians. Do you really think their mates would be okay with them going into these kinds of situations alone? And if they go with them, you will lose most of your senior Guardians."

Kian cursed, earning a surprised look from Ellrom, who was still learning the intricacies of spoken Earth language.

"Have you thought about the paranormals in Safe Haven?" Max asked. "Some of them have useful abilities, and they've been trained for precisely that kind of work."

Kian considered this, rolling the idea around in his mind like the whiskey on his tongue. "Most of them aren't particularly powerful," he said after a moment. "But there might be potential there. Come to think of it, Eleanor and Emmett themselves are a formidable duo with both being compellers. The problem is that they wouldn't want to leave Safe Haven. The place is Emmett's life's work. He's built something meaningful there, and I can't see him abandoning it for shadow games in foreign capitals."

"Then we're back to square one," Max said. "We need resources we don't have to fight an enemy that metastasizes rapidly."

The admission hung in the air like the smoke from their cigars. Kian felt the weight of it, the familiar burden of leadership made heavier by the miserable acknowledgment of inadequacy. He was used to finding solutions, to protecting his people through strength and strategy.

But what could he do when the enemy had more pieces on the chessboard?

"I'm in over my head," he said quietly, the words costing him more than he cared to admit. "We all are. Navuh is using his greatest advantage over us, which is the sheer number of peons he can move, and his second advantage, which is playing a game where they are writing the rules."

Kalugal leaned forward, concern replacing his usual calculated charm. "I've never heard you talk like this, cousin."

"Because I've never felt like this," Kian said honestly. "We've always been the shadows protecting humanity from the darkness. Our greatest weapon was our technological know-how, which allowed us to fuel progress, but that's not enough anymore, and I don't know what to do with the limited resources we have." He took another sip of whiskey, letting the burn ground him. "We need a damn miracle."

"Or better technology," Kalugal suggested. "Speaking of which, how are the plans for building new Odus coming along?"

Kian laughed, not even bothering to act surprised that Kalugal knew about the secret project. His cousin had intelligence sources everywhere—it would have been more shocking if he didn't know about the progress Kaia and William were making.

"Robots can't solve this problem," Kian said. "What we need is an alien invasion to unite humanity against a common threat."

The words were meant as a joke, but Kalugal's visible shiver reminded him that some jokes cut too close to uncomfortable truths.

"That's not funny," his cousin said. "We all know what happens when the Eternal King becomes aware of what's happening on Earth. An alien invasion wouldn't unite humanity—it would end it."

The reminder of that looming threat cast another shadow over their gathering, as if they didn't have enough problems with terrestrial enemies.

"You're right," Kian said. "Poor attempt at humor. But the point stands—we need something to fundamentally change the game's dynamics. The Brotherhood is winning because they're playing by different rules, and they started the game long before we realized what they were planning. We limit ourselves to protecting humanity's free will. They manipulate and control without conscience."

"So, we adapt our rules," Ell-rom said, then looked surprised at himself for speaking. "The honorable warrior who faces the dishonorable one must choose—maintain honor and die or adapt and survive to restore honor later. Perhaps it's time to consider which choice serves the greater good."

"Wise words," Dalhu murmured. "The cost of maintaining principle against unprincipled enemies might be catastrophic."

Kian had already resolved to use the same unprincipled tactics as the Brotherhood, so what Ell-rom had said wasn't anything new, but he was glad that others saw things the same way he did.

"The ends justifying the means," Orion said. "It's a dangerous philosophy."

"But is it more dangerous than allowing evil to triumph through our inaction?" Ell-rom countered.

They sat in silence for a moment, each lost in their own thoughts. The cigars had burned down considerably, and the whiskey glasses had been emptied and refilled. Outside, the afternoon was fading toward evening, though plenty of natural light was still reaching Kalugal's lounge.

"There might be another way." Din took a fortifying sip of whiskey before continuing. "The patterns of how civilizations rise and fall are always the same, and the Brotherhood's strategy isn't new, but neither are the counters to it."

"Go on," Kian encouraged.

"They're using humanity's divisions against itself," Din explained, warming to his topic. "Religious, political, economic—every fracture becomes a wedge they can exploit. But what if we focused on strengthening unity instead of just fighting their influence? Not through manipulation, but through improvement of human conditions?"

"We already do that," Brandon pointed out. "Medical advances, technological development, social progress—"

"Yes, but piecemeal," Din interrupted, then caught himself. "Apologies. What I mean is, we respond tactically to their strategic moves. What if we developed our own long-term strategy for human advancement? Not just preventing their victory, but making it impossible by eliminating the conditions they exploit?"

Intrigued, Kian leaned forward. "You're talking about social engineering on a massive scale, and I like where you are going with that, but I'm afraid that we are out of time. The game will be lost before we get the wheels spinning."

"The Brotherhood thrives on despair, on division, and on humanity's worst impulses," Din said. "What if we gave them something better to believe in?"

"Like what?" Orion scoffed. "A new religion?"

Din shrugged. "Why not? Religious fervor is the easiest to fuel. People love to proselytize."

Dalhu regarded him with a skeptical look. "There is something to it, but those who are zealots for whatever they believe in, either religion or ideology, will not be easy to convince to try something new, even if you come up with the most wonderful and uplifting version of either."

"People need hope," Max said. "The Brotherhood sells despair and somehow makes it palatable by promising rewards in the afterlife. It's the biggest con ever perpetrated against humans."

"How do you engineer belief?" Ell-rom asked.

"The same way they engineer despair," Din said. "Through stories, through media, through careful cultivation of cultural movements. The difference is we'd be cultivating growth instead of decay."

Brandon groaned. "That's exactly what the clan has done for decades, but the rules have changed on us. It used to be that a few Hollywood executives made all the decisions and dictated what the public was exposed to. That was the golden era of film and television. Now, every idiot with internet access is an influencer, and way too many are spewing hate. I'm sure that the Brotherhood is paying hundreds of them or even thousands to sow the seeds of despair to undermine societies all over the world."

"Humans are naturally inclined toward hope," Din argued. "They want to believe in better futures. I bet that we can counteract their hateful messages with fewer influencers and with much less money. Good will always triumph over evil."

Kian felt something shift in his chest—not quite hope, but perhaps hope's precursor. It wasn't really a viable solution, or a partial one, but Din's optimism was like a ray of sunshine in the darkness, and perhaps that was precisely what was needed, just amplified times a million.

"Where can I find a million Dins who will spread a message of hope?"

Kalugal chuckled. "Who owes you favors, cousin? I would start with them."

"They don't have to be people," Ell-rom said. "Artificial Intelligence can mimic a million influencers and spread positive messages to the world. I don't know how to make it work, but I'm sure William does."

"That's actually brilliant," Kian rose to his feet and walked over to the bar to refill his glass. "I'll talk to William, but someone needs to come up with the messages." He took a sip of the whiskey and looked at Ell-rom. "You were trained to become a priest. I know that you don't remember what you were taught, but you are still the most qualified among us to come up with something spiritually uplifting."

Ell-rom swallowed. "You can't be serious. I wouldn't know where to start."

"That's okay." Kian smiled. "I'm not expecting you to do it all. But if you can come up with a few positive messages, that could be a good start. Your Mother of All Life is a bit too harsh to be a good deity for this new religion, but maybe a mellower version will work."

Max joined Kian at the bar and refilled his glass. "I think a female deity is a good counter to the Brotherhood's evil male god. I'm sure that Ell-rom can make her more benevolent and less vengeful, but I don't like the idea of God having a gender. The humanization is diminishing. But then humans need something they can relate to, so there is that."

"It's still manipulation, you know," Orion pointed out. "Even if our intentions are pure. Isn't religion supposed to come from divine inspiration? Artificial Intelligence shouldn't write it."

Kalugal laughed. "You know what? I actually think that the original religion that the gods introduced to humans, the one all other religions eventually copied in one way or another, might have been written by an artificial intelligence. The gods surely had the technology."

It was a disturbing thought, but Kian was in no mood to examine what it implied.

"We should return to the others," he said. "They'll wonder if we've all died of smoke inhalation."

"The ventilation system is perfectly calibrated—" Kalugal began, then caught Kian's expression. "Ah. You're joking."

"I do that occasionally," Kian said dryly. "Don't look so shocked."

As they prepared to leave, Orion raised his glass

one final time. "To impossible challenges and improbable solutions."

"To family," Kalugal countered. "Blood, choice, and circumstance."

"To hope," Din added quietly. "However we choose to cultivate it."

As Kian drank, he felt the warmth of the whiskey mingle with something else—not an answer but a possibility. They faced impossible odds against a cunning enemy, but they had resources Navuh never would. They had diversity of thought, loyalty, and the kind of creative problem-solving that came from bringing together disparate perspectives.

FENELLA

The time spent with the children had managed to relax Fenella after the mini earthquake she'd experienced while holding that figurine.

The whole psychometry thing was unnerving.

She didn't like taking a ride on some stranger's memories, seeing and feeling things that she shouldn't. It wasn't about invasion of privacy since the guy was long gone by now, it was just creepy.

"So, your place or mine?" Din asked as they crossed the bridge that separated Kalugal's section from the main village.

The question was innocent enough, but the undertone in his voice made heat pool low in her belly. She glanced up at him, taking in the way the dark strands of his hair shifted in the light ocean breeze, the way his shirt stretched across his broad shoulders.

Five days.

Had it really only been five days since he'd arrived in the village? It felt like yesterday and like a lifetime ago at the same time.

"Shira is not home."

That was enough said, and Din got her meaning right away.

The glow from his eyes became visible in the fading light. "I like the way you think." His hand found the small of her back, the touch possessive in a way that sent pleasant shivers down her spine. "A late afternoon delight before your shift in the bar is a brilliant idea."

She liked the way he phrased it. There were clear advantages to having a boyfriend who had grown up in an era when words still mattered and a gentleman didn't use crude language when in the presence of a lady. It was such a refreshing change from everyone else she'd ever been with.

Not that she was much of a lady. She could cuss with the worst of them. But she still enjoyed being treated as one, and it incentivized her to act more cultured herself.

"It is, right?" She bumped her hip against his.

He leaned over and kissed her cheek. "A brilliant idea from a brilliant lady. You always know what makes me happy."

She stifled the urge to roll her eyes. Was there a healthy male who would not be happy with such a suggestion?

Instead, she said, "You're easy to please, Professor. Especially in bed."

"Every moment with you feels like a gift, in bed and outside of it." His voice dropped to that low register that made her pulse quicken.

"Careful, Professor. Keep talking like that, and I might say those words you are waiting for sooner than later."

Din stopped walking.

They were in the middle of one of the village's main pathways, busier than usual with residents enjoying the Sunday afternoon, but he didn't seem to care about their audience. "Then you'll be hearing much more of this from now on." He punctuated his words with a kiss that was anything but appropriate for public consumption.

His hands framing her face and holding her steady, he claimed her mouth with a thoroughness that made her weak in the knees. There was a fleeting moment of embarrassment when her mind was still aware of the people around them, but she didn't push him away or tell him to stop nor scold him for making a scene. Instead, she melted against him, her hands fisting in his shirt as she kissed him back with equal fervor.

"Oh, look!" someone said, the voice tinged with amusement. "They are filming a remake of *Twilight*."

"Where are the sparkles?" another voice said.

Behind Din's back, Fenella lifted her middle finger at the jokers, which elicited twin bouts of laughter.

Din didn't even break the kiss to respond to the two.

When she finally pulled away to take a breath, the spectators were gone, and she was a little dazed. "You're impossible."

"Impossibly in love with you," he corrected, looking entirely too pleased with himself.

As they resumed walking, Fenella was hyperaware of every point of contact between them—Din's hand on her back, the warmth of his body so close to hers. "This is nice," she said.

"I agree." He cast her a satisfied smile.

"I meant this." She waved a hand over the pathway. "Sunday afternoon in the village, with people just living their lives. No one running from anything, no one looking over their shoulder. It feels almost surreal. Utopian."

Din's palm moved from her back to capture her hand, his fingers intertwining with hers. "The castle in Scotland and its surrounding grounds are even more serene than this."

She tilted her head. "Do you like it better there?"

"That's a definite no." He laughed. "The castle is drafty, the plumbing and electrical systems are iffy, and we get rooms, not even apartments."

Fenella frowned. "Then how do you prepare your meals?"

"We have a dining hall, and we eat together, which is easy and practical until you get tired of the same cyclical menu and want something different, but it's an hour and a half drive to the nearest restaurant."

"I wouldn't mind communal meals. Atzil cooks not just for Kalugal but for all his men, and they all eat together. I think it's nice. It creates a sense of community."

Din chuckled. "And now their boss also treats them to after-dinner whiskey and cigars in his smoking lounge. I bet no one wants to quit their employment."

"Atzil has only good things to say about Kalugal." She turned to look at Din. "What did you boys talk about during your manly bonding time in the lounge? Besides comparing the size of your cigars, that is."

Din chuckled, but then the amusement slid off his face. "Kian's worried. More than worried, actually. He thinks the Brotherhood is winning, that we don't have the resources to counter their influence effectively."

"Well, that's cheerful." Fenella tried to keep her tone light, but unease crept up her spine. If someone as powerful as Kian was worried, what chance did the rest of them have?

"He actually said we need a miracle," Din continued. "I've never heard him sound so defeated. He was always the rock everyone depended on. I mean, we have Sari in Scotland, and she is great, but she's not a military gal. She's not exposed to the things Kian is."

"So, what did you do? Pat him on the back and pour him more whiskey to console him?"

"Actually..." Din rubbed a hand over the back of his

neck. "I made a few suggestions to counter the pessimism. An alternative, more optimistic approach."

That was interesting. "Do tell."

As they walked, Din explained his idea about countering the Brotherhood's influence not through cultural manipulation, but by fostering hope and unity instead of just fighting against despair and division. It was idealistic, maybe even naive, but Fenella was charmed by his earnestness.

"The last thing I expected from you was such optimism," she said when he finished. "I thought you were the brooding academic type, all doom and gloom about humanity's failure to learn from history."

"I surprised myself," Din admitted. "Usually, I'm not a glass-half-full type of guy, but someone had to counteract Kian's gloom and inject some hope into the conversation. When everyone's convinced the situation is hopeless, that becomes a self-fulfilling prophecy."

"Look at you, being all wise and philosophical." She squeezed his hand. "Though I have to admit that it's a bit naive, which is a funny thing to say about someone who's lived as long as you have and seen enough crap to sour them on humanity forever."

"Maybe that's exactly why I can still hope," Din said. "I've seen humanity at its worst, but I've also seen it emerge from those depths time and again and climb higher than it was before. Sometimes things have to become truly desperate before people rise against the tide of evil, but they always do. The Brotherhood wins when we forget that resilience, that capacity to fight for what's right."

There was something both beautiful and heart-breaking about Din's faith in humanity's better nature, especially when contrasted with her own hard-won cynicism.

When they reached Shira's house, Fenella knocked just to be sure and then opened the door a crack, peeking inside and sniffing. "No coffee smell and no television noise in the background. It seems like no one's home." She turned to Din and smiled. "Good news all around. Shira is not home, and we have plenty of time before my shift. The bad news is that I'm going to have to tell Atzil that I'll be leaving soon for Egypt. He's not going to be happy."

Din's hands settled on her shoulders, turning her to face him. "Don't worry about Atzil. He works for Kalugal, remember? He won't hold it against you, and he will take you back as soon as you return. I bet his bar never made as much money as when you were there."

"You might be right, but I wish I had more time to settle into my job." She stepped into the cool interior of the house. "I felt in my element for a change. I..."

The words died in her throat as Din kicked the door shut behind them and lifted her clean off her feet. Before she could do more than gasp, her back was against the wall, Din's body pinning her there as his mouth found hers in a kiss that made their public display seem chaste by comparison.

"Professor," she chuckled when he let her up for air, her legs automatically wrapping around his waist for balance. "What's gotten into you?"

"You," he said, his eyes blazing with an intensity that made her stomach flip. When his lips found her throat, she had to bite back a moan. "Everything about you drives me to distraction," he murmured.

"Oh, my. You are such a sweet talker," she accused, but her hands were already working at the buttons of his shirt, desperate to feel skin against skin.

"Truth teller," he corrected, carrying her down the hallway toward her bedroom with an ease that never failed to thrill her. Immortal strength was a beautiful thing when properly applied.

He set her on her feet just inside her bedroom door, and for a moment, they simply looked at each other. Fenella hadn't missed the desire burning in his eyes, and also something deeper, more meaningful. This wasn't just physical attraction, though there was plenty of that.

This was love, connection, recognition.

This was two souls finding each other despite impossible odds.

"You're incredible," Fenella said quietly, needing him to understand. "But I'm still not ready to say those three words to you."

"I know." He cupped her face. "I'm good with you just letting me love you."

The tenderness in his voice, the patience in his eyes —it undid something inside her. She'd spent so long protecting herself, building walls to keep others at a safe distance, yet Din didn't attack those walls or demand they come down. He simply stood outside them, steady and sure, waiting for her to open the gate.

"You really are too good to be true," she murmured, then pulled his head down for another kiss.

This one was different from the desperate passion against the wall. This was exploration, communion, a slow burn that built gradually until they were both breathing hard.

Din's hands tangled in her hair, angling her head to deepen the kiss, while hers mapped the planes of his chest through his partially unbuttoned shirt.

When they finally broke apart, Fenella felt like she was floating. "We have a few hours," she said, her voice husky. "Before my shift at the bar."

"Then we'd better make them count." The smile he gave her was pure wickedness.

"Is that a challenge, Professor?"

"More like a promise."

She laughed. "Bold words. Let's see if you can back them up."

"Oh, I intend to." He backed her toward the bed with predatory grace. "Thoroughly."

The back of her knees hit the mattress, and she sat down hard, looking up at him with anticipation thrumming through her veins.

Din knelt before her, placing his hands on her ankles, and removed her shoes. "Still thinking about disappointing Atzil?" he asked, pressing a kiss to the inside of her ankle that sent shivers up her leg.

"Atzil who?" she murmured, which earned her one of those rare full smiles that transformed his face.

"That's what I thought." He pulled her pants down with ease, and as his lips traced a path up her calf, Fenella let her head fall back, surrendering to the moment.

"Din?"

"Mmm?" He'd reached her knee, and the scrape of his stubble against her inner thigh was doing dangerous things to her composure.

"You are overdressed for the occasion, Professor."

His laugh rumbled against her skin. "Patience, my love."

14

DIN

With a hand on each knee, Din pushed Fenella's legs apart, lowered his face to the inside of one knee, and nipped lightly at the soft skin.

She squirmed, but he knew she liked a little teasing, and he planned to try more with her, but not just yet. They were still too new, and she was too traumatized and skittish for anything more daring than light nipping.

After licking the tiny sting away, he kissed the spot and continued inside her leg, nipping and licking and kissing on his way to her center.

Instinctively, Fenella tried to close her thighs, but he nipped her inner thigh in warning. "Don't." He planted an open-mouthed kiss on her moist folds. "Your smell is intoxicating."

She chuckled. "Is that good or bad?"

He looked up at her, amused, and smirked with a frown. "Of course it's good. What else could it be?"

"Toxic fumes can be intoxicating, you know."

His Fenella used humor like a weapon, which meant that she was nervous for some reason. Was it the light?

They hadn't made love in the daytime before, and some women were shy about being fully seen like this, but Fenella wasn't the shy type, and as an immortal, she knew he could see perfectly even when there was no light at all.

"I assure you that for me, your scent is the elixir of the gods." He held her gaze. "Do you want me to close the shutters?"

She nodded. "If you don't mind."

"I would crawl over broken glass for you." He reached for the remote on the nightstand. "But fortunately, that won't be necessary. All I have to do is press this button."

As the shutters lowered and the room darkened, Fenella released a relieved breath.

"Better?" Din asked.

"Much. Please continue."

He chuckled. "So bossy."

She threaded her fingers in his hair. "You like that about me."

"Yes, I do." Din dipped his head and licked over one side of her wet folds, wresting a powerful jerk out of her.

His hands clamped on both sides of her inner thighs, holding her in place. "Easy, love. Relax and enjoy the ride. I promise not to do anything too scandalous to you. Not today."

The scent of her arousal intensified, indicating that she was curious about what he meant by scandalous, but she didn't ask. Instead, she eased back and surrendered to the pleasure.

Parting her folds with several tender strokes, Din flicked his tongue over her clit, and when she jerked again, he flattened it over her entire entrance.

With a groan, Fenella let her knees fall apart, giving him better access.

"That's my girl." He gave her an appreciative lick before spearing his tongue into her weeping entrance.

Caught by surprise, she arched and threaded her fingers through his hair.

"Din," she murmured.

"I got you, love." He penetrated her with one finger, then two, and as he pumped them in and out of her, Fenella's hips moved on the mattress in a dance older than time. She was close, and when she erupted, it was going to be epic.

He would've liked to prolong the build-up some more, but the truth was that he was hanging by a thread and needed to be inside of her. But first, he wanted her to climax on his tongue.

Hell, he needed that.

Still pumping, he flicked his tongue over her clit,

once, twice, and as more moisture coated his fingers, he hooked them inside of her, pressing the tips against that special sensitive spot.

"Din," she groaned. "I'm so close."

Thank the merciful Fates.

He closed his lips over her clit and sucked.

As Fenella erupted, throwing her head back, she screamed something incoherent that might have been a Scottish curse, and as an outpour of wetness coated his tongue, he licked and sucked like a male possessed.

His shaft was desperate to replace his fingers, but he wanted to wrest every last drop of Fenella's first climax of the day before he started working on the second.

Helping her ride out her climax, he gently pumped in and out of her until her shudders subsided.

When her body stopped quaking and she pushed on his head, he knew she was ready for the next stage of the game.

"Din," Fenella said his name almost lovingly. "I need you inside of me right now."

"My sweet Fenella." He planted a soft kiss to her swollen folds before forcing himself to relinquish his bounty, just long enough to get naked like she'd asked him to do before they'd even started.

Fenella eyed his erection with hunger in her eyes. "This looks yummy, but right now there is only one place I want it in and it's not in my mouth."

And to think that she'd been bashful about making love with sunshine in the room.

He ran the crown over her drenched folds until it was covered in her juices and then pushed it inside of her, just a fraction, even though he could have rammed into her with one powerful thrust, and she would have been perfectly okay with that.

He wanted to savor this in the same way he wanted to savor every time they made love. Even a thousand years from now.

Fenella was too exquisite to rush.

Leaning over her, he rested his elbow beside her head and kissed her gently, tenderly, while pushing a little more.

When he finally let go of her mouth, she gave him one of her teasing smiles, gripped his bottom, and arched up, taking him all the way inside of her.

"That's better." Her eyes rolled back in her head. "Now move."

"So very bossy." He pushed one hand under her bottom, angling her up before retreating and surging back inside her with a powerful thrust.

"Yes," she hissed and opened her eyes. "More."

Rising on straightened arms, Din pulled almost all the way out and surged back again, watching where they were joined.

She moaned when he withdrew again, and then cried out when he drove inside her, repeating that curse she'd uttered before.

Once more, he withdrew and drove back inside, elation sweeping through him as Fenella lifted to meet his thrusts.

"Yes, love, just like that." He gradually increased the tempo, all along gazing into her eyes, making sure she was right there with him for the ride.

15

FENELLA

ifting on straightened arms, Din gazed into Fenella's eyes as he pulled out, and then pushed back into her with deliberate slowness that made her want to scream.

With his fangs fully elongated and his eyes blazing like twin flames in the dimness of the room, he looked magnificent, a little scary perhaps, but the love shining in his eyes counterbalanced the alien appearance.

The contrast between the predator and the lover fascinated her. It was a duality that probably existed in all immortals, but she had only experienced it with Din.

This powerful immortal male was in love with her.

How lucky could a girl get?

To think of herself as fortunate was so foreign to Fenella that she almost laughed.

She'd always thought of herself as unlucky, even cursed. Fifty years of running, of looking over her shoulder, of never staying in one place long enough to see the seasons change, hadn't been good to her. The trouble she'd gotten herself into hadn't been good either, and then the doctor was the ultimate bad luck. He was the definition of that. It followed her like a dark shadow that had never let go.

But she shouldn't allow dark thoughts to distract her from this goodness.

Not when Din was looking at her like she was precious beyond measure, like she was worth waiting fifty years for. The intensity of his gaze made her chest tight with emotions she wasn't ready to name.

It was too tempting to say the words to him now, to tell him that she loved him back as much as he loved her, but something inside of her pushed against it, a self-preservation instinct that was misfiring. The words lodged in her throat like shards of glass, beautiful and dangerous and impossible to speak.

Perhaps it was part of her PTSD. Her fight-or-flight response had never left, and her body was still convinced that she was fighting for survival. Even here, safe in the village, protected by immortals and gods and technology beyond human comprehension, some part of her remained that terrified woman who'd learned that attachment meant vulnerability, and vulnerability meant a fate worse than death.

She could show Din, though. Use her body to let him know the love was there, but it was trapped, too afraid to emerge. Her body had always been more honest than her words anyway. It couldn't lie, couldn't deflect with humor or sarcasm. When Din touched her, when he moved inside her like this, her body told him everything her mouth couldn't.

Heart swelling with emotion that she refused to verbalize, Fenella lifted to meet Din's increasingly hard thrusts. Each movement was a wordless declaration, each gasp a confession she couldn't voice.

"Yes, love, just like this," he praised, his Scottish accent thickening with arousal.

The endearment made her eyes burn with unshed tears.

Love.

He called her love so easily, so naturally, as if she'd always been his love, even during those fifty lost years. Maybe she had been. Maybe that's what true love was —not just the feeling, but the waiting, the hoping, the never quite giving up.

Wrapping her arms around him, she brought his chest down to hers, skin to skin, and the feeling of closeness was incredible. She could feel his heart hammering against her breast, matching the wild rhythm of her own. This was what she'd been missing all those years of empty encounters and lonely mornings. Not just the physical connection, but this meeting of souls that transcended the mere joining of bodies.

For a few moments, they rocked together like that, gentle despite the growing urgency between them. She breathed him in, that unique scent that was purely Din, mixed with arousal and the faint lingering trace of the cologne he'd worn to Kalugal's brunch. She wanted to memorize it, to carry it with her always, a sensory memory to chase away the nightmares that still plagued her sleep.

Din lifted his head, and the expression on his face changed from reverent and loving to possessive, almost savage. The shift sent a thrill through her that started at the base of her spine and radiated outward like lightning.

The apex predator emerged, but she wasn't afraid of him because he was hers.

The thought should have terrified her. Once, it would have sent her running. But now she reveled in it, in the knowledge that all that power, all that strength, was leashed by his love for her. He could break her so easily, could take whatever he wanted, but instead he gave and gave and gave some more.

She was ready for the wild ride that she knew was coming. She craved Din fully unleashed, needed to feel the depth of his passion, his control finally slipping.

When he guided her arms over her head and threaded his fingers through hers, she closed her eyes and surrendered completely. The position left her vulnerable, exposed, unable to touch him or control the pace.

Once, that would have panicked her. Now, it felt like freedom.

This was so good. So right. So everything she'd never known she needed.

With a groan that seemed to come from the depths

of his soul, he pinned their entwined hands to the mattress, and the tempo and power of his thrusts increased. The bed creaked beneath them, a rhythmic counterpoint to their ragged breathing.

Fenella was powerless to do more than receive the pounding. Even lifting to meet him halfway was impossible because he was driving into her with such incredible force. Each thrust pushed her higher, closer to that edge she could feel approaching like a storm on the horizon.

The coil deep in her belly was winding up again, another explosive climax building up momentum. She could feel it gathering, tightening, threatening to snap at any moment.

"Din," she groaned as the tightness became unbearable. "I need..." She didn't know what to ask for. Release? More? Him? Everything?

He seemed to understand without words. He always did. His lips found her throat, and she felt him inhale deeply, scenting her arousal, her need, her unspoken love.

Hissing against her neck, he flicked his tongue over the spot he was going to sink his fangs into. The wet heat of it made her shiver, anticipation mixing with arousal, a cocktail that left her dizzy. He adjusted his grip, locking her head between their joined hands, immobilizing her for his bite.

The position was primal, possessive, and it spoke to something deep in her, some ancient recognition of claiming and being claimed.

A split moment later, she felt his seed explode into her, hot and urgent, and the sharp burn of twin incisions piercing her neck. The pain was fleeting, instantly transformed into pleasure so intense it left her breathless. The coil sprang free, and an orgasm crashed over her even before the first drop of venom entered her system.

When it did, she climaxed again, and again, each wave more intense than the last, until she couldn't tell where one ended and the next began. She was drowning in sensation, in pleasure, in the overwhelming rightness of being in Din's arms, being loved by him, being his.

16

AREZOO

Arezoo held Cyra's tiny hand as they walked along the tree-lined path toward the playground. Her other hand gripped a canvas bag filled with water bottles, snacks, and the inevitable collection of toys that was necessary on an outing with her little cousins.

"I want to go on the big swing!" Rohan skipped ahead with the boundless energy of a six-year-old.

"Me too!" Arman followed.

"Don't rush ahead!" Arezoo called after them, using the same commanding tone her mother employed often and with great effectiveness. "Stay with me, or we are going back home."

The threat achieved the desired results, and the two little rebels slowed down, grumbling under their breath that she was worse than their mother.

Behind them, the older boys walked together, occasionally shoving each other in the way brothers did.

Kavir and Zaden considered themselves far more mature than the others, though they'd been just as eager to leave the house when their mother suggested the playground.

"Why can't we run ahead?" Kavir complained. "Maman says it's safe here."

"I promised your mother I'd watch all of you," Arezoo replied patiently. "And I can't do that unless we are all together."

The boys grumbled some more but stayed by her side.

Taking five kids to the playground was a challenge, but Kavir was right about the village being safe, and save for her, everyone had things they needed to do. Donya and Laleh were studying, and so were the other older kids.

It wasn't easy for any of them, and their mothers needed a break too. Between Yasmin's grief, the adjustments to their new life, and the challenge of homeschooling a horde of children for the first time, they had a lot to deal with.

"Look!" Cyra pointed with her free hand. "Your friend. The tall girl!"

Arezoo only had one friend in the village, and that was Drova, who also matched the description. Sure enough, she saw the willowy Kra-ell walking over to them, wearing something that looked a lot like her training uniform, just without the insignia marking her as a Guardian-in-training.

It seemed that everything Drova wore, even on

weekends when she wasn't training, was black cargo pants with a black T-shirt, sometimes with a matching jacket and sometimes without. Today, it was absent as it was getting too warm for that.

"Hello," Drova called out as she reached them. Her large, dark eyes swept over the group. "Heading to the playground?"

"Yeah. My mother and aunts needed some quiet time," Arezoo said, feeling a little self-conscious about her decidedly less cool appearance—a pair of loose jeans and a girly blouse with puffy, short sleeves. "I volunteered to take the little ones."

"You are a good daughter and niece," Drova said. "Small humans can be tiring, but not as tiring as small Kra-ell. Watching over them is like herding a bunch of demons." She tilted her head, studying the children who had gone unnaturally quiet at her approach. "I don't bite, you know. Not without provocation."

Rohan pressed closer to Arezoo's leg, while Arman tried to look brave despite the fear in his eyes. Even Kavir and Zaden, who were older and should have understood that Drova was joking, seemed a little scared.

"Drova is just being funny," Arezoo said, keeping her tone light and friendly. "And just so you know, she helped rescue me and my sisters and Azadeh. She even got injured doing that."

"You are very tall and skinny," Cyra observed with the directness of a four-year-old. "And your eyes are too big for your face. You need to eat more."

Drova's lips curved in amusement. "I'm a Kra-ell, little girl. We're built differently than humans." She glanced toward the playground. "Mind if I join you there?"

"I'd love that," Arezoo said, though she wondered what Drova could possibly find interesting about supervising a bunch of human children at a playground. "I could use some adult company to keep me sane."

As they walked, the boys gradually moved ahead, their natural energy overcoming their initial hesitation. Only Cyra remained pressed against Arezoo's side, stealing glances at Drova.

"Do you do this a lot? I mean, take care of the children?"

Arezoo chuckled. "I'm the oldest among my siblings and cousins. It kind of comes with the territory."

"I understand. Your mother and aunts depend on you."

At the playground, Rohan and Arman immediately claimed the swings, while Kavir and Zaden headed for the climbing structure, competing and shoving each other on the way to the top.

Boys were like monkeys, but Arezoo wasn't going to intervene. Not unless someone got hurt. So far, it looked innocent enough.

"Can you push me on the swing?" Cyra asked Arezoo, pointing to the smaller swings designed for younger children.

"Of course, sweetie." She lifted the little girl into the swing, making sure she was secure.

"I can push her," Drova offered, surprising Arezoo.

She hesitated, then nodded. "Just be gentle. She's small and she doesn't like to swing too high."

"I might be strong, but I know how to handle small things without breaking them," Drova said.

As she took over pushing Cyra, the child squealed with delight at the attention, forgetting her fear of the tall Kra-ell. Arezoo settled onto the bench and watched. It was strange seeing Drova playing with Cyra. It was like watching a tiger entertain a mouse.

"Higher!" Cyra demanded, her earlier fear completely forgotten.

"This is high enough for you," Drova said. "Arezoo wants me to be gentle."

"But I want to go higher!"

Drova shook her head. "We don't want you flying off to the moon."

"I want to see the moon!"

"Maybe when you're older and have wings."

The boys had abandoned the climbing structure and the swings, gathering near the open area beside the playground. Rohan and Arman were engaged in an impromptu wrestling match that looked about two seconds away from tears, while the other two watched.

"Boys," Arezoo called out. "That's enough!"

They paused, looking guilty, then separated with muttered complaints about who started what and walked over to where Drova was pushing Cyra on the swing.

"I heard that you are very strong," Rohan said.

"I am. Do you want to see how strong?"

Rohan nodded enthusiastically.

Drova spread her arms wide, holding them straight out from her sides. "I bet all of you together can't pull my arms down."

The boys exchanged glances, mischief and intrigue warring with their healthy fear of the Kra-ell.

"That will be easy." Arman pointed at her slender arms that didn't look like they could hold anything over a few pounds. "You're skinny."

"Skinny doesn't mean weak," Drova said. "But if you want to prove me wrong, try to pull down my arm."

"Me first," Arman insisted.

He approached cautiously and grabbed Drova's right arm with both hands, trying to pull it down with all his might. Drova's arm didn't budge. Not even a tremor.

"How do you do that?" Arman gasped, his face reddening with effort.

"Help your brother." Drova gestured with her chin at Zaden.

Before long, both of the older boys were hanging from one arm while Rohan and Arman attacked the other. The sight was comical. The tall, thin Kra-ell, standing perfectly still while four boys dangled from her outstretched arms, looked like a scarecrow with ornaments.

"This is impossible!" Zaden declared, his feet actually leaving the ground despite him being the oldest and tallest of the bunch.

"Kra-ell muscle fibers are different from human ones," Drova explained in a measured tone, as if she were giving a lesson rather than supporting the entire weight of four children. "We're much stronger than we look."

"Can I try?" Cyra called from the swing, not wanting to be left out.

"You're too small, sweetie," Arezoo said gently. "But you can cheer for the boys."

"Go, boys!" Cyra shouted gleefully. "Pull harder!"

The boys redoubled their efforts, grunting and straining, but Drova's arms remained perfectly horizontal. After another minute, she slowly lowered them so their feet touched the ground.

"That was amazing!" Arman exclaimed. "Are all Kra-ell that strong?"

"Most adults are," Drova confirmed. "Though some are stronger than others, just like with humans."

"Can you lift a car?" Rohan asked, his voice full of awe even before Drova answered.

"With ease, provided it's not a very big one."

"Could you throw a person?"

"Rohan!" Arezoo admonished, even though Drova could and would.

"Of course. But I wouldn't unless it was to protect

people that person was trying to hurt." She leaned closer to the little ones, nearly bending in half. "Can you keep a secret?"

The boys nodded eagerly.

"I don't need to throw people to stop them from harming others. I can command them to stop, and they will obey me. I have a special voice just for that."

The boys peppered her with more questions, clustering around her with the fearless curiosity of children who'd already decided that she was cool and not a threat. Even Cyra demanded to be lifted from the swing so she could join the group.

"Can you jump really high?" she asked.

"Higher than humans," Drova confirmed. "Want to see?"

"Yes, please."

Drova crouched slightly, then sprang upward in a movement so fluid it looked effortless. She easily cleared twice her own height, catching on to a branch, and hanging from it for a moment before jumping down and landing with barely a sound.

The children gasped in unison, then immediately began begging for another demonstration.

"One more and that's it," Drova said. "Then you go and play nicely while Arezoo and I get to chat in peace."

This time, she jumped lower but executed a perfect backflip at the apex before landing in the same spot. The children applauded wildly, and even Arezoo found herself clapping.

"I want to do that!" Arman announced.

"When you're older and immortal," Drova said. "For now, work on your strength and agility."

As the children reluctantly returned to the swings and climbing structure, pretending to have super strength as they played, Drova joined Arezoo on the bench.

"You've made their day," Arezoo said.

Drova shrugged. "It was fun. I grew up in a compound where the Kra-ell children mostly trained. I saw the human children engage in silly, playful activities, but until I moved to the village, I didn't understand why they wasted their time on such trivial things." She affected a smile, but on her Kra-ell face, it looked more threatening than reassuring.

Arezoo wondered what kind of childhood produced someone who could be both a deadly warrior and patient with small children.

"Were there playgrounds in your compound?" she asked carefully.

"We had training grounds. The closest thing to play was combat practice. The human kids just played ball in the dirt or hide and seek games."

The weight of that statement made for a charged and silent moment between them. Arezoo thought of her own cousins, of how their childhoods had been so much better than Drova's, despite the restrictions.

"I should thank you again," Arezoo said. "For the rescue, I mean. You are very brave."

"You've already thanked me multiple times."

"It doesn't feel like enough. You risked your life for strangers. You flew halfway around the world to liberate a bunch of women you didn't know from the evil people who did really bad things to us. I will be forever grateful to you."

Drova shrugged again, but Arezoo could see the satisfaction in her big, black eyes. "I didn't do it for you. I wanted to prove myself to my mother and to the Guardians, and because of my special ability, I was allowed to join the mission despite my age. I screwed up majorly, but I want to believe that I prevented casualties despite losing my voice amplifier and getting shot."

Arezoo appreciated the honesty, but she still thought that Drova was selling herself short. "You did your best, and without you, I wouldn't be here, sitting on a bench in one of the safest spots on earth, enjoying a sunny day with a friend."

After a long moment of just watching the children play, Drova turned to her. "Can I ask you something?"

"Of course. Anything."

"How do you like working at the café?"

That was an abrupt change of subject. "I like it a lot. Wonder and Aliya have been patient with my mistakes. And most of the customers are nice, except for—"

A commotion at the playground cut off her words. Arman had decided to try the monkey bars and now he had fallen and was sitting on the ground, holding his knee and trying very hard not to cry.

Arezoo rushed over to him, while Drova didn't seem overly concerned and stayed on the bench.

To her, a scraped knee was nothing. A small hurt that she had probably been told to ignore and keep on training.

The Kra-ell raised Spartans.

"Let me see," Arezoo said, examining his knee. It wasn't bad, just a surface scrape, but to a six-year-old it probably felt catastrophic.

"It hurts," Arman whimpered.

"I know, brave one. But look, it's just a tiny scratch. You'll have a battle scar to show everyone."

"A battle scar?" He perked up.

"All the best warriors have them," Drova said from behind Arezoo and then crouched beside them. "This one will heal quickly, but you can tell everyone you got it fighting monsters."

"Really?"

"Absolutely," Drova said with a perfectly straight face. "I saw the whole thing. You were very brave."

Arezoo opened the pack Yasmin had prepared for the kids and wasn't surprised to find a first aid kit. The boy hissed when she cleaned the scrape, but he was trying hard to be brave in front of Drova. When she applied a Batman Band-Aid, Arman's tears dried up, replaced by excitement about the battle wound and the cool Band-Aid.

"Can I have a battle scar too?" Rohan asked hopefully.

"No," Arezoo and Drova said in unison, making them both laugh.

"Scars have to happen naturally," Drova explained. "You can't plan them."

"Good afternoon, ladies," someone said from behind them, and Arezoo's stomach tightened when she recognized the voice.

Turning around, she plastered a smile on her face. "Hello."

Ruvon seemed lost for words for a moment, but then they spilled out of him in a rush. "I was on my way to the café, I mean to the vending machines, when I saw you here. I thought I would stop to say hello and see if you would like me to get you something while I was at it."

Every instinct screamed at her to refuse. The thought of accepting anything from a former Doomer made her skin crawl.

"I—" she started to decline.

"That would be nice," Drova interjected. "Black coffee for me, nothing added. Arezoo?"

Trapped by social courtesy and Drova's acceptance, she couldn't be rude, not when Ruvon hadn't done anything wrong.

"The same, thank you," she managed, the words feeling like sand in her mouth.

"Two black coffees," Ruvon repeated, a smile transforming his usually serious expression. "I'll be right back."

As he walked away, Drova looked at her with an amused expression on her skinny face. "He likes you."

"I know," Arezoo muttered, watching Cyra chase Rohan around the slide.

"He seems nice enough. A bit too timid for my taste, but nice."

Arezoo looked around to make sure the children weren't listening, then lowered her voice to barely above a whisper. "I want nothing to do with Doomers, even former ones. I've suffered enough at their hands."

The words came out harsher than she'd intended, carrying all the fear and anger she'd been holding bottled up inside.

Drova was quiet for a moment, her enormous dark eyes thoughtful. "What happened to you and your family was horrible. No one expects you to forget that, but you should consider that Ruvon being born into the Brotherhood doesn't automatically make him a monster. It just means he was born in the wrong place and probably suffered a lot."

"How can you say that?" Arezoo wrapped her arms around herself. "They're all monsters. They're raised to be that way. Once the lines of decency and morality are crossed, there is no coming back from that."

"It's true," Drova conceded. "They're raised in hatred, taught to see others as less than human, and conditioned to violence from birth. Most never escape that programming. But some do."

Arezoo shook her head. "If they escape the organization, it's only to do their own evil deeds, like the fake doctor who hurt us."

Drova's eyes softened. "Kalugal and his men escaped because they managed to break through the brainwashing. Kalugal is a compeller, so he must have freed those whom he believed were different. The fact that Ruvon escaped, that he abandoned that life and everything he'd been taught to believe, is actually a much stronger indicator of his character than where he came from."

"You don't know what they did to us," Arezoo whispered, tears threatening.

"No, I don't," Drova said softly. "And I'm not saying you have to do anything you're not comfortable with. You don't owe him or anyone else your time or attention. Your feelings are valid. Your caution is understandable."

"But?"

"But maybe consider that these men were victims too. Born into a system they didn't choose, brainwashed from birth, never given a chance to be anything else, but they still managed to break free."

As the children's laughter rang out across the playground, it was a bright counterpoint to the heavy conversation. Arezoo watched them play, thinking about innocence and choice, about the circumstances of birth versus the decisions people made.

"I still don't want anything to do with him," she said finally.

"That's your choice," Drova said. "Just remember

that this community is small. You'll be running into Kalugal's men regularly. Finding a way to coexist with them will make your life easier."

"Coexisting doesn't mean I have to be friendly."

"No, it doesn't," Drova agreed. "But it might mean accepting coffee when it's offered in kindness, if only to keep the peace."

Before Arezoo could argue further, Cyra ran over and tugged on her shirt. "I'm thirsty!"

"Me too!" Rohan added, appearing at her other side.

Thankful for the interruption, Arezoo dug into her bag for the water bottles she'd brought, and as she distributed them, she tried to push thoughts of Ruvon and former Doomers from her mind.

Still, Drova's words lingered.

The uncomfortable truths, or rather claims, were unsettling. The world had been simpler when she could divide people into clear categories of good and evil, victim and perpetrator, friend and enemy. This new reality, where former enemies walked the same paths and brought coffee as peace offerings, necessitated a kind of nuance she wasn't ready for.

It required the suspension of disbelief and the acceptance that redemption was possible even for monsters.

Once upon a time, Arezoo might have believed it, but not anymore.

17

KYRA

"You're quiet," Max said, his hand warm on Kyra's back as they strolled the village paths. "Thinking about the figurine?"

"Among other things." Kyra sighed. "I'm just not looking forward to leaving on another adventure when my sisters need me here."

"They'll survive without you," Max said.

"I'm not sure. I would feel much better about leaving if Jasmine would be here to help them, but she is coming with us. They will have no one to turn to."

"Your sisters are fighters too, in their own way. They'll manage. Besides, Onegus might decide that he can't spare me, and I'll have to stay behind. If so, I'll help them as much as I can."

Kyra stopped in her tracks. "You have to come with us. I'm not leaving without you."

Smiling, he cupped her cheek and leaned in to plant a kiss on her lips. "My warrior queen. If you give

Onegus the look you've just given me, he will insist on my going with you."

She chuckled. "You make me sound scary. I doubt your boss is impressed by a former rebel."

Every time she uttered the word 'rebel' it was accompanied by guilt. She'd abandoned her adopted ragtag family of rebels for her real family, and even though it was the right thing to do, she still felt horrible for doing it.

As they approached Soraya's house, the front door was open, and through it, Kyra could see all four of her sisters sitting in the living room.

"Looks like they're having a meeting," she murmured to Max.

"Without inviting you?"

"I'm inviting myself." Kyra knocked on the open door. "Hello there. Can Max and I come in?"

"Of course." Yasmin waved them over. "You're right on time."

She looked tired, grief still etched in the lines around her eyes, but there was also a new spark of determination in them that hadn't been there the day before.

Her sisters sat with cups of black coffee, all four looking excited. If Kyra didn't know better, she would have thought that one of them was expecting a child, but since they were all single at the moment, that wasn't an option.

Unless someone conceived before arriving and had just discovered it now.

"Who's pregnant?" She swept her gaze over her sisters.

Soraya snorted. "I hope it's you. None of us wants more children."

Kyra's hand instinctively went to her stomach. "I'm not, but the four of you look way too excited. What's going on?"

"Sit down first." Yasmin gestured toward the couch. "Can I get you both coffee?"

"Sure," Max said.

"Count me in." Kyra sat down. "Where are the children?"

"Arezoo took the little ones to the playground," Soraya said. "The older children are studying with Vrog's programs. They have a lot of catching up to do."

That explained the unusual quiet in the house.

Yasmin handed them each a cup of the strong, black brew that transported Kyra instantly back to the rebel camp and conversations over similar coffee while planning operations against the regime.

"How was the meeting at Kalugal's?" Rana asked, but there was an impatience in her voice that suggested she had other things on her mind.

Kyra took a sip of coffee. "Illuminating. Kalugal discovered a figurine in Egypt that was a stunning depiction of the Clan Mother. He wanted Fenella to do a reading of it. Jasmine and I were there to reinforce her ability. Long story short, it turns out that this figurine was modeled on an older and better one that had been created by Khiann's squire, who had appar-

156

ently survived the destruction of the gods' city to carve the likeness of the goddess and inscribe its base."

"That's amazing," Soraya said. "Did Fenella see all that just from touching the figurine?"

Kyra nodded. "We all saw it. I mean, Jasmine and I piggybacked on Fenella's vision, and we all saw the inscription when the carver looked at it, but we couldn't read the script. Luckily, the Clan Mother could, and she told us that the original artist was Esag, Khiann's squire. He made the figurine in honor of her memory, thinking that she had perished with the other gods." Kyra paused to take a breath. "That means I'll need to travel to Egypt soon to help search for him."

Her sisters exchanged looks.

"It's good we're having this meeting today, then," Soraya said, leaning back into her chair with the natural authority of the eldest. "You can help us before you go."

"With what?" Kyra put down her cup.

Another round of silent communication passed between her sisters before Soraya spoke again. "We want to open a store in the village."

The words hung in the air for a moment, unexpected and yet somehow perfectly logical.

"What kind of store?" Max asked.

"Like the neighborhood stores we had back home," Yasmin said, her hands gesturing as she spoke. "The ones on every corner where you could buy groceries, fresh bread, and some other baked goods."

"Candy," Parisa added. "Chocolates. The kids loved going to the store to get some treats."

"This place needs a store," Soraya said. "Every time we need groceries, it's a whole procedure of ordering them and then waiting for someone to deliver them because only members of the community can get in here. Even when we get cars of our own, it's a long drive to the nearest supermarket. I'm sure we are not the only ones who find it inconvenient."

"I hate ordering groceries," Rana said. "It sucks all the fun out of shopping. There's no browsing through produce, no haggling over prices, no aunties gossiping while they squeeze tomatoes to check for ripeness."

Kyra smiled. "You want to recreate a piece of home here."

"It's not about that," Soraya said. "We want to contribute, to earn our keep. I don't know what arrangement we can come to with Kian, but we can figure it out. Maybe a share of the profit for managing the place, or salaries, and some of it will be deducted for housing and everything else we've been getting for free."

Kyra understood, and she was proud of her sisters for their initiative.

"We can even sell home-cooked food." Parisa's usually quiet voice was firm with conviction. "I'm sure that will be in high demand."

"I'm not much of a cook, but I can handle the business side," Rana said. "I can keep the books, manage orders."

"We want you to talk to Kian for us." Soraya's dark eyes fixed on Kyra. "We were thinking of using one of the empty residential houses for our store."

Yasmin nodded. "We've already identified a few that might work—good locations and enough space for storage and display."

Her sisters had put considerable thought into this. "You've been planning this for a while."

Soraya shrugged. "It was easy to figure out what this place was missing, but we don't have the connections to put things in motion. The immortals have lived so long, they've forgotten some of the simple pleasures of life. When did any of them last argue with a shopkeeper over the price of eggplant? When did they gather somewhere just to share the small dramas of daily life?"

Kyra laughed. "Forget the haggling. No one does that here. And there is enough gossip going on in the café and the Hobbit Bar."

Soraya pursed her lips. "Well, if they don't like haggling here, we can live without it. It's less fun, though."

"Maybe we can also serve coffee," Rana suggested. "We could have a few tables outside in the backyard."

"I don't think Kian would agree to that." Kyra glanced at Max. "What do you think?"

"I think that a grocery store is a wonderful idea, but having it in a residential area is problematic. The other residents will not want the commotion disturbing their quiet. We will need to come up with another solution."

"Like what?" Kyra asked. "It's not like there are any empty spaces in the village square."

"There might be." Max rubbed a hand over his jaw. "We can build an extension behind the office building, but it's really up to Kian to decide."

"I'm sure Kian will love the idea," Kyra said. "I'll arrange a meeting with him for all of us. You should present this to him yourselves—he'll want to hear your vision directly."

Relief and excitement washed across her sisters' faces.

"We've already come up with preliminary plans," Parisa said, producing a folder from beside her chair.

Kyra took it and flipped through pages covered in her sisters' neat handwriting.

"This is impressive," Max said, reading over her shoulder. "You've really done your homework."

"We had help," Soraya admitted. "The girls searched online for prices for us."

"You've been busy." Kyra flipped through the folder again. "What about the children?" she asked. "Running a store is demanding work, and you are in charge of homeschooling here. It's not like the kids are at school most of the day."

"That's part of why we want to do it together," Soraya said. "We can rotate schedules and share child-care duties. The older children can help after their studies are done. It will be good for them to have responsibilities and be useful."

"The older boys in particular need purpose," Parisa said. "Arman still has nightmares."

"They are angry," Parisa added quietly. "So much anger. For us, leaving our home, for the immortals, for not saving Uncle Javad."

"The children need purpose, routine, and a sense of belonging," Yasmin said. "That's another reason the store is important. It will give them something to be a part of, to be proud of, a way to contribute to their new community."

"Essa has been incredible with the younger children," Soraya said, speaking of Yasmin's eldest. "He's stepped into his father's shoes, perhaps too much so. He needs to be a teenager, not a surrogate parent, but the only boys his age here are Kra-ell, and he doesn't feel comfortable around them."

Kyra marveled at how her sisters had woven together all these threads into a single solution, but she feared their expectations for this endeavor were inflated.

"Donya has made friends with some of the Kra-ell kids," Soraya said. "Initially, that worried me because they look so strange, but so far, there have been no issues. Laleh decided she wants to be a Guardian when she grows up." Her sister chuckled. "It's your fault, you know. Seeing female warriors opened up a whole world of possibilities she never imagined. I'm not saying I want her to fight, but seeing women in positions of strength, treated with respect—it's good for her."

"For all of them," Yasmin agreed. "This place offers them futures we couldn't have dreamt of back home." She looked at Kyra. "I really don't want you to leave right now. We need you."

"I know." Kyra leaned over and took her hand. "It's not like I will be gone for long, though. For the simple reason that Kalugal will need to return sooner rather than later."

"What about security" Rana asked. "Is Egypt safe?"

Kyra shrugged. "It has to be safer than infiltrating Revolutionary Guard installations."

"Don't joke about it," Yasmin scolded. "We've lost enough already."

The reminder of Javad's death cast a momentary shadow over the room. They'd all lost so much. Their homes, their loved ones, the lives they'd built over decades. But sitting here in Soraya's living room, surrounded by her sisters' determined faces, Kyra also saw what they'd gained.

"The store will be good for the village," she said, changing the subject back to safer ground. "The immortals need what you're offering, and not just the groceries. It's the rhythms of normal life."

"That's what we hope," Soraya said. "To build something lasting here, something our children can be proud of. A bridge between the world we left and the one we've joined."

"Have you thought about what you'll call it?" Max asked.

The sisters exchanged smiles.

"The Pearl," Rana announced. "It's Parisa's idea. After our mother."

"It's perfect," Kyra said.

"We want to paint the door blue," Yasmin added. "Like home. To ward off the evil eye."

"I'm sure Kian won't mind that," Kyra said, though privately she wondered what the architecturally minded immortals would think of such a departure from the village's Mediterranean aesthetic. Then again, Kalugal had his red door, so a precedent already existed.

18

AREZOO

"One more!" Drova encouraged as Arman struggled through his fifth push-up. "Keep your back straight."

"It's hard!" Arman grunted, his arms trembling.

"Hard things are worth doing," Drova said. "That's how you get stronger."

Cyra sat cross-legged beside them, counting loudly and not entirely accurately. "Seven, nine, eight!"

The scene felt surreal—a Kra-ell warrior running an impromptu boot camp for human children at a playground. But the boys were eating it up, despite sweating and grunting.

Focusing on her cousins, Arezoo didn't notice Ruvon returning until he was standing beside the bench and blocking the sun.

"Here is your coffee." He removed one of the paper cups from the cardboard tray and handed it to her.

"Thank you." She forced a smile as she took it.

"I also brought this." He pulled a small paper bag from beneath the carrier. "It's a Danish. I didn't bring more because I didn't know if you were allowed to eat this. I mean, if you and your family are following any dietary restrictions. But I can go back and get more."

She loved the Danishes from the café, and she was a little hungry. "We don't follow any dietary restrictions. Not anymore." She reached for the paper bag. "We are not religious, and we are very happy to be free of being forced to follow rules that were imposed on us. We are Persians, originally. Our ancestors were Zoroastrian and were forcefully converted. My grandmother was secretly a Zoroastrian, but my grandfather wasn't, and he ruled his house with an iron fist. Thankfully, my mother and her sisters were always rebels at heart and only appeared to accept the dogma to survive. They pretended to comply."

She didn't know why she was sharing all this with him. Perhaps she wanted to shatter any illusion he might have about her beliefs. She wasn't the meek and subservient woman he might have expected, being Iranian.

The truth was that Arezoo didn't know much about Zoroastrianism other than the few things her grandmother had told her about it in secret. Still, perhaps she should learn more about it now that she was free to do so and had access to nearly any kind of information she sought.

That was probably the greatest freedom of living in a country that didn't restrict access to knowledge.

Ruvon nodded. "I understand completely."

Did he?

"Does the Brotherhood have dietary restrictions?"

He shook his head. "We only did that when we were stationed in countries that had them. Mortdh's teachings did not include anything about food other than cautioning about indulging in excess."

Well, that made sense. Immortals didn't need to worry about things being healthy or unhealthy, and the comment on excess had probably been more about conserving resources than the health or well-being of the foot soldiers.

Still, she was surprised that he'd shared that with her.

When an uncomfortable moment of silence followed, Ruvon glanced at Drova, who was now demonstrating a complicated push-up routine and singing a catchy tune to accompany it.

"I should give Drova her coffee before it gets cold," he said. "I don't want to interrupt her routine, though. It's damn impressive."

Arezoo chuckled. "It is. I could never do that even if I trained for a hundred years. She's incredibly strong."

He cast her a look that was hard to decipher, but it was so intense that she had to look away.

"Drova!" she called out to hide her unease. "Your coffee is here."

Drova jumped to her feet with her usual fluid grace and sauntered over, not even breathing hard. "This is just what I needed. Thanks, Ruvon."

"You're welcome." He handed her the cup and put the cardboard tray on the bench. "That was an impressive performance."

"It was nothing." She waved a dismissive hand. "One of the Guardians saw it on YouTube or one of the other social media platforms and started doing it, and it caught on like wildfire. Everyone is doing it now in conditioning."

"It's a catchy tune," Ruvon said. "And it's challenging."

"Pfft." She snorted. "Not for me. But if you want, I can send you a link." She looked pointedly at his lean arms. "If you were a Kra-ell, those scrawny arms would be just fine, but you are an immortal, and you could benefit from some bulking up."

Arezoo was so embarrassed for Ruvon that her cheeks were flaming with heat. Were all Kra-ell so blunt?

For a long moment, the guy was speechless, and then he nodded. "You are right. It's just that I find physical training incredibly boring. I prefer to challenge my mind."

Oh, that was good, and Arezoo wanted to give him the thumbs up for the perfect retort.

Wait, why was she siding with the Doomer against her friend?

Drova laughed and clapped Ruvon on his back.

"Then watch some boring lectures while you are training if that's your thing."

"Good suggestion." He took a sip of his coffee. "I need to trick myself into liking the exercise."

It was a relief to see them reaching an under-standing and neither appearing offended. Perhaps there was a lesson to be learned from this. They each had said their truth as they saw it, and they were both smart about not taking offense just because they had different interests in life.

Drova took a long sip of her coffee, her dark eyes moving between them with poorly concealed amuse-ment. "I should get back to the kids before they decide to try something dangerous. Zaden's been eyeing that tree like he wants to climb it, and it's dangerous for a little human with tiny, worthless muscles."

"They're not worthless," Arezoo protested.

"You know what I mean." Drova waved a dismissive hand and walked away, leaving Arezoo with Ruvon.

"Would you like to sit?" she offered, gesturing toward the bench.

"Thank you." He sat, spreading his legs.

"Sorry about my friend. She has absolutely no filter." Arezoo eyed the Danish and debated whether she should offer him half.

"She's honest. I like it." He leaned forward, bracing his elbows on his knees and cradling his coffee cup between his palms.

Arezoo chuckled. "She's brutal, but then that's not a

168

big surprise. She's a pureblooded Kra-ell. They are known for that."

"So I've heard."

She lifted the pastry. "Can I offer you half?"

He hesitated. "Maybe just a little piece. You are hungry."

"I have snacks in my bag." She tore it in half and handed him the slightly bigger portion. "Enjoy."

The Danish was delicious—flaky pastry with a sweet cheese filling and a drizzle of icing. She ate it slowly, using it as an excuse not to talk while she studied him from the corner of her eye.

He wasn't handsome by immortal standards. Where most of the males she'd seen around the village were broad-shouldered and confidently attractive, Ruvon was slight, almost fragile looking. His features were pleasant enough but unremarkable, and he held himself with a hunched quality as if trying to take up less space in the world.

His lack of confidence was actually refreshing. Every other immortal male she'd encountered so far carried himself with the assurance of an apex predator, and it made the immortal males a little intimidating. Then again, Ruvon valued his mind, not his muscles, and the intensity of his intelligent gaze was as intimidating as, if not more so than, the swagger of the other immortals.

"The coffee's good," she said, needing to fill the silence. "Stronger than what usually comes from the vending machines."

"That's because it's a double shot," he said. "You can choose that when you order coffee."

How did he know that she liked her coffee strong?

He'd been watching her, she knew that, but she hadn't known that he'd been paying attention to small details like that.

It was flattering, but also a little creepy.

"Do you come to the playground often?" he asked.

"This is the little ones' favorite place in the village, so when their mothers need a breather, either I or one of the older kids brings them here."

"It must be nice to have a big family," he said.

Something in his tone made her look at him more directly. "Do you have family?"

"Not anymore. My mother passed away a long time ago, and so did my sisters. I didn't have any brothers, so it's just me now."

The words hung between them, heavy with unspoken history. Arezoo got curious despite her better judgment. "How old are you?"

"One hundred and thirty-seven."

The number made her stomach twist. He was old enough to be her great-great-grandfather, sitting here bringing her coffee and pastries like a schoolboy with a crush. But then, age meant little to immortals. Din and Max were both over five hundred years old, and neither Aunt Kyra nor Fenella seemed bothered by it.

"I still have a hard time reconciling immortal youthful looks with how old you really are," she said. "I can't imagine living so long."

"You learn to focus on the present instead of the past or the future."

Another long moment of silence followed, and Arezoo struggled to find something to talk to him about.

"What do you do for Kalugal?" she finally asked. "I mean, when you are not bringing coffee to thirsty humans and Kra-ell?"

He looked startled at her attempt at a joke, then his lips curved in a tiny smile. "I'm in charge of electronic security. Making sure our systems can't be breached, monitoring for threats, that sort of thing."

"That sounds complicated."

"It can be," he agreed, some of his awkwardness fading as he warmed to the subject. "Technology changes rapidly. What was secure yesterday might be vulnerable today. It requires constant adaptation."

"Where did you learn to do that? I can't imagine the Brotherhood had computer science programs."

His expression darkened, and she immediately regretted the question. "There was barely any education in the camp other than how to kill as many as possible as fast as possible. I could barely read and write when Kalugal took me under his wing. He taught me and the others, so we were at least literate. He could have just left us ignorant, but he wanted us to be more than what we'd been made to be. We were the lucky ones, and not just because Kalugal saw something worth saving in us. We were not as dumb as the average Doomer was back then."

Arezoo lifted a brow. "Back then? Are the Doomers smarter now?"

"Navuh is working on it. He finally realized that a dumb army of brutes is no longer what would win wars for him. He needed smarter soldiers, so he changed the kind of men he brought to the island to breed his warriors. The next generation of Doomers will be smarter and much more dangerous."

When he'd mentioned breeding, the fight or flight response kicked in, and Arezoo suddenly had a hard time getting air into her lungs.

"Are you okay?" He looked at her with worry in his eyes.

"I'm fine." She forced a smile. "So, how did you get from learning how to read and write to modern tech?"

"That happened much later. After we escaped and got to America, we needed to start from scratch, and Kalugal needed robust security because he feared Navuh coming after us. I discovered that I had a knack for it, and I've been teaching myself everything I could about the subject ever since."

"That's impressive," she said. "Teaching yourself such complex skills."

He nodded. "Thank you. I can't change where I came from, but thanks to where I am now, I can be whoever I want to be, and I owe it all to Kalugal."

"You really care about him."

"I owe him everything," Ruvon said with quiet intensity. "My life and my soul. If I'd stayed with the Brotherhood..." He trailed off, shaking his head. "I would have shriveled up inside. Kalugal gave me the chance to live a life free of hate and death."

Arezoo felt a shift inside of her, an uncomfortable loosening of the rigid categories she'd constructed. This man beside her, this shy and unassuming guy, was a survivor, just like her.

19

DIN

Fenella's blissed-out expression was the stuff dreams were made of, except fifty years of dreams paled beside the reality of her.

"I can practically hear the gears turning in that professor brain of yours," she said without opening her eyes.

How had she known that he was looking at her?

Din lifted her hand, pressing a kiss to her palm. "I'm not thinking. I'm cataloging, storing this moment away like a precious artifact."

She opened her eyes. "I'm not going anywhere, Din."

Was that a promise? It sounded like it, and he was going to pretend like it was.

"I know." He shifted and ran his hand down her back, capturing her ass and pulling her closer against his chest. "But I am a collector, not of artifacts but of moments. I record them and store them in the album inside my mind, so I can retrieve them anytime I want and refill my cup of joy. It has been empty for far too long."

She propped herself on an elbow, studying his face with those dark eyes that had haunted him for decades. "What was it like for you in the years I was gone? Did you think of me often?"

He knew she hadn't thought of him, so admitting that he'd thought of her was hard. Women did not appreciate men who fawned over them too much. They liked working for the attention they were getting.

"I was pretty lonely," he admitted. "But that's the lot of most immortals. We can't form relationships with mortals, and immortals who we are not related to are hard to find. So, I did what most of my clan members do and found fulfillment in studying a new field I was interested in and later working in it."

Her lips quirked up in a semi-smile. "I bet you rarely slept alone."

"Waking up next to a woman I had no interest in was not a good idea, so I made it a rule to always go home and sleep in my bed alone."

She nodded. "I was the same. That's why I never invited guys to my place. I always went to theirs so I could sneak out the moment they fell asleep."

His fangs started itching, which they shouldn't have since he'd emptied his venom glands only a couple of hours ago. "Perhaps we shouldn't talk about past lovers." He reached up to tuck a strand of hair behind her ear. "I'm jealous of any man you've spent any time with, even if it was platonic. Not a day went by that I didn't think of you, and I couldn't understand my obsession with a human I should have forgotten. I couldn't stand Max because he was a constant reminder of what I couldn't have."

"I hope you truly forgave him." Fenella cupped his cheek. "It wasn't his fault. He was there, and you weren't. Simple as that."

There was nothing simple about losing fifty years he could have spent with Fenella or all the suffering she'd endured during that time. But Max wasn't the one to blame.

Din was angrier with himself than he'd been with Max. If he hadn't been so hesitant, he would have approached Fenella first, and he would have been the one to induce her transition to immortality. But he'd chickened out, and his inaction resulted in Max seducing Fenella and turning her from a Dormant into an immortal without any of them being any the wiser.

Hell, if he wasn't such an asshole and had just accepted Max's apology, he would have pursued Fenella after Max had left, and he would have been there for her when she'd transitioned, explaining what was happening to her and bringing her into the clan's fold. They could have been together all this time.

The old pain lanced through him before he pushed it aside with an effort. "It's all in the past, love. We should focus on the here and now."

She smiled. "A borrowed bed in the middle of a

Sunday afternoon." There was humor in her voice. "Could be worse."

"But it could be better." He pulled her with him and shifted to his back so she was on top of him. "We can ask for our own place."

She was quiet for a long moment, and he could feel the tension in her body as she wrestled with what he'd suggested. "Eventually, we will, but we have the mission to Egypt coming up, and changing housing arrangements before we return doesn't make sense."

He was a little disappointed but also encouraged. She hadn't said no. She'd said not yet.

"I've been thinking about what Bridget said." Fenella laid her cheek on his chest. "About us being family."

The non-sequitur threw him. "You and your cousins?"

"Yeah, but it's more than that. This whole immortal community is connected in some way, and it all works. Some are tied by blood, while others are bound by choice and circumstance. I've spent so long running from connections, convinced that caring about people would only lead to pain. But maybe that's just another wall I built."

"Walls serve a purpose." Din caressed her back. "They protect us when we need protecting."

"But they also keep things out that might be good for us. I'm tired of living behind walls, Din. Tired of running, of always having one foot out the door. But I don't know how to be any other way. Staying put feels like a trap, no matter how hard I convince myself that it's not. I think I need a shrink."

"You can talk to Vanessa."

"She's busy."

"I know she is, but I'm sure she would find the time for you. Maybe she can give you some tools, so you can work on this on your own."

Fenella lifted her head and looked into his eyes. "That's a great idea. I hadn't thought of it like that. To me, a shrink is an office with a couch and a spectacled lady asking me how I feel about this or that."

He chuckled. "Real life is not like movies."

She pouted. "How would you know? Have you ever visited a psychologist's office?"

"Can't say that I have, but I know that Vanessa doesn't have a couch in hers."

"Oh." She laid her cheek back on his chest, her fingers tracing patterns on his belly. "What if I'm unfixable? What if this urge to flee never goes away? What if I'm too broken even for the mighty Vanessa?"

"You're not broken." He hooked a finger under her chin and lifted her head. "Wounded, cautious, skittish, but not broken. You just need more time to heal."

"How can you say that with such confidence, Professor?"

"Broken things can't connect, can't take risks. And you're doing all of those things. You have a new job you enjoy, you're making friends, and you're letting me love you." He smiled. "You're even worried about

178

disappointing Atzil. Those aren't the actions of someone who's broken."

The truth was that he was talking out of his ass because he knew next to nothing about psychology, but he knew that Fenella was strong. She was a survivor. Besides, all she needed was to believe in her ability to heal, and she would.

"Well, when you put it like that, Professor, who am I to argue?"

"I'm right and you know it." He shifted them so they were face to face on the pillow. "You're one of the strongest people I've ever met, Fenella. You survived things that would have destroyed others. And you're still here, still fighting, still capable of joy and connection and terrible jokes at inappropriate times."

"My jokes are excellent," she protested, but she was smiling.

"They're terrible and you know it." He kissed her nose. "I love them anyway."

"You love everything about me." There was wonder in her voice, as if she still couldn't quite believe it.

"Guilty as charged." He traced the line of her jaw with one finger. "Though I'm particularly fond of certain aspects."

"Oh?" Her eyes sparked with mischief. "Do tell."

"Well," he said, affecting his most scholarly tone, "from a purely academic perspective, of course, I find your rebellious streak particularly fascinating."

"Purely academic?" She shifted closer, her body pressing against his in decidedly non-academic ways.

"Absolutely. I'm conducting a thorough study of all your fascinating attributes. It's important to be comprehensive in one's research."

"And what have you concluded so far?"

He pretended to consider. "That further investigation is required. Extensive further investigation."

The sound of a throaty laugh warmed him from the inside out. "How fortunate that we have the time."

"About that..." He glanced at the bedside clock. "Don't you need to get ready for your shift soon?"

"I think we have a few more minutes to spare. I love cuddling with you in bed."

He pulled her closer. "I don't want to be responsible for you being late on your third night on the job."

"Look at you, being all responsible and considerate." She pressed a kiss to his chest. "It's presumptuous of you to think it's up to you to decide, but I find it oddly attractive."

"Everything I do is oddly attractive to you."

"Confident much?"

He trailed his hand down her back, satisfied when she shivered. "I've made a study of it, remember?"

"And they say romance is dead," she said with a smile. "You can make it up to me when we go to Egypt. I've never been there. What's it like?"

"Hot," he said. "Sandy. Full of tourists and merchants trying to separate them from their money."

"You're really selling it."

"But if you manage to filter out all the noise, there is something about it. The weight of history, maybe.

You can feel the age of the place in your bones. And at night, in the desert, the stars are incredible."

"Sounds lovely."

"Well, not really, but I love the history of it. The mystery. Every dig site could hold answers to questions we don't even know to ask yet." He paused. "I think you'll find it fascinating, even with the heat and the sand and the aggressive carpet sellers."

"Carpet sellers?"

"They're relentless. Jasmine will probably need to hold you back from throttling them."

She grinned. "You know me so well."

"I'm learning more every day."

20

AREZOO

Arezoo was getting tired just from watching her cousins, or maybe it was Ruvon's presence that was draining her energy. A war was waging inside of her between the effects of her trauma and her empathy, and it was all happening in her subconscious because she couldn't assign any conscious thought to it while watching the little devils.

Rohan and Arman were turning the slide into a fortress they needed to defend against imaginary invaders, while Kavir and Zaden practiced super-jumps from the swings, trying to recreate Drova's spectacular leap.

"Don't jump so high," Arezoo called out, her voice carrying the same cautionary tone her mother used. "You're not immortal yet, and you can get hurt."

Zaden rolled his eyes at her the same way she rolled hers at her own mother.

Soraya would have called it payback, and she would have been right.

Thankfully, Cyra was happy in the sandbox, using the paper cup from Ruvon's coffee delivery to build a palace.

Girls were so much easier to raise than boys. If she ever had kids, she hoped they would all be girls. Not that she would ever have children. If she turned immortal, which she should do sooner rather than later, her fertility rate would drop, and children would be unlikely.

Arezoo couldn't say she minded.

She took another sip of her by now cold coffee, hyperaware of the immortal male sitting beside her. Ruvon hadn't said much since their conversation about his past, seeming content to watch the children play while nursing his drink. The silence wasn't exactly comfortable, but it wasn't unbearable either.

"You know," Ruvon said, startling her, "you should come with me to the Hobbit Bar tonight."

She turned to look at him, noting how he kept his gaze fixed on the playground rather than meeting her eyes. "Why?"

"Fenella is working at the bar tonight, and rumors claim that she's very entertaining. She's been conducting psychometric readings on objects brought to her by bar patrons. Her readings are fake, of course, but they are a lot of fun. The whole village has been talking about it."

"Who says that she makes them up?" Arezoo frowned. "Psychometry is her talent."

"Oh, she is. That's what makes it entertaining. She might be getting real impressions from the objects, but then she turns them into wild tales. Last night, she told a Guardian that he had a passion for performing yoga in the nude on top of the roof of his house and howling at the moon."

Despite herself, Arezoo found her lips quirking up. "Maybe it's true?"

"It's not, but eyewitnesses report that everyone in the bar was laughing hysterically."

From where she was pushing herself ever higher on the remaining swing, Drova had clearly been listening. "Fenella sounds like fun," she called out, executing a graceful dismount that had the boys stopping to watch. "I'd love to check it out."

She sauntered over, her long legs eating up the distance in just a few strides. "We should go tonight. All three of us."

Arezoo's stomach tightened. "I've never had alcohol before."

"You don't have to drink anything alcoholic," Ruvon said. "I'm sure Fenella can make a mocktail for you."

"What's that?"

"Non-alcoholic cocktails," he explained. "All the presentation and flavors, but without the alcohol. You'd like them. I don't know what Fenella can make, but there is one that tastes like tropical paradise, with mango, passion fruit, and coconut. Or a more subtle one with cucumber and mint or pomegranate and rose."

Pomegranate and rose sounded like home, like the *sharbat* her grandmother used to make for special occasions. The memory brought an unexpected lump to her throat.

"I..." She paused, already knowing what the real obstacle would be. "I'd need to ask my mother's permission."

Ruvon's brow furrowed. "But you're an adult, right?"

As if that meant anything in her household.

Drova nodded in agreement. "You're what, nineteen? Twenty? Why would you need permission?"

Heat rose up Arezoo's neck. How could she explain? How could she make them understand that in her family, in her culture, unmarried daughters didn't do what they pleased, that her mother had already been through so much that she didn't want to stir things up, especially for something as inconsequential as going to a bar?

"It's just how things are in my family," she said quietly. "It's not that my mother is traditional, she's not. But we've lived a certain way, and it isn't easy to just switch gears and behave like we were born here in the land of the free. Things take time."

"I could come with you and talk to your mother," Drova offered. "I can convince her that it's perfectly safe, and that I'll be there too."

Something in Drova's tone made Arezoo's eyes narrow. "You're not planning to use your compulsion power on my mother, are you?"

Drova's eyes widened. "Of course not! I swear on my honor as a warrior that I would never use compulsion on your mother or any member of your family without their explicit permission."

The oath sounded formal, ritualistic even, but Arezoo wasn't entirely convinced. She'd seen how easily the immortals bent others to their will, how natural it seemed to them. Even if Drova meant her promise now, in the heat of the moment, faced with Soraya's temper…

"I appreciate the offer, but I think it's better if I talk to her alone."

Ruvon shifted beside her, and when she glanced at him, she caught something that might have been disappointment flash across his features before he smoothed them back to neutral.

"I'd be happy to pick you up from your home," he offered. "Properly introduce myself to your mother, if that would help. But if you prefer to meet me at the bar, that's perfectly fine too."

He was trying so hard to do this right, to respect her boundaries even if he didn't fully understand them.

"Meeting there would be better," she said. "If I can come at all. I'll call you if my mother throws a tantrum and forbids it."

"You'll need my number." He pulled out his phone.

"What's yours?"

She recited the number of the phone the clan had given her, watching as he typed it. When he finished, her phone buzzed with a text: *Ruvon - This is my number. Looking forward to tonight, but no pressure if it doesn't work out.*

"There," he said, tucking his phone away. "Now you can reach me either way."

She stared at the message on her screen, her throat suddenly tight. It was the first time she'd exchanged phone numbers with a guy who wasn't family. Such a simple thing, something her friends in Tehran had been doing since they started attending university, but for her, it felt monumental.

It was ridiculous because she wasn't even sure she was interested in Ruvon romantically, even though she no longer saw him as a threat or lumped him together automatically with the monsters who'd hurt her. The conversation about his past and his gratitude to Kalugal had shifted her perspective.

She felt guilty now for her initial prejudice.

He'd been a victim too, raised in brutality, denied education, denied choice. That he'd escaped and had built a new life, that he could sit here making gentle conversation about mocktails and respecting her boundaries, spoke to the quality of his character.

But understanding someone's story and being attracted to them were two different things.

The truth was that she wasn't attracted to anyone in the village, which was strange since most of the immortal males looked like they'd stepped out of magazines with their supernatural beauty. They were also polite and friendly, and she couldn't find any fault in any of them except perhaps being too perfect.

Maybe she was broken.

Maybe she considered all males a threat because of what had been done to her.

It wasn't rational. She knew that. Some of these immortal males, the Guardians, were saving girls like her from predators like the fake doctor. They were honorable, kind, and respectful. They would never hurt her.

But knowing something intellectually and feeling it were two different things.

When she thought about being touched by any man, her skin crawled. Her body remembered rough hands, violations, the helplessness of being examined like livestock. The fake doctor's face haunted her—so handsome and yet so evil, capable of such cruelty.

Perhaps that was the problem. All these males were just as handsome if not more so, and they reminded her of him.

Except, Ruvon wasn't as perfect as the others. Yet, still, she wasn't interested.

"Arezoo!" Cyra's voice broke through her spiraling thoughts. "Look! I made a tower!"

Grateful for the distraction, Arezoo rose and walked to the sandbox, making appropriate sounds of admiration for Cyra's architectural achievement. Behind her, she heard Drova challenge Ruvon to attempt her push-up routine, followed by his good-natured laughter and acceptance.

Arezoo needed to transition to immortality eventually. She knew that, too. Her mother and aunts were already discussing it in hushed voices when they thought the younger ones couldn't hear. The sooner the better, they said. While they were still young and healthy, while their children could grow up with immortal mothers.

But the transition required an inducer. An immortal male's venom delivered through a bite during...

She couldn't even complete the thought.

"What's wrong?" Cyra asked, tilting her head up at Arezoo with those overly perceptive eyes of hers.

"Nothing, sweetie. I was just thinking."

"Sad thoughts?" The little girl reached up with sandy hands. "You need a hug."

Arezoo bent down and accepted the embrace, sand and all. This was love untainted by complication—simple, pure, freely given. If only all affection could be so uncomplicated.

"Arezoo," her mother called from behind them.

She turned to see her mother standing at the edge of the sandbox with Yasmin.

"Maman." She straightened as Cyra ran to her own mother. "I thought you were in the house."

"Yasmin and I decided to come see how you were doing." Her mother's eyes turned to Ruvon, narrowing slightly. "Who is this?"

"This is Ruvon," Arezoo said, trying to keep her voice neutral. "He works for Kalugal and he's a friend of Drova's."

Ruvon rose to his feet and offered her mother a respectful nod. "It's a pleasure to meet you. Your daughter speaks highly of you."

It was a polite lie, but she appreciated the attempt at diplomacy.

"Does she?" Soraya's voice could have frozen the desert. "How nice."

An uncomfortable silence stretched until Drova, bless her complete lack of social awareness, broke it. "Ruvon and I invited Arezoo to join us at the Hobbit Bar tonight. Fenella, your newly discovered cousin, does these hilarious psychic readings that the whole village is talking about, and we thought it would be fun to see."

Arezoo wanted the ground to swallow her up as her mother's expression shifted from suspicious to thunderous.

"The bar," Soraya repeated flatly. "You invited my daughter to a bar."

"It's just for the entertainment," Ruvon said quickly.

"Thank you for the invitation," Soraya cut him off, her voice sharp enough to slice steel. "But Arezoo has responsibilities at home tonight. Come, daughter. It's time to go."

The dismissal was clear. Arezoo felt heat flood her face as she gathered her things, avoiding everyone's eyes.

"I'll call you," she managed to murmur to Ruvon as she passed.

His expression was understanding, sympathetic, and even. "Of course. Have a good evening."

As they walked away, Yasmin herding the protesting children, Arezoo could feel her mother's anger radiating like heat from a forge. The lecture would come later, she knew. For now, there was just this tense silence and the weight of conflicting expectations.

On the one hand, her mother wanted her to find a guy who would induce her transition, but on the other hand, she wanted to cloister her in the house. The two were mutually exclusive.

As her phone buzzed in her pocket, she pulled it out and saw a text: *I understand. The invitation stands whenever you're ready. No pressure. - R*

She deleted it before her mother could ask who was messaging her.

21

DIN

Fenella's damp hair hung loose around her shoulders, releasing the scent of her shampoo —floral with a hint of citrus that made him want to bury his nose in the dark strands.

"The black top with the lace detail or the plain one?" She held up both options, turning to face him where he sat on the edge of the bed.

"The one with lace," he said.

She smiled, that particular smile that made his chest tight with emotion. "Lace it is, then. Black is perfect for bartending. It doesn't show stains."

As she pulled the top over her head, Din thought about the velvet box sitting in his nightstand drawer in Thomas's place. For fifty years, he'd carried the brooch, and he wanted to give it to Fenella, but it never seemed like the right time.

Today felt special, though.

She hadn't told him she loved him, but he could

feel it in the way she looked at him, in the way she made love to him, in the knowing smiles she sent his way, which she didn't bestow on anyone else.

It still wasn't the best time, but he felt an urge to give it to her right now.

"Do I have toothpaste on my face or something?" Fenella smoothed her hand over the black top. "You're staring."

"No, you're perfect." He smiled. "Even if you had toothpaste on your face, but you don't."

"Flatterer." She turned back to the mirror, tilting her head to put on a dangling silver earring. "It's good for tips if I look nice."

A jolt of jealousy speared through him at her words. He didn't want all those males in the bar salivating after her. Everyone knew that they were together, but until their bond solidified, the vultures would continue circling, waiting for their chance to snatch a beautiful immortal female.

Perhaps he didn't have as much time as he thought he had to get her to fall in love with him. Maybe that was the reason he felt like he had to give her the present now.

Not that bribes would work on Fenella, but it was a gorgeous piece of jewelry, and it had cost him a small fortune. It should move the needle in his favor at least a little.

They still had over an hour before she needed to be at the bar, which gave him enough time to get it if he hurried.

"I need to run to my place." He rose to his feet. "I also need to change clothes."

She turned, eyebrow raised as she took in his appearance. "Why? You look nice. That shirt brings out your eyes."

He glanced down at the button-down he'd worn to Kalugal's. It was a nice dress shirt, which was a little much for a bar outing. "I need something more casual. I don't want to clean tables and move chairs in this one."

"Didn't stop you from helping last night when you were wearing a shirt just as nice."

"I've learned my lesson." He leaned over her and moved her hair aside to kiss her neck. "I think I have a black T-shirt I can wear."

She studied him for a moment, and he had the uncomfortable feeling she could see right through him. But then she shrugged. "Fine. I'll brew some coffee and make us sandwiches. We haven't eaten since brunch, and all the bar serves are mixed nuts and pretzels."

"That sounds perfect." He walked over to the door, pausing to take one more look at her. "I won't be long."

"You'd better not be. I make mean sandwiches, and they don't improve with age."

He blew her a kiss before closing the door behind him.

The evening was crisp as he jogged through the village paths toward Thomas's house. His mind was already in his bedroom, picturing exactly where the box sat in the bottom drawer of his nightstand, cushioned beneath academic journals he'd been meaning to read.

He heard the television blaring as soon as he opened the door.

Thomas was sprawled on the couch, beer in hand, watching American football, not proper football, which the Americans called soccer for some reason.

"Din!" Thomas raised his beer in greeting. "Perfect timing. The game just started. Grab a beer and join me."

"Can't, sorry. I'm in a rush. Fenella is waiting to have dinner with me before her shift at the Hobbit."

Once in his room, he closed the door behind him to block the television noise and went straight to the nightstand, pulling open the bottom drawer. Inside, beneath the stack of journals, was the small velvet box.

Din sat on the edge of the bed and opened it, needing to reassure himself that it was as beautiful and unique as he remembered.

The brooch didn't disappoint. It lay nestled in faded blue velvet, the silver tarnished to a lovely antique patina that enhanced rather than diminished its beauty. The Celtic knot-work pattern was as intricate as he remembered, endless loops and whorls that drew the eye inward to the center stone. The amber caught the light from his bedside lamp, glowing like aged whiskey, which had been his thought when he'd first seen it in that Edinburgh shop window.

He'd bought it just a week after meeting Fenella,

already so taken with her that he'd spent a small fortune on a gift he hadn't planned on and hadn't known when he would give. The piece had just called to him, and the moment he'd laid eyes on it, he'd known it should be Fenella's.

The elderly shopkeeper with knowing eyes had told him it was late Victorian, probably 1880s or 1890s. "A sweetheart's gift," she'd said with a smile. "See the pattern? Eternal love, no beginning and no end."

He'd carried it through every move, every change, every lonely decade of wondering if she was even alive. There had been chances to give it away, other women who'd passed through his life, but something had always held him back.

Subconsciously, he must have kept it for Fenella even though it had made no sense.

Stubborn, irrational hope.

Din closed the box with a soft snap and put it on top of the nightstand. After changing into a pair of jeans and a casual black T-shirt, he slipped the box into his pocket.

As he stepped out and headed for the front door, Thomas called after him, "Say hello to Fenella for me."

"Will do," Din promised. "You should stop by the bar after the game. See her in action."

"I might do that." Thomas saluted him with the bottle of beer.

As Din jogged back to Shira's place, the box

bouncing slightly in his pocket, his heart was racing, but not from exertion.

After fifty years, the moment was finally here.

Regrettably, it wouldn't happen over a candlelit dinner like he'd imagined, and the setting was far from perfect, but he felt the urge to do it now and not wait any longer.

Back at Shira's place, he found Fenella in the kitchen finishing the assembling of their sandwiches. She'd put music on, something jazzy and smooth that seemed to move through her as she worked, adding a subtle sway to her hips.

"Perfect timing," she said without turning around. "Coffee's ready, and I'm just finishing my culinary masterpieces."

"They look and smell amazing." He walked over to the coffee pot, needing something to do with his hands while his heart tried to return to a normal rhythm. "What did you put in them?"

"I'm not telling. It's a trade secret." She glanced over her shoulder with a grin. "Whatever I found in the fridge. Turkey, avocado, slices of tomatoes, arugula, and Dijon mustard."

"Sounds delicious." He poured two cups of coffee, adding cream to hers the way she liked it.

The domestic vibe of the moment struck him. He was standing in a kitchen with the woman he loved, preparing to share a meal before she went to work.

After decades of solitude, this felt almost miraculous.

"Here." She slid a plate across the counter to him. "Eat up."

He took a bite, the flavors barely registering. The box in his pocket felt enormous, obvious, as if it was glowing through the fabric of his jeans. How did people do this? How did they casually pull out jewelry between bites?

"Okay, what's wrong?" Fenella set down her sandwich, fixing him with those knowing eyes of hers that saw too much. "You've been weird since you got back. Weirder than usual, I mean. You're practically vibrating."

"Nothing's wrong."

"You are freaking me out." She frowned at him. "Spill. What's going on?"

He set down his coffee cup, decision made. This wasn't how he'd planned it, but then again, nothing with Fenella ever went according to plan. Their entire relationship had chaos written all over it.

Why should this be different?

"I have something for you," he said, pulling the box from his pocket and setting it on the counter between them.

She looked at the box, then at him, her expression shifting from curiosity to something more guarded. "Din..."

"It's not a ring, so don't look so panicked." He ran a hand through his hair. "I bought this fifty years ago. A week after we met, actually. I saw it in a shop window in Edinburgh, and I knew that you had to have it.

Don't ask me why. It was an impulse, an odd gut feeling."

Her hand moved toward the box, then stopped. "You held on to it through all those years?"

He nodded. "After the blowup, I swore I'd give it to the next woman I dated, but I could never go through with it. I carried it with me through every move, and I never found anyone I wanted to gift it to." He pushed the box closer to her. "Please. Just open it."

As she picked up the box with careful fingers, he felt like a cosmic circle was closing, and when she opened it, her soft intake of breath made all those years of waiting worth it.

"Oh, Din." Her finger hovered over the Celtic pattern, not quite touching the silver. "It's beautiful."

"It's Scottish. Late Victorian. The shopkeeper told me the pattern means eternal love—no beginning and no end." He was babbling now, but couldn't stop. "I know it's tarnished, but I didn't want to clean it. Seemed wrong to erase all those years. Like they are part of its story now. Our story."

She looked up at him, and her eyes were bright with unshed tears. "I can't believe you kept it for me even though you couldn't have known I was even alive."

He reached out, covering her hand with his. "It made no sense, and sometimes it just lay forgotten for years, but then I would find it again when I was packing, and I'd tell myself to donate it, sell it, give it away. But I never could."

She lifted the brooch from its velvet nest, holding it up to catch the kitchen light. The amber glowed, warm and rich like honey, like whiskey.

"I don't know what to say."

"You don't have to say anything." He took the brooch from her, fingers clumsy as he worked the old clasp. "May I?"

She nodded, and he moved behind her and gathered a bit of fabric from her black top, careful not to damage the delicate lace detail as he pinned the brooch just above her heart. The metal was cool under his fingers, but where his knuckles brushed her skin through the fabric, she was warm.

"There." He took a step back.

She turned to face him, one hand going immediately to the brooch. With the backdrop of her dark clothing and dark hair, the silver and amber seemed to glow, drawing the eye like a star in the night sky.

"How does it look on me?" she asked.

"Perfect." His voice sounded rougher than intended. "Absolutely perfect."

She rose up on her toes, pulling his head down for a kiss that was soft and fierce at the same time. Din could taste coffee and emotion, and for a moment, he thought that she might say the words he longed to hear.

When her lips parted, he held his breath.

"Thank you," she said instead. "I'll look at it properly later, really look at it when I can take my time. Thank you for never giving up on me."

Later, when she had time, her psychometric abilities might let her see more than just metal and stone. She might see the years of waiting, the hope and heartache, all the moments he'd held it and thought of her. All the times he'd almost given up but didn't.

"You're welcome," he said for lack of anything better to say. The words felt so inadequate for the magnitude of the moment.

She touched the brooch again, a gesture he suspected would become a habit. "I don't know if I should wear it to work. It's so distinctive that Atzil might have a problem with it."

"Tell him it's a present from me and I insist on you wearing it at all times as a good talisman." Din picked up his forgotten sandwich. "I actually believe that it is. Who knows, maybe holding on to it for fifty years was what brought you back to me."

"Perhaps it did." She looked down at the brooch. "It's gorgeous."

It wasn't the candlelit dinner he'd once imagined, it wasn't the perfect romantic gesture, but as he watched her clear their plates, the brooch glinting against her black top with each movement, he thought perhaps this was better.

Not a fantasy, but reality. Not perfect, but theirs.

Just like everything else about them, it was imperfect and absolutely right.

22

FENELLA

The brooch got a lot of curious glances, first from Atzil and then from the bar's clientele, but surprisingly, no one asked about it. They must have assumed that it had been a gift because someone like her would never buy a piece of such jewelry for herself.

It looked expensive, but even if she'd had the money, Fenella doubted she would have gotten something as big and as bold. It looked ridiculous on her simple T-shirt, and yet she wore it with pride that bordered on reverence.

It wasn't just that Din had held on to it for fifty years, though that alone would have made it precious. There was something about the brooch itself that was reassuring, comforting. It felt like an old friend found after a long separation.

The brooch was more than just a beautiful piece of jewelry.

It was special.

Maybe it was her newly discovered psychometric abilities playing tricks on her mind, but she could swear she felt a subtle pulse of energy from it, like Kyra's pendant but different. More subtle and patient.

Was it possible that the brooch could channel her abilities like Kyra's pendant channeled hers? The thought seemed fanciful, but then again, a week ago, she would have laughed at the idea of reading memories from objects or being descended from gods.

Her definition of possible had expanded considerably.

Someone cleared his throat, pulling her out of her head, and she realized that the vodka she'd been pouring into the shaker was overflowing.

"Sorry about that." She emptied the contents into the sink and started on the Moscow mule from scratch. "Lost touch with reality for a moment."

"It happens," the guy said with a smile. "Has the shaker revealed some hidden truths?"

She chuckled. "Even if it did, I wouldn't be able to understand them. I don't speak Chinese."

The guy cast an amused glance at Atzil. "I'm sure your boss has plenty of interesting stories to tell, and he's been using this same shaker for months."

Fenella shrugged. "You know that I'm making it all up, right?"

The guy arched a brow. "Not all of it."

She was about to come up with a rebuttal when the bar door opened and Ruvon walked in.

He paused just inside, scanning the half-empty room with uncertainty. Then his gaze landed on her, and he offered a tentative smile and made his way to the bar.

"Evening, Ruvon," she greeted him. "What can I get you?"

"Just a beer, please. Whatever you have on tap." He sat on the barstool next to the talkative client.

During Kian's party, Ruvon had said something about coming over to hear her amusing readings, but he was early. She wouldn't start the performance until the bar was full and all the patrons were at least slightly drunk.

It was no fun performing for sober immortals.

Perhaps Ruvon realized his mistake because his eyes kept darting toward the door.

"Expecting someone?" she asked as she put the beer in front of him on the bar.

He accepted it with a nod of thanks. "I'm actually waiting for a friend, but I'm not sure she'll come."

"She?" Fenella raised an eyebrow. Had he asked Shira out on a date?

Perhaps that was what they'd been talking about during Kian's birthday celebration.

"Would this mysterious friend happen to have red hair and freckles?"

Ruvon looked confused. "No, I'm waiting for Arezoo."

Fenella nearly dropped the bottle she'd just picked up. "Arezoo?"

He nodded, taking a sip of his beer. "We met at the playground, and I invited her, but she wasn't sure she could come."

"Of course she won't," Fenella said, shaking her head. "Her mother would never allow it. Besides, isn't she a little too young for you?"

"She's of legal age, isn't she?"

"Well, yes, she is. But she lived a very sheltered life, and then bad things happened to her. She's not ready to date a guy who is older than her great-grandfather."

He frowned. "I'm one hundred and thirty-seven, which makes me younger than most immortals in the village. I don't see why I shouldn't court Arezoo."

Fenella had forgotten that age was a relative thing in the immortals' village.

The gap between her and Din was more significant than the gap between Ruvon and Arezoo, but that was just chronological age. The experience gap went the other way.

"She's not ready, Ruvon. You'd have more chance of success courting her mother."

He winced, looking dejected. "Her mother is scary. Arezoo is kind and I like her, not her mother."

Fenella couldn't argue with that, and she felt a pang of sympathy for him. He looked so lonely.

She filled up a small container with pretzels and put it in front of him. "You don't have to sit here at the bar looking like someone stood you up. Din is sitting in the back corner at his usual table. You could take this bowl of pretzels to him and join him."

Ruvon glanced toward the back of the bar, where Din had indeed claimed his regular spot, already armed with a beer and reading on his phone. "Maybe he doesn't want to be bothered."

"It's a bar, Ruvon, and the moment it becomes crowded, which it soon will be, people will not let Din hog a whole table for himself, and he'll have no choice but to share. He might as well start with you."

That earned her a small smile. "When you put it that way…"

Ruvon picked up his beer and phone, then paused. "If Arezoo does show up..."

"I'll point her your way," Fenella promised. "Though honestly? Don't hold your breath."

As Ruvon made his way to Din's table, Fenella smiled at her guy and signaled as best she could that he should invite Ruvon to sit with him.

Poor guy. He had no chance with Arezoo or her mother. The daughter needed time to get over her trauma, and a former Doomer wasn't the best candidate to help her with that, even if he was the nicest immortal.

"First reading of the night!" A cheerful voice interrupted her musings.

The same immortal who'd kicked off her impromptu psychic performance the night before slid onto a barstool with a grin. "I brought something different this time." Graham produced a fountain pen from his jacket pocket. "This baby's twenty-six years old. Maybe it'll be more talkative than my watch."

Fenella looked around the bar, debating if it was the right time for her first reading. It was far from full, but what if Sunday nights were slower than Fridays and Saturdays, and this was as crowded as it would get?

"It's still early, but I'll do it for you." She accepted the pen, wrapping her fingers around it. For a moment, she thought she felt something, a whisper of emotion, perhaps a ghost of a memory, but it was so faint she couldn't be sure if it was real or just her imagination filling in the blanks.

Still, she closed her eyes and made a show of concentrating. After a suitable dramatic pause, she gasped.

"Oh my," she said, opening her eyes wide. "This pen has a confession to make."

"Does it now?" Graham leaned forward, his eyes full of eager anticipation.

"It seems," Fenella said in a stage whisper, "that this pen has been living a double life. By day, it signs important documents and writes thoughtful letters. But by night..." She paused for effect. "It composes terrible poetry about cheese."

Graham burst out laughing. "Cheese?"

"Oh yes. Odes to cheddar, sonnets to Swiss, haikus about gouda." She handed the pen back with a solemn expression. "Your pen has hidden depths, my friend. Hidden dairy depths."

"I'll never look at it the same way again," Graham said, still chuckling as he pocketed the pen.

Thankfully, her prediction of a slow night had proven to be false, as more and more customers began arriving, and soon Fenella found herself in the familiar fast pace of the previous nights, mixing drinks, inventing outrageous psychometric readings, and keeping the crowd entertained.

Still, tonight was a bit different, and she wondered if the brooch had something to do with it, or was it her growing comfort with the village community. She definitely felt more grounded than before. More confident.

When she picked up a car key for her next reading, she was surprised to feel a flicker of something, like a faint impression of urgency, of someone racing against time. The sensation was gone as quickly as it had come, leaving her uncertain whether she'd imagined it.

She covered her momentary disorientation by launching into a tale about the car key's secret desire to unlock a door to another dimension where everything was made of chocolate. The owner, a Guardian named Kri, protested loudly that her keys would never betray her for confectionery, no matter how tempting.

Throughout it all, Fenella found herself unconsciously touching the brooch, her fingers drawn to the amber stone, and each time she did, she felt that same subtle pulse of energy.

She must be imagining it—a mystical placebo effect.

"New jewelry?" Ingrid asked, her sharp eyes

missing nothing. "It's lovely. A bit old-fashioned for my taste, though. Antique Scottish?"

"I believe so," Fenella said, her hand going to the brooch again. "It's a gift from Din."

Ingrid grinned. "That's nice. He must have brought it with him from Scotland."

"He did. He bought it for me when we first met half a century ago and kept it for all those years even though he had no reason to believe he would ever meet me again or that I was even alive."

"That's love." Ingrid sighed dramatically. "It's irrational."

Before Fenella could respond, another wave of customers arrived demanding drinks and entertainment in equal measure, and she threw herself back into the performance.

As the night wore on, she noticed something interesting. The faint impressions she was getting from objects seemed to be growing slightly stronger. It was nothing dramatic, just moments when she picked up an item and felt something. An emotion, a fleeting image, a whisper of memory that vanished before she could grasp it.

The brooch seemed to be amplifying her abilities even if only slightly.

Or was she simply becoming more attuned to her gift through practice?

Either way, she made sure to keep her actual impressions to herself, sticking to her invented tales.

The last thing she needed was to accidentally reveal something private that should remain that way.

"Your wallet is judging your spending habits," she told one customer with mock severity. "It's particularly offended by that impulse purchase of a singing fish plaque last month. Where did you even hang it?"

"How did you know? I mean, that's ridiculous!" the man sputtered, his face reddening as his friends roared with laughter.

That had been pure coincidence, but Fenella had learned to run with whatever reactions she got. "The wallet never lies," she intoned solemnly, handing it back.

A singing fish was a stupid decoration, but it wasn't anything to be ashamed of. It was innocent enough.

She was just reaching for another object when the door opened, and a mane of dark hair caught her eye. For a wild moment, she thought it was Arezoo, proving her wrong about her mother's iron grip, but it was just a dark-haired immortal female, one she'd seen the two previous nights.

Poor Ruvon. She glanced toward the back table where he still sat with Din. At least he had company, even if it wasn't the company he'd hoped for.

The thought occurred to her that Ruvon, despite being more than a century old, seemed as young as Arezoo in some ways or even younger. There was an uncertainty about him, a hesitancy that spoke of someone still finding his place in the world. Maybe that's why he was drawn to her—not despite the age difference but because of it. In terms of romantic experiences, they might be more evenly matched than the numbers suggested.

Or maybe she was overthinking it. Maybe Ruvon just liked Arezoo because he was attracted to her. After all, men were simple creatures when it came to romance. They were either drawn to a particular female or not.

23

AREZOO

rezoo sat cross-legged on her bed, staring at the phone in her hands. Ruvon's number glowed on the screen, saved just hours ago at the playground. The first phone number she'd ever received from a man who wasn't family.

She should delete it. That would be the smart thing to do. Delete the number, forget about the bar, forget about the mortifying embarrassment she'd felt when he'd asked her mother's permission to take her out on a date and had gotten dismissed like a bothersome pest.

Her thumb hovered over the delete button.

A sharp knock on her sliding glass door made her jump, the phone tumbling from her hands onto the bedspread. Her heart raced as she stared at the closed shutters. Who would be knocking on her door at this hour?

Maybe it was Azadeh? Her cousin wouldn't be out

this late, and if something happened to anyone in her family, they would come through the front door instead of knocking on her screen.

The knock came again, more insistent this time.

Arezoo remained frozen. Should she call for her mother?

When her phone buzzed with an incoming text, she grabbed it, and the name on the screen was enough to clarify who was banging on her shutters.

It's me outside your door. Let me in.

Arezoo exhaled slowly, tension draining from her shoulders. It was just Drova.

She typed back quickly. *I can't open the shutters. They come down automatically at night.*

She'd tried, but the button wouldn't respond.

The answer came in a moment later. *Turn off the lights first, dummy. It's a safety mechanism to prevent someone from accidentally raising the shutters when the lights are still on.*

That made sense. Why hadn't she thought of that?

But wouldn't the sound of the shutters opening wake her mother?

What if it did, though? It was just Drova. Her mother might disapprove of the timing of the visit, but she would allow it. Probably.

After switching off the lights, Arezoo pressed the button again, and the shutters responded, rising with a mechanical whir and a rattle that seemed impossibly loud in the quiet night. Drova's silhouette appeared against the starlit sky, tall and impossibly thin, her large eyes reflecting the scant light available.

"Finally." Drova stepped in after Arezoo unlocked the door and slid it open. "You can close the shutters now and turn on the lights."

When illumination flooded the room, she found Drova examining her space with those unnerving eyes, taking in the neat desk, the bedspread, the complete absence of personal touches.

"Your room looks like a hotel," Drova said. "Where's all your stuff?"

"This is my stuff," Arezoo said, gesturing at the few items she'd accumulated since arriving at the village— some clothes in the closet, a few books on the desk, her phone charger.

"Sad, but familiar." Drova flopped onto the bed with less grace than usual, her long limbs sprawling. "I was in the same situation when I first got to the village. We came with nothing, even less than this. You need to get a couple of posters to liven up the space, or a lava lamp. It was one of the first things I got for my room."

"Did you come here to critique my decor?"

"No." Drova sat up, her expression turning a little scary. Determined. "I came to break you out of this prison." She sounded dead serious. "The bar. Tonight. You and me." Drova's grin didn't soften her friend's predatory determination. "You're not a child, and it's time your mother acknowledged that."

Arezoo could practically hear her mother

complaining about Drova being a bad influence on her. This would prove her right and endanger the only friendship she had in the village.

"Absolutely not." She backed away from Drova.

"You can't let your mother control you forever." Drova bounced on the bed, looking excited by her own rebellion. "You're nineteen. You're an adult, and that's why we have to go."

"That's not how it works in my family."

"It's how it worked in your family when you lived in Iran. You are free now to live however you want. No one is going to stop you unless you do something illegal."

"Like what?"

Drova winced. "Like compelling people to steal things for you. But we are talking about you now, not me."

Arezoo sank onto her desk chair, wrapping her arms around herself. "Family is not just about respecting or disrespecting traditions. It's about caring for one another and not being selfish. It's about obligations."

"Bullshit," Drova said succinctly. "It's about fear. Your mother is afraid of losing control, and you're afraid of disappointing her."

The words stung because they were true. Arezoo had always been the good daughter, who never caused trouble and was always helpful. But then what choice did she have? Her father was a controlling, borderline abusive jerk, and her mother was bitter but still doing her best to raise three girls. She'd needed Arezoo's help, and she needed it still.

"You don't understand," she said. "My mother needs me."

Drova sighed. "I know, but you can be there for her and still have a life, right? You are working at the café, earning your own money, and meeting people. You just need to set boundaries."

Arezoo snorted. "She'll just tell me that as long as I live under her roof, I have to obey her rules."

Drova leaned forward. "Then maybe you should move out. As an adult, you can apply for housing and get to live with a roommate instead of your family." Her black eyes flickered red for a moment, taking Arezoo aback. "We could move in together. Get our own place. I'm not eighteen yet, but I'm a Guardian in training, and I'm considered an adult in the Kra-ell community. I can convince them to approve it." She grinned. "And don't worry. I won't be using compulsion. My persuasion powers and charm should be enough."

That sounded tempting, but premature. "I can't. Not yet, anyway."

"Why not?" Drova pinned her with a dark glare. "Your mother would disown you? Drag you back by your hair? She might get upset at first, but she'd get over it."

"Are you unhappy living with your mother?" Arezoo asked, deflecting from her own situation.

Drova shrugged. "Jade doesn't try to control my life

or anything. And Phinas, her immortal mate, is cool. But I'm ready for my own space. Aren't you?"

Arezoo tried to imagine a home where she could do what she wanted and could come and go without explanation. The image was thrilling, but she wasn't ready for that much independence yet.

Until Drova came up with the rebellious suggestion, it hadn't ever crossed Arezoo's mind that she could move out and live on her own. She needed time to get accustomed to the idea, to prepare her mother and her aunts, so when the time came, they wouldn't be as shocked.

"I can't right now," she said finally. "My mother and aunts need me, especially now, with the store they're planning. Someone has to watch the children, help with inventory, be there for them."

"You can do all that while living somewhere else," Drova pointed out. "It's not like you'd be moving to another planet. Just to a different house in the village."

"I need time to think about it," Arezoo said.

Drova's expression turned skeptical. "Sure you do. Just like you needed time to think about calling Ruvon, or standing up to your mother, or to think about actually living your life instead of just existing in it."

The words were like a series of punches to her stomach, each one finding its mark. Arezoo wanted to protest, to deny the accusations, but her throat felt tight with unshed tears.

"Come to the bar with me," Drova said, her voice

softer now. "Just for an hour. One drink—hell, one mocktail. Take that first step. Trust me, rebellion gets easier with practice."

"You sound like you're speaking from experience."

"I am." Drova's grin returned, sharp and proud. "First time I defied my mother, I thought lightning would strike me down. When it didn't, I realized the sky wasn't going to fall just because I made my own choices. They were bad ones, but they were mine, and everything worked out okay. Using my compulsion was wrong, but it revealed my powers, and Kian decided that instead of punishing me, he could use me, and I got to join the Guardian Force."

Arezoo's resolve started to waver. The idea of walking into the bar and sitting down like she'd seen young women do in the movies was exciting, liberating. The rebellious aspect was much more tempting than meeting Ruvon.

"My mother would know," she said.

"So what? Let her know. Let her rage, cry, and guilt you. Then what? She can't actually stop you." Drova stood, stretching her long limbs. "The door's right there. All you have to do is walk through it."

"With you."

"With me," Drova confirmed. "I'll be your body-guard against maternal guilt. I'm very good at being intimidating, and I don't mean compulsion. I'm scary enough as I am."

She was, and her arguments were convincing, but so were Arezoo's.

The bar wasn't as important as peace and harmony in her family. She could do without the adventure, but she couldn't do without the love and support of her family.

"I can't," she said again, but this time with more conviction. "I'm not ready. Please stop trying to convince me because nothing you say is going to work. This is not the right time for rebellion."

Drova studied her for a long moment, those large eyes seeing too much. "When will you be ready? When you're fifty? A hundred? Because newsflash—immortality means you could spend centuries being not ready."

The thought was sobering.

"I promise that I won't wait that long. I just need a little more time to think, to plan. I can't, just can't."

"Yes, you can." Drova rose to her feet and walked toward the sliding door. "The only thing stopping you is you." She paused, one hand on the light switch. "Ruvon's at the bar, waiting for you. Did you at least text him that you are not coming?"

Arezoo winced. "Not yet. I was about to when you knocked on the shutters and scared me to death."

That was a lie. She'd meant to delete Ruvon's contact from her phone so she wouldn't be tempted to talk to him.

"Text him. It's not fair to leave the guy hanging."

The expression sounded strange to her, one more of those lost in translation, but she could infer what Drova had meant from the context.

"I will. I promise." After a short pause, she added, "I'm not ready." She hated how small her voice sounded.

"Let me know when you are ready to fly the coop." Drova flicked off the light, raised the shutters, and slipped out into the night with barely a sound. Arezoo quickly lowered them again, sealing herself back in her safe, dark room.

The only light was the soft glow her phone's screen emitted from where she'd left it on her bed.

Arezoo picked up the phone and dictated a message to Ruvon because her written English wasn't good enough to type it. *Sorry, but I can't come. I hope you are enjoying your evening.*

She powered down the device so she wouldn't have to see his response.

As she lay in the dark, Arezoo thought about Drova's words, about rebellion getting easier with practice.

The first step was the hardest, and after that, if the sky didn't fall, the next one was less difficult, and the next one after that even less so.

It was probably true, and one day she would find out, but it wouldn't be tomorrow or even a week from now. She was in no rush to embrace her independence.

24

FENELLA

The disappointment on Ruvon's face was hard to miss as he pulled out his wallet to close his tab for the night.

Fenella rang up his drinks and handed him the printout. He'd had three beers over the course of four hours and had nursed them slowly while he'd waited. "I hope you'll have better luck next time."

He nodded. "I knew she wouldn't come. I shouldn't have invited her. She's too young, too sheltered, and too new to freedom."

"That's a smart observation." Fenella ran his credit card. "I mean, about her being too new to freedom. I guess that's true for the entire family except for Kyra, who was a rebel for many years."

Ruvon pocketed the receipt without glancing at it and inserted a folded bill into the tip jar. "Thank you," he forced a smile. "Goodnight, Fenella."

"Goodnight." She watched him leave, realizing that he hadn't asked for a reading.

Poor guy. She hoped he would find someone who would appreciate him. And to think that only two days ago she'd regarded him with suspicion just because he was a former Doomer and an awkward fellow.

The bar had mostly emptied out, Sunday nights proving to be indeed quieter than the weekend rush. People were getting ready to start their workweek, and retired earlier, but a few stragglers remained, finishing their drinks and conversations. The energy had shifted, though, from lively to languid.

When the door opened, Fenella was surprised to see her roommate walk in, and given her thunderous expression, her date hadn't gone well.

"I need a drink," Shira announced as she collapsed onto a barstool.

Fenella raised an eyebrow. "Rough night?"

"Yeah, you can say so." Shira groaned. "I must have the worst taste in men. It takes real talent to always choose the deadbeat losers."

"Same guy as last time?" Fenella mixed her friend a pear martini and dropped a lychee fruit inside.

Shira laughed. "Fates, no. I never hook up with the same guy twice." She lifted the martini gratefully. "New guy, same bullshit. But this drink looks awesome. Thank you."

"You're welcome. What happened?"

Shira took a long sip before answering. "Everything was fine at first. Decent conversation, good chemistry. Then we get back to his place, and it turns out that he lives with his mother."

Fenella chuckled. "Is that so bad? A good son is a good partner. Everyone knows that."

Shira frowned. "Really? I thought that mama's boys are bad."

"There is a difference between a good son and a mama's boy. I assume that your date was the latter kind?"

Nodding, Shira took another sip from the martini, nearly finishing it. "He introduced me to his mother as if I were his fiancée, talking about a barbecue at his sister's next weekend and how she would be delighted to know that I was a librarian because she loves reading." Shira shuddered. "I mean, we hadn't even gotten our clothes off yet, and he's already planning our future. Talk about a major turn-off."

"The horror," Fenella said dryly, but she was smiling. "A guy actually wanting to see you again."

"You don't get it." Shira drained the rest of the martini, popped the lychee into her mouth, and pushed the empty glass to Fenella for a refill. "This was excellent. Can I have another?"

"The same? Or do you want something new?"

"The same," Shira confirmed.

"Coming up."

"Anyway. As I was saying, I was very clear with him about what I wanted. One night, no strings, no follow-up, and then he goes and introduces me to his mama."

"You're certainly an atypical librarian," Fenella observed, starting on the second martini.

"What's that supposed to mean?"

"I always pictured librarians as hopeless romantics, reading raunchy romance novels under their desks when no one is looking. You are the opposite of romantic. Most people who talk about free love and no boundaries usually mean they want to sleep around without consequences. You actually follow through on the philosophy."

Shira took a sip of the fresh drink. "Exactly! Is it so hard to understand? I'm an immortal. Even if I wanted a relationship, I can't have it, and feelings are my kryptonite." She dug out the fruit and put it in her mouth. "I can't do them," she said after swallowing. "I just want good sex with no emotional entanglements. Why is that so complicated?" She gulped the rest of the martini and pushed the glass back to Fenella. "One more."

Fenella lifted a brow. "Are you sure?"

"Yeah. This glass is really small, and I'm a sucker for lychee."

From across the bar, Atzil cleared his throat loudly. "It's closing time, people. Finish your drinks and go home."

When several grumbled complaints sounded, he shook his head. "I've got breakfast to cook for Kalugal's men tomorrow, and I need my beauty sleep."

The stragglers complained but began gathering their things. Sunday nights, the bar closed at midnight instead of staying open until two in the morning or even later.

Despite Atzil's announcement, Shira didn't budge from her spot and asked for another drink.

Fenella humored her but cautioned that this would be the last one.

When all the customers except Shira had filed out, Din walked up to the bar. "Take her home. I'll stay to help Atzil with cleanup."

Her roommate looked like she could use the company, and Fenella was grateful for Din's thoughtful consideration.

He was one in a million.

Scrap that—one in a billion.

"I don't want to keep taking advantage of you. It's not fair that you're doing this every night."

"Just on the weekends, and my motives are selfish." He waggled his brows. "The sooner you are done, the sooner I can get you in bed. But if you really want to pay me back, you can help me grade papers."

She laughed. "I don't know anything about archaeology."

"Neither do my students, apparently." His expression was perfectly deadpan. "You'd be amazed at some of the things they come up with. Last semester, one student actually wrote that time-traveling tourists most likely built the pyramids."

Shira snorted into her martini, the sound somewhere between a laugh and a hiccup. "That's actually not the worst theory I've heard."

"See?" Din's eyes crinkled with amusement. "You can help me grade, too."

Shira lifted her glass in a salute. "You've got it, Professor. I know a thing or two about archaeology. Probably enough to grade your students' papers."

Fenella wasn't sure whether Shira was drunk, boasting, or was actually knowledgeable on the subject.

Din leaned in to kiss her cheek, his lips warm against her skin. "Take care of your friend. Do you want to come over to my place later?"

She glanced at Shira, who looked to be in a much better mood now than she had been when she'd entered the bar. "I think I'll stay with Shira and call it a night. It's been a long day."

He looked a little disappointed. "Then I'll see you tomorrow morning for breakfast."

"You've got it." She cupped his cheek. "I'll make you a killer omelet with mushrooms, onions, and feta cheese."

"Sounds yummy," Shira slurred. "Can I get an omelet too?"

"Sure." Fenella took off her apron and stuffed it in her bag to take home to launder. "Come on, light-weight," she said to Shira, who was swaying slightly on her barstool. "Let's get you home before you fall over."

"I'm not drunk," Shira protested, but she let Fenella steady her as she stood. "Just pleasantly buzzed."

"Sure you are." Fenella handed Shira her bag, which

she'd forgotten about. "That's why you're listing to starboard."

"Maritime references? Din's rubbing off on you?"

"He's an archeologist, not a sailor."

"Whatever." Shira let Fenella guide her toward the door.

The night air was cool and crisp, carrying a salt tang of the ocean despite the distance. Shira breathed deeply, and Fenella could practically see her metabolism kicking into high gear, processing the alcohol with familiar immortal efficiency.

"I hate how quickly we sober up," Shira muttered. "What's the point of drinking if you can't stay properly drunk?"

"To enjoy the taste?" Fenella suggested.

"True. Your pear martinis were delicious. Now that I know how good you are, I'll come every night of the weekend."

Fenella arched a brow. "You doubted my ability?"

"Not at all. I was sure you were good, but you are excellent, and you are also a mind reader. How did you know that I love lychee? You never even asked me what drink I wanted."

Fenella frowned. "I just know what people like. It's probably an instinct all experienced bartenders develop."

"Oh, please." Shira waved a dismissive hand. "They don't. Just accept the compliment."

Fenella chuckled. "Fine. It must be one of my many innate talents."

They walked in silence for a few minutes, their footsteps echoing on the quiet paths. The village at night had a different quality than during the day, a little spooky because the only light came from the moon and stars.

"Do you think something is wrong with me?" Shira asked out of the blue.

Fenella glanced at her friend, surprised by the question. "Not at all. Why?"

"Everyone else seems to want to be in a relationship. They want to experience the connection, the feelings, to find their forever person." She kicked at a pebble on the path. "But I just don't want that. The thought of being tied to one person forever makes me want to run screaming. I like doing my own thing, which is reading most of the time, or sketching, or just watching shows or movies, and I don't want to have to think about what someone else wants and compromise. Does that make me a narcissist?"

Fenella shrugged. "I don't know what the definition of a narcissist is."

"I do, and I'm not that, but I wanted to know what you think."

"Sorry to disappoint you. So, what's a narcissist?"

"Someone with a grandiose sense of self-importance, lack of empathy for others, a need for excessive admiration, and the belief that one is unique and deserving of special treatment."

"I've met many people like that, but you are not one of them. You are just different. One of a kind."

Shira might be a little egotistical and socially unaware, but she wasn't the other things in that description.

"Different." Shira snorted. "One of a kind. That's a nice way to put it."

"Hey." Fenella stopped walking, forcing Shira to stop too. "Look at me."

Shira met her eyes reluctantly.

"There's nothing wrong with knowing what you want, or what you don't want. The only problem is when other people don't respect that."

"Like Mr. Mama's boy tonight."

"Yeah, like him."

They resumed walking, and by the time they reached the house, Shira seemed to have sobered up. The fast immortal metabolism was both a blessing and a curse—great for recovering from injuries or illnesses, less great when you actually wanted to maintain a buzz.

"Thanks for walking home with me," Shira said as she opened the door. "Though I wasn't really that drunk."

"I know. But Atzil wanted to close early, and it gave me an excuse to leave too, and thanks to Din, I could."

Shira studied her for a moment. "He's a good guy."

"Yeah, he is."

"Don't screw it up."

Fenella rolled her eyes. "Thanks for the vote of confidence."

Shira dropped her purse on the console next to

the front door and kicked off her heels. "I watch you with him, and sometimes I see this look on your face, like you're waiting for the other shoe to drop. Like you're just counting down until something goes wrong."

Was she?

"I'm not."

"Yes, you are, and I get it. Trust me, I understand self-sabotage better than most." She sighed. "Forget what I said. I get philosophical when drunk." She yawned. "Fates, I'm exhausted. I'm going to bed."

"Sleep well."

"Yeah, you too, but shower first. You smell like a distillery."

"Noted."

Fenella waited until she heard Shira's bedroom door close before heading to her own room.

She stripped off her work clothes, which did indeed reek of alcohol, but not before removing the brooch and setting it carefully on the bathroom vanity.

The shower was blissfully hot, washing away the residue of the evening along with the tension in her muscles.

Shira's words kept echoing in her head. Was she really waiting for things to go wrong?

Maybe.

Probably.

It was hard to shake fifty years of survival instincts, during which she'd learned that something always went wrong. Life was chaotic, and happily-ever-afters belonged in fairy tales.

After toweling off and slipping into a pair of sleep shorts and a tank top, she sat cross-legged on her bed, the brooch cradled in her palms. The metal was cool against her skin, the amber stone reflecting the light from her bedside lamp.

She'd felt things from it earlier—fleeting impressions, whispers of memories. But there had been nothing concrete to latch on to.

What if she tried with more deliberation?

The two real readings she'd managed had been with Kyra and Jasmine's help, their combined abilities amplifying her own. Alone, she probably couldn't access the deeper layers of memories trapped in objects. But maybe she could sense something about Din from this piece that he had held close to his heart for so long.

Closing her eyes, Fenella let herself relax, let her mental walls down. She didn't force it, didn't grasp for visions. She just held the brooch and breathed, letting whatever wanted to come through find its way to her.

At first, there was nothing. Just the weight of the metal in her hands and her own heartbeat.

Then, like smoke curling at the edges of her consciousness, images began to form. Hazy, dreamlike, more impression than clear vision.

A shop window in Edinburgh, rain streaking the glass. Din's face reflected in the glass, looking less weighted by years, as something caught his eye. The brooch, displayed on faded velvet, seemed to glow in the gray Scottish morning. It hadn't been tarnished as it was now. Someone had polished it so it shone.

A certainty flooded through him. Not a thought but a knowing: *this belongs to her.*

The memory shifted, blurred, re-formed.

Years later. An apartment somewhere—London? The wallpaper suggested the 80s. Din packing boxes, preparing for another move. Finding the brooch wrapped in tissue at the bottom of a drawer. The way his hands stilled. The ache in his chest as he remembered dark hair and clever eyes and a laugh that made him feel alive.

Another shift.

The new millennium. Din at a desk surrounded by papers, grading by lamplight. The brooch sitting on the desk like a paperweight, a talisman, a reminder. His fingers brushing over it absently as he worked.

More moments, flowing faster now. The brooch traveling through decades in pockets, drawers, and safes. Always kept, never forgotten.

The visions faded, leaving Fenella gasping as if she'd been holding her breath. Her cheeks were wet.

When had she started crying?

But there was more. Deeper memories. Older.

The silver itself held memories, ancient and fragmentary. Images so faint she could barely grasp them —hands shaping metal with tools she didn't recognize. A woman's face, beautiful and strange, framed by starlight. Love and loss and time beyond measure.

Those visions slipped away like water through her fingers, too old and alien to hold. But Din's memories remained, warm and present and achingly real.

Fenella opened her eyes, still clutching the brooch. Her chest felt too full, like her ribs might crack from the pressure of emotion inside her.

Fifty years. He'd loved her without hope, without reason, without even knowing if she lived.

She thought of all the women who must have passed through his life in those years. Beautiful, available, uncomplicated women, but he couldn't allow himself to love any of them because they were human, their lives fleeting in the span of his endless immortality. So, he'd kept the brooch and kept loving a ghost who by all reason should have been dead.

The stirring in her chest was familiar now, no longer frightening but still overwhelming.

Love.

She loved Din.

But saying it, acknowledging it, and making it real was terrifying.

What was stopping her?

Fear, obviously. Fear that things would sour like they had before. Fear that love was just another trap, another cage, another thing that would eventually be used against her.

Maybe she needed to test him. Poke at him, push his buttons, see how much he was willing to take. See if his patience had limits, if his love came with conditions.

The thought made her uncomfortable. It felt manipulative, childish. But the scared part of her, the part that had kept her alive for fifty years, whispered that tests were necessary.

Better to know now than later.

Better to find the breaking point before she got in too deep.

Except she was already in too deep, wasn't she?

The way her heart lifted when she saw him, the way her body fit against his like coming home, the way even thinking about pushing him away made her chest ache—all of it pointed to a truth she'd been dancing around since he'd told her that he loved her.

Din loved her, and she loved him back, and it should be simple, but simple had never been her style.

25

KIAN

As a knock sounded on Kian's partially open office door, Jackson poked his head in. He smiled and rose to his feet.

"Come in." He offered the young immortal his hand. "Thank you for making time in your busy schedule."

"I'm honored to be invited." Jackson shook his hand with a grin spreading over his handsome face. "It was such a nice surprise to see your text last night."

"As soon as Kyra told me her sisters' idea, I knew you were the guy to call. I know that shopkeeping isn't your area of expertise, but you must know a lot about commercial refrigerators and where to shop for supplies."

Despite his young age, Jackson was a successful entrepreneur who ran several commercial bakeries and supplied coffee shops and restaurants throughout Los Angeles. And to think that he had started out as

Nathalie's assistant in her father's coffee shop only a few years ago.

His rapid success was awe-inspiring.

"I do." Jackson pulled out a chair next to the conference table. "And I'll gladly show them the ropes."

Kian was surprised. "Do you have time for that? You are always running around."

"I was." Jackson leaned back in the chair. "I'm finally making enough money to employ good help, so I can focus on expanding my empire or take my mate out on all the dates I couldn't take her out on when I was running like crazy, trying to do everything myself."

"Glad to hear that. How is Tessa doing? Is she still working for Eva?"

"Part-time," Jackson said. "She dedicates two days a week to the halfway house. It's important for the girls to see someone who was in their situation and who has mostly healed. She also helps Ella with the fundraising, although Jacki has taken over that part since she got the government to contribute to the cause. The female is a genius."

Kian chuckled. "She is. Or perhaps she just knows humans better than we do. I never expected it to be so easy, nor was I aware of how much of taxpayers' money was being squandered on fake causes. At least ours is real, and all the funds go to the rehabilitation effort. No one's getting rich from it."

Nodding, Jackson crossed his arms over his chest. "If I knew that the real money was in politics and not in commerce or industry, I might have chosen a different career."

With his looks and his charm, Jackson could have done great in politics, but as an immortal he couldn't afford to be in the public eye, so that had never been an option for him.

"I'm glad you've chosen to get into the baking business. Kyra and her sisters are going to be here any moment, and I want to brief you first about their idea."

Jackson leaned forward. "You mentioned that they want to open a grocery store. The refrigeration and freezer units won't be a problem—I have good contacts in the commercial wholesale equipment. The real challenge is the supply chain because we can't get deliveries to the village. Only our people can do that."

"Right. So, what do you suggest?"

"Get them a large van, maybe two, equipped with the same security features as all our other vehicles. They could make supply runs themselves and load up at various wholesale locations around LA." Jackson pulled out his phone, scrolling through his notes. "I can introduce them to my suppliers."

"That could work."

"I can also help them set up accounts or even funnel their purchases through my accounts. That might make things easier for them at the beginning. If they need help with the business side of things, I can give them a few pointers, but I don't have time to hold their hands throughout it. They would have to take a course or figure out things for themselves."

"Of course," Kian said. "I'm thankful for all the help you are offering. It's more than I expected."

As another knock sounded at the door, Kian rose to his feet again and walked over to welcome Kyra and her four sisters.

"Good morning," he greeted them and offered his hand to Kyra first.

"Good morning." She smiled as she shook his hand. "Thank you for agreeing to see us on such short notice."

"I liked your idea, and I brought in an expert." He motioned at Jackson. "Please, sit down, and I'll introduce everyone." He gestured to the chairs around his conference table.

When they were all seated, he took his place at the head of the table. "Let me introduce Jackson. He runs a successful food service empire, and he is the one supplying our café. He's kindly agreed to help with your venture."

"Thank you," Soraya said, studying Jackson with the shrewd assessment of someone who'd learned to judge character quickly. "We appreciate your assistance."

"Happy to help," Jackson replied. "I understand you want to open a grocery store. It's a great idea. The village needs one."

The sisters exchanged glances, and Kian saw some of their tension ease. They'd prepared for resistance, he realized. Instead, they were met with enthusiasm.

"We have a proposal," Soraya said, producing a thin folder. "We've run some numbers."

For the next twenty minutes, the sisters presented their plan with impressive thoroughness. They'd thought through product selection, pricing strategies, operating hours, and division of responsibilities. Rana would handle the business side, while Soraya, Parisa, and Yasmin would run the store, each specializing in their chosen departments.

"We identified three possible locations," Rana said. "All are currently vacant. We marked them on the village map in the folder."

He flipped to the appropriate page. "I appreciate the thought you've put into this, but having a commercial operation in a residential area could be problematic. The neighbors might object to the increased foot traffic."

When the sisters' faces fell, Kian continued, "That doesn't mean we can't make this work. We just need to find the right spot."

"What about the village square?" Parisa suggested tentatively. "Maybe next to the café?"

"We don't have any vacant space there," Kian said. "And I'm reluctant to sacrifice any of the green areas. The greenery and open spaces are important for the village's atmosphere, and we use them for celebrations. It would be a mistake to sacrifice any portion of it for a new building."

"What about the area behind this building?" Kyra

said. "Max said that the slope that goes down can be partially reclaimed."

Kian pictured the area she meant. It was a steep hillside. "To build anything there would require significant grading and reinforcement."

"But it's possible?" Soraya pressed.

"Theoretically, yes." Kian found himself warming to the idea. "We could grade a shallow terrace that could accommodate a long and narrow building."

"It would block the first-floor windows of the offices facing the ravine," Jackson pointed out.

"Not if we build several feet below the current ground level," Kian said. "We can create a walkway down to it."

The sisters looked excited, hope brightening their faces.

"Let's go take a look." Kian rose from his chair.

The group filed out of his office and down the stairs. Kian led them through the building's rear exit to the area in question. The morning sun highlighted the slope's gradient—steep but not impossible.

"Here," Kian said, gesturing to a relatively flat area a few feet below where they were standing. "Perhaps the roof of the new structure could create a terrace for the office building."

He could picture his smoking setup there instead of the roof, but on second thought, it would be less private, so it had better remain where it was.

Jackson nodded. "I love it. We can put a few

vending machines against the office building's wall, and some tables and chairs. A new recreation area with a spectacular view."

"I'll ask Gavin, our architect, to sketch out a few ideas," Kian told the sisters.

"How long would construction take?" Yasmin asked quietly.

Kian calculated mentally. "Between the design and construction? Two to three months, but the problem is the availability of the crews I use for projects in the village, which might delay the project for a few months, if not more. I'll need to check with the contractor."

The sisters exchanged glances, and Kian read the disappointment in their expressions.

"We hoped to open the store sooner," Rana said.

"Let's go back to my office and talk it through," Kian suggested.

Once they were reseated around the conference table, Kian addressed the issue that seemed to trouble them. "Why are you in a rush to open the store?"

Soraya straightened her shoulders. "We need to start earning money. We've been living off the clan's charity since we arrived, and we appreciate the generosity, but we don't feel comfortable living on charity."

"We need to contribute," Parisa said. "We want to feel useful."

Kian understood. Pride was universal, crossing

cultural and temporal boundaries. The store wasn't just about earning a living—it was about reclaiming dignity.

"We don't need to wait for the new building," he decided. "You can start small in one of the houses as a temporary location, and when the permanent structure is complete, you'll move there and enlarge your operation. You'll need the time to learn anyway, right?" He swept his gaze over them. "As far as I know, none of you have run a store before."

Relief was written over all their faces.

"You are very wise, Mr. Kian," Soraya said. "Your suggestion is perfect."

He chuckled. "Just Kian, and thank you for the flattery, but it's not needed. I'll ask Ingrid to identify the best available house. Ideally, it would be close to the village square, but we might need to relocate some residents."

"We shouldn't," Parisa interrupted, then blushed. "I mean, we don't want to uproot anyone. That wouldn't be right."

"The community is flexible," Kian assured her. "Some of our single members might actually prefer to move to a newer section. Ingrid has a gift for making these arrangements work for everyone involved."

"The house closest to the square would be ideal for foot traffic," Jackson noted. "Even as a temporary location. It would be the least disruptive to the neighbors."

"I believe that one's currently occupied by two

young engineers," Kian said. "They like being close to the pavilion, but I don't think it will be difficult to convince them to relocate, especially if I get them their own golf cart."

Parisa regarded him with a big smile on her face. "Can we get our own golf cart as well? I mean for the store. I'm thinking of the logistics of carrying supplies from the parking structure to the store."

"That would be prudent," Kian agreed.

"Speaking of logistics," Jackson said, "I can take you ladies on a shopping excursion to show you the wholesale markets, introduce you to suppliers, and help you understand the LA food distribution network."

"Can we leave the village?" Rana asked Kian.

He chuckled. "You are not prisoners here, and to run a grocery store, you will need to make regular supply runs. I think it's a great idea to have Jackson show you around so you can familiarize yourselves with the territory."

"When can we go?" Soraya asked.

"I can take you tomorrow," Jackson said. "I was planning on visiting some of my suppliers anyway."

"We accept your generous offer," Soraya said. "Thank you."

"Excellent." Jackson turned to Kian. "Do you want me to coordinate security or do you want to handle that?"

"I'll speak to Onegus. If he can spare Max, I think

that should be enough. It's not like we expect an ambush in one of the markets."

"Right." Jackson stood up. "Traveling with five ladies, I'd rather be cautious." He turned to the sisters. "Be ready at nine tomorrow morning and wear comfortable shoes. We'll be doing a lot of walking."

26

FENELLA

"Have fun." Din pulled Fenella into his arms. "And be careful out there."

She rolled her eyes. "What possible dangers can await me in wholesale vegetable markets?"

"Oh, I don't know. You seem to be a magnet for trouble."

There was something to what he was saying, but since she was traveling with Kyra, her sisters, and Max, Fenella doubted that anything worse than sore feet awaited her.

"I'll be fine." She stretched on her toes and kissed his dimple. "Max is coming with us. I'm sure he will be armed to the teeth."

"I hope so." For a change, there was no note of jealousy in his tone at the mention of Max.

"You know, you can still change your mind and

come along." She pulled out of his arms. "It would be fun to explore the city together."

He sighed. "I wish I could, but I have a virtual stack of final papers to grade, and each is about a hundred pages. It will take me weeks to go through them all."

"Poor baby." She cupped his cheek. "Well, good luck with that. I'm planning on having lots of fun with Kyra and her sisters."

"Are any of the girls joining you?"

"I don't know. I didn't ask Kyra when she called to invite me. I was too surprised by the gesture, but I assume that the girls are staying behind to watch their younger cousins."

Kyra had said that it was an opportunity for Fenella to get out of the village, and she knew how stifled Fenella felt about being cooped up in the small community.

The truth was that the urge to escape and disappear into anonymous crowds had subsided since she'd started her job at the Hobbit, but some of it was back after a whole day of inaction on Monday.

Well, there was the action in bed with Din, but that had only filled up a couple of hours. She'd visited the gym, had taken a swim in the pool, and even checked out Ingrid's design center to see which houses were available, but none of that had been enough to stifle the simmering disquiet under her skin.

"Do you want me to walk with you to the parking structure?" Din offered.

"I know the way. Start on those papers, Professor."

When she got out of the elevator on the parking structure level that Kyra had indicated, Fenella immediately spotted the group of ladies clustered together right outside the entrance. Next to them, Max stood with another guy she didn't recognize, who was leaning against a pillar.

"Am I late?" Fenella said as she joined the group.

"You are right on time." Kyra patted her shoulder. "We are early because we are all excited. Jackson is picking us up with his van."

"Awesome." Fenella nodded at the sisters, still learning to match names to faces. Soraya was the eldest, and the one she remembered most easily. She nicknamed her the dragon mom. Yasmin was easy to identify by the grief that was etched in the lines around her eyes. But she wasn't sure who Rana was and who Parisa was.

"Morning, Fenella," Max said. "Let me introduce you to Theo. He's going to accompany us today."

The guy dipped his head in greeting. "Nice to meet you, Fenella. I've heard so much about your readings at the Hobbit Bar."

She smiled. "You should come this weekend and bring an object. I'll do a reading for you."

Max cleared his throat. "We might leave for Egypt beforehand. I don't think that arrangement will take an entire week."

"Right." Her smile wilted.

Normally, she would have been super excited about a trip to a place she hadn't visited yet, but working at the Hobbit was satisfying in a way she hadn't experienced in any other job before. She'd always loved bartending and everything that came with it, but her nightly performances and the attention and laughter they garnered kind of rounded the experience, turning the bartending from a job to a calling.

It was so silly to think of it that way. It wasn't like she was saving lives or making life-changing discoveries. But this was what made her happy, her little corner of the universe that she was the star of, where she shone.

"The Hobbit is not going anywhere," Theo said. "It will still be there when you return from Egypt."

"That's right." She gave him a smile. "And you should come then. By the way, why do we need two Guardians for a shopping trip? Are the wholesale markets really that dangerous?"

Max's lips quirked in a half-smile. "They're not, but Kian thought that the sisters would feel safer with an escort. They are a little skittish after what they've been through."

"Kian is just being overprotective," Rana said. "We are tougher than we look."

"We appreciate the gesture nonetheless," Soraya said with a glare at her sister.

As a large van pulled up in front of them, the driver's door opened to reveal a man who made Fenella's eyebrows shoot up to her hairline.

Even by immortal standards, he was devastatingly

handsome—chiseled features, perfectly styled blond hair, and a smile that could cause traffic accidents.

Surprisingly, though, she felt no stirring of attraction even though his looks were precisely what she'd used to go gaga over. Now, she appreciated his beauty in a detached way, like admiring a particularly well-executed piece of art. Pretty to look at, certainly, but it stirred nothing in her belly. That particular sensation seemed reserved exclusively for her professor.

"That's Jackson," Max said. "He's a prodigy, a self-made millionaire at twenty-three."

So young?

Wow, the guy was really something, but there was still nothing.

Jackson smiled. "Thank you for the glorious introduction." He opened the side sliding door. "Ladies, please take your seats."

"Fenella," she introduced herself, shaking Jackson's offered hand. "I'm tagging along to help carry bags and provide moral support."

"The more the merrier," Jackson said. "Help yourselves to the water bottles in the cooler."

They climbed into the van, the sisters taking the middle rows while Max and Theo claimed the back. Fenella slid in beside Kyra, who grabbed her hand and squeezed.

"Thank you for coming," Kyra said.

"Thank you for inviting me. I get antsy when I have nothing to do."

As Jackson pulled out of the parking structure,

Rana leaned forward. "Do you know any Persian markets?"

Jackson glanced at her through the rearview mirror. "I have to admit that I'm not familiar with any. My suppliers are wholesale operations. But let me find out." He pulled out his phone and activated the voice assistant. "Please provide a list of Persian markets in the Los Angeles area, including locations and distance."

The surprisingly pleasant female voice began listing options, and Jackson's eyebrows rose with each addition to the list. "Wow. There are quite a few." He glanced back at them. "I had no idea there were so many Persian supermarkets throughout the city."

"Arezoo says that Los Angeles has one of the largest Persian populations outside of Iran," Soraya said. "Apparently, many settled here after the revolution."

Fenella hadn't known that, but then the Persian diaspora hadn't been a subject of interest to her, even though her travels had somehow led her to Iran. She should have known better, but it was water under the bridge now.

"We want to see what's offered in those markets," Parisa said. "So we can emulate it in our store."

"We need spices that we can't find in the regular supermarket," Yasmin said. "Even for our own cooking at home."

"And the bread," Rana added with a dramatic sigh. "The bread here is nothing like home."

"Don't get her started on bread." Parisa chuckled.

"She'll lecture you for an hour about the proper way to make *sangak*."

"It's an art form!" Rana protested, which set off an argument among the sisters about various Persian breads that was accompanied by a lot of hand gesturing and bouts of laughter as they teased one another mercilessly.

It was enviable, and Fenella wished she had sisters to banter with like Kyra had. She could barely remember her brother, and even when she'd still lived at home, they hadn't been close.

"Wholesome Choice is one of the larger ones according to the reviews," Jackson said. "And it's not too far."

Agreement rippled through the van, and soon they were on the freeway, but Fenella couldn't tell in which direction they were heading. Not that it mattered. She watched the city roll by, marveling at how different it was from the isolated beauty and safety of the village.

There weren't many people on the sidewalks, actually almost none, but the vehicle traffic was heavy, and everything seemed to be moving at a fast pace.

"This is real life," Kyra commented quietly beside her. "The village seems like a utopian dream." She turned to Fenella. "Do you miss it?"

She chuckled. "We've only been gone for less than an hour, so no, I don't miss it yet."

Kyra punched her shoulder playfully. "I mean life on the outside, among humans."

Fenella considered the question. "Yeah, but seeing

it now up close, I'm less nostalgic. Not that it's bad. The streets are clean and there are no beggars on every corner, but still. It's not the village."

Jackson snorted. "We are in the better parts of the city. Some areas are drowning in trash, and drug addicts loiter on the streets. Naturally, I wouldn't take you there, but you should know that they exist even here, in one of the richest cities in the world. It's shameful, really, but it is what it is."

When Jackson finally pulled into a sprawling parking lot, Fenella glanced at the façade of the market, which featured both English and Persian script. Colorful displays of fresh produce were visible through the large windows. It looked clean and well-organized.

"Here we are," Jackson announced. "Wholesome Choice Market."

Max and Theo exited first, doing a subtle but thorough scan of the parking lot before nodding to the ladies and offering them a hand to help them out of the van.

As they approached the entrance, the automatic doors slid open to reveal a produce section that made Rana gasp with delight. Mountains of fresh herbs filled the air with fragrance—mint, basil, cilantro, and others Fenella couldn't identify. Pomegranates were piled high in pyramids, along with citruses of all kinds.

"Oh, look!" Parisa rushed to a display of fresh figs. "When was the last time we had proper figs?"

"And dates," Soraya added, examining the variety with a critical eye. "These are Mazafati dates from Bam. The best kind."

The sisters dispersed through the produce section like children in a candy store, calling out discoveries to each other, while Max and Theo looked distressed because they couldn't keep up with all of them.

Fenella was happy with following Kyra as she trailed after her sisters with an indulgent smile.

"*Torshi*!" Yasmin exclaimed from an aisle filled with glass jars. "They have proper *torshi*!"

"What's *torshi*?" Fenella asked.

"Pickled vegetables," Kyra said. "Every family has their own recipes. According to Soraya, our mother used to make the best *torshi-e bademjan*—pickled eggplant. She learned from her mother, who learned from hers and so on."

Jackson lingered behind, making notes on his phone as the sisters rattled off products they wanted to stock.

"This is unbelievable," he said to Soraya as she explained the different types of rice and their uses. "I had no idea there was such variety. My knowledge of Middle Eastern cuisine is limited."

"Persian cuisine," Rana corrected with a touch of heat. "It's distinct from Arab food, though people often confuse them."

"My apologies," Jackson said sincerely. "Please, educate me. I want to understand."

That seemed to be the right response. Rana

launched into an explanation of Persian culinary traditions as they led him toward the spice section. In contrast, the others followed, which seemed to make Max and Theo happy because the sisters were all clustered together.

"Saffron," Parisa breathed, handling a small container with reverence. "Real saffron, not the fake stuff they try to pass off in regular stores. It's so expensive, though."

"What's the difference?" Theo asked.

"Oh, you poor, poor man," Soraya said with something approaching pity. "Let me show you."

What followed was an impromptu lesson in spices that was too much information for Fenella, and definitely for the Guardians, who had probably never cooked anything more elaborate than steak.

Max caught her eye and smiled. "They are so happy," he said quietly. "This is the first time I've seen them so animated."

"Food is home in a way that's deeper than geography."

"You're philosophical for a Tuesday morning," Max teased. "Is the professor rubbing off on you?"

"He is," she admitted with a grin. "All those deep conversations over coffee."

After the spice aisle, in which the sisters had lingered way too long, they moved on to a section dedicated to fresh bread, and the sisters nearly wept over the *sangak*. Then it was dried fruits and nuts, tea supplies, and elaborate containers of rose water and orange blossom water.

"We need to stock all of this," Yasmin said. "Not just for us, but for the others in the village who might want to try new things."

"You can post recipes on the clan's bulletin board," Jackson suggested.

Soraya beamed like Fenella had never seen before. "I'm inviting you and your wife to dinner. You have to taste my *tahdig*."

"What's that?" Fenella asked.

"The crispy rice from the bottom of the pot," Parisa explained. "It's impossible to explain. You have to taste it to understand."

Jackson nodded. "I'm sure Tessa will be delighted to try your special dishes. I don't think she's familiar with them."

KYRA

K yra drifted behind her sisters as they pushed overflowing carts down the aisles of the supermarket. Soraya and Yasmin led the charge, consulting lists and debating quantities, while Parisa and Rana collected more items, their voices a comforting hum in Kyra's ears.

Their carts were filled to the brim with everything from canned goods to fresh produce. The shelves were a blur of color and brand names that Kyra barely recognized. She had never been one for shopping trips. Most of her remembered life, she'd acquired supplies by raiding the regime's installations.

The domestic scene felt alien yet familiar in some way, a reminder of bonds she'd been robbed of by time and cruelty.

She and Fenella hovered near the edge of the group, slightly apart but content to be included. The air was thick with the scent of disinfectant and artificial citrus, overlaid by the sharper tang of coffee from the in-store café.

It was a mundane backdrop for the tension coiling beneath her skin.

Instinctively, she reached for her pendant, closing her hand around the stone and taking comfort in its cool reassurance.

Was it cool, though?

It felt a little warm, but that could be just warmth from her body. She'd been walking for what seemed like hours, trudging through every aisle multiple times as her sisters searched for items.

"Do you think it's enough sugar?" Yasmin asked, balancing a jumbo bag on her hip.

"Two bags are enough," Parisa said as she eyed the bag. "Unless you want to focus on selling sweets."

"Not just sweets," Yasmin said as she dropped the bag into her shopping cart. "But you can never have enough sugar or flour."

"That's true," Parisa agreed.

Ahead of them, Soraya leaned over her cart to rearrange the contents to make room for a crate of canned olives.

"Apparently, one can never have enough olives either," Fenella whispered in Kyra's ear.

Kyra chuckled. "They are like kids in a candy store. Not that I know what kids in a candy store look like, but I imagine this is it."

Fenella shrugged. "You and me both, sister. I don't think I've ever been to a candy store."

The carts creaked as they kept going, forming a mini caravan as they finally headed toward the checkout lanes.

"Thank God," Fenella murmured. "Or the merciful Fates. I thought they would never be done."

"Isn't there anything you want to get?" Max asked from behind her. "Some Persian sweets, perhaps?" He dangled a box of candied fruit in front of her.

"You remembered." She snatched the box from his hands. "I love these."

Max looked smug, and Kyra felt a pang of jealousy over the history those two shared. She'd thought she was over that, and mostly, she was, but here and there the reminders irked. Did Max even know what her favorite sweets were?

"I got one for you as well." He produced another box from behind his back. "I know that you don't like things that are too sweet, but I thought you should try these. They are sweet and tangy at the same time."

Warmth spread through Kyra at his words, and she took the box from his hands. "Thank you. I would love to try them."

Soraya looked over her shoulder at the boxes of sweets with a disapproving expression on her face. "Those will rot your teeth, but since you don't need to worry about that, enjoy."

"Thank you," Kyra said with a smile. "I intend to."

She had no memories of their childhood together, and sometimes the weight of the years lost with her sisters felt as heavy as the years lost with her daughter.

However, in the short time since they'd been reunited, she'd seen flashes of what might have been. Soraya's competence, Yasmin's empathy, and Parisa's attention to detail. And Rana's sarcasm. She wondered which traits they had inherited from their mother, and which from their father. She didn't remember either, but her father had been the one who enabled all her suffering, so she hoped that she and her sisters were more like their mother than him.

They were stubborn and fierce, and watching them pile groceries onto the conveyor belt, Kyra realized that bonds of blood ran too deep to be erased.

As they reached the cashier, Jackson stepped forward, his wallet already in hand. "I'll cover it."

Soraya's head snapped up. "Absolutely not."

Jackson gave a half-smile, tilting his head. "You can pay me back once your store turns a profit."

Soraya's expression softened. "I appreciate the offer, Jackson. But we have credit cards that Kian gave us. We can pay for the groceries, and once we turn a profit, we will pay him back for this and everything else we've bought since he has given us refuge."

"What's the difference?" Jackson tried to argue.

Kyra put a hand on his arm. "My sisters are stubborn, and they don't back down. It's futile to try to negotiate with them."

Sighing, Jackson stepped back and slipped his wallet into his pocket. "It's a shame, really. I get points for buying stuff, and I use that for travel."

Kyra had a feeling that he was just saying it to give

Soraya an incentive to let him pay, but her sister just nodded and smiled, not taking the bait.

Suddenly, her sister's smile wilted, replaced by a panicked expression, and then she ducked her head, signaling to her sisters to do the same.

"What's wrong?" Kyra's hand landed on the pendant again, and this time it definitely felt warmer than what it could've absorbed from her body.

"A Revolutionary Guard." Soraya's voice was barely audible. "Over by the other cashier. He knows me, and he knows Rana. If he sees us, he'll tell Fareed, or worse, send the Doomers after us."

The words sliced through the air like a blade. Kyra scanned the closest checkout lane, trying to spot the threat. Her sisters were keeping their heads down and looking even more conspicuous as they attempted to make themselves invisible.

Without their headscarves and dressed in Western clothes, they should be harder to recognize, but if the guy was someone who had been a guest at Soraya's house, he might see past the superficial changes.

Sensing that something was afoot, Max and Theo got closer.

"What's going on?" Max whispered in her ear.

"Soraya and Rana need to leave. You and Theo pretend to be their husbands and walk them out of here."

Max gave her a curt nod and stepped to Soraya's side, slipping his arm around her shoulders. "Come on, love. Let's go get the car. Jackson can take care of the rest."

Theo offered Rana his arm with a murmured, "Shall we?"

Only Yasmin and Parisa remained, their wide eyes fixed on Kyra as they tried to stay shielded behind Jackson's tall frame.

She saw him then, a stocky man at the other line with bushy eyebrows who was looking their way, passing over Yasmin and Parisa and landing on Soraya.

His eyes widened, recognition flashing like a spark. "Soraya!" he called out.

Kyra felt her stomach drop. "Max, get him!" she hissed.

Max didn't hesitate, but he misunderstood, and instead of reaching into the guy's head and thralling him to forget what he had seen, he lunged across the other conveyor belt and seized the man by the collar, dragging him bodily to the floor.

A loud crash echoed through the market as the man's grocery basket clattered over, scattering cans and packages.

People gasped. One woman screamed in alarm. Others backed away.

Theo pulled a thin wallet from his back pocket and flashed a card with a flick of his wrist. "ICE," he said in a calm, authoritative tone. "Federal agents. Everyone, step back."

The whispered panic surged into a full retreat.

Customers scurried away, abandoning their carts as they fled for the exits. Even the cashier froze, her mouth working soundlessly.

Kyra's brow furrowed. "What's ICE?"

"I'll explain later," Theo muttered.

Max hauled the dazed man to his feet and delivered a swift, economical punch to render him limp. "We're leaving. Now."

They abandoned the groceries, pushing the carts aside as they hustled toward the exit.

Soraya clutched Kyra's arm, her voice thin and shaking. "If there's one of them, there'll be more. They'll come for us."

"Calm down," Max said. "We'll question this guy and find out if there are others. Jackson—get us out of here."

They burst out into the parking lot, reaching the van in seconds. Jackson had the doors open with a remote, and they piled in, Max still holding the unconscious man as if he weighed nothing.

Kyra slid into a seat next to her sisters, and Max commandeered the back with the unconscious Revolutionary Guard. As the engine roared to life and they peeled out of the lot, Jackson grumbled under his breath, "I'll have to swap the plates on the van."

"We'll worry about it later," Max said. "Take us to the warehouse. We need to check this guy for trackers before we bring him to the dungeon."

Jackson looked at him through the rearview mirror. "I don't know where this warehouse is."

Theo pulled out his phone. "I'm sending you a pin."

Kyra took Soraya's trembling hand. "Don't worry. The Guardians are going to sort it out. You are safe."

Soraya nodded, but she was still breathing shallowly, fighting panic.

As the van sped toward the warehouse, Kyra had a feeling that their world had just shifted once again.

MAX

The tires of the van screeched as Jackson took a sharp turn, the unconscious Revolutionary Guard sliding across the floor despite Max's grip on him. In the middle row, Kyra's sisters huddled together like frightened birds, their earlier shopping euphoria gone.

"There is no need to rush," Max told Jackson. "Slow down."

The guy might be an exceptional entrepreneur, but he didn't have what it took to be a Guardian.

Not everyone did, and that was fine.

"I just want that filth gone from my van," Jackson grumbled. "I want to forget that any of this happened."

"Me too," Soraya said. "Where are we going?"

"We need to make a couple of stops," Max said, keeping his tone calm and reassuring. "Standard procedure when we capture an enemy operative or even when we save someone is to check them for tracking devices."

Soraya nodded. "I remember. The handsome doctor checked all of us before we were allowed into the village."

"These days, you can't be too careful," Jackson said from the driver's seat. "They might have trackers sewn into clothing, embedded in shoes, or even subdermal implants."

"That's why we are stopping at the warehouse first," Max said. "The next stop is the keep, where Jackson will drop Theo and me off with the prisoner, and then take you ladies back to the village."

"What's in the warehouse?" Fenella asked.

"We have equipment there like what Julian has in his van. Scanners and other things."

The guard stirred, a low groan escaping his lips. Without hesitation, Theo delivered another precise blow to his temple, rendering him unconscious again.

"How hard are you hitting him?" Rana asked, her eyes wide. "If you kill him, you won't learn anything from him."

Max stifled a chuckle. He'd thought she was asking because she was concerned for the man, but she was only worried about him being well enough to give them the information they needed.

Theo actually looked offended. "I'm a professional, ma'am. I know exactly how much force to apply."

Humans had soft skulls, so Rana's caution was

justified. It had happened on occasion that they had unintentionally killed a scumbag that they'd only meant to keep unconscious.

"He'll just wake up with a killer headache," he murmured.

The warehouse was a nondescript gray building in an industrial area, surrounded by similar structures, and Jackson pulled around to the back, where a loading dock provided cover from prying eyes.

"Everyone, please stay in the van until we are back," Max said as Jackson parked.

"I'm coming with you." Kyra unbuckled her seatbelt.

Max caught her hand and squeezed it gently. "We're going to have to strip the dude naked for the scan. Unless you are keen on seeing a Revolutionary Guard's equipment, and I'm not talking about weapons, I suggest that you stay here."

Fenella snorted. "Count me out. I never want to see such a horror show."

Even Soraya cracked a smile.

"I've seen naked men before," Kyra protested. "What's the big deal?"

It was a big deal to him, and he tried to convey it in the look he gave her. "Trust me, you don't want to. From what I can see, personal hygiene isn't high on his priority list."

That got a chorus of disgusted sounds and snorts from the sisters, which was exactly what Max had intended—anything to break the tension and pull them out of the spiral of fear.

All that adrenaline coursing through their bodies wasn't good for them. They weren't immortal yet, and excess of fear and stress hormones wreaked havoc on the human body. Even he knew that.

"Fine," Kyra conceded. "But hurry."

Max hauled the unconscious guard out of the van. The man was heavier than he looked, soft around the middle, probably from eating too much Persian rice.

The warehouse door opened to Max's palm print on the scanner, and he walked in with the prisoner draped over his shoulder.

He dropped him on the metal examination table. "Start stripping him while I call this in."

As Theo started on the guard's clothes, Max dialed Onegus's line.

"Max," the chief answered on the second ring. "I hear you had some excitement at the market."

"News travels fast," Max said. "Where did you hear that?"

"Fenella just called Din, and he panicked and right away called Kian."

"I see." Max leaned against another examination table. "We have the Revolutionary Guard who recognized Soraya and Rana at the Persian market. We are in the warehouse, checking him for trackers, and from here we are heading to the keep. Jackson will drop us off and continue with the ladies to the village."

"Hold on, I'm patching Kian in."

There was a brief silence, then Kian's voice came through the conference call. "Hello, Max. What's going on?"

Max quickly summarized the events at the market, from Soraya's recognition of the guard to the neutralization of the threat.

"That was quick thinking," Kian said when he finished. "If he'd had time to make a phone call or send a text, we could have had a serious problem on our hands."

"Actually, it was Kyra who told me to grab him," Max admitted. "I just followed her instructions."

Kian chuckled. "Her instincts are better than most. She's been dealing with those thugs for over twenty years."

Max felt a surge of pride for his mate. "That she has."

"I'll meet you at the keep," Onegus said. "This man might be here on vacation, visiting family, or he might be part of a cell. We need to find out what we are dealing with."

Max wanted to say that he didn't need Onegus's help to interrogate a human, but, of course, he didn't.

"Understood. We'll be there in about forty-five minutes."

"Take your time," Onegus said. "It will take me at least that long to get to the keep, and I don't want you rushing the search. Make sure he's clean before you bring him in."

"Yes, sir."

Max ended the call and turned to see that Theo had completely stripped the guard and was feeding his clothes into the scanner piece by piece. The machine beeped as it analyzed each item.

"Two phones," Theo reported, holding up the devices. "One in his pocket, one sewn into the lining of his jacket. Also, a smartwatch, and what looks like a GPS tracker in his shoe."

"Paranoid bastards," Max muttered. "Or maybe just well-equipped. Put everything in the signal-proof box."

"We'll need to vacate this warehouse," Theo said.

Max shrugged. "We keep moving the equipment around anyway. It's not a big deal. But we might be able to release him before anyone notices he's missing and bothers to check his whereabouts. Help me get him in the body scanner," he said, not because the guy was too heavy for him to carry alone but because his body was like a noodle, which was difficult to maneuver.

He was pale and soft, with a significant paunch and body hair in unfortunate places. Max was glad he'd kept Kyra in the van—not out of jealousy, but because no one needed to see this.

As they put him on the scanner platform, the device hummed to life, bathing the guard in blue light as it checked for subdermal implants or other hidden devices.

"Clean," Theo announced after several moments. "No implants."

"Good. Let's get him dressed and out of here."

They pulled a set of scrubs from a supply cabinet, which the clan kept there for exactly this purpose. The light blue fabric made the guard look like an escaped hospital patient, which wasn't far from the truth.

Max gathered the man's original clothes and shoes and put them into an insulated bag and zipped it. It wasn't as good as the box, but since they'd already scanned the clothes, he wasn't really worried about that. The phones and tracker were in the signal-proof box, which Theo would deliver to William to take apart.

Max hoisted the unconscious guard over his shoulder in a fireman's carry while Theo grabbed the box and the bag and held the door open for him.

When they emerged from the warehouse, the van's occupants all looked their way through the open side door.

"Did he have any trackers?" Kyra asked.

Max nodded. "In his shoe. But it's in the box." He pointed to Theo. "No signal can go in or out of this thing."

That alleviated some of the tension in the van.

"You see?" Kyra said. "The clan has the best protocols for keeping everyone safe. You have nothing to worry about inside the village. No one can find you there."

"But what if he was there looking for us?" Soraya asked. "That would mean that they know we are in Los Angeles."

"That's not likely," Max said as he climbed into the van with the guard slung over his shoulder, careful not to let his head hit the door frame. "I think it was pure coincidence, but we will know more after we interrogate him. Onegus is meeting us in the keep."

"I'm coming with you," Kyra said.

The dungeon wasn't a place she should see right now. They had prisoners there that the Avengers had brought from the raids on the pedophile rings—more guinea pigs for Ell-rom to test his strange ability on.

"Your sisters need you right now," he said, knowing it was an argument she couldn't refute.

Kyra's shoulders sagged, but she nodded. "Okay. But you call me the moment you know something."

"I will," Max promised.

The guard began stirring again as they pulled into the keep's parking garage.

"Should I?" Theo asked, raising his fist.

"No," Max decided. "He'll need to be conscious soon anyway. Just watch him. If he starts to thrash about, hit him again."

When they reached the lowest level where the clan's vehicles were parked, Jackson waited for the gate to slide open and then eased the van as close to the entrance as he could get.

Max leaned over to kiss Kyra's cheek. "Jackson will take you all back to the village. Get some rest and try to relax." He swept his gaze over the worried faces of her sisters. "It's over. No one knows you are here."

Once he and Theo disembarked with the prisoner

between them, the van pulled out, made a K-turn, and left through the gate to start its ascent back to street level.

"Do we put him in a cell or an interrogation room?" Theo asked.

"Interrogation room three is vacant, and it has a cot we can put him down on."

29

FENELLA

The afternoon sun felt too bright as they emerged from the keep's underground parking structure, as if the world above was trying to pretend the darkness below didn't exist. Fenella squinted against the glare, her hand unconsciously going to the brooch at her chest. It had a calming effect on her, helping her realize that a chance encounter with some Revolutionary Guard thug was nothing for her to worry about.

She'd dealt with worse.

Much worse.

But the sisters looked shaken, their earlier excitement about the shopping trip completely evaporated. Soraya's face had aged ten years in the past hour, deep lines bracketing her mouth. Rana kept glancing over her shoulder as if expecting pursuit, and Parisa hadn't spoken since they'd left the keep. Yasmin just looked sad, but then that was what she usually looked like.

Poor woman.

"How about we go now to one of the wholesale places I wanted to take you to originally?" Jackson looked at them through the rearview mirror. "Or we can check out that specialty foods market in Koreatown. They have amazing kimchi, and the chance of meeting any Iranians there is zero."

"No." Soraya's voice cut through his enthusiasm like a blade. "No more shopping. I need to go home. I need some relaxing tea, but first, I need to hold my daughters tightly to stop shaking."

The raw emotion in her voice made Fenella's chest tight. She understood the need to retreat to safety, to surround herself with the familiar after danger had brushed too close. But she also knew that giving in to that fear, letting it drive her back into hiding, was not the answer.

"We should eat something first," she suggested. "It's been hours since any of us has eaten anything, and that's part of what is making us nervous."

"I'm not hungry," Parisa said quietly. "I just want to go home. Please."

The fear in her voice was palpable, and Fenella felt a flash of anger—not at Parisa, but at the men who'd made her afraid, who'd stolen her sense of safety in her adopted country. One chance encounter in a massive city, and they were all ready to barricade themselves back in the village.

"Don't let them win," Fenella said, turning in her seat to look at the sisters. "One random meeting with some asshole who's now held in the keep and being interrogated, and you are going to run scared? That's exactly what they want. They want you to be afraid, to hide, to be small."

"Easy for you to say," Rana snapped. "You don't know what it's like."

"I know about running," Fenella said. "I know about being afraid, about looking over your shoulder, about seeing threats in every shadow. I did it for fifty years. And you know what? The fear doesn't go away just because you hide. It gets worse."

Silence filled the van, heavy and uncomfortable.

Then Jackson cleared his throat. "I know the perfect place for lunch. It's a little café where I started my career in baked goods, and it is now run by another clan member. Ruth took over when I left." He glanced at them in the rearview mirror. "The sandwiches are incredible, the coffee is perfection, and there is absolutely no chance of meeting any Revolutionary Guard in there. What's more, it's only fifteen minutes away, while it's at least an hour to the village."

Fenella's mouth watered at the mention of sandwiches. "That's perfect. We eat, we regroup, we let the adrenaline settle. Then we go home."

Soraya sighed, the sound deep and weary. "Fine. But after we eat, we go home. No more adventures today."

"Deal," Fenella agreed, pulling out her phone. "I just need to call Din and let him know that we are not

275

heading straight home. He's probably wearing a hole in the floor with his pacing."

It occurred to her then that all of them had been referring to the village as home, and it had felt so right that she hadn't even noticed.

She hit his number, and he answered before the first ring finished.

"Fenella? Are you on your way back?"

The worry in his voice made her heart sing and ache simultaneously. "We're making a quick stop for sandwiches and coffee. Jackson knows a safe place that is run by a clan member."

"I wish you would come straight home." The worry shifted to something closer to frustration.

"I'm hungry, Din. It's been a long, stressful day, and we need food. I'll bring you a sandwich."

"I don't want a sandwich. I want you here, safe, where I can—" He cut himself off, and she could practically see him running his hand through his hair in frustration.

"That's sweet, Din. Really. But we can't live our lives in fear and hide in our little hidey-holes."

"This isn't about hiding. It's about being sensible. You were just involved in a security incident that required Guardian intervention."

Fenella rolled her eyes. "You make it sound like an international incident. It was just a chance encounter with someone from Soraya's past. Don't make it into such a big deal." She glanced at the sisters, who were pretending not to listen to her conversation. "You can't be with me twenty-four-seven, Din. Life is full of hazards, and you can't protect me at all times. It's impractical and it would be suffocating."

The silence on the other end stretched so long that she wondered if the call had dropped.

"Din? Are you there?"

"I'm here." His voice was quiet, controlled. "I understand that you feel that way, but I would be ecstatic to be with you every minute of every day. Not to guard you, or restrict you in any way, but just to be with you. Obviously, it's not the same for you, which is, well… not ideal."

He was hurt.

"Din, I didn't mean—"

"I know." He sighed. "You need your space. You're still figuring out how to be in a relationship after so long alone. And I am too. It's as new to me as it is to you. But when something like this happens, when you're in danger and I'm not there… it kills me."

Fenella closed her eyes, pressing her fingers to the brooch. She could feel the echo of his emotions in it—not through any psychometric gift, just through knowing him.

"I'm sorry," she said softly. "I'm not used to having someone worry about me."

"Get used to me worrying about you because you matter to me," he said.

"I'm beginning to understand that." She opened her

eyes, watching the city scroll past outside the windows. "We'll be back in less than two hours, and I'll bring you a tasty sandwich."

"I don't care about the sandwich."

"I know. But I'm bringing you one anyway. Because that's what people do when they—when they care about each other, they bring food."

She'd almost said it. Almost said the words he longed to hear. But not over the phone, not in a van full of people, not when her nerves were still jangling from the afternoon's events.

"Be safe," he said finally.

"Always am," she replied, which was true and false at the same time.

She'd tried to be safe, to take care of herself, but it hadn't always worked.

"Bye, Din."

After she ended the call, Kyra touched her shoulder. "He loves you."

"I know," Fenella said. "That's what makes it so hard."

"Love is supposed to be hard?" Yasmin asked, a bitter edge to her voice. "I thought it was supposed to make everything better."

"Love makes everything more," Fenella said, thinking it through as she spoke. "More wonderful, more terrible, more complicated. When you love someone, you give them the power to destroy you and trust them not to use it."

"That's scary," Parisa said. "And also overly dramatic. Sometimes love can be quiet and sensible."

Fenella chuckled. "I guess everyone has their own definition of love."

30

MAX

Interrogation room number three was bare except for a metal table, two chairs, and a narrow cot against one wall.

The guard occasionally stirred, indicating that he was coming around, but he seemed in no rush.

Max turned to the chief. "Do you want me to throw some water on him?"

"No need. He's coming around," Onegus said, and as if to prove him right, the man groaned and shifted.

They waited in silence as consciousness returned. The guard's eyes fluttered open, unfocused at first, then sharpened with alarm as he took in his surroundings.

"Where—" He tried to sit up, then groaned and grabbed his head. "What did you do to me?"

He was pretending to be much more disoriented than he really was. Otherwise, he would have spoken in his native Farsi and not in heavily accented English.

"We gave you a nap," Max said conversationally.

The guard's eyes darted between them. "You're making a big mistake. Why did you take me? There will be consequences—"

"Please," Onegus said calmly. "We can do without the theatrics. Just take a seat in the chair so we can talk like civilized people."

The guy hesitated only for a second before doing as Onegus had commanded and moving from the cot to the chair. That was also the moment he realized that he was no longer wearing his clothes but was dressed in blue scrubs.

"What is this?" He waved a hand over the clothes. "I demand to speak to the Iranian consul—"

"What is your name?" Onegus asked as calmly as before. "After all, we cannot contact the consulate without knowing who you are."

The guard gaped at the chief. "Rashid Mohammadi."

"Good. Now, Rashid, you're going to answer all our questions truthfully and completely. Understand?"

"Yes," the man said, his eyes looking a little glazed over.

Human minds were remarkably easy to influence, especially when the immortal doing the influencing was as skilled as Onegus. He wasn't a compeller, but thralling worked just as well on humans when applied with skill and precision, and the chief had Rashid completely under his thrall.

"Why were you at the Persian market today?" Onegus asked.

"Shopping," Rashid answered. "I wanted to get some saffron and proper rice."

"You recognized someone you didn't expect to see there. Who were they?"

"Soraya. Wife of Colonel Fareed. And her sister Rana." Rashid's brow furrowed slightly, as if trying to remember through fog. "They were missing. Thought to have been abducted by the rebels, them and their children and their two other sisters and their children. When I left Iran, Colonel Fareed was still waiting for a ransom demand. I was shocked to see them in Los Angeles, free and looking like wanton kafirs. No hijab. Western clothes. But I still knew it was them. I wanted to call in and report what I saw, but then this one jumped me." He pointed at Max. "Where is my phone? Why am I here?"

"Why indeed?" Onegus steepled his fingers. "What are you doing in Los Angeles, Rashid?"

The guy hesitated.

Onegus leaned forward. "Tell me everything, Rashid. You want to tell me everything you know."

"We're part of a major operation." The guard's expression grew animated. "Coordinated attacks across the city." A hint of pride crept into his voice. "We'll strike fear into the hearts of the infidels."

Max's heart started racing as he realized that the merciful Fates might have orchestrated the chance encounter with Soraya to save countless lives.

"What kind of attacks?" Onegus asked, his voice carefully controlled despite how tense his posture had become.

"Bombings. Multiple targets—shopping centers, transit hubs, entertainment venues." Rashid's eyes gleamed with fanatic fervor. "Maximum casualties. We have enough explosives to make September 11 look like fireworks."

The casual discussion of mass murder turned Max's stomach. He couldn't fathom what drove people to such insanity.

It must be the Brotherhood's influence. They didn't care how many humans died in the pursuit of their goal of world domination.

"How many cells are there in the city?" Onegus asked.

"Four. Each cell has its own targets and timetables." Rashid straightened in his chair, clearly proud of being part of something he considered important. "We have fighters from the special forces to assist us."

Onegus and Max exchanged a quick glance. "Special forces?" Onegus asked. "What makes them special?"

"They're the elite," Rashid said, his voice taking on an almost reverent tone. "The best of the best. Stronger, faster than normal soldiers. They can do things that seem impossible."

"Elaborate," Onegus commanded. "Give me an example."

"I've seen one lift a car like it weighed nothing."

Rashid's eyes shone with admiration. "And when they run, they are faster than cheetahs. They are enhanced, but no one knows how. It's classified." He leaned forward as if to tell them a secret. "Sometimes their eyes glow in the dark. Like animals, and sometimes it looks like they have fangs. Maybe they are jinn."

Doomers. As Max had suspected, the Brotherhood was behind this barbaric plan to cause mass casualty events in Los Angeles.

"How many of these special unit soldiers do you have?" Onegus asked.

"Two or three per cell. They are in charge of the operation. We follow their orders."

"But you outrank them, right?" Max asked, picking up on something in Rashid's tone.

The guy's face twisted with resentment. "Rank means nothing to them. They have authority that comes from higher up. We have to obey them."

Of course they did. The Doomers were probably thralling them to follow their commands.

Onegus leaned back. "Let's go back to Colonel Fareed's missing wife. You said that he thinks rebels took her."

Rashid nodded. "He's been going crazy since his wife disappeared."

"He's searching for her?"

"Not exactly searching," Rashid admitted. "He thinks the rebels took her, his daughters, and the rest of his wife's family as retaliation. He's been interrogating every rebel sympathizer he can find." A slight smirk crossed his face. "Personally, I think she ran away. The colonel is not an easy man to get along with, and his wife was a hardheaded woman. They didn't get along. But then the daughters went missing first, and Soraya was distressed. But seeing them here, dressed like Western whores..." He shook his head. "That proved that I was right, and they had all escaped. The daughters going missing first must have been staged, and Soraya put up a good act."

Max could feel his temper rise at the disgusting display of misogyny, but he kept his expression neutral.

"Back to the cells," Onegus redirected. "Give me the locations of all of them."

Rashid recited addresses without hesitation, and Max memorized them even though everything was being recorded and they could get the transcript later.

"What's the timeline for these attacks?" Onegus asked.

"Soon. The first one is scheduled for two weeks from now. A big concert in the Glen Helen Amphitheater." He waved his hand. "That harlot Lasusa will be shaking her half-naked ass, and we will send it straight to hell where it belongs, along with all the little harlots that shake their asses to her music." Pride colored his voice again. "Los Angeles will burn, and America will remember that the Islamic Republic's reach is long."

Chills ran down Max's spine as he imagined the carnage. The Glen Helen had a capacity of tens of thousands, and Lasusa was known for filling up stadiums, mostly with preteen girls and their moms.

"Do these special unit soldiers stay with you, or do they stay somewhere else?" Onegus asked.

"They have their own rooms, but we all stay together in the rented mansions." He grinned. "No one thinks to look for revolutionaries in expensive houses."

Revolutionaries, right. Mass murderers. Monsters. That was what they were.

"Where do you store your explosives?" Onegus continued with the questioning.

"With us, of course. We can't just leave them lying somewhere for someone to find. They are not dangerous without the detonators."

Onegus continued the interrogation for a while longer, extracting every detail about the planned attacks, the cell structures, communication protocols, and the enhanced soldiers and their habits. By the end, they had a comprehensive picture of a terror network with embedded Doomer operatives.

"Alright, Rashid," Onegus said. "You are going to forget everything that happened to you today, and you are going to get up, walk over to the cot, and go to sleep. You won't wake up until I tell you that you can. Understood?"

Rashid nodded, walked over to the cot, and lay down.

A moment later, he was snoring.

"Talk about luck," Onegus said, turning to Max.

"What do you want to do with him?" Max asked.

Onegus rubbed a hand over the back of his head. "I'm thinking. We can't let the others know that we are on to them. We can either arrange a fatal accident for him, so his disappearance will be explained that way, or we can use him to infiltrate the cells. To do that, though, I will need Kalugal or maybe even Toven to compel him. Thralling is too limited. We would also need to implant him with a tracker."

"I have a better idea," Max said. "Remember the tiny drones the gods brought with them from Anumati? We can ask them for one and have eyes and ears in Rashid's cell without having to rely on him reporting back."

"That's brilliant." Onegus smiled. "I need to call Kian."

31

FENELLA

J ackson pulled up in front of a charming two-story building, with the café occupying the lower portion, but the sign didn't say Nathalie's Café or Ruth's Café. It had a guy's name, which was confusing.

"Is this the right place?" Fenella asked Jackson. "It says Fernando's Café."

"That was Nathalie's stepfather. It was his place, and she didn't change the name when she took over."

Fenella had a feeling that there was a story there, but this wasn't the time to hear it. Or maybe it was?

Kyra's sisters could use a distraction, and what better way to take their minds off what had just happened than a good story about someone else?

When they walked in, they were greeted with a warm smile by a petite, dark-haired woman and the enticing aromas of coffee and baked goods.

"Jackson filled me in," she said without preamble.

"You've had quite the afternoon. Sit wherever you're comfortable. Coffee is on the house, and I'll bring out a selection of sandwiches." She smiled at the sisters. "Any dietary restrictions?"

They exchanged glances, and then Soraya lifted her chin. "None. We don't accept any more restrictions apart from those we find morally justified."

Yasmin grimaced. "I don't want to eat pork. I have nothing against the rest of you eating it, but it just grosses me out. Pigs are filthy."

Fenella shook her head. "It's a common misconception. They like to wallow in mud to regulate their body temperature because they don't have many sweat glands, but if given a choice, they keep their environment clean and do their business away from where they sleep. That being said, I don't eat pork either because pigs are as smart as dogs, and you can actually keep them as pets. But to each her own. I don't judge."

Ruth smiled. "There are plenty of other options that would delight any palate."

"Thank you," Soraya said.

After all the ladies had squeezed into a large corner booth and Jackson pulled a chair up to the table, Soraya let out a breath. "Look at us. We are practically rebels." She turned a fond smile at Kyra. "You are no longer the only one."

Kyra chuckled. "I've noticed, but you don't have to abolish all the traditions you grew up with at once. You can take your time and get rid of them slowly."

"I don't do slow." Soraya straightened her back. "It's

just not how I'm made. I like to think of myself as decisive and assertive, and after spending a lifetime resenting the restrictions that have been placed upon me, I don't want to wait to shrug them all off."

Fenella regarded her with a sardonic smile. "Does that include letting Arezoo go to the perfectly safe Hobbit Bar in the perfectly safe village?"

Soraya swallowed. "She's too young to be going to bars. The drinking age in California is twenty-one, isn't it? Arezoo is only nineteen."

That was a good argument, but Fenella was ready with a retort. "In Scotland, the drinking age is eighteen, and in other places it's even younger than that. Besides, she doesn't have to consume alcohol while she's there. She can drink a mocktail or a soda. She needs to socialize so she can find a nice immortal to induce her transition."

Soraya's shoulders slumped. "Yeah. You might be right. I'm just not ready for my baby to be all grown up. I need her to stay my little girl for a little while longer."

Fenella crossed her arms over her chest. "As hard as it is to believe, I still remember being Arezoo's age, and I was already working in a bar, serving drinks, even though my father didn't like it one bit. You are fortunate that Arezoo is such a good daughter, and it's unfair of you to exploit her need to please you to stifle her growth as a person. Let her go, Soraya. Let her make her own decisions and her own mistakes. She's not in any danger inside the village."

Realizing that she'd lost the argument, Soraya looked to her sisters for support. "What do you think, Kyra? Should I allow Arezoo to go to the bar?"

Kyra didn't answer right away. After a long moment, she took a deep breath and leveled her gaze at Soraya. "I didn't do any parenting, and my daughter grew up without me, so I'm not really qualified to answer your questions, but I can tell you that her father was a lot like you, and it didn't end well. The moment she could, she stopped listening to him and did what she pleased, and she always resented him for not respecting her choices. They were practically estranged for many years."

"You don't want that to happen," Parisa told Soraya. "Arezoo needs to live free of oppression and spread her wings. You did a good job raising her, and now you need to take a step back and limit yourself to giving advice when she asks for it."

"The man at the market," Rana suddenly interjected. "He looked at us like—like he owned us. Like we were property that had been stolen, and he was going to return us to our rightful owners. Just like—" She broke off, shuddering. "I never again want to feel like I don't matter, like I am less because I'm a woman. We are the givers of life, and we should be cherished and revered, not diminished, dehumanized, and humiliated at every turn."

"We thought we were beyond their reach out here," Yasmin said. "What were the odds of stumbling upon someone who knew us in a market halfway around the world?"

"Maybe it was fated," Jackson said. "Thanks to you, we might have found a secret Revolutionary Guard cell in Los Angeles. I bet they are not here to protect the Iranian consulate or some prominent visiting Iranian figure. They are up to no good."

Ruth, arriving with a platter of sandwiches and a carafe of coffee, put an end to the speculation. Still, even though Fenella's main interest at the moment was filling up her ravenous tummy, her mind kept churning over possible reasons for the Guard's presence in Los Angeles.

Could he be just visiting family?

According to Arezoo's internet research, many former Iranians were living in the city, and the number of Persian markets proved it, so it was entirely possible that the guy was not on any official business.

She could text Max and ask him what they'd found out so far, but she didn't want to interrupt what he was doing.

"Eat," Yasmin commanded her sisters with maternal authority. "Everything looks worse on an empty stomach."

Fenella paused with the half-eaten sandwich in her hand, noticing that Soraya and Rana were still looking at the offering as if it was going to jump up and bite them.

"You have to try this." She waved with the remaining piece of the sandwich, "It's superb. The bread is so fresh and tasty. I think they bake it in-house."

"We do," Ruth said from behind the register. "Every morning. Wait until you taste our pastries. I'll bring them out when you are done with the sandwiches."

With what looked like a monumental effort, Soraya lifted a pastrami sandwich to her mouth and took a bite. Her eyes widened. "It's incredible." She turned to Rana. "You have to try it."

Letting out a breath, Rana did as her sister commanded and took a bite, and then another, each one seeming like she had to force herself to chew.

It made Fenella think about fear and freedom and about the cages people built for themselves and the ones others tried to force them into. The sisters had escaped a restrictive society and even physical captivity, only to imprison themselves in fear.

"After we're done eating, we're hitting another Persian market," she announced and then turned to Jackson. "Do you have time to take us?"

He shook his head. "Not today, but I'll try to clear some time later this week."

"I don't know about that," Soraya said. "We can find another solution. Ordering our supplies online shouldn't be all that difficult, correct?" She looked at Jackson as if he held the secret to their salvation. "Maybe we can pay a clan member to deliver them to the village. You probably don't go shopping for the things your bakeries need yourself, right? You get them delivered."

He nodded. "I can set up accounts with my wholesalers for you, and I can ask around if anyone is willing to drive a delivery van to the village."

"Don't do this." Fenella swept her gaze over Kyra's sisters. "Don't let fear rule you. It's not like it's going to happen again, and if it does, we will discover more undercover plots to damage this beacon of freedom for the world." She smiled at the sisters. "You said that you were all rebels. Prove it."

Parisa nodded. "The store means freedom, independence, a new life. We need to be a lot braver if we want to embrace all of what we can have here."

"You fight by not giving up," Fenella said. "By not giving in, by going back out there and buying your damn refrigerators and stocking your shelves and building your dream."

KIAN

O negus's face filled most of Kian's monitor, with Max taking just a corner of the screen. They were sitting in the cramped Guardian office in the dungeon, and the grim set of their jaws hinted that he was not going to like the news the two were about to deliver.

"We have a serious problem," Onegus said. "The Revolutionary Guard that Max grabbed at the market was not visiting family in Los Angeles. He's part of a terror network planning massive attacks across the city. The first target is the Lasusa concert at the Glen Helen Amphitheater, which is scheduled for Saturday, two weeks from now."

Kian had been prepared for bad news, but this was like dunking in ice water, burning and freezing at the same time. This was a venue that would hold tens of thousands of people, and a Lasusa concert was certain to be sold out, filled with crowds of young teenagers and their parents.

Any terror attack was evil, but this plan was particularly sinister.

"These people are the devil's minions."

Onegus nodded. "The devil is walking the streets openly, waving his wand of destruction and not even bothering to pretend to be something other than pure evil."

Neither of them believed in such an entity, but given how successful the forces of darkness had been lately, it almost seemed plausible.

Kian raked his fingers through his hair. "What else did you get out of him?"

"His name is Rashid Mohammadi, and he's a commander in the Iranian Revolutionary Guard." Onegus leaned back and crossed his arms over his chest. "Naturally, ISIS or some other terror group is going to assume responsibility for the attacks because that's how the Mullahs operate. They use proxies or pretend to use them when they are not effective enough to carry out their objectives. That's the gap the Brotherhood fills. Anyway, he gave us everything he knew. Four cells are operating in the city, each with specific targets and enough explosives to make September 11 look like, and I quote, 'fireworks.'"

Max leaned toward the camera. "Each cell has what Rashid called special-forces soldiers embedded within them. He says that they are enhanced, stronger, and faster than humanly possible. He also said that sometimes their eyes glow, and he caught a glimpse of fangs. He thinks they're jinn."

"Doomers," Kian said flatly.

On the screen, Onegus and Max nodded.

He'd noticed this latest pattern of the Brotherhood taking an active part in criminal activity and terrorism. The first hint of this was when they encountered Doomers working with the drug cartels in Mexico, and then what Yamanu and his team encountered in Iran.

It was a worrisome escalation.

Was Navuh targeting Los Angeles now because he suspected it was the clan's location? Or were similar cells operating in all the major cities, and they were planning a coordinated attack that would cripple the United States?

"We need to bring Andrew and Turner into this," Kian said. "We were lucky to stumble upon the plot right here in Los Angeles, but they might be planning more terror attacks in other major cities. Andrew might be able to find more intel, now that we know what to look for, and Turner has connections that he can mobilize across the nation."

"And then what?" Onegus asked. "Because Doomers are likely embedded in each cell, we will need to deal with the threat ourselves, and depending on the scope of the threat, it may be beyond our capabilities."

"Let's first find out all we can." Kian leaned back in his chair. "We can dial in our solutions when we have a better grasp of the threat. What else did he tell you?"

For the next several minutes, Onegus recounted the information he'd extracted from the guy. Four cells, each with twelve to fourteen humans and two to three Doomers. They used rented mansions in upscale neighborhoods where no one would expect terrorists to hide. The concert was just the first target, and it was what his team was working on. Another team was working on a shopping center, while the two others were making plans to blow up the control tower at the airport and to cause significant damage to the Los Angeles port.

"Those are some lofty aspirations," Kian said. "But they are all doable. Security is not top-notch at any of these locations."

"The humans think they're striking a blow for their cause," Onegus concluded. "But they are just puppets. The Doomers are pulling their strings through a combination of thralling and ideological manipulation."

"Navuh's getting bolder," Kian muttered. "He used to work through proxies, but he's no longer bothering with that. Did he get impatient? And if so, why?"

Onegus shrugged. "Who knows what goes through the despot's mind? He might have amassed so many immortal warriors that he doesn't know what to do with them, or he might be listening to a new advisor who is pushing him to move things faster to achieve his goal of global domination. Regrettably, it seems to be working. Perhaps building momentum emboldens his followers."

"That's possible. We need to gather more intelligence," Kian said. "Rushing in blind could be catastrophic."

"That brings me to my idea of using Rashid as our unwitting spy," Onegus said. "We can send him back with false memories and monitor him by using one of those tiny drones that the gods used to spy on us."

That was a great idea, but the drones were the property of the gods, and Kian wasn't sure they would give them up. He still remembered how careful they had been with their irreplaceable collection.

"That depends on whether the gods will be willing to part with their little marvels. It's not like they can get more once what they brought with them is gone."

"We are talking about saving tens of thousands of lives," Max said. "Most of them are still children. It's worth the sacrifice of one of their drones."

The moral mathematics was simple when stated so starkly—one piece of irreplaceable technology against tens of thousands of innocent lives. Still, Kian couldn't force them to give up the tech. He could only ask.

"I'll speak to Aru," he said.

"If we want to use Rashid to spy for us, we need to move fast." Onegus leaned toward the screen. "He's been missing for hours already, and his buddies are probably wondering where he is and why he isn't answering his phone. We need him back on the street with a plausible story before they get suspicious."

"I'll summon Aru right away," Kian said. "And Toven—we'll need his compulsion abilities to implant deep, unshakeable false memories in Rashid's mind. In the meantime, think of something that can explain his absence, the time gap, and the radio silence. I'll also get in touch with Andrew as soon as he's reachable. His expertise on counterterrorism might come in handy, not to mention his access to the government's surveillance resources."

Onegus nodded. "I'll keep Rashid sedated until we are ready to release him."

"There's one more issue I want to bring up," Max said. "Once we have intelligence from all four cells, we'll need to hit them simultaneously. Any delay between strikes and the others will scatter like roaches when you turn on the light."

"We'll need four Guardian strike teams," Onegus said. "Plus backup. That's a significant portion of our forces. We will have to cancel rescue operations for a couple of nights, but this is more important."

"What do we do with them?" Max asked. "Capture or kill? And then there is the issue of explosives. If we want to confiscate them, we will need trucks to transport them and a place to store them that's outside the city."

"One thing at a time," Kian said. "We'll figure it out."

"We can't use Yamanu for more than one location," Onegus pointed out. "Not if we are hitting them simultaneously. We will need cover stories for the ones he can't cover. Perhaps we could use SWAT uniforms or the FBI. The problem is that people who live in those upscale neighborhoods have connections, and they will call their friends to find out what's going on."

"Those are solvable problems," Kian said. "I'm more concerned with the Brotherhood knowing who took out their cells. We are the only ones who can take out Doomers. Then again, I'm tired of playing defense. Navuh needs to learn that attacking humans in our territory comes with consequences."

The words hung in the air, carrying implications beyond this immediate crisis. For centuries, the conflict between the clan and the Brotherhood had been a shadow war, fought through proxies and influence rather than confrontation. But times were changing. The stakes were rising. And the old rules no longer applied.

On the screen, Max and Onegus nodded, but the chief did so with much less enthusiasm than Max. He wasn't convinced that Kian's new approach was correct.

"I'll let you know when the team I'm assembling can make it to the keep. I hope they can all make it within the next hour or so." Kian shifted back to practical matters.

"Good," Onegus said. "The sooner we wrap up this portion of the plan, the better."

Kian crossed his arms over his chest. "There's something else that's bothering me about this. This feels like more than just terrorism. It feels like the opening move in something on a bigger scale."

On the laptop screen, Onegus and Max exchanged

glances. "Do you think this is a distraction for something even larger?" Onegus asked. "It doesn't get much bigger than blowing up a venue full of kids."

"It might be a probe," Kian said. "They know that we are located somewhere in the wider Los Angeles area, and they might be testing our responses. While we're focused on these attacks, what else might Navuh be moving into place?"

It was paranoid thinking, but paranoia had kept his clan alive for millennia, and Kian had learned the hard way not to underestimate Navuh.

Onegus shrugged. "Their main goal since forever was to eradicate the clan and the Clan Mother. They may be hallucinating that in the chaos, we will lower our guard and reveal where we are located. But right now, we need to focus on the immediate threat and the many thousands of lives that hang in the balance."

"True. Carry on, gentlemen."

After terminating the call, Kian scrolled through his contacts until he found Aru's and initiated the call. As he waited for the god to answer, he stared out his office window at the village below and the café that was bustling with activity. None of the people enjoying their coffees and the company of friends and relatives knew how close their city had come to devastation, how many would have died if not for a random encounter in a Persian market.

The Fates worked in mysterious ways, turning Soraya's recognition by a Revolutionary Guard from a potential disaster into an opportunity to save thousands.

The Fates were indeed merciful for orchestrating this chance encounter.

However, divine intervention wasn't enough, and the rest of the work had to be done by the community members. The invincible Guardians of everything that was good and decent about humanity.

"Kian?" Aru answered. "How can I help you?"

"I need one of your tiny spy drones. Untold thousands of human lives depend on it."

There was a pause. "When do you need it?"

"Right now. How soon can you be in my office with the drone?"

"I'll get Dagor, and we will be right over."

33

FENELLA

When the van entered the tunnel leading to the village, Fenella sighed in relief. Despite the brave face she'd shown Kyra's sisters, she had been shaken by what had happened.

It was proof that the outside world was still a scary place, and it was good to return home, to safety, to Din.

As she saw him waiting for her in the parking garage, her heart leaped. It did that complicated thing where warmth and feeling battled for dominance.

He'd been waiting for her, probably pacing the concrete like a caged panther since the moment she'd texted him that she was almost home.

She let Kyra and her sisters exit the van first and was the last to disembark.

"Thank you," she told Jackson. "Next sandwich is on me."

He waved a dismissive hand and closed the van doors from his control center up front. He'd told them that he was going back to work, so she wasn't surprised when he did a K-turn and headed back into the vehicle lift that would take the van down to the tunnel.

The man had been patience personified, letting them decompress at the café and then entertaining them with stories about his rock band days while driving them back home.

Turning to Din, Fenella smiled. "Have you been pacing the parking garage since the moment I texted you?"

"You know I have." His eyes swept over her, checking for damage as if she'd been in actual combat rather than shopping. When his gaze landed on the brooch still pinned to her shirt, something in his expression softened. "How was Ruth's café?"

"Awesome," she said, glancing at the sisters who were heading to the elevator that would take them up to the glass pavilion. She lowered her voice. "I played shrink, trying to convince a bunch of scared women not to hide forever in the village, which was a bit hypocritical of me, since that's precisely what I wanted to do."

"Oh, sweetheart." He pulled her into his arms for a fierce hug. "I'm never letting you out of my sight again."

"Careful with the box." She took a step back. "You'll smash the sandwich I brought you." She handed it to him. "And don't talk like that. It stresses me out even more than encountering a Revolutionary Guard in a Persian market and watching Max tackle him to the floor."

Din looked confused, her meaning lost on him, but before he could figure it out, Kyra waved at them from the elevator while holding the door from closing. "Are you two coming?"

"Yes, we are." Fenella took Din's hand and walked with him into the waiting lift.

It was a bit crowded in the cab, and Fenella found herself pressed against Din's side, the scent of him familiar and soothing. It was nice to have someone worry about her and wait for her return.

When they emerged into the glass pavilion, she immediately noticed that something was different about the displays along the walls. "Are those new?" She pointed to a case that contained an artifact that hadn't been there when she'd left this morning.

"Kalugal must have refreshed the exhibits," Din said, moving closer to examine the piece. "He told me that he likes to rotate his artifacts, so all the good pieces get to shine. That's Mayan, I believe. Classic period, probably from Palenque."

Fenella shook her head. "He just casually has price-less artifacts lying around to redecorate with?"

Kyra touched her shoulder. "We're heading home. Thank you for coming today and for what you said to my sisters. They needed to hear it."

"I just told them the truth," Fenella said. "Fear is a prison you carry with you. Trust me, I'm an expert."

Kyra nodded. "Regrettably, I'm an expert too."

"I know." Fenella took her hand and gave it a reassuring squeeze. "We were hell buddies, you and me."

"That's one way to put it." Kyra patted her shoulder and turned to follow her sisters.

"That one is new too," Din said, pointing to the next case. "Baltic amber, probably Neolithic. See how the beads are graduated in size? That's typical of—"

If she let him, he would talk for hours explaining about each artifact, and although she was fascinated, she was also tired and wanted to get home.

"Din." She tapped the box he was now carrying. "Your sandwich is going to turn into a soggy mess if you don't eat it soon."

He looked at the box like he'd forgotten it existed. "Right. Where would you like to eat? Shira's place or Thomas's?"

They needed to get a place of their own. By now, it was pretty obvious that she wasn't going anywhere, and that Din wasn't going back to Scotland, and that they were going to be together for the foreseeable future. Well, there was the excursion to Egypt, but after that, they should get a place of their own.

Fenella was no longer scared of committing to their relationship.

"Maybe we could just go to the café and order coffee," she suggested. "I could use a cappuccino, and before you ask, yes, I know I already had coffee at

Fernando's, but that was a while ago, and not that good if I want to be honest."

"I wasn't going to say anything." He took her hand. "The café sounds lovely."

The place was mostly empty in the late afternoon lull, caught between the lunch crowd and the dinner rush. Wonder wasn't there, and Aliya was all by herself because Arezoo had to stay home and watch her cousins while her mother and aunts went shopping.

After the chaos of the day, Fenella appreciated the quiet.

They claimed a corner table by her favorite tree, and Din unwrapped his sandwich with the reverence it deserved. The first bite made his eyes close in appreciation.

"Good?" she asked, though his expression had already answered.

"Excellent," he managed around a mouthful. "Can I offer you the other half?"

Always so considerate, always such a gentleman. She was really lucky to have the Fates choose him for her.

Look at her, being spiritual and all.

"I ate at Fernando's." She waved to get Aliya's attention. "Can we get two cappuccinos, please?"

"Of course," Aliya called out. "Coming right up."

As they waited for their coffees, Fenella enjoyed watching Din eat the sandwich with the focused attention of someone who'd learned not to take good food for granted. There was something endearing about the way he savored each bite.

When her phone buzzed, she expected it to be Kyra for some reason, but when she pulled it out of her purse, Atzil's name flashed on the screen.

"That's a surprise," she muttered. "Hello, boss."

"Fenella!" Atzil's voice boomed through the speaker with enough enthusiasm to make her hold the phone away from her ear. "I have a proposition for you."

"If it involves me learning to cook, the answer is no."

His laugh was rich and warm. "Nothing like that. I want you to work every night until you leave for Egypt, if you can. I've been getting calls and texts for the past two days with customers begging for it, and the bar has never been so busy as when you're performing your readings."

Every night was a lot, but it was also exactly what she needed—structure, purpose, and money.

"Do you want me to run it by myself?"

It would have been impossible to do during the weekend, but on weekdays the place wouldn't be as busy, so maybe she could pull it off by herself or with a little bit of help from Din.

"I wouldn't dream of leaving you to handle everything on your lonesome. I'll be there with you from opening to closing."

"What about your duties at Kalugal's?" she asked. "You cook breakfast, lunch, and dinner for his entire crew. That's a lot of work."

"It won't be the first time I've pulled double duty," Atzil said. "Ingrid keeps telling me that if I want to grow the business, I need to seize opportunities. And you, my dear, are the best opportunity the Hobbit has seen since its opening."

The compliment warmed her more than it should have. "When do you want me to start?"

"Tonight?" The hope in his voice was almost comical. "If you're available, of course. I was thinking of opening at nine in the evening and closing at one in the morning. That's only four hours. I can manage that in addition to my cooking duties during the day."

Fenella glanced at Din, who was watching her with an unreadable expression. "Tonight works."

"Excellent! I'll post it on the bulletin board so everyone knows. And as we agreed, you get to keep all the tips."

It was on the tip of her tongue to ask him for a better hourly rate as well, but she didn't want to be greedy. The tips alone were enough to cover most of her needs. After all, it wasn't as if she had to pay rent or utilities.

While she had been on the phone, their cappuccinos had arrived, and Fenella took an appreciative sip. "These are better than what Ruth makes at Fernando's, but don't tell her I said that."

"Your secret is safe," Din said, but there was something careful in his tone. "Every night is a lot, and after the excitement of today, you should rest instead of working."

His concern for her well-being was sweet, but she was perfectly capable of evaluating what she could and couldn't do, and she didn't appreciate being given unsolicited advice. She never had.

"It's only for a few days." She wrapped her hands around the warm cup. "Depending on when we leave for Egypt."

"That's even more reason not to exert yourself. A lot is riding on your ability, and if you arrive there exhausted, your performance might suffer."

She had a feeling that her performance was the least of his worries, and that what he wanted was to have more of her time.

"I need this," she said. "When I'm behind that bar, making drinks and telling ridiculous stories, I know who I am, and everything feels right." She smiled. "I get to shine."

"And when you're not behind the bar?"

The question hung between them, heavier than it should have been. When she wasn't behind the bar, she was just Fenella—a survivor who'd gone through too much and wanted to forget.

"It's still difficult," she said finally. "But I'm working on it."

Din reached across the table, his fingers brushing hers where they curved around the cup. "I'm here to help in any way I can. Just tell me what you need, and I'll do whatever it takes to get it for you."

"I know that you are here for me." He was constant,

steady, and patient in a way that made her feel both treasured and trapped. "It's just—"

Her phone buzzed again, saving her from finishing that thought. This time it was Shira.

"Where are you? I have gossip that cannot wait."

"The café," Fenella said. "What kind of gossip?"

"The kind that involves Ruvon mooning around the library all afternoon, asking about Persian poetry. I'll give you three guesses who he's trying to impress, and the first two don't count."

It wasn't hard to guess who Ruvon wanted to impress, unless he had decided that the older ladies were an easier conquest.

"Are you home?" Fenella asked.

"Yes."

"We'll be there in a few minutes, so you can tell me all about it when we get there. We are just finishing our cappuccinos at the café. And by the way, I have juicy gossip for you too."

Shira squealed in delight. "I can't wait."

Ending the call, Fenella smiled at Din. "Apparently, we're needed for an emergency gossip session."

"We?" He raised an eyebrow. "I didn't hear her inviting me."

"Consider yourself drafted." She stood, downing the rest of her cappuccino in one go. "You like Shira, don't you?"

"I tolerate Shira," he corrected, standing as well. "There's a difference."

As they left the café, Fenella reached for his hand,

threading their fingers together like it was the most natural thing in the world.

The walk back to Shira's house was comfortable, their joined hands swinging slightly between them. The village paths were busy with the late afternoon crowd—people heading home from work, others going to the gym, nearly all either nodding and smiling or calling out greetings.

Fenella realized with a start that she knew most of their names already.

When had that happened? When had she become a member of the community?

"What are you thinking about?" Din asked.

"I was just realizing that this place feels like home now, and that's new for me."

"New in a good way or a bad way?"

"Jury's still out," she said, but squeezed his hand to take the sting out of the words.

When they reached the house, Shira yanked the door open before they could knock. "Finally! Come in."

"Does this gossip require wine or hard liqueur?" Fenella asked. "Because if I'm working tonight, I should probably stick to coffee or tea."

"Coffee it is," Shira declared, dragging them toward the kitchen. "Sit. I'll make it while I talk."

"Not for me," Din said. "I'm all coffeed out."

"Tea, then?" Shira asked.

"Sure. Whatever tea you have is fine."

As Shira bustled around the kitchen, she launched

313

into her tale. Apparently, Ruvon had spent his entire afternoon in the library, checking out books on Persian history and poetry and asking Shira for advice about romantic gestures that a young, shy woman might find acceptable.

"He actually asked if I thought roses were nice or too cliché," Shira said, setting mugs in front of them. "I told him yes, obviously they were overdone, but he looked so crestfallen that I had to suggest alternatives."

"Let me guess," Fenella said. "You told him to write her a poem."

"I told him to be himself," Shira corrected. "And just to be on the safe side, I told him to get chocolates. I don't know any woman who doesn't appreciate a box of quality chocolate."

Din shifted beside Fenella. "Isn't Arezoo a bit young for him?"

"She's nineteen," Fenella said. "That's adult by any standard. And honestly? They might be good for each other. He needs someone to draw him out of his shell, and she needs someone who's very patient. I can't see Arezoo with any of the overconfident immortal males with all their swagger. A shy guy is perfect for her. He would bring out her maternal instinct."

"Listen to you, playing matchmaker," Shira teased. "Next, you'll be hosting dinner parties and setting up blind dates."

"People like to talk to bartenders, and I have a good eye for people. I'm uniquely qualified to do just that."

Shira pursed her lips. "And you really think that a

geeky former Doomer and a sheltered Iranian young woman are a good match?"

Fenella shrugged. "Sometimes the unlikely pairings are the ones that work best."

She felt Din's eyes on her, but didn't look at him. They were certainly an unlikely pairing—the quiet, studious professor and the skittish bartender. But somehow, against all odds and her self-destructive tendencies, they worked.

"Speaking of work," Shira said, "I saw on the bulletin board that you'll be at the bar every night until you need to leave for your trip."

"News does travel fast here," Fenella muttered. "Atzil just asked me less than half an hour ago."

"He posted it on the bulletin board the second you hung up. The guy knows how to capitalize on a good thing."

She laughed. "I have to admit that I enjoy the attention, but all I do is pour drinks and make up ridiculous stories about people's belongings. It's hardly a transformative experience."

"It's entertainment," Din said. "And connection. People come to see you because you make them laugh, and for a few minutes, they get to be part of something fun and light. That's important. I bet that for some it's better than therapy."

Fenella looked at him, startled by the insight. Maybe there was real value in bringing levity to immortal lives that could become weighted down by centuries.

"Thank you. That was a very nice thing for you to say, and very smart."

"Must be all that time I spent with artifacts," he said with a perfectly straight face. "Wisdom through osmosis."

Shira snorted. "More like you've been reading my self-help books. That sounded like something from *Understanding your Emotionally Unavailable Partner*."

Fenella's mouth dropped open. "You didn't."

Din's expression turned sheepish. "I needed a break from grading papers, and it was just lying there on the coffee table. I got curious."

"I've also noticed that you were leafing through the one about love languages," Shira continued mercilessly. "Did you ever figure out if Fenella prefers acts of service or gifts? Because that brooch suggests—"

"Okay, that's enough," Fenella interrupted, though she was fighting not to laugh. "Why are you home anyway, Shira? It's too early."

"I was on the first shift today," Shira said cheerfully. "Which means I started early and finished early, and now I have all evening to embarrass both of you until you leave for the bar."

"Actually," Fenella said, standing, "I need to get some rest before heading to work. And shower. And possibly burn my clothes because they smell like Persian market and panic sweat."

Shira's eyes widened. "You said that you had some gossip of your own. Spill!"

"I'm surprised the rumor machine hasn't put that

one into production yet." Fenella told Shira about the encounter at the market, and that Max had taken the man to the keep for interrogation.

"You are right. That's a lot of excitement," Shira agreed. "Poor women. They finally gathered the courage to leave the village, and that happened to them. I bet they won't want to leave for a long time now."

"I believe that I convinced them that living in fear was not the way."

Now Fenella only had to convince herself, and all would be good.

When she and Din headed to her bedroom, Shira made exaggerated kissing noises, which Fenella responded to with a decidedly rude gesture that only made their host laugh harder.

In her room, Fenella kicked off her shoes and sank onto the bed. The adrenaline from the day's adventures was wearing off, leaving her feeling wrung out and slightly shaky.

"You shouldn't work tonight." Din sat on the bed beside her. "Atzil would understand if you needed a night to recover."

"From what? Shopping?" She shook her head. "I'm fine. Besides, I function better when I'm distracted."

He studied her for a long moment. "You know that running toward something is just as much an escape as running away, right?"

The observation hit closer to home than she cared to admit. "Maybe. But at least I'm running toward something useful and beneficial. You've just said how I was helping people, uplifting their moods and all that crap."

"Fenella—"

"I know what you're going to say," she interrupted. "That I don't need to keep moving, that it's safe to be still, that you're here and patient and all the other lovely things that make me feel like the world's biggest ass for not being able to just enjoy you the way I should and the way you deserve."

Din pulled her against his side. "That's not what I was going to say at all."

"No?"

"No." He pressed a kiss to the top of her head. "I was going to say that I'm glad you have something that makes you happy."

His acceptance undid a knot in her chest. "You're too good for me."

"Rubbish," he said. "We're exactly right for each other. It just took us fifty years to figure it out."

She turned her face into his shoulder, breathing him in. "I don't deserve you."

"You deserve everything," he said fiercely. "Love, happiness, safety, purpose. All of it."

"Din..."

"And I'm going to keep telling you that until you believe it," he continued. "Even if it takes another fifty years."

"God, I hope not," she muttered against his shirt.

His chest rumbled with quiet laughter. "Me too. My patience is legendary, but even I have limits."

She pulled back to look at him. "What happens when you reach them?"

"Then I seduce you with my vast knowledge of Neolithic pottery until you capitulate out of sheer boredom," he said solemnly.

"Your pillow talk needs work," she informed him.

"I'll add it to my research list," he promised. "Right after *'Understanding your Emotionally Unavailable Partner, Volume Two.'*"

"There's a volume two?"

"There's always a volume two. That's how they get you."

Despite the stress of the day and the fear and restlessness that still lurked at the edges of everything, Fenella laughed. Real, genuine laughter that came from deep in her chest and loosened all those tight muscles she hadn't noticed had been that way for a very long time.

"There," Din said with a smile. "That's better."

"I really do need to shower," she said. "And change. And mentally prepare to tell fortunes for drunk immortals."

"Then I'll leave you to it." He stood but stopped at the doorway. "Do you want me to come with you tonight?"

She was surprised he was asking. "Sure. If you want to."

He grinned. "There is nowhere I'd rather be."

"Come back in an hour. We'll have dinner together."

Fenella wasn't at all hungry after all the sandwiches she'd consumed, but she would be in an hour, and she didn't like to be away from Din for too long. It was kind of pathetic to become so attached so quickly, but she didn't have the energy to fight it anymore.

"I'll bring steaks."

She laughed. "Is Thomas okay with you raiding his freezer?"

"I'm paying him back with fine whiskey. He's very happy with the exchange." He blew her a kiss before heading for the door.

After Din left, Fenella sat on her bed for another moment, her hand going to the brooch still pinned to her shirt. The metal was warm under her fingers, pulsing with that subtle energy she wasn't sure was real or imagined.

Every night at the bar until the trip to Egypt wasn't going to be easy, but then nothing worth having ever was.

34

KIAN

The keep's conference room had hosted many crucial meetings over the years, but Kian couldn't recall one where the stakes were as high and urgent as this. So many thousands of lives hung in the balance, most of them children who just wanted to see their favorite pop star perform.

It was strange to think that the tiny spy drone Aru was going to pull out of a metal case might be the thing that would prevent the disaster from happening.

"Originally, we brought a hundred units with us," Aru said. "But we're down to sixty-five. I hope we can figure out a way to retrieve this one when it's done its job or when it needs recharging."

Not for the first time, Kian wished they could take apart those marvelous devices and make more of them, but Anumatians were clever and protected their tech from getting copied by making everything solid state. Any attempt at tampering resulted in the destruction of the device.

Dagor flipped open his laptop. "I will fly the drone. Someone inexperienced will not be able to hide its presence as well, and we really can't afford to lose this guy, and not just because it's irreplaceable. If they succeed, we will no longer have eyes and ears in their den of malice."

"I remember the basics from your last demonstration," Kian said, "but that was a while ago. Perhaps you could refresh our memories?"

Aru lifted what looked like a miniscule metallic insect from the case and held it delicately balanced on his forefinger. The drone was the size of a mosquito and nearly invisible with its translucent, tiny wings and even tinier body that was made from materials not found on Earth.

"The exterior is adaptive," Dagor said, taking over the technical explanation. "It can adjust its surface properties to match ambient lighting conditions, making it effectively invisible to the naked eye. It's nearly silent, beyond the range of human hearing, and barely registers on ours. The best part of operating it remotely is my ability to park it somewhere safe while the host is not moving. It can be a wall or a shelf, which makes discovery even less likely. When the host is in motion, I can attach it to the back of their shirt or somewhere else on their person that is not visible to them or anyone interacting with them.

Andrew, who had been silent until now, cleared his throat. "What about detection with equipment?"

Dagor shook his head. "These drones emit no electromagnetic signature that Earth technology can detect. It operates on different principles and is made from materials that will not show on any of your scanners."

"It can be detected with the help of MRI if the tech is paying close attention," Andrew said.

Dagor smirked. "That's why it won't go into the scanner with the host but gets parked on a nearby surface."

"How does it transmit data then?" Andrew asked.

"Quantum entanglement," Dagor said. "Distance is irrelevant. The connection is instantaneous and cannot be intercepted or detected. The only limitation is energy. It can last a long time, but if it flies a lot, it will need to be recharged."

Kian chuckled. "With all its other wonders, I would think that it could also self-charge."

"The size is the problem," Dagor said. "Something had to give. If it were even a little larger, it could have been self-charging. But then it wouldn't have been as effective at spying."

"It's remarkable technology," Toven said. "I wish I could visit Anumati one day and experience all of its wonders."

Aru was thoughtful for a moment. "You are a full-blooded god, so there might be a way to smuggle you onto one of our ships, but I wouldn't risk it. The

Eternal King has spies everywhere, and some can read minds. No one is safe on Anumati."

Toven smiled indulgently. "It was just a bit of wishful thinking. My place is here, on Earth, with my immortal mate."

Aru nodded. "So is mine. At some point, we will have to fake our deaths convincingly enough so no one will come looking for us. But even if we manage a successful fake, we can't allow another team to replace us."

There was a long moment of silence as everyone present was reminded of the real danger looming over the clan and all of humanity. The Eternal King, the absolute ruler of Anumati and the entire galaxy it controlled, could destroy Earth with one command, and he would do that without giving it a second thought once he realized how close humans were to interplanetary space travel.

"Let me show you the control interface," Dagor said, pulling up an application on his laptop.

That part Kian remembered well. It was surprisingly simple, like a computer game, but Dagor was right about the importance of having experience with it and knowing when to move it and where to.

"How does it attach to the host or the wall?" Andrew asked.

"That's the elegant part. Watch." Dagor set the drone on the conference table and moved his finger on the trackpad. The tiny device suddenly sprouted microscopic legs, scurried across the surface with unsettling speed, and then attached itself to Aru's sleeve.

"It made a little bit of noise," Onegus said.

"That's why it's important to know when to move it and when not to," Dagor said.

Kian turned to Toven. "This compulsion will be a little complicated. We need Rashid to visit a public location regularly so that Dagor can retrieve the drone and recharge it periodically. Implant in his mind a love for a particular coffee shop that he will feel compelled to visit at least every other day, have coffee, and sit there for at least fifteen minutes."

"That shouldn't be too complicated." Toven leaned back. "You just need to show me the coffee shop and what they serve. It also should be close to where he lives."

"I'm on it." Onegus flipped his laptop open. "I'll provide you with this information in a moment."

"Did you think about a story to put into his mind?" Kian asked Onegus.

"Andrew and I discussed this while waiting for Aru and Dagor to arrive," Toven answered instead. "The ICE story provides perfect cover, as Andrew confirmed that there is no record of this guy entering the country legally. At least not under his real name. Immigration enforcement raids are common enough in Los Angeles that his cell won't question it."

Andrew picked up the thread. "We'll implant memories of him escaping ICE agents by sneaking out of their processing center, where they left him to wait with a large group of detainees, unrestrained. He went to an adjacent building and hid in a dumpster for hours, waiting for nightfall to avoid capture. The fear, the adrenaline—it'll explain his absence and any disorientation he feels. As for why he wasn't answering either of his phones, he will remember turning them off to avoid them accidentally giving off a sound that would reveal his hiding place."

"The beauty of it is that it reinforces their existing paranoia." Toven smiled. "The government finding out about them is a constant stressor, and fear of discovery is deeply ingrained in their psyche."

Kian considered the plan. "If he's been hiding in a dumpster, he should smell like garbage."

"I'll handle that," Max said. "His stuff didn't smell fresh to begin with, but I'll just put his clothing into the trash in the kitchen and give it a few stirs. Maybe I'll open a can of sardines and throw it in there for good measure."

Andrew snorted. "That will make him convincingly rank."

"I'm glad we have that covered." Kian turned to Toven. "The question is how to motivate the guy to get involved with as many of the meetings as possible and maybe even spy on the Doomers."

Toven's expression grew contemplative. "I can implant a subtle suggestion of burning curiosity and being helpful by serving his superiors in every capacity he can, so he will stay close to them. I might also implant a suggestion to find out what the so-called enhanced soldiers are doing. It can't be anything too dramatic that will conflict with his established personality and his position, though. His associates know him. If he suddenly becomes overly eager, they'll suspect something."

"Subtle is good," Onegus said. "We don't need him to be a spy, just to be present where our drone can get us the information we need."

Andrew checked his watch. "We should move soon. Rashid has been missing for nearly five hours now. Much longer and his story becomes harder to sell."

"Agreed," Kian said. "Dagor, where will you monitor the drone from?"

"Anywhere, really. I should probably stay in the keep because it's closer to everywhere Rashid might be going, and I would appreciate the use of your penthouse if it's available. I would like to get Frankie here as well."

"Of course," Kian said. "I'll get Okidu to come over and prepare a few days of meals for you so you won't have to bother while you work."

"No need." Dagor waved a dismissive hand. "Frankie will take care of me."

"Okay." Kian drummed his fingers on the conference table. "Toven, Max, and Dagor, please prepare the prisoner. Max, you will deposit Rashid in the dumpster next to ICE's holding center." He turned to Andrew. "I need you to stay a little longer to discuss the breach of security and possible other locations of infiltration. Your department messed up."

Andrew nodded. "Big time. I need to look into how these Revolutionary Guards and their Doomer handlers flew under the radar. Once I figure that out, I will have a pattern to look for."

Kian nodded. "That's good. Are there any concerns we haven't addressed?"

Toven shook his head. "We should go and take care of Rashid."

Max rose to his feet. "Follow me, gentlemen."

35

AREZOO

"Do you want more tea?" Arezoo asked her mother as she placed a plate of cookies on the coffee table.

Her mother was still in emotional turmoil after the incident at the market, and sweets always helped her calm down.

"No, thank you, sweetheart." Her mother smiled. "Come sit with me."

When Arezoo did, her mother took her hand. "A Revolutionary Guard, just standing there in the market," she said again, as if repeating it would make it less shocking. "If Max hadn't acted so quickly..."

"But he did," Yasmin said from where she sat at the dining table, cradling her own cup of tea. "The immortals are going to keep the man locked up or erase his memory of seeing us and let him go. There is nothing to worry about."

Yeah, as if.

If there was one, there were more, and the thought of those men walking free in Los Angeles made Arezoo's stomach churn.

The fact that her own father belonged to their organization didn't make things easier. Growing up, there had been plenty of times she'd been afraid of him, but after her abduction, that fear had been amplified by loathing. He might not have been involved in that operation or even known who had taken them, but the fact that those were the kind of people he associated with and was loyal to was enough to make Arezoo actually hate him.

"There must be more of them," Parisa echoed Arezoo's thoughts.

"Not necessarily," her mother said firmly, though Arezoo caught the uncertainty in her eyes. "Los Angeles is full of Persians. He was probably visiting family."

"There is no point in guessing," Rana said. "We are just stressing ourselves needlessly. When they are done interrogating him, I'm sure they will let us know what he was doing there." She pushed to her feet. "Azadeh and I should go home." She headed down the hallway to get her daughter from Donya and Laleh's room.

"She's right." Her mother sighed. "Fenella said as much, and given that she's an elder compared to us, I listened to what she had to say."

Her mother rarely listened to anyone's words of wisdom except her own, so that was surprising.

"What did she say?" Arezoo asked.

"It was about embracing our newfound freedoms and not letting fear control us." Soraya paused, as if gathering courage. "She convinced me that I should not stop you from going to the bar." She cast Arezoo an accusing look. "I didn't know that you and Fenella had got so close that you complained to her."

"I didn't. It must have been Drova. She probably talked to Fenella at the bar."

That seemed to mollify her mother. "I'm glad that you didn't badmouth me to a practical stranger."

"I would never do that, Maman." Arezoo lifted their still joined hands and kissed the back of her mother's. "I love you and respect you, and I'm grateful for all the sacrifices you've made for us."

There had been countless times when her mother had come between their father and Arezoo and her sisters, protecting them from his wrath when he'd found fault with something trivial any of them had done, or just when he was angry and needed to take it out on someone. Arezoo had seen and remembered each instance, and she admired her mother's courage.

Tears shone in Soraya's eyes. "You are the best daughter a mother could hope for, and I was doing you a disservice by trying to keep you from being the young woman that you are." She patted the back of Arezoo's hand. "Go to the bar, mingle with immortals and Kra-ell, and find a male who respects you. That's more important even than love."

The words hung in the air like a foreign language

that Arezoo couldn't quite translate. She stared at her mother, certain she'd misheard.

"Really? You are okay with me going to the bar?"

"If you want," her mother said, looking like each word pained her. "I'm not telling you to go, but you're nineteen, you're an adult, and we're not in Iran anymore. I was already married when I was your age, but I didn't select my husband. My father did, and I agreed because it was hammered into my head that a dutiful daughter must obey her father, and frankly, I didn't have a choice. You have all the choices that I was denied, so if you want to go, you should."

Aliens landing outside the living-room window would have been less shocking, but then her best friend was an alien, so that didn't hold as much of a shock factor as it had before her life had been turned upside down.

Still, her mother was the most stubborn person she knew, and this change of heart was unprecedented and staggering.

"I've been holding on too tight," Soraya continued. "I was trying to protect you from a world that's already hurt you so badly, but keeping you from spreading your wings isn't protection. It's just another cage."

Tears pricked at Arezoo's eyes, and she threw her arms around her mother. "Thank you," she whispered against Soraya's shoulder. "You are the best mother. Thank you."

Soraya held on tightly, and Arezoo felt her mother's tears dampen her hair. "Just be careful," Soraya murmured. "And don't drink too much so you have your wits about you. Better yet, avoid drinking altogether if possible. And come home at a reasonable hour. And—"

"Maman." Arezoo pulled back with a watery laugh. "I'll be fine. It's just the village bar, not a nightclub in Hollywood." She extracted herself from her mother's embrace. "I have to call Drova and tell her the good news. She'll be so happy."

"I'm glad she's your friend." Her mother wiped tears from her lashes with the sleeve of her shirt. "She's formidable, and no one will bother you with her by your side."

That had probably been a big factor in her mother's decision to ease the rules. She knew that Arezoo would be safe with Drova around.

In her room, Arezoo dropped onto her bed and took a moment to catch her breath and internalize the fact that her mother had finally seen her as an adult.

When she finally called Drova, the girl answered almost immediately. "I've heard what happened. My mother told me that someone recognized your mother and her sisters in a city market. Are they okay? I mean, it must have been scary for them."

It was incredible how fast rumors spread in the village, and Arezoo wondered how long it would take before everyone would know that she was now free to visit the bar, and by everyone, she meant Ruvon.

"They are fine. A little shaken but getting over it. That's not why I'm calling, though."

"Oh yeah?" Drova must have heard in her tone that she had something exciting to share because she suddenly sounded more curious than worried. "What is it?"

"The incident must have unsettled my mother's foundations because she came home and told me that I'm free to go to the bar if I want to."

"Thank the Mother of All Life! We are going tonight."

Arezoo laughed. "It's Tuesday. The bar isn't open on weekdays."

"It is now. There was an announcement on the bulletin board. The Hobbit will be open every night until Fenella leaves for her trip. Everyone wants to catch her readings while they can."

Arezoo's stomach did a double flip. She'd been expecting to have days to prepare mentally for her first bar visit. "I don't know if I can tonight."

"Yes, you can," Drova said firmly. "I'll pick you up at nine so we can get there right as it opens. It'll be packed because everyone wants a reading. Bring an object for Fenella to read."

36

DIN

"That was so good." Shira wiped her mouth with a napkin. "Thank you for cooking the steaks."

"You are welcome." Din rose to his feet and started collecting the plates.

"Stop," Shira commanded. "I'll clean up. You two need to rest a little before going to the bar." She gave him a very obvious wink that made Fenella roll her eyes.

"Much appreciated," he said, offering Fenella a hand. "Shall we?"

"Yes, we shall." She let him pull her up. "I'm stuffed."

"Nonsense, love. You ate just one steak."

She gave him a mock glare. "Are you kidding me? Each of those steaks could feed a family of four. Where does Thomas even get them?"

"I don't know, but they are very good." He put his

hand on the small of her back and led her to the bedroom.

"How much time do we have?" Fenella asked, closing the bedroom door behind them and leaning against it for a moment, watching him.

Din glanced at his watch. "Plenty. Nearly three hours." He plopped down on one of the armchairs facing the sliding door and the garden beyond, his long legs stretching out in front of him. It was getting dark, but there was still some time before the shutters went down.

It was peaceful, and after enduring Shira's exuberant chatter for over an hour, he appreciated the quiet. Din was sociable when required, but it was tiring to him. He preferred silence and solitude—except when it came to Fenella. He never got tired of hearing her talk or watching her do the most mundane things.

He just loved everything about her.

"Since there is still plenty of time before my shift…" Fenella sauntered over to him and sat on his lap. "Let's make it count." Her hands were already sliding up his chest.

"I like the way you think." He wrapped his arms around her, one hand splaying across her lower back to hold her secure.

When she tilted her face up to his, he captured her lips in a kiss that was gentle at first, a greeting, a promise. But then Fenella made that soft sound in her throat that drove him wild, and pressed her soft breasts to his chest, and all thoughts of taking it slow flew out the window.

His hands tightened on her, and when she whispered his name in that particular tone that never failed to undo him, his control snapped.

He rose to his feet with her in his arms and with purposeful strides crossed the short distance separating the sitting area from the bed, laid her down with surprising gentleness, and then followed, careful to keep his weight on his elbows.

He paused, just looking into her eyes and marveling at what he found there—the lust, yes, but more importantly, the complete trust. Finally, she was letting him love her without walls or barriers.

He loved her, and she loved him back, but was still too afraid to say the words.

"You are thinking too much." She lifted a hand to his cheek. "I can practically see your professor brain cataloging and analyzing."

"Occupational hazard." He traced his lips over the line of her jaw. "That's what I'm paid to do."

"Thinking is overrated." She arched beneath him. "Let your body rule you for a change and give your brain a break."

"I need an incentive," he teased.

She pushed on his chest until he was on his knees between her legs, then removed her shirt in one fluid move. "Is that what you had in mind?"

Din just stared at the perfection of her, his vocabulary momentarily deserting him. "Take off your bra," he commanded, his Scottish accent thickening.

"Yes, sir." She reached behind her back, released the hook, and then slid the straps down her arms with excruciating slowness.

Din felt his fangs beginning to elongate. "Just a reminder, we are a little short on time."

"You wanted an incentive." She pulled the bra cups off and tossed the undergarment aside. "I'm simply providing what you requested."

He licked his lips. "Yes, you are." He lowered his mouth to her right nipple and gave it a gentle kiss before turning to the other one and greeting it similarly.

"Just a reminder, Professor. We are short on time," she threw his words back at him, but her voice came out breathy with need.

He chuckled against her nipple and then took it between his lips and sucked.

Fenella moaned, her arms coming up and her fingers threading into his hair, holding him close.

He feasted on her for a moment longer, alternating between gentle and firm, reading her responses and adjusting accordingly, but was keenly aware that they didn't have a lot of time for extended foreplay.

Letting go, he leaned back and removed his shirt. The rest of his and her clothing followed in a tangle of fumbling hands and breathless laughter, and when they were finally skin to skin, Fenella's mouth found that spot on his throat just under his jawline that always made him groan.

He was inside her within a heartbeat, and as she held him tightly to her, he got lost in her touch, in the slide of skin against skin, in the catching of her breath, in the incoherent endearments she murmured against his shoulder.

It was a familiar dance by now, passionate in the intense way of new lovers, but saturated in the deeper connection of two souls recognizing each other across time and space.

"I love you," he said, the words coming unbidden but never unwelcome.

He'd say them a thousand times if that's what it took for her to believe them, to accept them, to return them.

Fenella's eyes flew open, meeting his, and for a moment, he thought she might finally say them back. He saw the words forming, saw her lips part, saw the internal struggle play out in her eyes.

Instead, she pulled his head down and kissed him with a fierce tenderness that said everything she couldn't yet manage to say.

It was enough. For now.

Some walls took time to crumble. He'd already waited fifty years, and he could wait a little longer for those words, when every touch, every look, every soft sigh already told him the truth she couldn't yet verbalize.

AREZOO

A rezoo stood before her closet in a state of complete panic. Every piece of clothing she owned seemed wrong. Too conservative or too casual. Not that she had much to begin with, and she'd worn all of it to work at the café.

What was she supposed to wear for her unsupervised adult outing?

A knock on her door interrupted her mental spiral. "Come in," she called.

Laleh poked her head in, took one look at the clothes strewn across Arezoo's bed, and grinned. "I've heard the incredible news. Do you need help getting ready?"

"Desperately," Arezoo admitted.

Her sister entered and began sorting through the options with the critical eye of a fifteen-year-old who'd been consuming Western fashion content at an alarming rate since gaining internet access.

"This." Laleh held up one of the two pairs of jeans Arezoo owned. "With this." A deep blue blouse that was a little fancier than basic. "You can borrow a necklace from Maman to spruce it up. Accessories show you made an effort without trying too hard."

"Did you learn that from a YouTube video?"

"So what if I did? I've watched so many makeover videos that I'm an expert on Western fashion by now. This outfit says that you are confident and yet approachable. I can send you a link to a video about signaling that you are interested. Apparently, the average guy needs no less than thirty signals to realize that a woman is interested in him."

Arezoo's eyes widened. "Thirty? I don't know how to signal even once."

"I can show you." Laleh pretended to scan the area and then lingered on Arezoo a moment longer before continuing her scan. "See? That signals that you are intrigued. Next time, add a smile to that."

That sounded reasonable, but thirty times? She would look like an idiot. "What else?"

Laleh continued to demonstrate, touching her hair, her neck, and her jaw. It wasn't suggestive, but it seemed to signal insecurity more than anything else.

"How is that supposed to convey that I'm interested?"

"Pheromones," Laleh deadpanned. "Every time you touch your face or neck, it supposedly releases pheromones, and guys get a subconscious message that you are available and interested."

"That's ridiculous. You shouldn't believe everything that you see or hear on the internet."

Laleh shrugged. "Try it and see what works. I'd love to be able to validate or dismiss any of these tips, but for that, I will need to test them personally, and the only immortal boy my age in this entire village is already spoken for. He's in love with a girl that didn't transition yet. There are the Kra-ell boys, but they are too alien-looking and too intense. I'd rather stick to the immortals who look like humans." She grinned. "Very hot humans. Regrettably, I'm off limits until I'm seventeen, so all I can do is drool."

Arezoo shook her head. "Who are you and what have you done with my baby sister, who until recently still played with dolls?"

"The internet," Laleh said. "I realized that at my age, I should be much more aware of boys."

"You should do nothing of the sort." Now she sounded like her mother. "What I meant is that you shouldn't feel pressured to grow up too fast. If you still want to play with dolls, that's perfectly fine. We are destined to become immortals, so there is no rush to do anything. You can enjoy your childhood for as long as you want."

Laleh nodded. "I know. Do you want to know the real reason I still played with dolls at fifteen?"

Arezoo frowned. "Wasn't it because you enjoyed it?"

Laleh shook her head. "I knew that Father was looking to marry off all three of us, and I was scared that he was going to do it before I finished high school. I acted like a little girl so he wouldn't even think of that. But then we were taken, and our abductor didn't care what I acted like. He touched me as if I were a woman, but I didn't want his hands on me." She shuddered. "When we were rescued, I clung to my shield, pretending to be younger than I was, but when I started to feel safer, I dropped the act and started researching. I found a lot of help on the internet."

Arezoo felt guilty for not realizing that before. She'd been so focused on her own survival that she hadn't noticed her sister doing the same in her own way.

"You are so brave." Arezoo hugged her. "Braver than I am."

Laleh pulled away. "Are you still scared?"

Arezoo sighed. "I'm not scared, but I'm not ready to flirt or signal that I'm interested because I'm not. I can't think of a male that way without remembering what was done to me. To us. Drova doesn't understand that because she's never been in our situation, but you do."

Laleh nodded. "I do, but I won't let fear rule me. If I do, he wins. You know what I mean?"

"Yeah, I do." Arezoo sat on the bed. "But I'm not as strong as you."

It was strange to hear herself saying it. Arezoo had always thought that as the eldest, she had to be strong for her sisters, but she'd been wrong about Laleh. Her youngest sister had their mother's backbone, and she was much more calculated and crafty than Arezoo had ever suspected.

"You are the strongest of us," Laleh said. "You are just burdened with the weight of carrying us and Mother on your shoulders. You don't need to. Not anymore. Take care of yourself. Find out what makes you happy."

She chuckled. "When did you get so smart?"

"I told you. The internet, and also from talking to the clan's therapist. Vanessa is nothing like what you imagine a psychologist is. You should give her a try."

Arezoo winced. "She's busy, and there are many people who need her more than I do. When she's done with them, I'll put my name on her waiting list."

Laleh regarded her with eyes that were much older than they should be. "You always put everyone else's needs before your own, but whatever. I'm not going to talk you into calling Vanessa right now. Just give it some thought, okay?"

Arezoo nodded. "I will."

Laleh made a sound indicating she doubted it, then leaned to kiss Arezoo on the cheek and left the room.

By the time nine approached, Arezoo had changed outfits three times before returning to Laleh's original suggestion. She'd applied a little makeup, just mascara and lip gloss, and let her hair fall loose around her shoulders.

The doorbell's ringing sent her heart racing. She

grabbed her phone, put it in one pocket of her jeans and the lip gloss in the other, and headed for the door.

Donya had already let Drova in, and the Kra-ell girl standing in their living room looked nothing like the warrior woman Arezoo was familiar with.

Drova had gone through a jaw-dropping transformation.

Instead of her utilitarian ponytail, her black hair fell in soft curls around her shoulders, and it was clear that someone had styled it to look that way. She wore makeup that emphasized her huge, dark eyes, making them seem mysteriously beautiful rather than unnervingly large. Black jeans hugged her impossibly long legs, and a pink t-shirt that showed a strip of her extremely narrow midriff made her look almost breakable. A black leather jacket was thrown over it, completing the look.

"You look..." Arezoo searched for words. "Really nice. But isn't it too warm for a leather jacket?"

Drova grinned, the expression transforming her angular features. "It is, but isn't it cool? I've wanted one forever, ever since I saw Aliya wearing one. After I got my first pay as a Guardian in training, I ordered it, and it finally arrived today."

It suddenly occurred to Arezoo that beneath the alien features and the warrior vibe, Drova was just a teenage girl who got excited about leather jackets and spent time curling her hair for a night out.

"It is very cool," Arezoo agreed, feeling some of her

nervousness ease. "You look like you stepped out of a magazine or a movie set."

"Good movie or bad movie?"

"Definitely good. Like one of those action films where the heroine kicks ass and looks amazing doing it."

Drova preened. "That's exactly what I was going for. You look nice, too. Are you ready to go?"

"I am." Arezoo said goodbye to her mother, who seemed like she was clenching her teeth not to say anything.

She gave them a nod and a tight smile. "Enjoy your evening, girls."

As they started walking toward the new section of the village where the bar was located, Drova offered her a hand. "It's probably too dark for you to see."

There were no streetlights in the village, but the sky was clear and the moon provided enough illumination.

"I can see just fine, but thanks for the offer."

Drova pushed her hands into her pockets. "Are you nervous?"

"I am," Arezoo admitted.

"Everyone will be too busy trying to get Fenella's attention for readings to even notice you," Drova assured her. "And if anyone bothers you, I'll give them my scary Kra-ell look."

"You always look scary," Arezoo teased, then immediately worried that she had offended her friend.

But Drova just laughed. "Everyone knows it's just for show and that I'm adorable."

"Adorable might be pushing it."

"Striking? Memorable? Unforgettable?"

"Definitely unforgettable," Arezoo agreed.

As they neared the Hobbit, Arezoo could hear noise spilling out onto the street—laughter, conversation, the clink of glasses.

Her steps slowed.

When they got inside, the sounds intensified. The bar was packed, just as Drova had predicted.

Every table was occupied, and people stood in clusters wherever space allowed. The air smelled of alcohol and perfume and something indefinable that hinted at excitement.

"Wow," Arezoo breathed. "It's really crowded in here."

"Come on." Drova took her hand, using her height advantage to navigate through the clusters of people. "Let's get to the bar."

They ended up squeezed into a corner near the bar itself, with barely enough room to stand without pressing against strangers. Arezoo tried to make herself smaller, acutely aware of every accidental touch.

"What do you want to drink?" Drova asked, having to raise her voice over the noise.

"Something without alcohol," Arezoo said. "I believe it's called a mocktail?"

"On it." Drova turned to the bar, using her height to

catch the bartender's attention. Not Fenella because she was at the other end, holding court with some object in her hands, but the bar owner himself, who looked harried but happy.

While Drova ordered, Arezoo studied the faces of the patrons, most of whom she recognized from the café, but seeing them here, relaxed and laughing, was different.

"One virgin mojito for you." Drova pressed a glass into Arezoo's hand. "And a real one for me."

The drink was pretty, with mint leaves and lime floating in clear liquid. Arezoo took a tentative sip and found it refreshingly tart and sweet.

"Good?" Drova asked.

"Very."

"Ladies and gentlemen!" Fenella's voice rose above the noise. "Who's ready for some psychometric readings?"

The crowd cheered, and Arezoo found herself caught up in the energy. She watched as Fenella held up an old pocket watch.

"This distinguished timepiece," Fenella said dramatically, "has a confession to make. It's been living a double life!"

"Oh no," the watch's owner said with played-up concern. "What has it been up to?"

"By day, it keeps perfect time for important meet-ings and appointments," Fenella continued. "But by night..." She paused for effect. "It runs backwards, trying to return to the year 1887, when life was simpler and it didn't have to deal with daylight saving time!"

The crowd erupted in laughter, and even Arezoo giggled. The absurdity of it, the way Fenella delivered the lines with such conviction, was infectious. She didn't know that her newfound cousin was such a good performer.

It seemed that blood, no matter how diluted, was still thicker than water. Fenella and Jasmine both thrived on the adoration of a crowd.

"Furthermore," Fenella added, "it's been having an affair with the grandfather clock in the living room. They synchronize every midnight!"

"That hussy!" the owner exclaimed, playing along. "And here I thought we had something special!"

As the performance continued, the tension in Arezoo's shoulders eased. This wasn't the den of iniquity her mother had probably imagined. It was just people having fun, laughing at silly stories, and enjoying each other's company.

"She is amazing." Drova nudged her. "Do you want to hand her an object?"

"I didn't bring anything," Arezoo admitted. "But maybe—"

The words died in her throat as the door opened and Ruvon walked in. He stood by the entrance, scanning the crowd, and when his eyes landed on her, his face brightened.

"Did you tell him I was going to be here?" Arezoo hissed at Drova.

"I might have mentioned that to someone," Drova said innocently. "You know how news travels in the village."

"Drova!"

"What? He's nice. You're nice. Nice people should talk to each other."

Ruvon was already making his way toward them, and Arezoo's flight instinct kicked into overdrive. "Let's go. Before he gets here."

"Not a chance." Drova's voice turned firm. "You wanted to come to the bar. You're here. You don't get to run away just because a guy who likes you showed up."

"But—"

"No buts. You need to develop a backbone, girl. I guarantee that you can survive talking to a guy for a few minutes. You've talked to him plenty at the playground."

Before Arezoo could argue some more, Ruvon reached them, looking nervous, which was usual for him, or maybe just when he was around her.

"Hey," he said, his voice barely audible over the bar noise, shoving his hands into his pockets. "It's really crowded tonight."

"Everyone wants to see Fenella perform before she leaves for Egypt," Drova said. "Can I get you a drink?"

"I'll get it myself," Ruvon said quickly.

As he turned toward the bar, Arezoo grabbed Drova's arm. "Let's go now. Before he comes back."

She was dimly aware of how ridiculously she was

acting, and that it would be terribly rude and hurtful to give Ruvon the slip, but she was driven by an irrational need to flee.

"No way, Arezoo. Ruvon is just a dude—a shy, awkward dude who thinks you're special. Give him a chance. Talk to him. It's not like anyone expects you to go home with him."

Arezoo nearly choked on her drink. "Don't even say things like that to me. You are fueling my panic attack."

Not really, but maybe a guilt trip would get Drova to be more cooperative.

"Five minutes," Drova bargained. "Give him five minutes. If you still want to leave after that, we'll go. But first, finish your drink and watch Fenella make someone's car keys confess to secret dreams of being a guitar pick."

Arezoo snorted despite herself. "She said that?"

Drova nodded. "According to Fenella, that one over there," Drova pointed to where Fenella was holding up a key ring, "wants to run away and join a rock band."

"That's funny and completely ridiculous."

"That's the point. The ridiculousness of her readings is what makes them fun. If she gave real readings, I bet they would be boring because, let's face it, most people are boring."

Arezoo took another sip of her mock mojito, using the glass as a shield. Around them, the crowd laughed at another of Fenella's silly revelations.

Five minutes. She could manage for five more minutes.

"Okay," she said quietly.

"Okay?"

"Five minutes. But if I want to leave after that—"

"We leave," Drova promised.

Arezoo nodded and turned her attention back to Fenella's performance, determined to focus on the entertainment rather than the anxiety churning in her stomach. She'd taken the first step by coming here. Now she just had to survive the next five minutes, one second at a time, even if it involved talking to Ruvon.

KIAN

The war room in the underground structure beneath the village was once again in use.

Maps and surveillance photos were tacked up in neat rows on the wall, and grainy drone footage of terrorists entering and leaving their rented houses was displayed on a large screen, each occupying a quarter of the available landscape.

Due to the scope of the threat Kian had assembled an extensive team, and they were all seated around the conference table, waiting for Onegus to give them updates about the information that had been collected so far.

In the meantime, Turner was jotting down notes on his ever-present yellow pad, Aru and Dagor were sipping coffee, William and Roni were conferring over an open laptop, and Andrew was looking at the intel pinups lining the wall. All the head Guardians were in attendance as well, their grim faces mirroring Kian's own. In addition, Max and Magnus had been invited to take part in the meeting.

The two were on their way to becoming head Guardians themselves, and Onegus had decided that they should be there.

"Let's do this." Onegus stood and pointed at the screen that was showing real-time footage. "Thanks to the overhead drones and Dagor's tiny spy transmitting from the inside, the intelligence gathering was relatively easy, and we have a lot of information on the enemy. Fortunately, Rashid's been moving between all four cells, and the spy drone attached to him enabled us to have operational internal pictures of all four locations."

On screen, the interior of an upscale mansion appeared; it was clear as if someone had filmed it for a documentary. Men moved about, a name tag hovering over each one's head, added by the software on Dagor's laptop. When clicked, a pull-down menu appeared with all the information gathered about the person, and the profiles were updated in real time.

Onegus continued. "The Doomers are running the entire operation. The human terrorists, including our friend Rashid, are essentially puppets."

"Thralled?" Andrew asked from his position near the maps.

"It seems more fundamental than that," Onegus said. "This is sustained, systematic brainwashing, which means that we cannot override it with our own thralling. We've listened and watched enough exchanges to realize that the Doomers are using a combination of thralling, ideological reinforcement, and fear."

"That's what Navuh has always done," Kian said. "What surprises me is that the technique was taught to the rank and file. Doesn't it make them realize that they are being manipulated in the same way?"

"People are dumb," Anandur said. "Doomers and humans alike are very easily manipulated, and Navuh is an expert at it. They all believe in his so-called cause and are willing not only to kill for it but also to die for it."

"The humans are almost irrelevant," Turner offered. "Every major decision, every tactical choice, comes from the Doomers. The assets, which is how they refer to the Revolutionary Guards, are true believers who don't even realize they're being controlled. Our focus should be on them. Neutralize the Doomers and the rest will fall like dominoes."

"Let's see the explosives cache," Kian said.

Onegus switched the display. The image that appeared evoked several juicy curses. The walls of a basement room were lined with enough explosives to level several city blocks.

"Combined, there is enough there to kill over a hundred thousand people," Onegus said. "And that's a conservative estimate. The concert is just the opening act. While everyone is still reeling from that, their next target is a shopping center during peak hours, then the airport, and lastly the port. The idea is to break the spirit of the nation and show them that nowhere is safe, and that terror can strike anywhere, anytime. They are hoping to paralyze the population with fear and deliver a major economic blow. That's why they chose Los Angeles. It's the second-largest metropolitan economy in the United States, following New York, but since it's more spread out, it's easier to hide in. Moreover, they have already struck New York. They want to outdo Bin Laden."

Bhathian nodded. "They want maximum psycho-logical impact. Hit when people feel safest, then hit again while they're terrified and vulnerable."

"Precisely," Onegus agreed. "The concert is in eleven days. The next attack after that is scheduled to follow within forty-eight hours while the city is still reeling from the first strike."

"The Brotherhood's signature move," Anandur murmured. "Create chaos, then step into the power vacuum."

Kian walked over to the wall of maps, studying the red pins. Four cells, four locations spread across the sprawling city. They would need to hit them all simul-taneously. Any delay and the others would scatter to the winds.

"Any thoughts?" The question was for everyone, but collectively, all eyes turned to Turner.

"Four strike teams," Turner lifted his eyes after a quick glance at his notes. "Striking simultaneously with perfect coordination is a must. There is no margin for error." After a short pause to collect his thoughts or to let others interject, Turner continued in his dispassionate tone, "We must deploy over-whelming force to prevent anyone slipping by us, or, worse, getting to the explosives before us."

"I've been working on team compositions," Onegus said, pulling up another display. "It would have made things significantly easier if we had four compellers, neutralizing the humans and immortals at once, but we only have one in the force, unless we can get Toven and Kalugal's help. Otherwise, we should use Drova with the team taking out the concert cell. That's the most immediate threat."

Kian shook his head. "I don't want her partici-pating in this. We used her in the pedophile ring bust because there were children involved, and we couldn't risk the Doomers using them as shields. That's not the case here. We've been dealing with Doomers for centuries without the benefit of compulsion, we can keep doing that like we've always done."

Onegus nodded. "I also wish we had four Yamanus, but since we have only one, we need cover stories for the other three teams."

"Not necessarily," Turner said. "What's the driving time between all these locations?"

Onegus's calculating gaze indicated he understood what Turner was suggesting. "Two hours should do it. Yamanu can drive from place to place, putting entire city blocks into a deep sleep, including the human minions working for the Doomers. That will make our job easier."

Kian looked at Yamanu. "Do you see a problem with that? Will you be able to repeat the feat four consecutive times?"

The Guardian stood and stepped up to the map to better understand the distances involved and the routes he'd need to take, and to get a better sense of the geographic and urban nature of the areas he would need to thrall, while everyone waited patiently for his assessment.

Turning back to Kian, Yamanu nodded. "I can handle it. I suggest we predefine the routes and have Roni on standby in case we need to reroute traffic or any other agency that may hinder my ability to make it to all four locations in the time allotted. Having another car driving the route with me might be prudent, just in case the car I'm in is disabled."

"Great points, Yamanu. Roni, can you please meet with Yamanu to coordinate?" Kian asked.

"Naturally." Roni smiled at Yamanu. "Don't worry. I'll have you covered."

"What about government resources?" Kian asked, looking at Andrew. "Should we let them know?"

"If we fail or succeed only partially, I will inform the local authorities. They will need to block off the areas and get a massive emergency response put together."

With so many tons of advanced explosives under the control of terrorists, many things could go sideways, fast.

"So the humans, both the terrorists and the neighbors, will be out of the picture courtesy of Yamanu," Max noted. "That leaves the three or four Doomers at each location for us to deal with. Should be fun!"

The comment got laughs out of some of the Guardians, and Kian noticed the shadow of a smile on Turner's face.

"How many Guardians can you spare for each location?" Turner asked Onegus.

The chief consulted his notes. "Considering we'll need at least three transports per site, need to secure Julian in the warehouse where we'll be scanning the scum for trackers, and still need to protect the keep and the village, the maximum team size we can allocate to each cell is twelve Guardians including the team leader."

"You insult us, chief." Anandur held a hand to his chest, feigning great offense. "Are you suggesting that twelve of us are needed to take down three Doomers?"

Turner answered for the chief. "We cannot allow any of the Doomers or Revolutionary Guards to slip by us and disappear into the night. We also cannot allow enough time for anyone to get to the explosives, which might be rigged and ready to trigger. That means securing the perimeter, which means more Guardians than would be needed just to neutralize three or four Doomers. We also have to be ready for the unexpected. So, if twelve is the best we can do, I'll take it. If we could spare twenty per cell, though, I would have preferred it."

"Actually, we can improve our odds still. While I

can't give you twenty Guardians per cell, I can give you twelve that will perform as twenty, or better," Kian said.

"Don't say Kra-ell," Max murmured.

Kian smiled. "No, not the Kra-ell, though they've certainly proved themselves. They are not trained for these kinds of operations." Kian looked around to see if anyone had picked up on what he was thinking. "Guardians have bested the Kra-ell once, and they can certainly best these Doomers."

That was an elephant-sized hint, and Kian could see they all got it.

"Hell yeah!" Anandur enthused. "It's been a while since we played with the exoskeleton suits. I hear we have upgraded them lately." Anandur raised an eyebrow, looking at William.

"Yes, we improved the electronic package, the battery efficiency, and the external coating. These suits are now barely visible at night. We used a special matte coating that is almost light inert."

"We will need to train on the new features and get comfortable with the suits anew. It has been a while," Bhathian said.

"I will arrange for a two-day refresher for every-one." Onegus turned to William. "Can you spare a couple of hours to walk us through the changes you implemented?"

William nodded. "Tell me when and where and I'm there."

"There's the issue of the aftermath," Kri said. "Even

if we successfully neutralize all four cells, the Brotherhood will know it was us because no one else can pull off an operation like that against Doomers."

"They know we are here," Kian said. "It will confirm it for them, but I'm not too worried."

Kian had already decided he wanted Navuh to know who had thwarted his evil plans and let him wonder how the clan had discovered them. He wanted the despot to lose sleep, wondering who'd betrayed him and how.

"We may be able to clean up the scene so it looks like there was no struggle if we can neutralize all of the Doomers before they can react. But that is not likely to happen. Besides, it is time to put the Brotherhood on notice—come too close and suffer the consequences. In this city, we call the shots. I want Navuh to get this message loud and clear. Moving forward, he is no longer the hunter but the hunted. We will hunt the Brotherhood at will."

Onegus arched a brow. "We didn't hunt them. We discovered the plot by chance."

Kian smiled. "That's the beauty of this. Imagine the resulting paranoia. They will be running around looking for the traitors."

Given the chief's thoughtful nod and Max's grin, it seemed that he was not the only one thinking that was a good idea.

39

FENELLA

The bar was nearly empty despite it being the weekend, which was just as well since Fenella's heart hadn't been in her performances tonight. She'd fumbled through a few half-hearted readings, telling one Guardian his wallet harbored secret dreams of becoming a purse and another that his car key was conspiring with his phone to hide from him every morning. The usual laughter had been forced, the energy flat.

The Guardians had been quiet and brooding, preparing mentally for the mission, and everyone else had sensed that something was off. Those who didn't know about the discovery of the most evil plan she could imagine must have attributed her bad mood to her having a fight with Din or some other inconsequential thing.

If only it were that simple.

Fenella wiped down the bar with mechanical movements, her mind churning with the snippets of conversation she'd overheard throughout the evening. A Lasusa concert. Thousands of kids. Bombs. The words kept circling in her head, making her stomach twist with each pass.

Monsters. That's what they were. Not the humans or even the Doomers themselves—she'd learned enough to know that most were victims of their twisted upbringing and their leaders' brainwashing, but the ones orchestrating this? Devils in human form. Satan's minions were planning to murder children for their sick purposes, whatever those might be.

In her opinion, the aim was simply to propagate evil and cause suffering.

"Another round," Max slurred from his spot at the bar, pushing his empty glass toward her.

He and Din both were looking properly sloshed. Max's usually perfectly styled hair was disheveled, his shirt untucked, and Din had that loose-limbed quality of the thoroughly drunk. They'd been at it for hours, putting away enough alcohol to fell a small army.

"You two are cut off," she said, though she was already reaching for the bottle. Who was she to judge? The little she'd pieced together made her want to join them in oblivion.

"Nonsense," Din declared, his Scottish accent thicker than usual. "We're merely... adequately lubricated for important discussions."

Max snorted. "Important. Right. Your delusions of grandeur are not important to anyone other than you. You are not some kind of ancient warrior god."

"Not a god," Din corrected with the pedantic precision of the very drunk. "But I was quite formidable in my day, and you know it. Do you remember the Battle of Calleh? Not on the battlefield, mind you, you were busy keeping our people safe from the aftermath. But the skirmishes that followed?" He made a slashing motion with his hand. "I took more than my share of heads."

Fenella's hand stilled on the bottle. She'd never heard Din talk about his past like this. The professor who graded papers and got excited about pottery shards had apparently been, at some point, cutting off heads in the Scottish Highlands.

"That was nearly five hundred years ago." Max laughed. "Modern warfare is nothing like the Highland raids you remember. You can't just charge in with a claymore anymore."

"I've kept up with the times," Din insisted, swaying slightly on his barstool. "I know how to use firearms. I've been to the range."

"The range." Max's voice dripped with condescension. "Shooting paper targets is not the same as engaging Doomers at close quarters. They know how to kill us."

Din snorted. "And we know how to kill them. So what?"

Fenella poured herself a generous measure of whiskey, not bothering with ice. If they were going to have this conversation, she needed fortification. The burn down her throat was welcome.

"I should help," Din said stubbornly. "You need every able-bodied—"

"We have enough bodies, and they are well trained." Max cut him off. "You think you can just strap on an exoskeleton and become a superhero?"

"Exoskeleton?" Fenella interjected. "Seriously? Like bugs?"

Max turned to her, his eyes taking a moment to focus. "Those are military-grade powered armor suits. Makes us as strong as the Kra-ell, actually stronger. We fought them while wearing those suits. They are bulletproof, too. But they're not easy to operate." He looked back at Din. "I have plenty of experience in operating a suit, and yet I spent all day yesterday and today relearning how to move in one without putting my fist through a wall or tripping over my own feet. The strength amplification is incredible, but it takes finesse to control."

"I can learn," Din insisted drunkenly.

"In time, maybe." Max shook his head, the movement making him grip the bar for balance. "We're hitting them tomorrow night, Din. Tomorrow. There's no time for you to learn, no margin for error. One person who doesn't know what they're doing could get the whole team killed." He shook his head again.

"Why am I even entertaining your delusions instead of going to sleep?"

Tomorrow night.

Fenella's blood chilled.

The attack was tomorrow night. She'd known that, but hearing it said aloud made it real in a way that contracted her chest.

"Tell him," Max said, turning to her. "Tell him he's being an idiot."

She looked at Din, seeing past the drunken bravado to the frustration beneath. He wanted to help, to protect, to be useful. It was who he was at his core—someone who took care of others. But Max was right, and Din's good intentions didn't qualify him for modern warfare.

"Din," she said softly, reaching out to touch his hand. "There are other ways for you to help. You're not a fighter anymore, nor do you want to be." She smiled. "Remember? You never liked being on the force."

"You just don't think I'm capable," he said, making a pouty face that made her want to laugh.

She stifled the urge. "I think you're very capable, but I also think you're drunk and talking nonsense. Tell me about these battles you fought. Tell me about the glory of taking heads."

She hoped it would be enough to get him off the subject, but he was apparently too drunk to think straight.

"It wasn't glorious." His jaw tightened. "It was necessary."

"You see? You didn't enjoy being a soldier, and suddenly you remember those horrible days as if they were the highlight of your existence."

"After the battle, the Highlands were in chaos. Whole families were slaughtered, women and children put to the sword. We couldn't save them all, but we tried."

Max had gone quiet.

He'd been there, fought alongside Din.

"There was this village," Din continued, his words slightly slurred, but his eyes distant. "They came back for the women and children. We were there that time." He took a long swallow of whiskey. "Seven of us against thirty of them. But we were immortals, and they were human. The odds were stacked in our favor."

"What happened?" Fenella asked even though she really didn't want to hear any more gory details.

"We killed them all." The words were flat, matter-of-fact. "Had to. If even one escaped to report unnaturally strong men defending the village, it would have brought a witch hunt down on us. We made sure none escaped. I personally took eight heads that day."

The bar was silent except for the hum of the refrigerators.

"There was this girl who couldn't have been more than fifteen," Din continued. "She watched from her doorway as I cut down a soldier who couldn't have been more than three years older than her. I will never forget the look in her eyes, gratitude and horror.

That's what glory looks like. That's what being a warrior means. Doing terrible things because the alternative is worse."

"Exactly," Max said, lifting his glass. "And that's why you can't come tomorrow, because you remember their faces. Because it costs you something every time. The Doomers? It costs them nothing. They've been trained since birth to feel nothing but hate and loathing. They kill with glee and laugh as they torture."

Din looked like he wanted to argue, but Fenella saw the moment he accepted the truth of Max's words.

His shoulders slumped. "I hate feeling useless."

"You're not useless," Fenella said. "You're just not a soldier, and neither am I. That doesn't make us less valuable."

"She's right." Max took a long swig from his drink. "We all have our roles to play, and those roles are only somewhat flexible. Guardians, even those who retired, train for a full month every year to stay updated and in shape, but you quit the force so long ago that you don't have the benefit of even that. My role is to put on that exoskeleton tomorrow night and make sure those bombs never go off. Yours is to be here when we get back, preferably with a bottle of very expensive whiskey."

"When you get back," Fenella repeated. "You say that like it's guaranteed."

Max's smile was sharp. "It is. We've been doing this for a long time, Fenella. We know what we're doing, and the exoskeletons are extra insurance. They make us practically invincible and unstoppable."

"Why not use them all the time then?" she asked.

"They are cumbersome, and sometimes speed and agility are more important than power and dependability. They're also not exactly subtle—hard to do undercover work when you're wearing one of those. We look like alien invaders in them."

Fenella poured another round despite her earlier threat to cut them off. They all needed it tonight.

"Tell me it's going to work," she said. "Tell me those kids at the concert are going to be safe."

"They're going to be safe," Max said with absolute conviction. "Yamanu is going to put entire neighborhoods to sleep so we can work without interference from the neighbors, and the humans in those cells are going to be deep asleep as well. We'll go in, neutralize the Doomers, and secure the explosives. By Monday morning, it'll be like the cells never existed."

"What happens to the Doomers?" Din asked.

Max's expression darkened. "They go to the dungeon for questioning, and after that, it's up to Kian what he wants to do with them. The humans are disposable."

The casual discussion of violence should have bothered Fenella more than it did. But all she could think about was those kids at the concert, excited to see their favorite singer, having no idea how close they would come to death.

"I understand Din's frustration," she said. "I also

wish I could do more. My stupid bar tricks feel pretty worthless compared to what you're doing."

"Your 'stupid bar tricks' make people happy," Din said, reaching for her hand. "That's not worthless. That's... that's necessary. We need joy to balance the darkness."

"A drunk philosopher," Max observed. "The most annoying kind."

"Better than a belligerent drunk," Din shot back.

"I'm not belligerent. I'm righteously determined."

"You're both ridiculous," Fenella said, but she was smiling.

The banter was helping, easing the knot of tension in her chest. Tomorrow night, Max and the other Guardians would risk their lives to save thousands. Tonight, she could pour drinks and pretend the world wasn't teetering on a knife edge.

"One more round," Max said. "Then I really need to get some sleep."

She wondered why Kyra was letting him get drunk in the first place, and why she wasn't there to keep an eye on him, but perhaps because she was a fighter herself, she understood that he needed this.

"One more," Fenella agreed, reaching for the bottle. As she poured, she caught Din watching her with those intense eyes that seemed less clouded than they should be, given the copious amounts of whiskey he'd consumed.

"What?" she asked.

"I love you," he said.

She smiled, the words she wanted to say in return lodged in her throat like always, held there by irrational fear. Instead, she leaned across the bar and kissed him, tasting whiskey and promise.

"I know," she whispered against his lips.

Max cleared his throat. "Still here. Still conscious. Still not interested in watching you two make out."

Fenella pulled back with a smirk. "Sorry."

"Don't be. Just save it for when I'm gone." He downed his whiskey in one go and stood, swaying slightly on his feet. "And on that note, I'm out of here before Kyra sends a search party after me."

"Max," Fenella called after him as he neared the door. When he turned back, she said, "Be safe."

His cocky grin softened into something more genuine. "Always am, love. Always am."

After Max left, the bar felt too quiet without him, too empty with just the two of them and Atzil cleaning up in the kitchen.

"He's going to be fine," Din said, though she wasn't sure if he was trying to convince her or himself.

"I know." She didn't, not really, but what else could she say? That she was scared? That the thought of losing any of them made her throat clog with panic?

"Close up time," Atzil called. "You two don't look like you'll be any help cleaning tonight. Do you need help getting home?"

"I'm fine," Din said, though his attempt to stand suggested otherwise.

Fenella rounded the bar and slipped under his arm,

371

steadying him. "Come on, Professor. Let's get you home." She cast Atzil an apologetic glance. "Sorry about not helping, boss. I can come back after I put Din in bed."

He waved a dismissive hand. "Don't worry about it. Get your man home."

MAX

The exoskeleton hummed as Max powered it up. Through the suit's enhanced optics, part of William's latest upgrades, he could see heat signatures inside—three Doomers moving on the upper floors, and twelve humans scattered throughout, deep in Yamanu-induced sleep.

"Strike One in position," he said into the comm.

"Strike Two in position," came the response from Bhathian's team across the city.

"Strike Three ready," Anandur confirmed.

"Strike Four standing by," Magnus reported.

Max checked his chronometer: 0059 hours. The neighborhood slept under Yamanu's influence, a blanket thrall that would hold until he made another round through the four locations and released it. If he did nothing, the thrall would eventually weaken and evaporate, but it might take days, and that was dangerous. The less time the humans spent sleeping unnaturally, the better.

"Simultaneous breach in thirty seconds," Onegus's voice came through the command channel. "Start the countdown on my mark. Now!"

In addition to himself, Max's team included eleven Guardians in matching exoskeletons, their armor making them look like something out of a science fiction movie. The recently added camouflage of a matte black surface absorbed light, turning them into shadows with substance. He still wasn't entirely comfortable with the servo-assisted movement, but two days of intensive training had given him enough proficiency to work with.

"Ten seconds," he told his team.

Breach team Alpha, headed by Conrac was in charge of the basement and securing the explosives. Thar's team was tasked with securing the perimeter, and Zolen's breaking in through the back. Max and his team were about to charge through the front and head straight for the Doomers.

It had all been rehearsed enough times for each Guardian to know precisely what his task was, but things never went according to plan, and shit happened more often than not.

"Five seconds."

Max gripped the specialized battering ram with the suit's mechanical fingers like it weighed nothing. Even if the door was reinforced with steel, which many of the doors in this upscale neighborhood were, it wouldn't stand a chance.

"Three... two... one... Breach!"

The ram connected with devastating force, and the door exploded inward, torn from its hinges. Max flowed through the opening, his movements relatively smooth despite the bulk of the exoskeleton.

The interior was dark, but the suit's optics rendered everything in sharp clarity. Not that immortal eyesight needed the enhancement, but it was nice to see so clearly.

Expensive furniture, Persian rugs, the trappings of wealth hiding a nest of killers. Two human guards were slumped in chairs by the entrance, lost in Yamanu's thrall.

The suit's feed indicated that the basement and back teams breached successfully as well. The visuals superimposed on a corner of his visor were another benefit of using the suit. No comm confirmations were needed.

He leaped directly to the second-floor gallery, his men landing with loud thuds all around him. It was a calculated risk since their combined weight could overcome the gallery's structural supports, but the element of surprise was worth the risk.

Not even three seconds had elapsed since the door was breached, and the Doomers were already on them.

They were fast. But not fast enough.

Max's reflexes kicked in, the suit responding to his

commands with just the slightest delay. He leaped, bringing his arm up just in time to block a blow aimed at his head. Without the suit's helmet, it would have likely knocked him off his feet, but with it, it would have been an inconvenience that may have given his opponent a momentary edge. Not something he was willing to do.

"Surprise, asshole," Max growled, driving his armored fist into the Doomer's solar plexus. The impact lifted the immortal off his feet, sending him crashing through a wall.

"Contact with two more Doomers, second floor, east wing!" Thar's voice came through the comm.

"Moving to support," Raith confirmed.

Max pursued his target through the hole in the wall. The Doomer should have been knocked out, but he was already rolling to his feet.

Tough bastard.

They collided in the center of what had been a library and reading room. The Doomer was fast, trained, and enhanced beyond what his immortal strength should have afforded him. Max suspected drugs, but even though they could make the guy stronger, faster, and more resilient, they couldn't protect his body from the massive damage of the amplified force behind every punch Max delivered.

The problem was that Max was slower with the suit, and the Doomer could simply outrun him, but the guy wasn't smart enough to exercise that option and charged.

"This is going to be fun." Max simply lifted him bodily and slammed him through a desk.

Wood exploded into splinters. The Doomer tried to roll away, but Max's suit electronics and algorithm let him track the movement. His armored boot came down where the Doomer's head had been a microsecond before, cracking the floor.

"Don't play with your prey," Onegus's amused voice came through the com. "Neutralize him and bag him."

"Let me have my fun, chief. An opportunity like this doesn't come often."

"You're not human," the Doomer snarled in accented English, his fangs fully extended.

"Neither are you," Max replied, catching the knife the Doomer threw at him with an armored grip. "But I'm better equipped."

He tossed the knife aside and head-butted the Doomer, the helmet crushing the warrior's nose in a spray of blood. As the Doomer reeled, Max followed up with a precisely measured strike to the temple— enough to incapacitate, not enough to shatter. He didn't want brain matter on his visor.

Besides, they needed to bring the Doomers in for interrogation.

The guy dropped like a rag doll.

"One down," Max reported, producing zip-cuffs designed to hold immortals. "Status?"

"Still engaged!" Thar said. Sounds of combat filtered through the helmet's speakers.

"Seems like I'm not the only one playing with my prey."

Max headed in the direction of the noise as fast as the exoskeleton allowed, its weight making stealth impossible.

He found Thar and Raith locked in combat with the remaining two Doomers in an upstairs hallway. The exoskeletons should have made it a walk in the park, but these Doomers were obviously on some enhancing drugs that made them stronger, faster, and more determined to keep fighting.

They were also smarter, using their unimpeded speed and confined space to limit the exoskeleton's advantages.

Max charged ahead like a battering ram.

The Doomer engaging Thar saw him coming and tried to evade, but Max's momentum was unstoppable, and they went through a wall together, plaster and wood exploding around them.

They tumbled into a bedroom where two humans were obliviously asleep in their beds. Max exploded downward, driving the Doomer into the floor hard enough to crack through it. A quick strike to the jaw, enhanced by the suit's augmented force, and the second Doomer was out.

"Clear!" Raith called from the hallway. "Third target subdued!"

"Basement team, report," Max ordered as he secured his prisoner.

"Holy shit, boss." Conrac's voice was tight with stress. "You need to see this."

Max's blood chilled. "The explosives?"

"Enough to level six city blocks. And it's all rigged. Dead man's switch on the wall. If we'd come in hot without knowing..."

"Don't touch anything," Max ordered. "I'm coming down."

He found his team in a basement that looked like a terrorist's wet dream. The walls were lined with military-grade explosives, enough to turn the concert venue into a crater. But worse was the detonation system—sophisticated, with multiple redundancies and what looked like a pressure switch connected to the door, which mercifully his guys carefully bypassed.

"Can you disarm it?" Max asked.

Darven, their explosives expert, was already removing the exoskeleton gloves to examine the system. "Maybe. Give me twenty minutes of absolute silence. I need you all to clear out."

"You've got it." Max switched channels. "Strike One to Command. We have the concert cell secured. Three Doomers in custody. Explosives are rigged with anti-tamper devices. Darven is working on it. The ones in the other locations are probably rigged too. Proceed with caution."

"Copy that, Strike One," Onegus said. "Strike Three has already reported a similar setup. Strikes Two and Four report clean captures and explosives secured. Theirs weren't rigged."

Max allowed himself a moment of satisfaction. Three cells down, one to go. But they weren't done yet.

"Movement!" Thar's voice crackled through the comm. "Someone's coming—shit, they're not affected by the sleep!"

Max's head snapped up. A fourth Doomer? They'd only counted three on surveillance.

"Positions!" he barked, moving toward the stairs. "Conrac, stay with Darven. Allow no one through this door till he says it's safe. Everyone else, with me!"

They met the newcomer in the mansion's foyer—definitely a Doomer.

Max expected him to turn around and flee, or pull out a gun and shoot, but the guy unexpectedly charged right at him instead.

What the hell?

Maybe the drugs they were on addled their brains.

As if to confirm his suspicion, the Doomer laughed maniacally. "The Brotherhood will always win, you alien scum. You think you've won? This is just the beginning."

Max wanted to laugh. The idiot really thought they were alien invaders? It was almost worth it to let him escape so he could bring the news to his bosses.

The Doomer moved fast, but Max was ready, his armored fist meeting the guy's face with devastating force that had him flying backward. He landed on his feet though, blood streaming from his ruined nose. "I will kill you! Demon!"

"Look who's talking." Max engaged again.

The fight was different—this Doomer was craftier, using techniques Max had not encountered before. He went for joints, trying to damage the exoskeleton's servo mechanisms.

"The bombs here are nothing," he hissed, going for psychological warfare. "There are many more. We have hundreds of cells, thousands of bombs. You can't stop us."

Max knew it was a lie, an attempt to distract him. But for a split second, doubt crept in. What if they'd missed something?

That momentary pause was all his opponent needed. The Doomer's fangs found a gap where only a thin membrane covered his neck. Pain flared as they penetrated, drawing blood and about to pump venom.

Not going to happen.

Max triggered the exoskeleton's electrical discharge. Another upgrade from William. It coursed through the armor's surface, channeled directly through the Doomer's fangs, and everywhere he was touching the suit.

The guy convulsed as his nervous system overloaded.

"Shocking, isn't it?" Max quipped as his opponent collapsed, twitching.

He made a mental note to personally thank William for this feature.

"Command, we have one more Doomer to add to our collection. He wasn't on our intel."

"That's concerning," Onegus said. "There might be another cell we are not aware of. Bag him. We'll sort it out later. Make sure the explosives are disarmed."

The additional Doomer had taken Max's mind off that issue, but now he was back to stressing over that.

The next fifteen minutes passed like hours while Darven worked on the explosives.

In the meantime, Max and his team stored the Doomers in a specially reinforced transport van. They, along with the sleeping terrorists in a second transport, would be taken to a warehouse where Julian would scan them for trackers, and their clothing and devices would be stored in secure, signal-blocking containers. All the Doomers were injected with tranquilizers to keep them under till they could be placed in holding cells in the keep's dungeon.

It occurred to Max that they might be running out of space there.

Good times.

"Got it," Darven finally announced, sagging with relief. "We can get in and start moving the explosives out."

"Outstanding work," Max said. "Strike One to all teams. Concert cell fully secured."

They loaded the explosives into a truck that would proceed to a warehouse located far from any populated areas.

As dawn approached, Max stood in the empty mansion, surveying the damage. Broken walls, shattered furniture—the detritus of violence. But no bodies.

All in a night's work.

41

KIAN

ian's eyes darted from one screen to the next as he monitored four simultaneous operations across Los Angeles. Beside him, Onegus, Turner, Andrew, William, and Roni did the same.

"Strike Three to Command," Bhathian's voice came through the speakers. "Site secured. Three Doomers, fourteen humans in custody. Explosives located and disarmed. No complications."

"Copy that, Strike Three," Onegus responded. "Load the transports and clear the site."

One corner of Kian's mouth lifted in a smile. Trust Bhathian to make it sound routine, as if neutralizing a terrorist cell was no more challenging than a morning training exercise.

"Strike One reports similar success," Onegus updated, glancing at his screens. "Max's team encountered an unexpected additional Doomer."

Andrew leveled his gaze at the chief. "That wasn't in our intelligence."

"No, it wasn't." Onegus's jaw tightened. "Either our surveillance missed him, or he arrived after Dagor recalled the spy drone. It could also mean there is a fifth cell we are unaware of. We need to interrogate these Doomers as soon as possible so we can find out. We don't have the luxury of missing any of them."

Kian nodded. "We are heading to the keep first thing tomorrow morning."

Onegus chuckled. "I know it's hard to tell in the underground what time it is, but it's already morning."

"Let me rephrase that," Kian said. "As soon as the Doomers are secured in the dungeon, you and I are heading to the keep. Neither of us is going to sleep until we know for sure that we are not missing another cell loaded with explosives."

Before the chief could respond, another voice crackled through the comm system.

"Strike Four to Command." Magnus's tone was all business. "We have the site secured. I'm happy to report that there's significant structural damage. Some of the guys got overly enthusiastic."

Kian couldn't help but smile. Talk about sending a message to Navuh...

"Define significant," Onegus said.

"Structural integrity is questionable. Several walls were destroyed, with at least two of them being load-bearing. Additionally, one of the Doomers attempted to trigger the explosives manually. Dustin stopped him, but it was close. If he'd been half a second slower..."

The unfinished sentence hung in the air. The explosives in each cell could level several city blocks. If even one had detonated, the death toll would have been catastrophic.

"Understood, Strike Four," Onegus said. "Good work. Special thanks to Dustin from all of us."

"What about Strike Two?" Kian said, noting they hadn't heard from Anandur's team yet.

"Strike Two, copy?" Onegus repeated.

Static filled the war room for several heartbeats before Anandur's voice came through. "Strike Two is still engaged. Facing heavier resistance than expected. These Doomers are on some kind of enhancing drugs and better trained than the others."

Kian exchanged a look with Onegus. "Clarify."

"Four Doomers, not three," Anandur reported. Sounds of combat filtered through—gun shots, crashes, grunts, the distinctive whine of exoskeleton servos under strain. "They must have seen us coming because they were ready for us. Probably perimeter cameras that the crew outside didn't catch."

"Do you need reinforcements?" Onegus asked.

"Negative." A crash echoed through the comm, followed by Anandur's grunt. "We've got—shit, watch the explosives! Secure that detonator!"

As the comm cut to static, Kian found himself standing, though he didn't remember rising from his chair. Every instinct screamed at him to suit up and join the Guardians in the field, even though it was entirely irrational.

By now, he should have gotten used to observing missions from a distance instead of being right there with his Guardians, but whenever things went south, he felt this irrational urge to be there and help.

As long seconds passed, Kian could hear his own heartbeat, steady despite the adrenaline coursing through his system.

"Strike Two to Command." Anandur's voice returned, steadier now. "Site secured. Four Doomers in custody, one seriously injured but alive. Brundar took some damage to his exoskeleton, but he's functional. Explosives secured, but barely so. One of the bastards had his hand on the trigger when Marco tackled him."

"Anyone else hurt?" Onegus asked.

"None. But I have to admit that I was thankful for the exoskeleton. I don't know what they were on, but they were a challenge even with the suits. Without them, we would have had a much harder time."

"Wrap up the operation as planned and clear with your team," the chief instructed. "Good work. We'll see you all at the debriefing."

As Anandur acknowledged the order, Kian turned to study the wall-mounted map of Los Angeles. Four red pins marked the neutralized cells. Four disasters averted. But his mind was already racing ahead.

"Enhanced Doomers," he murmured. "Do you think it's systemic or the locals dipping their fingers into the drug cookie jar?"

"They weren't expecting us," Turner said. "So, they had no reason to get jacked up. I don't know what game they are playing, but we will soon find out."

Navuh's every move was calculated, part of some larger strategy. There had to be a reason for this.

"What's the status on explosive removal?" Kian asked.

Onegus checked the screens. "Trucks are at all sites. Strikes One and Three report explosives loaded and en route to the warehouse. Two and Four are still loading."

The warehouse was in an industrial district forty miles outside the city, far from any residential areas. Not ideal for long-term storage, but it would do until they could arrange something more secure. The sheer volume of explosives recovered made Kian's blood run cold. Each cell had enough to create massive casualties. Combined, they could have turned downtown Los Angeles into a war zone.

Where had they even gotten that much?

He turned to his brother-in-law. "Andrew, we should try to figure out where all of these explosives came from and how they made their way into the city without anyone the wiser."

Andrew nodded. "Indeed, I intend to secure a sample of the cache for analysis to identify the source. If it's in our database, we'll figure it out."

"Command, Strike One," Max's voice interrupted his thoughts. "We're clear of the site. Prisoners are secured and in transport. Note that our party crasher means a possible fifth cell."

"We'll find out after interrogating them," Kian said. "Good work, Max."

"Well, thank you, boss," Max replied with his usual irreverence, but Kian heard the exhaustion beneath the playful tone. "Oh, please thank William for me. The upgrades were very useful, especially the electrification of the suit's exterior skin. Our party crasher found that one particularly shocking."

"Strike Four to Command," Magnus reported. "Explosives loaded, but we have a problem. Local PD is responding to a noise complaint from the neighbors. Someone must have been immune to Yamanu's thrall and heard the walls coming down."

"I'll handle it," Roni said, pulling up LAPD dispatch on his screen. A few quick keystrokes later, and the patrol car would be redirected to a 'more urgent' call across town. "Magnus, you have fifteen minutes to clear the scene."

"Copy that. Strike Four moving out."

As the teams reported their successful extractions one by one, Kian allowed himself a moment to process the magnitude of what they'd prevented.

The casualties would have been staggering, and the worldwide aftershocks possibly more so. The event could have started a catastrophic chain reaction of events that went far beyond the local casualties.

Tonight, the clan had taken a firm stand and handed the forces of darkness a significant blow. The terrifying part was that they'd stopped it with seconds to spare and purely by chance.

42

DIN

The noise hit Din before he'd even fully entered Kyra's house—a cacophony of voices, laughter, and the distinctive chaos that only a gathering of children could produce. He paused in the doorway, momentarily overwhelmed by the sheer energy contained within the living room.

"Din! Fenella!" Kyra's voice cut through the commotion as she waved them over. "Come in."

This was a celebration of Max's safe return, and Kyra had invited the entire family, which in her case was a small clan. All of her sisters and their kids were there, and also Jasmine and Ell-rom.

The house had been transformed into what looked like a Persian feast. Every available surface held platters of food—fragrant rice dishes, stews that filled the air with saffron and herbs, flatbreads still warm from the oven, and an array of sweets that had the younger children circling like hungry sharks.

391

Din felt distinctly out of place.

His experience with children was limited, and he had never been comfortable around them. Although he had to admit that there was a positive energy in the joyful chaos, with kids ranging from toddlers to teenagers all talking over each other and buzzing around like wind-up toys.

"Here." Max pressed a cold beer into his hand. "You look like you need this."

"Thanks." Din took a grateful sip. "Quite the gathering." He lifted his beer and clinked it with Max's. "Congratulations on the mission. I understand that everything went well?"

"There were a few hitches, but the objectives were achieved. We had a surprise visitor, and we feared that there was a fifth cell somewhere, but Kian took Toven to the keep to interrogate him, and it turned out that he was just a recent arrival. For now, there will be no terror attacks in the greater Los Angeles area, but we need to stay alert. Once the idea gets into their heads, they will keep trying."

"Well, thank the merciful Fates that this time you got them all." Din clinked Max's bottle again and took a long swig from his.

Max's face lit up as he surveyed the controlled chaos. "Isn't this great? I love big families. When I fell for Kyra, I had no idea I was getting an entire clan as part of the deal." He grinned. "Best bonus package ever."

Din watched as one of the smaller boys chased his

brother around the coffee table, nearly upending a plate of cookies in the process. Yasmin scooped them both up with a mother's ease, redirecting their energy toward the pile of toys in the corner.

"I can see the appeal," Din said diplomatically, though privately he wondered how anyone maintained sanity in such an environment.

His gaze found Fenella across the room, and his chest tightened with familiar warmth. She sat on the floor surrounded by a gaggle of girls, from a tiny one in a pretty, girly dress to four teenagers in jeans and T-shirts who looked like they had been born and bred in California and not recent arrivals from a country that restricted the freedoms of women. Each of them held out an object and was asking for a reading.

Fenella took the doll that the small girl handed her. "This is a brave warrior," she said solemnly, holding up the doll. "She has been through many battles at tea parties. She's been force-fed seventeen thousand cups of imaginary tea and lived to tell the tale, but she asks to be fed no more."

The girls dissolved into giggles, and even serious Arezoo cracked a smile from her perch on the arm of the sofa.

"She looks happy," Max observed, following Din's gaze.

"She does. Last night, she was terrified for you and the other Guardians."

"She told you that?"

"She didn't have to." Din took another sip of his

beer. "She barely managed any readings, and when we got home, she couldn't sleep. When you texted me this morning that it was all done and everyone was safe, she cried in relief."

Max shifted uncomfortably. "I told her that we would be fine. We were never in any real danger."

"Bullshit," Din said. "But I appreciate the attempt at reassurance."

For a long moment, they stood side by side, watching the chaos. It was quite entertaining, but the noise was fatiguing, and Din was contemplating how long they needed to stay not to offend anyone.

"Can you believe what almost happened?" Max's voice dropped. "If we hadn't stumbled upon that guy in the market…"

"Thank the merciful Fates that you did."

Din had never been particularly spiritual, but recent events had made him reconsider. "Maybe it was all fated."

Max nodded, taking another swig from his bottle of Snake Venom.

"Uncle Max!" One of the boys tugged at Max's jeans. "Come see what we built!"

"Duty calls," Max said with a grin, allowing himself to be dragged toward a block construction in the corner of the living room.

"Uncle Max." Din chuckled. "I never thought I'd hear anyone calling him that."

"You look a bit overwhelmed." Fenella slipped her hand into his.

"Can you blame me?" He waved his beer bottle at the crowded living room.

She laughed. "Want to escape to the porch for a minute?"

"Fates, yes."

They slipped out the sliding door onto the patio. The evening air was cooler, quieter, though the sounds of the celebration still filtered through the glass.

"Big families can be overwhelming." Fenella leaned against the railing. "I'm not used to that either, but it's nice, in small doses, that is. After a while, all I want is to get away from the noise."

"Speaking of getting away. Has anyone made arrangements for the Egypt trip? Given everything that happened?"

"No one's told me anything, but I assume that Kian had his hands full with preventing his city from exploding."

"Are you disappointed?"

She tilted her head. "No, I'm glad. It gives me more time at the Hobbit." A smile played at her lips. "I like what I do there."

"My mate is the village's latest celebrity," Din teased.

She arched a brow. "Mate?"

"I mean girlfriend. It's just that no one uses that term around here."

"I like the sound of mate. It's like a romantic partner who is also a friend."

Din let out a relieved breath. "Good. I was afraid I scared you with that slip-up."

"We should go back in," Fenella said after a moment. "The food is incredible, and Rana will be offended if we don't have thirds."

"Thirds? I didn't have firsts yet."

"Then we definitely need to get you started."

Din groaned. "I don't know if I can handle thirds."

"I'm sure you'll survive."

When they rejoined the celebration, Din got pulled into a conversation with Soraya about the grocery store plans. Her enthusiasm was infectious as she described their vision for bringing authentic Persian products to the village.

"The architect is ready to show us some preliminary drawings for the building," she said. "I'm so excited."

"So am I," Rana said. "I can't believe that Kian had time to even call the architect with everything that was going on. I'm just glad that it's over and we can go back to making big plans." She rubbed her hands. "Our store is going to be spectacular."

Dinner progressed with multiple courses and constant encouragement to eat more, but as the evening wore on, the energy gradually shifted from manic to mellow. The younger children curled up on the sofa and the rug, their energy spent, and conversations became quieter, more intimate.

Din found himself actually enjoying the atmosphere, to his surprise. There was something deeply satisfying about being accepted into this extended family unit, even as a peripheral member.

"Time to go, Professor." Fenella patted his arm. "I need to change before my shift."

He was actually sorry to leave.

They made their rounds, saying goodbye, accepting hugs from the sisters and sticky kisses from some of the younger children.

Max caught them at the door. "Thanks for coming. Kyra and I plan to stop at the bar later on."

"Awesome." Fenella grinned. "Bring Jasmine and Ell-rom. They look like they could use some adult company after this."

They all looked at the couple. Jasmine was fine, but Ell-rom looked like he was pained.

"No worries," Max said. "I'll drag them to the Hobbit whether they want to go or not."

Once they were out the door, Fenella took Din's hand. "That was nice."

"It was," Din agreed. "Overwhelming, but nice."

"Could you see yourself with something like that? A big family, I mean?"

He smiled. "It's not in the cards for immortals. We'll be lucky to have one child." He frowned. "I mean, if you want that, and when you want that."

She laughed. "That's okay. You don't have to keep apologizing for thinking of our future and me as your mate."

"You're okay with that?"

"I just said that." Fenella stopped walking and

turned to face him with a strange expression on her face.

"What?" he asked.

Instead of answering, she wrapped her arms around his neck and kissed him. Not a quick peck or casual gesture, but something more intentional. When she pulled back, Din was breathless.

"What was that for?" he asked.

"I was exercising what I told Soraya earlier." Her hands still rested on his shoulders, her eyes serious. "Every moment in life needs to be cherished, not squandered in fear or hesitation. Life needs to be lived courageously."

"Fenella—"

"No, let me finish." She took a deep breath, and he could see her gathering her courage like armor. "Last night, when Max and the others were out there, all I could think about was how fragile everything is. Even immortal lives can be snuffed out in an instant."

Din stayed silent, sensing she needed to work through this at her own pace.

"I've been such a coward," she continued. "You've given me everything—patience, understanding, love— and I've given you scraps. Half-measures and almosts."

"That's not true—"

"It is, or it was, but I'm done with that. I'm not going to live in fear anymore, and I'm not going to deny you what you deserve to hear me say."

Din's heart was pounding so hard he was sure she could feel it where her hands rested against his chest.

"I love you, Din."

The words hung in the air between them, simple and perfect and everything he'd waited for so long to hear. For a moment, he couldn't speak, couldn't breathe, couldn't do anything but stare at the woman who'd just given him the gift he'd begun to think might never come.

"Say something," Fenella whispered, and he realized there was vulnerability in her eyes, as if she wasn't sure of his response even though he'd told her he loved her so many times before.

"I love you too," he said, the words rough with emotion. "Fates, Fenella, I love you so much I don't have words for it in any language, ancient or modern, and I speak over twenty-five of them."

She laughed. "Always the professor."

"Always *your* professor," he corrected, pulling her close. "For as long as you'll have me."

"Forever sounds about right," she murmured against his chest.

As they stood in the jasmine-scented darkness, holding each other, Din felt something fundamental shift in his chest, a locking into place of pieces that had been floating loose for half a century.

"We need to get home," he said eventually, though he didn't loosen his hold.

"We do," she agreed, not moving either.

"You'll be late, and Atzil will wonder where you are."

"Let him wonder," she said, but stepped back and continued walking.

Everything looked different somehow—the familiar paths, the houses they passed, even the stars above. The world hadn't changed, but Din's place in it had.

"I'm going to say it a lot now," Fenella warned as they reached Shira's house. "I love you at completely inappropriate times. While you're talking to others or grading papers or cooking steaks with Shira's apron on."

"I'll cope somehow," Din said dryly.

She grinned. "I love the way you use sarcasm when you're emotionally overwhelmed."

"I'm not emotionally overwhelmed."

"I love it when you lie badly, too."

He pulled her back for another kiss. "Go change for work before I decide to take you to bed instead."

"Tempting," she murmured against his lips. "But Fenella the psychometric bartender can't just not show up."

"I love you," he said, just because he could, because she'd finally given him permission to say it, knowing it would be returned.

"I love you too," she said easily, as if the words hadn't been trapped behind walls of fear for what had felt like eternity. "Now stop making me all emotional. I need to be funny and irreverent in less than an hour."

Later, as they walked toward the Hobbit, her *I love*

you still echoed in his ears, and Din couldn't imagine being anywhere else.

"Hey," Fenella said as the Hobbit came into view. "Want to know what tonight's special reading theme is going to be?"

"Tell me."

"Love stories. Every object will have a secret romantic past that is either deeply moving or hilariously awkward."

"Knowing you, it will be both."

"I love that you know me so well," she said, then laughed. "God, I really am going to be insufferable with this, aren't I?"

"Completely," Din agreed. "It's going to be glorious."

COMING UP NEXT
The Children of the Gods Book 97
Dark Rover's Shire

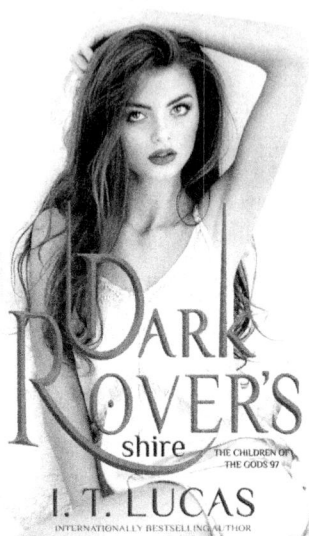

Fenella has finally found home in the village and Din's arms, but just as she's learning to trust in forever, duty calls them across the world. Armed with her growing psychometric abilities and backed by her newfound family, Fenella must help unravel a five-thousand-year-old mystery that could change everything.

NOTE

Dear reader,

I hope my stories have added a little joy to your day. If you have a moment to add some to mine, you can help spread the word about the Children Of The Gods series by telling your friends and penning a review. Your recommendations are the most powerful way to inspire new readers to explore the series.

Thank you,

Isabell

THE CHILDREN OF THE GODS ORIGINS

1: GODDESS'S CHOICE

When gods and immortals still ruled the ancient world, one young goddess risked everything for love.

2: GODDESS'S HOPE

Hungry for power and infatuated with the beautiful Areana, Navuh plots his father's demise. After all, by getting rid of the insane god he would be doing the world a favor. Except, when gods and immortals conspire against each other, humanity pays the price.

But things are not what they seem, and prophecies should not to be trusted...

THE CHILDREN OF THE GODS

THE DARK STRANGER TRILOGY

1: DARK STRANGER THE DREAM

2: DARK STRANGER REVEALED

3: DARK STRANGER IMMORTAL

Syssi's paranormal foresight lands her a job at Dr. Amanda Dokani's neuroscience lab, but it fails to predict the thrilling yet terrifying turn her life will take. Syssi has no clue that her boss is an immortal who'll drag her into a secret, millennia-old battle over humanity's future. Nor does she realize that the professor's imposing brother is the mysterious stranger who's been starring in her dreams.

Since the dawn of human civilization, two warring factions of immortals—the descendants of the gods of old—have been secretly shaping its destiny. Leading the clandestine battle from his luxurious Los Angeles high-rise, Kian is surrounded by his clan, yet alone. Descending from a single goddess, clan members are forbidden to each other. And as the only other immortals are their hated enemies, Kian and his kin have been long resigned to a lonely existence of fleeting trysts with human partners. That is, until his sister makes a game-changing discovery—a mortal seeress who she believes is a dormant carrier of their genes. Ever the realist, Kian is skeptical and refuses Amanda's plea to attempt Syssi's activation. But when his enemies learn of the Dormant's existence, he's forced to rush her to the safety of his keep. Inexorably drawn to Syssi, Kian wrestles with his conscience as he is tempted to explore her budding interest in the darker shades of sensuality.

THE DARK ENEMY TRILOGY

4: DARK ENEMY TAKEN

5: DARK ENEMY CAPTIVE

6: DARK ENEMY REDEEMED

Dalhu can't believe his luck when he stumbles upon the beautiful immortal professor. Presented with a once-in-a-lifetime opportunity to grab an immortal female for himself, he kidnaps her and runs. If he ever gets caught, either by her people or his, his life is forfeit. But for a chance of a loving mate and a family of his own, Dalhu is prepared to do everything in his power to win Amanda's heart, and that includes leaving the Doom brotherhood and his old life behind.

Amanda soon discovers that there is more to the handsome Doomer than his dark past and a hulking, sexy body. But succumbing to her enemy's seduction, or worse, developing feelings for a ruthless killer is out of the question. No man is worth life on the run, not even the one and only immortal male she could claim as her own.

Her clan and her research must come first.

6.5: My Dark Amazon

When Michael and Kri fend off a gang of humans, Michael is stabbed. Though his immortal body recovers quickly, the injury to his ego takes longer to heal, putting a strain on his relationship with Kri.

THE DARK WARRIOR TETRALOGY

7: Dark Warrior Mine

8: Dark Warrior's Promise

9: Dark Warrior's Destiny

10: Dark Warrior's Legacy

When Andrew is forced to retire from active duty, he believes that all he has to look forward to is a boring desk job. His glory days in special ops are over. But as it turns out, his thrill ride has just begun. Andrew discovers not only that immortals exist and have been manipulating global affairs since antiquity, but that he and his sister are rare possessors of the immortal genes.

Problem is, Andrew might be too old to attempt the

activation process. His sister, who is fourteen years his junior, barely made it through the transition, so the odds of him coming out of it alive, let alone immortal, are slim.

But fate may force his hand.

Helping a friend find his long-lost daughter, Andrew finds a woman who's worth taking the risk for. Nathalie might be a Dormant, but the only way to find out for sure requires fangs and venom.

DARK GUARDIAN TRILOGY

11: DARK GUARDIAN FOUND

12: DARK GUARDIAN CRAVED

13: DARK GUARDIAN'S MATE

What would you do if you stopped aging?

Eva runs. The ex-DEA agent doesn't know what caused her strange mutation, only that if discovered, she'll be dissected like a lab rat. What Eva doesn't know, though, is that she's a descendant of the gods, and that she is not alone. The man who rocked her world in one life-changing encounter over thirty years ago is an immortal as well.

To keep his people's existence secret, Bhathian was forced to turn his back on the only woman who ever captured his heart, but he's never forgotten and never stopped looking for her.

DARK ANGEL TRILOGY

14: DARK ANGEL'S OBSESSION

15: DARK ANGEL'S SEDUCTION

16: DARK ANGEL'S SURRENDER

The cold and stoic warrior is an enigma even to those closest to him. His secrets are about to unravel...

Brundar is fighting a losing battle. Calypso is slowly chipping away his icy armor from the outside, while his need for her is melting it from the inside.

He can't allow it to happen. Calypso is a human with none of the Dormant indicators. There is no way he can keep her for more than a few weeks.

DARK OPERATIVE TRILOGY

17: DARK OPERATIVE: A SHADOW OF DEATH

18: DARK OPERATIVE: A GLIMMER OF HOPE

19: DARK OPERATIVE: THE DAWN OF LOVE

As a brilliant strategist and the only human entrusted with the secret of immortals' existence, Turner is both an asset and a liability to the clan. His request to attempt transition into immortality as an alternative to cancer treatments cannot be denied without risking the clan's exposure. On the other hand, approving it means risking his premature death. In both scenarios, the clan will lose a valuable ally.

When the decision is left to the clan's physician, Turner makes plans to manipulate her by taking advantage of her interest in him.

Will Bridget fall for the cold, calculated operative? Or will Turner fall into his own trap?

DARK SURVIVOR TRILOGY

20: DARK SURVIVOR AWAKENED

21: DARK SURVIVOR ECHOES OF LOVE

This was a strange new world she had awakened to.

Her memory loss must have been catastrophic because almost nothing was familiar. The language was foreign to her, with only a few words bearing some similarity to the language she thought in. Still, a full moon cycle had passed since her awakening, and little by little, she was gaining basic understanding of it--only a few words and phrases, but she was learning more each day.

A week or so ago, a little girl on the street had tugged on her mother's sleeve and pointed at her. "Look, Mama, Wonder Woman!"

The mother smiled apologetically, saying something in the language these people spoke, then scurried away with the child looking behind her shoulder and grinning.

When it happened again with another child on the same day, it was settled.

Wonder Woman must have been the name of someone important in this strange world she had awoken to, and since both times it had been said with a smile it must have been a good one.

Wonder had a nice ring to it.

She just wished she knew what it meant.

DARK WIDOW TRILOGY

23: Dark Widow's Secret

24: Dark Widow's Curse

25: Dark Widow's Blessing

Vivian and her daughter share a powerful telepathic connection, so when Ella can't be reached by conventional or psychic means, her mother fears the worst.

Help arrives from an unexpected source when Vivian gets a call from the young doctor she met at a psychic convention. Turns out Julian belongs to a private organization specializing in retrieving missing girls.

As Julian's clan mobilizes its considerable resources to rescue the daughter, Magnus is charged with keeping the gorgeous young mother safe.

Worry for Ella and the secrets Vivian and Magnus keep from each other should be enough to prevent the sparks of attraction from kindling a blaze of desire. Except, these pesky sparks have a mind of their own.

DARK DREAM TRILOGY

26: DARK DREAM'S TEMPTATION

27: DARK DREAM'S UNRAVELING

28: DARK DREAM'S TRAP

Julian has known Ella is the one for him from the moment he saw her picture, but when he finally frees her from captivity, she seems indifferent to him. Could he have been mistaken?

Ella's rescue should've ended that chapter in her life, but it seems like the road back to normalcy has just begun, and it's full of obstacles. Between the pitying looks she gets and her mother's attempts to get her into therapy, Ella feels like she's typecast as a victim when nothing could be further from the truth. She's a tough survivor, and she's going to prove it.

Strangely, the only one who seems to understand is Logan,

who keeps popping up in her dreams. But then, he's a figment of her imagination—or is he?

DARK PRINCE TRILOGY

29: Dark Prince's Enigma

30: Dark Prince's Dilemma

31: Dark Prince's Agenda

As the son of the most dangerous male on the planet, Lokan lives by three rules:

Don't trust a soul.

Don't show emotions.

And don't get attached.

Will one extraordinary woman make him break all three?

DARK QUEEN TRILOGY

32: Dark Queen's Quest

33: Dark Queen's Knight

34: Dark Queen's Army

A former beauty queen, a retired undercover agent, and a successful model, Mey is not the typical damsel in distress. But when her sister drops off the radar and then someone starts following her around, she panics.

Following a vague clue that Kalugal might be in New York, Kian sends a team headed by Yamanu to search for him.

As Mey and Yamanu's paths cross, he offers her his help and protection, but will that be all?

DARK SPY TRILOGY

Jin possesses a unique paranormal ability. Just by touching someone, she can insert a mental hook into their psyche and tie a string of her consciousness to it, creating a tether. That doesn't make her a spy, though, not unless her talent is discovered by those seeking to exploit it.

DARK OVERLORD TRILOGY

Jacki has two talents that set her apart from the rest of the human race.

She has unpredictable glimpses of other people's futures, and she is immune to mind manipulation.

Unfortunately, both talents are pretty useless for finding a job other than the one she had in the government's paranormal division.

It seemed like a sweet deal until she found out that the director planned on producing super babies by compelling the recruits into pairing up. When an opportunity to escape the program presented itself, she took it, only to find out that humans are not at the top of the food chain.

Immortals are real, and at the very top of the hierarchy is Kalugal, the most powerful, arrogant, and sexiest male she has ever met.

With one look, he sets her blood on fire, but Jacki is not a fool. A man like him will never think of her as anything more than a tasty snack, while she will never settle for anything less than his heart.

DARK CHOICES TRILOGY

41: DARK CHOICES THE QUANDARY

42: DARK CHOICES PARADIGM SHIFT

43: DARK CHOICES THE ACCORD

When Rufsur and Edna meet, the attraction is as unexpected as it is undeniable. Except, she's the clan's judge and councilwoman, and he's Kalugal's second-in-command.

Will loyalty and duty to their people keep them apart?

DARK SECRETS TRILOGY

44: DARK SECRETS RESURGENCE

45: DARK SECRETS UNVEILED

46: DARK SECRETS ABSOLVED

On a sabbatical from his Stanford teaching position, Professor David Levinson finally has time to write the sci-fi novel he's been thinking about for years.

The phenomena of past life memories and near-death experiences are too controversial to include in his formal psychiatric research, while fiction is the perfect outlet for his esoteric ideas.

Hoping that a change of pace will provide the inspiration he needs, David accepts a friend's invitation to an old Scottish castle.

DARK HAVEN TRILOGY

Welcome to Safe Haven, where not everything is what it seems.

On a quest to process personal pain, Anastasia joins the Safe Haven Spiritual Retreat.

Through meditation, self-reflection, and hard work, she hopes to make peace with the voices in her head.

This is where she belongs.

Except, membership comes with a hefty price, doubts are sacrilege, and leaving is not as easy as walking out the front gate.

Is living in utopia worth the sacrifice?

Anastasia believes so until the arrival of a new acolyte changes everything.

Apparently, the gods of old were not a myth, their immortal descendants share the planet with humans, and she might be a carrier of their genes.

DARK POWER TRILOGY

Attending a charity gala as the clan's figurehead, Onegus is ready for the pesky socialites he'll have a hard time keeping away. Instead, he encounters an intriguing beauty who won't give him the time of day.

Bad things happen when Cassandra gets all worked up, and given her fiery temper, the destructive power is difficult to tame. When she meets a gorgeous, cocky billionaire at a charity event, things just might start blowing up again.

DARK MEMORIES TRILOGY

53: DARK MEMORIES SUBMERGED

54: DARK MEMORIES EMERGE

55: DARK MEMORIES RESTORED

Geraldine's memories are spotty at best, and many of them are pure fiction. While her family attempts to solve the puzzle with far too many pieces missing, she's forced to confront a past life that she can't remember, a present that's more fantastic than her wildest made-up stories, and a future that might be better than her most heartfelt fantasies. But as more clues are uncovered, the picture starting to emerge is beyond anything she or her family could have ever imagined.

DARK HUNTER TRILOGY

56: DARK HUNTER'S QUERY

57: DARK HUNTER'S PREY

58: DARK HUNTER'S BOON

For most of his five centuries of existence, Orion has walked the earth alone, searching for answers.

Why is he immortal?

Where did his powers come from?

Is he the only one of his kind?

When fate puts Orion face to face with the god who sired him, he learns the secret behind his immortality and that he might not be the only one.

As the goddess's eldest daughter and a mother of thirteen, Alena deserves the title of Clan Mother just as much as Annani, but she's not interested in honorifics. Being her mother's companion and keeping the mischievous goddess out of trouble is a rewarding, full-time job. Lately, though, Alena's love for her mother and the clan's gratitude is not enough.

She craves adventure, excitement, and perhaps a true-love mate of her own.

When Alena and Orion meet, sparks fly, but they both resist the pull. Alena could never bring herself to trust the powerful compeller, and Orion could never allow himself to fall in love again.

DARK GOD TRILOGY

59: DARK GOD'S AVATAR

60: DARK GOD'S REVIVISCENCE

61: DARK GOD DESTINIES CONVERGE

Unaware of the time bomb ticking inside her, Mia had lived the perfect life until it all came to a screeching halt, but despite the difficulties she faces, she doggedly pursues her dreams.

Once known as the god of knowledge and wisdom, Toven has grown cold and indifferent. Disillusioned with humanity, he travels the world and pens novels about the love he can no longer feel.

Seeking to escape his ever-present ennui, Toven gives a cutting-edge virtual experience a try. When his avatar meets Mia's, their sizzling virtual romance unexpectedly turns into something deeper and more meaningful.

Will it endure in the real world?

DARK WHISPERS TRILOGY

62: DARK WHISPERS FROM THE PAST

63: DARK WHISPERS FROM AFAR

64: DARK WHISPERS FROM BEYOND

A brilliant scientist and programmer, William lives for his work, but when he recruits a young bioinformatician to help him decipher the gods' genetic blueprints, he finds himself smitten with more than just her brain.

With a Ph.D. at nineteen, Kaia is considered a prodigy and expects a bright future in academia. But when William invites her to join his secret research team, she accepts for reasons that have nothing to do with her career objectives. Wiliam's promise to look into her best friend's disappearance is an offer she just can't refuse.

DARK GAMBIT TRILOGY

65: DARK GAMBIT THE PAWN

66: DARK GAMBIT THE PLAY

67: DARK GAMBIT RELIANCE

Temporarily assigned to supervise a team of bioinformaticians, Marcel expects to spend a couple of weeks in the peaceful retreat of Safe Haven, enjoying Oregon Coast's cool weather and rugged beauty.

Things quickly turn chaotic when the retreat's director receives an email with an encoded message about a potential new threat to the clan.

While those in charge of security debate what to do next, Safe Haven's first ever paranormal retreat is about to begin, and one of the attendees is a mysterious woman who makes Marcel's heart beat faster whenever she's near.

Is the beautiful mortal his one truelove?

Or is she the harbinger of more bad news?

DARK ALLIANCE TRILOGY

68: Dark Alliance Kindred Souls

69: Dark Alliance Turbulent Waters

70: Dark Alliance Perfect Storm

A daring operation half a world away devolves into a full-scale crisis that escalates rapidly, requiring the clan's full might and technological wizardry to manage and survive.

Hardened by duty and tragedy, Jade is driven by a burning desire for revenge. When Phinas saves her second-in-command, Jade's gratitude quickly becomes something more.

DARK HEALING TRILOGY

71: Dark Healing Blind Justice

72: Dark Healing Blind Trust

73: Dark healing Blind Curve

The sanctuary is Vanessa's life project. The monumental task of rehabilitating the traumatized victims of trafficking doesn't leave much time for personal life, let alone dating or finding her one and only.

When Kian asks her to help the Kra-ell, she's torn between her duty to the sanctuary and a group of emotionally wounded aliens who no other psychologist can treat.

She's the only immortal with the necessary training to get it done.

The Kra-ell culture and the purebloods' nearly androgynous alien looks shouldn't appeal to her, and yet, she finds one of them disturbingly attractive.

Is it the dangerous vibe he emits?

Does it speak to her on a subconscious level?

Or is it her need to put the broken pieces of him back together?

And why is he interested in her?

She cannot offer him a fight for dominance like a Kra-ell female would, but some strange and unfamiliar part of her wishes she could.

DARK ENCOUNTERS TRILOGY

74: DARK ENCOUNTERS OF THE CLOSE KIND

75: DARK ENCOUNTERS OF THE UNEXPECTED KIND

76: DARK ENCOUNTERS OF THE FATED KIND

Convinced that her family is hiding a terrible secret from her, Gabi decides to pay them a surprise visit.

Something is very fishy about the stories her brothers have been telling her lately. Her niece, a nineteen-year-old prodigy with a Ph.D. in bioinformatics, has gotten engaged to a much older guy she met while working on some top-secret project, and if Gabi's older, overprotective brother's approval of the engagement wasn't suspicious enough, he also uprooted his family and moved to be closer to the couple.

What Gabi discovers when she gets to L.A. is wilder than anything she could have imagined. Her entire family possesses godly genes, her brothers and her niece have already turned immortal, and she could transition as soon as she finds an immortal male to induce her. Finding a suitable candidate in a village full of handsome immortals shouldn't be a problem, but Gabi's thoughts keep wandering to the gorgeous guy she met on her flight over.

Could Uriel be a lost descendant of the gods?

He certainly looks like them, but that doesn't mean that he's a good guy or that he's even immortal. He could be a descendant of a different god—a member of an enemy faction of immortals who seek to eradicate her family's adoptive clan, or what is more likely, he's just an extraordinarily good-looking human.

DARK VOYAGE TRILOGY

As Annani and Syssi set out to unravel the mysteries of Syssi's visions about the gods' home world, the long-awaited wedding cruise sets sail with Aru, Gabi, and Aru's teammates on board.

While the gods find themselves surrounded by immortal clan ladies eager for their affections, they soon discover that destiny has a different plan for them.

DARK HORIZON TRILOGY

80: DARK HORIZON NEW DAWN

81: DARK HORIZON ECLIPSE OF THE HEART

82: DARK HORIZON THE WITCHING HOUR

What begins as a carefree vacation quickly spirals into a heart-pounding adventure when a chance encounter with a mysterious woman entangles Margo in a shadowy world of deceit and danger.

Meanwhile, aboard the Silver Swan, the Fates weave their intricate web. Armed with Margo's photograph, Frankie is on a mission to match her with the last unmated god. Despite his initial disinterest, the image consumes Negal, and when Margo's situation becomes dire, the once indifferent god is compelled to join the frantic rescue mission.

DARK WITCH TRILOGY

83: DARK WITCH ENTANGLED FATES

84: DARK WITCH: TWIN DESTINIES

85: DARK WITCH: RESURRECTION

Jasmine's quest for her Prince Charming takes an

unexpected turn when she finds herself on a luxurious cruise ship steeped in secrets. Navigating a tangled maze of destiny, intrigue, and desire, she discovers that the key to unlocking her future may lie in the very cards she's been dealt.

DARK AWAKENING TRILOGY

86: DARK AWAKENING: NEW WORLD

87: DARK AWAKENING HIDDEN CURRENTS

88: DARK AWAKENING ECHOES OF DESTINY

"Your destiny awaits across the stars," Ell-rom's mother told him. "The seer foretold your future. You will live, and you will thrive, and you will be safe."

The seer's prophecy has come true. Ell-rom and his sister are safe, surrounded by people who care for them and want to help them heal, which is in stark contrast to where they came from. On Anumati, they were considered abominations because of their mixed heritage. As half gods and half Kra-ell, they would have been eradicated if ever discovered.

But even as he clings to that thought like a talisman against the darkness, he can't shake the lingering sense of unease, the feeling that something lurked in the shadows of his past, something dark and dangerous that is much worse than his inability to tolerate the taste of blood.

What is it about him and his sister that he is not supposed to let anyone see?

After millennia in stasis, Morelle is lured out of her slumber by a seductive storyteller with a velvet voice. As she awakens to twenty-first-century Earth instead of the primitive planet she's been expecting, she struggles to adapt, but thankfully she does not have to do it alone. She has her twin brother to guide her, and a charming stranger who refuses to leave her side.

———

Some warriors are born. Others are chosen by fate and forged by circumstances. In the mountains of Kurdistan, a mysterious woman fights for freedom while her own past remains locked away.

Stay tuned as the truth about Kyra's disappearance begins to unravel.

97: Dark Rover's Shire

For five decades, Fenella has led the life of a ghost, wandering from place to place and relying solely on herself. Now, while seeking refuge in the immortals' hidden village, she uncovers an unexpected connection that may inspire her to stay longer than she planned.

Din has held a torch for Fenella for half a century. Yet, instead of the spirited bartender he fell for, he encounters a hardened, disillusioned nomad who struggles to remain in one place for long.

Some secrets are meant to remain buried, while others are destined to be revealed, and sometimes, luck is simply a matter of being in the right place at the right time.

The Children of The Gods Series Bundled Sets

Dark Stranger Trilogy

Includes a bonus short story:

The Fates Take a Vacation

Dark Enemy Trilogy

Includes a bonus short story:

The Fates' Post-Wedding Celebration

Dark Warrior Tetralogy

Dark Guardian Trilogy

Dark Angel Trilogy

Dark Operative Trilogy

Dark Survivor Trilogy

Dark Widow Trilogy

Dark Dream Trilogy

Dark Prince Trilogy

Dark Queen Trilogy

Dark Spy Trilogy

Dark Overlord Trilogy

Dark Choices Trilogy

Dark Secrets Trilogy

Dark Haven Trilogy

Dark Power Trilogy

Dark Memories Trilogy

Dark Hunter Trilogy

Dark God Trilogy

Dark Whispers Trilogy

Dark Gambit Trilogy

Dark Alliance Trilogy

Dark Healing Trilogy

Dark Encounters Trilogy

Dark Voyage Trilogy

Dark Horizon Trilogy

Dark Witch Trilogy

Dark Awakening Trilogy

Dark Princess Trilogy

MEGA SETS

The Children of the Gods: Books 1-6

1: EL OSCURO DESCONOCIDO EL SUEÑO

2: EL OSCURO DESCONOCIDO REVELADO

3: EL OSCURO DESCONOCIDO INMORTAL

EL OSCURO ENEMIGO

4- EL OSCURO ENEMIGO CAPTURADO

5 - EL OSCURO ENEMIGO CAUTIVO

6- EL OSCURO ENEMIGO REDIMIDO

LES ENFANTS DES DIEUX

DARK STRANGER

1- DARK STRANGER LE RÊVE

2- DARK STRANGER LA RÉVÉLATION

3- DARK STRANGER L'IMMORTELLE

FOR A **FREE** AUDIOBOOK, PREVIEW CHAPTERS, AND OTHER
GOODIES OFFERED ONLY TO MY **VIP**S,

JOIN THE VIP CLUB AT ITLUCAS.COM

TRY THE SERIES ON

AUDIBLE

2 FREE audiobooks with your new Audible subscription!

PERFECT MATCH SERIES

Vampire's Consort

When Gabriel's company is ready to start beta testing, he invites his old crush to inspect its medical safety protocol.

Curious about the revolutionary technology of the *Perfect Match Virtual Fantasy-Fulfillment studios*, Brenna agrees.

Neither expects to end up partnering for its first fully immersive test run.

King's Chosen

When Lisa's nutty friends get her a gift certificate to *Perfect Match Virtual Fantasy Studios*, she has no intentions of using it. But since the only way to get a refund is if no partner can be found for her, she makes sure to request a fantasy so girly and over the top that no sane guy will pick it up.

Except, someone does.

Warning: This fantasy contains a hot, domineering crown prince, sweet insta-love, steamy love scenes painted with light shades of gray, a wedding, and a HEA in both the virtual and real worlds.

Intended for mature audience.

Working as a Starbucks barista, Alicia fends off flirting all day long, but none of the guys are as charming and sexy as Gregg. His frequent visits are the highlight of her day, but since he's never asked her out, she assumes he's taken. Besides, between a day job and a budding music career, she has no time to start a new relationship.

That is until Gregg makes her an offer she can't refuse—a gift certificate to the virtual fantasy fulfillment service everyone is talking about. As a huge Star Trek fan, Alicia has a perfect match in mind—the captain of the Starship Enterprise.

THE THIEF WHO LOVED ME

When Marian splurges on a Perfect Match Virtual adventure as a world-infamous jewel thief, she expects high-wire fun with a hot partner who she will never have to see again in real life.

A virtual encounter seems like the perfect answer to Marcus's string of dating disasters. No strings attached, no drama, and definitely no love. As a die-hard James Bond fan, he chooses as his avatar a dashing MI6 operative and to complement his adventure, a dangerously seductive partner.

Neither expects to find their forever Perfect Match.

My Merman Prince

The beautiful architect working late on the twelfth floor of my building thinks that I'm just the maintenance guy. She's also under the impression that I'm not interested.

Nothing could be further from the truth.

I want her like I've never wanted a woman before, but I don't play where I work.

I don't need the complications.

When she tells me about living out her mermaid fantasy with a stranger in a Perfect Match virtual adventure, I decide to do everything possible to ensure that the stranger is me.

The Dragon King

To save his beloved kingdom from a devastating war, the Crown Prince of Trieste makes a deal with a witch that costs him half of his humanity and dooms him to an eternity of loneliness.

Now king, he's a fearsome cobalt-winged dragon by day and a short-tempered monarch by night. Not many are brave enough to serve in the palace of the brooding and volatile ruler, but Charlotte ignores the rumors and accepts a scribe position in court.

As the young scribe reawakens Bruce's frozen heart, all that stands in the way of their happiness is the witch's bargain. Outsmarting the evil hag will take cunning and courage, and Charlotte is just the right woman for the job.

MY WEREWOLF ROMEO

The father of my star student is a big-shot screenwriter and the patron of the drama department who thinks he can dictate what production I should put on. The principal makes it very clear that I need to cooperate with the opinionated asshat or walk away from my dream job at the exclusive private high school.

It doesn't help matters that the guy is single, hot, charming, creative, and seems to like me despite my thinly-veiled hostility.

When he invites me to a custom-tailored Perfect Match virtual adventure to prove that his screenplay is perfect for my production, I accept, intending to have fun while proving that messing with the classics is a foolish idea.

I don't expect to be wowed by his werewolf adaptation of Red Riding Hood mesh-up with Romeo and Juliet, and I certainly don't expect to fall in love with the virtual fantasy's leading man.

THE CHANNELER'S COMPANION

A treat for fans of *The Wheel of Time*.

When Erika hires Rand to assist in her pediatric clinic,

she does so despite his good looks and irresistible charm, not because of them.

He's empathic, adores children, and has the patience of a saint.

He's also all she can think about, but he's off-limits.

What's a doctor to do to scratch that irresistible itch without risking workplace complications?

A shared adventure in the Perfect Match Virtual Studios seems like the solution, but instead of letting the algorithm choose a partner for her, Erika can try to influence it to select the one she wants. Awarding Rand a gift certificate to the service will get him into their database, but unless Erika can tip the odds in her favor, getting paired with him is a long shot.

Hopefully, a virtual adventure based on her and Rand's favorite series will do the trick.

THE VALKYRIE & THE WITCH

After breaking up with my boyfriend, I vow never to date a physician again and avoid workplace romances like the plague. Seeking an escape from bad memories and hospital politics, I apply for a job at the Perfect Match Virtual Fantasy Studios, where I hope to explore fantastical scenarios and beta-test new experiences.

I have no intention of entering a new relationship anytime soon, but it is difficult to ignore Kayden, a fellow trainee who's good-looking and charming but regrettably has aspirations of becoming a physician.

Hoping never to get paired with him to beta test an experience, I choose the Valkyrie adventure. It seems like a safe bet to avoid a guy like him, who would never select an experience where the female is the kick-ass heroine and the man only gets a supporting role. However, the algorithm has other plans in store for us. It seems to think that we are a perfect match.

Adina and the Magic Lamp

In this post-apocalyptic virtual reimagining of Aladdin, James, the enigmatic prince, and Adina, the fearless thief, navigate the treacherous streets of Londabad, a city that echoes London and Ahmedabad and fuses magic and technology. In the face of danger, the chemistry between them ignites, and the lines between prince and thief, royalty and commoner blur.

Perfect Match Bundle 1
Includes Books 1-5

FOR EXCLUSIVE PEEKS AT UPCOMING RELEASES & A FREE I. T. LUCAS COMPANION BOOK

JOIN MY *VIP CLUB* AND GAIN ACCESS TO THE VIP PORTAL AT ITLUCAS.COM

TO JOIN, GO TO:

http://eepurl.com/blMTpD

INCLUDED IN YOUR FREE MEMBERSHIP:

YOUR VIP PORTAL

- READ PREVIEW CHAPTERS OF UPCOMING RELEASES.
- LISTEN TO GODDESS'S CHOICE NARRATION BY CHARLES LAWRENCE
- EXCLUSIVE CONTENT OFFERED ONLY TO MY VIPS.

FREE I.T. LUCAS COMPANION INCLUDES:

- GODDESS'S CHOICE PART 1
- PERFECT MATCH: VAMPIRE'S CONSORT (A STANDALONE NOVELLA)
- INTERVIEW Q & A
- CHARACTER CHARTS

If you're already a subscriber and you are not getting my emails, your provider is sending them to your junk folder, and you are missing out on important updates. To fix that, add isabell@itlucas.com to your email contacts or your email VIP list.

**Check out the specials at
https://www.itlucas.com/specials**

Printed in Dunstable, United Kingdom